unattached

Also by Kristin Lee Johnson:

unprotected

unattached

Kristin Lee Johnson

North Star Press of St. Cloud, Inc.
St. Cloud, Minnesota

Cover design by Gary Johnson

ISBN: 978-0-87839-800-3

First edition: September 2015

Printed in the United States of America.

Published by:
North Star Press of St. Cloud, Inc.
P.O. Box 451
St. Cloud, MN 56302

www.northstarpress.com

Acknowledgements

As in my previous book, it is imperative to note that this is fiction. None of the characters or plot lines in the story were based on my family, my coworkers, my clients, or me.

I love to write about the power of family, and the blurring between friendship and family. I can write about it because I am lucky enough to live it every day. I want to thank those family and friends who have been so supportive by reading, editing, proofing, and encouraging me throughout my work on this book. A huge thank you to Lisa, Abby J., Michelle, Melissa, Abby V., Bonnie, Ellie, Katie, and Julie.

Thank you to North Star Press for taking the leap a second time and publishing this book.

Special recognition goes to my husband, Gary, for his ability to understand my ramblings and turn ideas into an image. It's such a thrill that his photo and cover design set the tone and introduce readers to the story.

And I dedicate this book to my family—Gary, Abby, Sam, Gracie and Lucy. You are my inspiration and my reason for everything.

chapter one

He loved to bounce that baby boy on his knee. Never much interested in girls, he ignored their first child, a daughter with a cap of blonde fuzz and a dimple in her left cheek. His friends, annoyingly married for the past year, had finally had their boy. His boy. He caressed the baby's head and wondered how old the little man would be before he would start spending the night with his favorite uncle.

LEAH DANCO DIDN'T sleep anymore. Not the full, doctor-recommended eight hours, anyway. Leah's nights involved hours of fitful rolling on her aged queen-sized bed with a deep divot in the middle from years of sleeping alone. This spring morning her insomnia had been interrupted with an ominous phone call from sheriff's dispatch at 3:00 a.m.

When the sun finally emerged that first Friday morning in May, Leah had already showered and was wrestling with her home-highlighted blonde frizz. If left alone, her hair would add at least two inches of fuzzy height to her barely five-foot frame, so her mornings always began with the aggravation of coaxing her hair into compliance. Annoyed with the stringy, crunchy results, she switched around a few of the studs in the upper cartilage of her left ear. The studs always cooperated, so at least she could control that much of her appearance. Leah had just turned thirty-five and worried that years of hard living had taken their toll, so she took the bright spots in her appearance where she could find them.

The best part of the day was that it was Friday. She could wear jeans. As a social worker who investigated allegations of child abuse, sometimes perks of the job were hard to find. The 3:00 a.m. phone call was from a dispatcher asking if a social worker wanted to ride along with a uniformed officer to Children's Hospital, where a toddler was being airlifted with life-threatening abuse injuries. The interviews could wait until morning, Leah told her. It was going to be an ugly day.

TWENTY MINUTES LATER, breakfast bar and Diet Coke tucked in her giant purse, Leah stood on the steps outside of Terrance County Human Services like the soles of her hiking sandals were glued to the sidewalk.

Going inside meant facing the day—kids who were angry, anxious or traumatized. Defensive, sobbing, or absent parents. Today, it meant finding answers and justice for a broken baby who just a few hours ago was safe and healthy and whole.

AN ANGRY PALL FELL over the child protection staff as their supervisor, Max, read the hospital report. Max, who looked vaguely like Barack Obama without the big ears, tried to keep his voice neutral, but he was growing more agitated with every sentence.

"Infant was airlifted to St. Paul Children's Hospital with multiple fractures to the skull, ribs, right tibia, and fibula. Multiple contusions on the face, neck, abdomen, back, buttocks, and legs. Infant entered Emergency Department at 01:43 a.m. lethargic and non-responsive, accompanied by the mother, who smelled of alcohol."

The group was quiet with the shared understanding of what the report meant. Toddlers' legs didn't break easily. More cartilage than bone, a toddler's limbs bent before they broke. If there was a fracture, child abuse was often suspected. Spiral fractures, the result of twisting or yanking, often occurred when a parent grabbed a child by the arm or leg and twisted or yanked hard. While parents usually did not intend to injure their children this way, they were not taking the care needed with a young body.

Rib fractures were more concerning. They were rarely accidental in small children. At times a child could break an arm or a leg jumping off play equipment. Rib fractures were the result of blows to the body, or a crushing or compression injury. Skull fractures were equally divided between accidents, such as falls, or abusive acts such as throwing or shoving a child.

When a child had all three injuries—broken legs, a skull fracture, and fractured ribs—that child had either fallen out a four-story window, or someone beat the heck out of that poor baby.

"Holy shit! Who the hell's that mother? Do we know her?" Leah always had a propensity for cursing, and her mouth was out of control with reports like these.

"Jill did one child welfare assessment two years ago. Mom tested positive for marijuana when she was five months pregnant. Jill did a brief assessment and offered services. Mom declined. Baby was negative for all substances at birth." Max leaned forward on the oblong table and closed the file with a heavy sigh. "We're waiting to hear how he does in surgery. They need to remove a section of his skull to control brain swelling, and he needs a surgical set for the right tibia fracture."

"Oh, my God," Zoe whispered, a tear hitting the table with a quiet splat. Zoe was the foster care licensor and mother of two-year-old miracle twins, born after years of fertility treatments. Her babies were a few months older than Baby Ben.

"I want it," Leah said. "Let me find the bastard who did this and hang him up by his nuts."

"Fine by me," Jill said, pushing her chair away from the table. Jill and Leah were the two investigators and sometimes wrestled for the "fun" cases. "I'll take five easy cases before I take another murder case."

"This baby isn't going to die." Amanda was quiet but firm. The newest member of their staff, Amanda Danscher, had a history that matched many of their clients'. Recently engaged to the newest assistant county attorney, she found herself the object of envy instead of the pity that she had come to expect. She was smart, compassionate, and Leah's good friend. "So who do they think did this?"

"Equal bets on the mom's boyfriend or the mom herself," Max said.

"Why equal bets?" Jill asked. "I don't remember this girl well, but she didn't seem vicious."

"Easy money says she's covering for her boyfriend," Max said. "But Kemper thinks there could be more to it." Pete Kemper, the senior investigator for Terrance Police Department, was known for being able to get a confession out of just about anyone. If he hadn't made a major mistake early in his career, he probably could have run for sheriff or worked for the Bureau of Criminal Apprehension. Instead, he was bright, highly respected but unpromotable.

Maddie, their wide eyed receptionist, stuck her head in the door. "Hospital social worker wants a call back ASAP."

"Got it," Leah said, gathering her calendar and notebooks.

Max handed her the two-page intake form. "Good luck."

AFTER SHE WENT THROUGH the basic paperwork to get the report opened into a case file, Leah made a quick call to the hospital social worker, and then to Pete Kemper, gathering her notebook and purse as she spoke.

"Hey, Kemp," she said through teeth clenching the intake form.

"Hey, when are you getting here?"

Leah had a hand free to grab the form from her mouth. "I'm leaving right now. How long have you been at the hospital?" Leah shoved everything in a tattered messenger bag and grabbed the keys for county car #2, the best of the dilapidated fleet of county vehicles.

"The baby was flown here sometime after midnight, and I got here at 4:00 a.m. I've been watching the mom. Something is up with her. She's twitchy and has been on her phone the entire time. She's upset but not *upset.* My ex would be out of her mind if one of our girls was in the hospital for a stomachache, let alone brain surgery. I've just been talking to a nurse—"

"Kemp, quit talking to people without me. Go get yourself a breakfast burrito and sit your ass down in the cafeteria."

"Yeah . . . no. There's no way I'm eating hospital food."

"Then go read the paper. Don't start these interviews without me, Kemp. Do you hear me? Don't do it." Leah waved at Maddie at the front desk as she headed out the front door and across the street to pick up car #2.

"Settle down, Danco. I haven't talked to anyone other than the doctor and that nurse. And some social worker who keeps coming over here. And I talked to the mom for, like, two minutes."

"Dammit, Kemp, get the hell away from those people until I get there. Nothing's going to change in the next hour. Team investigations, Kemp. TEAM!"

"It was one time, Leah." They were supposed to conduct investigations together, and last year Kemper had completed every interview in a high profile abuse case, and then suddenly "remembered" that he was supposed to contact Social Services immediately. "I'm gonna wait for you." She heard the smile in his voice, and it ticked her off even more.

"It was more than one time. Go take a nap in your car. I'll be there by ten."

LEAH DROVE SEVENTY-FIVE MILES per hour just in case Kemp got stupid and decided to talk to someone anyway. Leah was glad to be an investigator, enabling her to interact with a family a short time, usually forty-five days, and then either close the case or pass it on to one of the ongoing case managers. When it was determined a family needed services and support to avoid future abuse or neglect, they were transferred for ongoing case management with either Jackie,

Roberta, or Amanda. The three of them were all able to form relationships with families in their own way, knowing that the basis for most behavior change was relationship. Leah preferred to keep her interactions with families short, knowing she wasn't good at relationships.

Leah parked at the top of the ramp closest to the building, barely noticing that the chill in the air was finally gone. May in Minnesota could be anywhere from thirty to eighty degrees and this May had been bitterly cold so far, but there was finally the hope of spring in the air.

Using the emergency room entrance turned out to be a mistake. After weaving through a maze of nondescript corridors and wondering if she should have left a trail of breadcrumbs to find her way out, Leah found Investigator Kemper outside of the PICU, where Baby Ben would soon be returning from surgery. Pete Kemper was blond and slightly balding ("That's my natural hairline!" he swore to anyone who would listen), wearing his uniform of a polo and worn-out khakis. Kemp, already tan from many weekends spent on his boat, had permanent, deep laugh lines around his eyes casting doubt on whether he ever took anything too seriously.

Kemp switched off his phone and nodded at Leah. "I've got uniform guys patrolling the boyfriend's house to see what he does. It looks like he's just camped out there. He doesn't work, but was on probation for a long time for DUIs, driving after revocation and crap like that."

"So who's your money on?" Leah leaned against the dingy, tiled wall, standing close enough to smell that his deodorant was working. Old Spice . . . delicious. Kemper was old school in the best way.

"Baby is going to be in recovery for about an hour, the nurse said. I want to take a run at Mom right now before she gets all caught up in taking care of the baby . . . I mean, that sounded terrible . . . but you know what I mean."

Leah did know what he meant. The mom's place would be to take care of her son, but their place was to figure out what happened to him. They both knew that, for now, they needed to pull themselves away from the human reaction to how the baby was doing, because it would make it almost impossible to focus. Outrage would settle into an angry simmer and sit in the backs of their minds as they conducted their interviews. In reality, that latent rage often stayed much longer, dull and heavy, slowly burning them out interview by interview.

Protocol said they were supposed to see Ben, but he was in surgery so they would have to return another day.

"Let's find the mom," Leah said. "I've got this."

TWENTY MINUTES LATER they were in a family meeting room just off the PICU, furnished with a large painting of Jesus surrounded by children, two vinyl couches and a small table with several boxes of tissues. Leah sat across from Jenny Huffman, and Kemper was to Leah's left.

"We don't want to take a lot of your time, Jenny," Kemper said softly. "This is obviously a very difficult time for you." Jenny looked like hell, with heavy mascara clouds under her eyes, tufts of chin-length black hair matted into nests around her head, and teeth badly in need of orthodontia. And a toothbrush.

"No, I understand I have to talk to you." Her voice was surprisingly soft.

"So you were at Beaches Bar last night." Kemp had already learned that much before Leah had arrived. *Damn him.*

"Yeah, I work the 3:00 to 11:00 at the ethanol plant, but we got out early. I just found out I passed the nursing boards so I'm officially a nurse." A smile escaped, despite her son clinging to life a few rooms away. "Me and two other girls promised each other we'd go out when we all became real nurses. We went to Beaches over in Wisconsin because they were having dollar taps." Her eyes flitted up as she realized she may have said the wrong thing. "We only had a couple. Then I wanted to get home. Joe had been watching Benny all night, and I just wanted to see them both."

Leah noted her eyes lit up about the nursing boards and became nervous when she moved on to the taps, but the hysterical eyes of a terrified mother just weren't there. Kemp was right. She was upset, but she wasn't *upset*, about her son. Was she in shock, or was there more to it than that?

"What did you find when you got home?" Kemp's voice was sympathetic.

Jenny's eyes shifted and she paused like she was seeing it again. Finally: "Joe was asleep on the couch. It looked like he just passed out. I, uh, was tired. It was after midnight so I just went straight to bed. I was kind of pissed, you know, that he was drinking. Or at least it seemed like he was. I went to bed, and then I got up to use the bathroom, so I checked on Benny." Didn't go straight to her son when she got home. Checked on him as an afterthought.

"What did you see when you checked on Ben?" Kemp's smooth voice irritated the crap out of Leah during interviews like this, but it worked.

"I didn't see it at first," Jenny said, smoothing her ratted hair away from her face. "It looked like he had a runny nose. I wiped his nose, but it felt weird. It was oily or something." Leah recalled that cerebrospinal fluid dripped out of his nose, according to the ER report. Her stomach dropped a bit, but she tried to ignore her nausea and focus. "He didn't move when I wiped his nose. He always moves, so I shined my phone on his face. That's when I saw the black eyes. I picked him up and he was limp, and he felt funny. He was lumpy in the wrong places. I called for Joe, but he didn't move. I called 911."

Factual, some shell shock, but there should be more emotion. For pity's sake, her son was lumpy because his bones were broken, and he was leaking fluid from his brain. Jenny's eyes were glassy, and Leah still wasn't sure what she was seeing in Jenny's vacant expression. Leah glanced at Kemp, but his face was neutral, which meant he wasn't sure yet either.

"Jenny." Leah started, and paused. "What do you think happened? You're his mama. I think you know." Kemp sat back in his chair, letting Leah take a run at Jenny.

"I . . . I don't know." Eyes downward. She knew something.

"Jenny." Leah leaned forward with her hands out, feeling like she could pull the information out of her if she asked the right questions. "I'm not saying that you saw it happen. But this is your boy, and he's hurt." When Leah said that Jenny didn't see it, she realized she believed it. Jenny didn't do this. This mother was passive and disconnected, but Leah's gut told her that Jenny wasn't capable of something this violent. Mothers almost never were.

Kemp came forward. "This is your chance to tell us everything we need to know, Jenny. What aren't you saying?" He felt it, too—Jenny was holding on to something they needed to know.

Jenny just stared at Kemp.

"Jenny, what do you need to tell us? For your son."

Jenny slid around in her chair, pushed her hair back, slid her hands along the table. "He drinks a lot." Her words came out even softer.

Leah sat still. Expectant. Kemper took her cue and didn't move. The awkward silence usually made people keep going.

A tear threatened and Jenny stared at the ceiling. "He . . . uh . . . he . . ." her voice shook more as the tears fell. "He isn't nice when he drinks."

"Has he hurt you?" Leah asked the question—they both knew it would be better coming from her.

She shook her head in an almost involuntary reaction, but the tears betrayed her, and him.

"What has he done?" Kemper sat forward protectively.

"He's so great most of the time. You should see him with Benny. They just love each other, and Benny almost prefers Joey over me." *He prefers Joe*—Leah made a mental note.

"But . . ." Leah prompted as patiently as she could.

"But when he's drunk, he's a different guy. We just stay away from him. But then he promised me he would quit." She paused with a shudder. "He was just out cold last night, the way he gets when he's so drunk he just passes out. He says he blacked out and doesn't remember anything."

"What does he usually drink? Will we find bottles around?" Kemper was always thinking about evidence.

"He likes vodka and whiskey, but I didn't see any around. I was pissed when I came home and saw him passed out, because he usually stays up all night and plays *Call of Duty*. Since he was asleep, I knew he had to be drinking . . . but no, I didn't see any bottles." Overall, she wasn't much help. Didn't see anything. No obvious evidence.

"Has he ever hurt Ben?" Leah slipped the question in quietly so that Jenny would stay in her rhythm and answer.

"What do you mean by hurt him?" Jenny asked, not realizing her question just gave them their answer.

"Did he spank too hard, slap him, grab him . . ." With some people, they had to be very specific. Parents universally deny that they "abuse" their kids, but oftentimes if they asked the question differently (i.e. "Have you ever left a mark on your child from hitting or grabbing too hard?") the answers changed.

Jenny shrugged and shuddered a bit. "He's never spanked him or slapped him. He wouldn't do those things. But he's . . . grabbed him before. Like, he'll grab Benny's arm and pull him to his room, and he's pulling way too hard. He's left, like, these light little bruises around his arm." Jenny grimaced and wouldn't look at them, ashamed to admit that her boyfriend hurt her son. "I've talked to Joe about it before because I don't like it when he's rough like that. But Benny can also get wild, so you have to be firm with him." Jenny buried her face in her hands. "I just don't even know what to think anymore. I know Joe couldn't have done this, but I also know someone did something horrible to him. If not Joe, who?"

"That's a good question, Jenny. Could it be anyone else?" It was the right question, but Leah was afraid it would give her an easy out.

"How long were you away from Ben?" Kemper clarified.

"I never went home after school." Jenny squinted, trying to remember the day, hours but eons ago. "All day, I guess. I was at my friend's house helping her move until I had to go to work at three." A picture was emerging of a mom who worked full time, went to nursing school, and still took opportunities (like helping a friend move) to be away from her son for long periods. Jenny's schedule meant Joe did most of the parenting, and statistically the people most likely to abuse children are the moms' boyfriends. "So he had Benny from then until I got home at midnight." Jenny paused. "That's a long time," she thought out loud, her eyes meeting Leah's, searching for judgment. Leah met her gaze and forced her face to stay blank. Jenny shifted away and seemed to be remembering something else.

"What is it?" Leah asked quietly.

Jenny looked back at Leah, shaking her head slightly. "Are you gonna arrest Joe?"

Leah looked at Kemper. He studied Jenny's face before answering. "Should we?" He tilted his head slightly, watching her closely now.

"I . . . I don't know. Maybe?" Her chin quivered as she seemed to play out the scene of Joe's arrest in her head.

"What do you think should happen to someone who hurts a child like this?" It was one of their most important questions, and Kemp asked it casually, but still watching her every move.

"I don't know . . ." She answered, her mind clearly somewhere else.

"Jenny." Leah spoke slowly to be sure to get Jenny's full attention. "We're asking what should happen to someone who shakes, or punches, or kicks a baby so hard that five of his ribs crack." Leah could feel her composure slipping, and could see Jenny losing hers as well. "Your son's skull bones broke apart so far the fluid that protects his brain leaked out his nose. Bruises cover his body—"

Kemper put his hand on Leah's knee, signaling her to stop.

A horrible sound had emanated from Jenny, somewhere between a moan and a scream. Jenny wrapped her arms around herself as her body quaked with sobs. Leah's words broke the shell-shocked veneer, and Jenny caught her breath long enough to say, "Fry that fucker," before she slumped over the table in a heap of tears, anger, and fear.

It was the answer they were looking for. Jenny didn't hurt her boy. And Ben had his mother on his side.

ON THEIR WAY BACK to the parking ramp, Leah asked before Kemp could scold her. "You think I went too far?"

Kemp shrugged. "She was glazed over. Shut down. You could just see her feeling sorry for Joe, all while her baby's brain is leaking."

Leah was walking faster and faster, the image of the baby's damaged body seeping under her skin. Making it hard to focus. He had to become "the baby" in her mind, as it was too difficult to think clearly if she allowed him to have a name and an identity.

As they reached the end of the parking ramp, Leah threw her hands up. "I can't find my car," she growled. "I never used to lose my car before I started this job."

"Leah." Kemp was behind her and grabbed her arm, his touch making her jump.

Her head dropped. She knew she had crossed a line this time. "Don't say it," she said, not turning around.

"The doctors will help him. Our job is to find the guy who did this and get him in jail. You gotta take a step back."

Leah gulped back a sob, turned around and started walking back to the parking ramp elevator. She remembered she wasn't even on the right side of the ramp, let alone the correct floor. "I told you not to say it," she snapped over her shoulder.

THEY BOTH MADE GOOD TIME to their meeting with Assistant County Attorney Jacob Mann at his office. Leah and Kemp squeezed around the chairs in his tiny office to sit across from him at his desk.

"What if we don't get him to give it up?" Kemp asked. They discussed the interview with Jenny, including Jenny's belief Joe was the only one with Ben all day.

"You need something else that ties the boyfriend to the assault," Jacob said conclusively. "The baby is seriously injured, and she assumes he was the only one there. But she wasn't there, so she can't say what happened at her house all day. We gotta hear what this guy has to say for himself and go from there."

"What if he lawyers up?" Kemp asked.

"I still don't think you have it." Jacob was relatively new, but was well respected and knew child abuse cases. "A soft confession might do it, at a minimum."

"How soft?" Kemp asked with a grin. A soft confession was a vague term for an acknowledgment that it was possible that he could have hurt Ben.

"Medium soft at best." Jacob said. "But face it. This guy would be an idiot to admit to anything, because so far we've really got nothing tying him to the crime other than the rather obvious fact that he did it."

"So he needs to admit." Kemper said with finality.

THE INTERVIEW ROOM at the Law Enforcement Center was eight feet by eight feet at the most, with two institutionally uncomfortable couches placed perpendicular to each other and a small coffee table between them. Jacob Mann sat behind the two-way mirror with Rick Jordan and Gordy Hoffbrau, the head of investigations and heir apparent to be chief of police. Kemper didn't like Rick, the newest patrol officer to be moved up to investigator. Kemp and the five other investigators were tight, and they all showed Kemp the respect he thought he deserved. Rick Jordan kissed only one ass, and it wasn't Kemp's. Rick had his sights on Gordy's job, and his lack of respect for the elder investigators put him at immediate odds against all of them. Kemp didn't want him there, but Gordy, who enjoyed having his ass kissed, insisted.

Leah didn't have as much of an issue with Rick as she did with Gordy. He was smart, savvy with technology, and seemed to have a sixth sense about criminals, especially drug dealers. In the late 1990s, Gordy solved one of Terrance's rare murders using some sophisticated computerized evidence analysis, and was rewarded with the promotion to head of investigations. Leah didn't doubt his skill, but she had a visceral reaction to him—the way he guffawed with the male detectives but could barely muster a hello for her or any other female in the room. It didn't help that Gordy had multiple health issues including some kind of autoimmune disease that covered his body in red and purple blotches. Leah swore her dislike was purely about his being a jackass and had nothing to do with his appearance. It was hard to know what came first—women rejecting Gordy, or Gordy patronizing and ignoring the women in the room.

Kemper decided he wanted to interview Joe in the soft interview room, with more comfortable seating usually used for interviewing victims. He hoped the more casual setting would put him at ease. He'd have to read Joe his rights, but then Kemp planned to be as mellow and ingratiating as the law allowed.

Officers had gone to his home and asked Joe to go to the Law Enforcement Center for an interview, but he could drive himself because he wasn't under arrest. Kemp met him in the lobby and led him to the interview room, where Leah was already waiting.

"Make yourself comfortable," Kemp said. Knowing this was their guy, Leah pushed down the urge to treat Joe like the abuser that he was. He was skinny, with a light puberty mustache, jeans hanging low on his hips, and a mullet grazing his bony shoulders. He sat down on the couch across from Leah, nervous.

"Hey, I really want to thank you for coming in," Kemp said in his best guy-to-guy voice.

"No problem." Joe rubbed his hands on his dirty jeans. Sweaty palms.

"So, technically I have to read you your rights." Kemp took out the required laminated card and read the abbreviated Miranda warning quickly, his tone almost apologetic. Leah watched Joe's eyes grow wide as the reality of the situation sank in.

Kemp placed the card back in his notebook and smiled at his new buddy Joe, who still had barely uttered a word.

"So, you okay if I just ask you a couple of questions?" The implied question was really whether Joe was going to ask for an attorney.

"Sure," Joe squeaked, then cleared his throat and shuffled on the hard sofa. "Sure," he tried again, his voice finding a manlier octave. No attorney. Their first small victory.

"We're here because of Ben's injuries," Kemp started, and then frowned. Leah could see him struggling to find words to make the horrific injuries sound somehow less severe. He was not going to admit unless they could make this assault seem understandable, even justifiable under the circumstances. In criminal sexual conduct cases, sometimes that even meant making it seem like the victim seduced the perpetrator. It was an acceptable amount of deception allowed by the law. In this situation, finding the angle, the justification, for beating the hell out of a two-year-old was going to be quite a challenge.

"Boy, those toddlers are tough, aren't they?" Leah blurted out. "Always getting into things. You have to follow them 24/7." Leah didn't have children, but remembered her coworker, Zoe, talking about the chaos of parenting her twins when they were one year old.

Joe seemed to exhale a bit. "Ben started walking at nine months. He was hell on wheels. He still gets into everything. One time he got into the refrigerator and dumped out every jar and bottle he could. Ketchup and pickles and mayo . . ." Joe's voice drifted off, hesitant and nervous again.

"I sure remember that," Kemp said, picking up the thread. "I have two girls, and I was ready to give them away at that age. Man was that hard, having them wreck everything, make messes everywhere." Joe nodded and looked back and forth between Leah and Kemp, searching their faces.

"How many messes did he make yesterday?" Leah asked smoothly.

"I . . . I'm not really, uh . . ." *Joe should not play poker,* Leah thought. Fear lit up his face like a beacon.

"Yesterday kinda fuzzy?" Kemp asked knowingly. "Got a headache today? Do you need some water? Leah can grab you some water if you want some." *Oh yeah,* Leah thought, *the woman can fetch you a cool beverage.*

"Sure, yeah, that'd be good." Joe said. With her back turned, Leah smiled with all of her teeth at Kemp, and stepped out to find Joe a glass of water. Gordy met her in the hallway with a water bottle.

"This guy is guilty as fuck," Gordy whispered.

Leah nodded, avoiding his deep-set, watery eyes, and got back into the room quickly. Joe wordlessly took the bottle and downed a third of it, wiping his mouth with the neck of his grubby t-shirt. Leah gave him a thin, encouraging smile and resumed her seat .

Kemp continued to chit chat about the challenges of parenting, treating Joe with the utmost courtesy and respect. Leah watched Joe's face carefully, noticing how he nodded quickly anytime Kemp made a point. Pete Kemper was the consummate "cool jock" in high school classification terms, and Joe was the typical stoner. Back in the day, Joe had probably never received such respect from someone of Kemp's stature. Joe wanted Kemp's approval, and this was working in their favor.

"So what do you like to drink? I'm guessing after a day of chasing the kid around all day, you're ready for a cold one." Kemp flashed a conspiratorial smile, like he would crack a beer with Joe right now if he could.

"Uh . . ." Joe glanced at Leah, and she wondered if she should leave. Occasionally, offenders needed to make their confessions "man to man." She nodded encouragingly, hoping she could find a way to stay.

"Whiskey Cokes, usually," Joe finally said.

"Oh, yeah," Kemp said with a friendly grin. "There's nothing like settling into your chair at the end of the day and having a whiskey and Coke." Joe's face burst into a grin. Just two drinking buddies telling stories now.

Leah knew then she was out of this conversation. The "good ol' boy" approach was working too well. She simply nodded and smiled and tried to encourage him along.

"Any buddies stop over last night?" It was one of his most important questions, needed to establish or rule out the possibility of other suspects, but Kemp slid it in like it was nothing.

Joe's face became clouded with confusion. "Well, my buddy was supposed to stop by, but I guess he never did." The two most important words in that sentence were *I guess.* Joe was so drunk he didn't know if his friend was there or not. It was an important point to clarify.

"So he never made it?" Kemp asked.

He let out some sort of noise that was probably supposed to be a laugh, but Joe was so nervous it came out as a honking snort. "He must not have. He was gonna borrow my truck, but I still have my truck, so he never came."

"You don't remember for sure?" Kemp asked casually.

Nervous snort again. "The whole night's pretty fuzzy, actually."

"That happens," Kemp said understandingly, and Joe's body relaxed into his chair for the first time since they started the interview.

Gradually, Kemp shifted the conversation around to the injuries. "So the kid's got some broken bones. Some bruises. What happened?"

"I don't know, man," Joe said quickly. "I seriously don't. I swear to God, I don't know what happened." He clutched his hands together, which were shaking wildly.

"You don't seem like a bad guy," Leah said, seeing her chance to score an important point. Leah wasn't one of the cool kids in high school, but she was pretty enough and held her own. She was banking on Joe wanting her approval, too.

"I'm not a bad guy," he exhaled quickly. "I'm not. I'm really not."

"Nobody said you were," Leah said, looking at him as sincerely as she could. "These things happen in the blink of an eye. Taking care of kids is the hardest job in the world, and those frustrations, the fatigue–they can pile up fast. You have a few drinks to take the edge off, and it helps. But the booze can also make you do things you'd never do sober. We see it every day." Joe was nodding.

"I don't drink that much during the week at all. But then Friday night comes and, sometimes, I just kinda cut loose." Joe stopped making eye contact, getting absorbed in what he was saying. They both knew to stay silent and let him talk. "I take Ben everywhere. He's my buddy. We get along great most of the time. But I think he's getting his back teeth or something, because he just whined and cried and flipped out and shit all day long."

"Man, that sounds rough," Kemp said, not interrupting, trying to encourage.

"It was." Joe slumped forward and shakily rubbed his hands through his greasy thin hair. "I love that kid."

Leah took the leap. "We know you love him. But you were drinking, and he was fussy. Is that when it happened?"

Joe cringed and dropped his head. "No." It was a whisper. Not a forceful one.

"Is it possible, Joe, that you hurt Ben last night?" A soft confession would allow him just to endorse the possibility he could have done it.

Joe shook his head. Not forcefully. "I can't even remember last night."

"Joe," Leah began. "Ben got hurt last night, and his doctors are trying to help him. But we need to know what happened to him." Leah leaned forward, smelling his hangover, trying to force the contempt and judgment off her face.

"I. Don't. Know." His chin quivered slightly.

"I know it's pretty unclear," Kemp went on, "but I'm asking you to try to think back and really remember. What did you do to Ben last night?" The shift was subtle, but Kemp took it to an assumption that Joe hurt him.

Joe paused for a second and then words starting tumbling out. "All I know is he wouldn't go to sleep. I just wanted him to go to sleep because he was just flippin' out all day. I put him in his crib, turned off the light and left him in there. He was kinda screaming, and I just couldn't stand it anymore, so I walked away." His voice was getting quieter and quieter until it was almost a whisper.

"But then you went back in," Kemp said.

"I don't remember."

"You were drunk, and you lost it with him," Kemp persisted.

Joe held his head in his hands, his shoulders shaking. Leah's heart was pounding. They were so close, but they needed him to say it. Kemp leaned in close, his words quiet but clear. Clear enough for the jury to hear on the videotape. "You were drunk, and you were fed up with the crying, and you went in there and made it stop. Didn't you?"

Joe held up his hands in defeat. "I guess I did." His face contorted as he heard the words out loud, his world changing in that moment when he confessed to first degree assault of a child.

chapter two

LEAH WAS IN KEMP'S OFFICE, typing up notes on her laptop. Most of the office and plainclothes staff had already left for the day, and Kemp was helping the uniformed officers get Joe booked into jail. All the lights in the investigative wing shut off, and Leah left them off, appreciating the calm of the dark office. She called Max and filled him in about the day. When she told him they got the confession, Max whooped and told her she'd earned the rest of the week off.

"It was Kemp," she told Max. "He did it again."

"Yes, I did, didn't I?" Kemp strolled into his office, the unmistakable glow of victory on his face. Leah smirked at Kemp as she said goodbye to Max.

"You had help, Mr. Arrogant."

Kemp closed the door behind him, the dark office lit only by the flickering glow of the laptop.

"I did have help. It was both of us." Kemp pushed the lock on the door, a slow grin spreading across his face. He took the computer off Leah's lap, set it next to her, and pulled Leah out of her chair and up next to him.

"Damn right it was both of us," she said under her breath, his face coming close to hers. And as he kissed her, the tension and anxiety and anger from the day dissolved into frantic, sweaty, slightly desperate sex. Leah's last clear thought was that she was glad she wore her new bra. Kemp liked the front hooking kind he could pop off quickly, before dispatchers or a custodian wandered into their hallway and found them in a tangle on the institutional carpet.

AFTERWARD, STILL ON THE FLOOR, Leah wrapped herself in a silver thermal blanket she pulled out of an emergency road kit she found under Kemp's desk. Without a trace of shyness, Kemp stood up and found a bottle of water and two protein bars.

"Dear God, I'm starving." Leah caught the bar he tossed and tore off a bite.

"I'm still full from my hospital-issue breakfast burrito," Kemp said as he pulled on his boxers and t-shirt.

"Mhm." Leah, still focused on the bar, scanned the room for her underwear.

"Let's go get some real food." Kemp reached a hand out to help Leah up.

Leah looked up and finally made eye contact. "You wanna go out? Together?"

He shrugged and grinned. "Yeah. Why not?"

There were a hundred reasons why Leah should not have dinner with her fellow investigator that night. But Leah ignored all of them and took Kemp's hand.

WHEN LEAH FINALLY ARRIVED home it was after 10:00 p.m. Dinner was at Las Margaritas, and Leah ate everything on her plate, including almost the entire appetizer of guacamole with chips. Kemp was amused at her voracious appetite and took credit for "tiring her out." They had never been out together other than an occasional quick lunch during a day of interviews. Leah was uncharacteristically quiet. It was one of the many times she wished she could have had a drink to take the nervous edge off. But after spending the early part of her twenties in a drunken haze, she had "taken the cure." She had spent the last nine years sober and was left on her own to deal with her social awkwardness and occasional depression.

Kemp had two big margaritas and was all smiles. She didn't know what she hated more, the fact he could have two margaritas and stop, or that the case wasn't getting to him the way it got to her. *Spinal fluid leaking out of his nose . . . lumpy in the wrong places . . .* Kemp had photos, but she avoided them so far, needing to keep her head clear until after the interviews. Images swirled in her head throughout dinner, distracting her from Kemp's play-by-play of the interview and how they had walked Joe into his confession.

When dinner was over, Kemp accompanied her to her car and wanted to come home with her. She laughed him off, trying to appear casual despite the lusty affection in his eyes. Not only was the case clouding her judgment, but she needed time to process what was going on with the two of them. He seemed to want to "go public" with whatever it was that they were doing, but Leah had barely acknowledged it to herself.

Leah leaned up against her car, and Kemp surprised her by kissing her goodnight, resting his hands on her hips, his stubble from the day scratching her chin. The parking lot behind Las Margaritas was dark, but there were still people around. Leah broke away quickly, leaving him disappointed and questioning, and she headed home.

Their fling, or whatever it was, had started two years ago at the county Christmas party. While the dinner was tame, the real party started after the county commissioners left. The alcohol was flowing freely. The hard-core partiers had stayed for the band, and coworkers from every department were dancing together, somehow finding a way to shove past the constraints of workplace etiquette to put their hands on each other and bump into each other sweatily on the dance floor. Leah had stayed at a table with the newly separated Kemp and some of the jailers, who told bawdy stories about prison body searches and finding inmates in compromising situations. She was pounding Diet Cokes that night, missing alcohol but knowing she would have been on the dance floor had she been drinking, and was thus grateful not to have to deal with that on Monday morning. On her third trip to the restroom, she met Kemp in the hallway outside the restaurant. Having moved out the month before, he seemed to be pacifying his grief and anger with copious amounts of beer. He came out of the restroom and without missing a beat, wrapped his arms around her waist and kissed her. Forceful and sloppy, the taste of beer on his lips was delicious and forbidden. He broke away and wandered back to their table, neither of them acknowledging the kiss for the rest of the night.

As she pulled into her driveway, Leah's phone buzzed. She cringed, knowing her real friends would not call after ten on a Friday. While she wondered when 10:00 p.m. became the end of the night instead of the beginning, she pulled out her phone and checked the caller ID: Terrance County Government Center. That could mean two options—work or her brother, Luke. She hoped for work.

"Leah? Thank God you answered. You gotta come get me."

"I need to bail you out, you mean. Right, Luke?" Family ties superseded good boundaries and common sense, especially when it came to her alcoholic, criminal, marijuana-dealing only sibling.

"No. There's no bail. I'm just booked and released this time. It was only a DAR." Driving after revocation. Luke had lost his license years ago after numerous DUIs, but that detail had never kept him from being behind the wheel.

"I should let you walk home."

Silence on the other end. "I know. I'm such a shit," he muttered. The remorse only came after the offense, and never seemed to be enough to keep him from doing it the next time.

"Fine. I'll be there in ten."

LEAH'S BROTHER WAS UNFORTUNATELY, but intentionally, named Luke. As in Luke and Leah from Star Wars, although many true fans over the years had informed her that Princess Leia spelled her name differently. Their parents were endlessly geeky, and often intoxicated, Star Wars fanatics.

As she pulled up to the jail, which was across the street from the Social Services building, Leah sat low in her seat and hoped she wouldn't see any officers coming or going from work. Thankfully, her brother came running out quickly. A former jock until he got kicked off the basketball team for bad grades, Luke had just turned thirty and his lifestyle was beginning to catch up with him. He was panting as he pulled her door shut.

"Hey," Luke muttered.

Leah nodded her irritated greeting.

"Thanks for picking me up." Luke's dirty-blond hair was falling in his eyes, making him look younger, but his smoker's cough and lined face gave away years of hard living. "Were you awake?

"It was 10:30 when you called," she said, indignant with his arrogant, albeit correct, assumption that she had nothing else to do on a Friday night but pick him up. "Yeah, I was awake. I was actually just getting home."

"That's cool. Where were you?" He pulled a pack of cigarettes out of a large plastic bag labeled PERSONAL BELONGINGS that the jailers had put into storage for him.

"Don't even think about it."

"Sorry, sorry." Luke shoved the cigarette back in the pack and clutched the crinkly package in his fist. He needed the smoke, but Leah let the craving be another punishment for his latest screw-up. Leah turned the corner toward Luke's apartment when he cleared his throat nervously. "Um, would it work if I crashed at your place tonight?"

"What?" Leah groaned. "Luke . . . why? What's going on? What else did you do?"

"I didn't do anything. I swear. There's just some shit going down at my apartment, and I want to clear out of there for a while." Luke was looking out the window, avoiding Leah's eyes.

"Do I even want to know who you're living with? Are you dealing again?"

Luke tried to look hurt, but couldn't pull it off. It was actually a relief he wasn't the type of criminal who could look his sister in the face and lie to her. He had a shred of conscience left. "One of the guys at my place has some shit going down with his brother. I just wanna clear outta there for a few days. That's all."

The answer should have been no, without a doubt, but as always, Leah found herself nodding. "No drugs, no smoking, no booze, no girls." It was her typical speech, but she stumbled on the part about girls. Luke pretended to be a womanizer, but they both knew he couldn't keep a girl around for more than a night. Luke was messed up when it came to relationships. They both were. She didn't bother to ask when he would be leaving, because it was probably better if he stayed. Plus, and she never wanted to admit this to anyone, let alone Luke, it was nice to have someone else around.

LUKE SLEPT LIKE A LOG in the spare bedroom of Leah's small, nondescript three-bedroom rambler on the bad side of town. The railroad tracks were thirty yards from her back door. If a train ever derailed, her house would probably be crushed.

Leah awoke early on Saturday morning and headed out for a run with her neighbor, coworker, and the newest of friends, Amanda. Leah had admitted to Amanda she had her pegged wrong when she first started at Terrance County. Wearing high heels and tight skirts, Amanda had the look of a sorority girl, and Leah was prepared to dislike her from day one. Leah learned Amanda was intuitive, darkly funny, and a fast learner, traits that came from her chaotic and sad childhood.

Amanda was waiting outside her equally nondescript rambler, which was all but given to her by her father, the former judge, Matthew Bach. In the county's most recent scandal, Judge Bach left the bench after failing to recuse himself from a messy child protection case in which Amanda was the social worker, and she was also, impossibly, Judge Bach's illegitimate daughter. It was jaw dropping, but both the former judge and Amanda seemed to come through unscathed. He and Amanda had forged an awkward but comfortable relationship, all things considered.

Amanda was standing in the driveway, stretching her long legs, when Leah jogged up to her. The morning held the promise of some real warmth later in the day, and they were both optimistically dressed in shorts and t-shirts.

"Is Jake already out?" Jacob was also an early riser and often ran in the mornings, but not with Leah and Amanda because he would never be able to keep up. Leah was ready to talk a little shop with Jacob about the case and try to unload the weight off her shoulders that made her sleep more restless than usual.

"No, we were up kinda late last night so he's sleeping in." Amanda avoided Leah's eyes.

"You two were doing it all night long, weren't you?" They really were a disgustingly happy couple.

"You know I'm not answering that." Amanda pulled her hair into a high ponytail and started jogging down the driveway. Amanda was several inches taller, but Leah was a more experienced runner. They kept a good pace together, and by the end of the block they found their rhythm.

They ran in silence for several minutes, climbing hills and negotiating a long area without sidewalks. Amanda asked about the case, so Leah was able to unload. She described Jenny's black-rimmed, absent eyes, and Joe's pathetic evasiveness.

"But he still confessed, even though he didn't remember anything?" Amanda asked, breathing a little harder as they climbed the last hill before they returned to their neighborhood. "How does that work?"

Leah felt a flash of irritation as Amanda asked the question that had been hovering just under her consciousness. "Nobody is going to confess to something they didn't do."

"Well, yeah, but how does he know he did it if he blacked out?"

"Have you ever blacked out?" Leah asked, her irritation growing.

"I don't know," Amanda said, not seeing, or perhaps ignoring, Leah's attitude. "I had my years of partying, but even when I couldn't remember what happened, as soon as people started talking about it, it came back."

"It doesn't happen that way in a real blackout," Leah said, the conversation adding to the heat of the day.

"You're making my point, aren't you? If he blacked out, then he has no idea what he did."

"Well then it wasn't a real blackout, was it?" Leah slowed to a walk for their last block, hands on her hips.

"I'm not trying to piss you off," Amanda said. "I just don't get it, I guess."

"The guy confessed. What's to get?" Leah wanted to start running again to burn off the growing frustration. This run was supposed to make her feel better.

"I'm sorry. It's great that he confessed. Jake didn't mention anything last night, so he must have felt good about it, too." Amanda tried to get her friend to hear her out, but Leah kept walking. "Leah!"

Leah stopped. "Shit." She turned to face Amanda. "It doesn't feel right," she admitted.

Amanda crossed her arms and pondered the implications. "Does it matter that it doesn't feel right? A confession is a slam dunk, right?"

"Wrong," Leah shook her head. "A confession is actually one of the weakest ways to get an arrest, because the offender can 'take it back,' so to speak, and then you could be done. We don't have a witness or any concrete evidence on him. It was like he knew no one else could have done it, so he just gave it up."

Amanda nodded, still processing. "But is there anyone else who could have done it? Doesn't it pretty much have to be him?"

"I guess so," Leah said. "But a guy can be guilty as shit, and that doesn't mean he's going to get convicted." They had arrived back at Amanda's driveway, and Leah was even more frustrated. "And a guy can look as guilty as shit, and not be."

"Let's not think about any more work today," Amanda said. "You wanna come in for a glass of water . . . some coffee . . . a huge caramel roll to offset all that running?"

"Nah, I'm gonna head home and run my head under the shower." As if the stress of the case could just wash away.

"Zoe texted that she wants to barbecue tonight. Do you have any plans?"

"Nope. It must be my turn to have everyone over," Leah said. "I'll text Zoe, and you guys can come over around six. And no work talk!"

Easier said than done.

READYING HER HOUSE for company turned out to be the ideal distraction. Leah dragged Luke out of bed, and together they hosed down her deck and furniture, and he mowed the lawn and watered the grass while Leah cleaned the house, windows open and music blaring. Leaves were finally fully grown in, and many trees in their neighborhood were blossoming with richly fragrant pink and white blooms. It was a glorious spring day, and the horrific images and questionable confession of the case were finally fading.

Judging by the huge mess, Luke had already become too comfortable in the spare bedroom, but he left before her guests arrived and promised to be gone all night. She had to fight the urge to ask where he would be.

Zoe and her husband, Sam, arrived first, their two-year-old twins in tow. Zoe had recently cut ten inches off her stick-straight black hair, leaving a shoulder-grazing bob that several fellow employees had copied already. It was impossible not to like Zoe, and she was well-respected by the entire staff. Only when she was really comfortable and sometimes a little drunk did she reveal a shockingly dirty sense of humor that had left Amanda and Leah in hysterics at numerous dinners and shopping trips.

Leah had set up her office with a napping corner and put all of her breakables out of reach. Zoe and Sam's pig-tailed daughter, Olivia, was out cold. Zoe carried her inside and laid her on the blankets, and then headed back out with Olivia's twin brother Dylan. Sam was chasing Dylan away from the railroad tracks when Amanda and Jacob walked up the driveway with a bottle of wine and a pan of brownies. The deck on Leah's house spanned most of the back of the house and wrapped around the side so that the cul-de-sac was visible. Leah was just setting a platter of chips and salsa on the patio table when a truck pulled into the driveway, and Kemp climbed out and made his way to the backyard.

"Why, Pete Kemper," Jake said with a smirk. "Whatever are you doing at our friend Leah's home?" Jake's smarmy grin told Leah he knew way too much.

Leah could not figure out what had made Kemp so suddenly forward. While Zoe introduced Sam to Kemp, Leah went inside and banged around in the kitchen getting the steaks and chicken ready for the grill. She turned around to find Kemp standing inches from her face.

"Jeez!" Two steaks slid off the platter and onto the floor.

Kemp picked up the steaks, rinsed them off in the sink and put them back on the platter. "No harm no foul."

She just glared. "Those steaks were ten bucks a pound."

Kemp flashed his big-man-on-campus grin. "You look all pissy. Why're you so mad?"

"I did not invite you to my home." Leah couldn't look at him when he stood that close. Aside from the numerous investigations, they had been together on his office floor a dozen times since their first sloppy Christmas kiss, but this kind of eye contact was rarely part of their interaction. He smelled like beer and fabric softener, and she wondered if a part of his overwhelming appeal was that being with him always felt destructive and wrong.

It was also strange to have him in her kitchen, out of context. He was in jeans and a t-shirt when she was used to seeing him in khakis . . . or in nothing . . . It was disconcerting and somehow felt more intimate than being naked.

"Are you trying to be my boyfriend, Kemp? Are we going steady now?" She was trying to force a light tone but didn't even convince herself.

"You bet I'll go steady with you. I'll call it anything you want." Her back was against her refrigerator, and a magnet souvenir from the North Shore was pressing into her shoulder blade. He rested his arms on either side of her so she was trapped. He was being so damn forward it made her queasy, but that also could have been from his hot beer breath. Unable to make eye contact, Leah stared at the logo on his U2 concert t-shirt.

"Where is this coming from, Kemp? Why are you suddenly so interested in being a couple?"

"Why do you look so scared?" Kemp asked with a flash of hurt behind his eyes. "I'm a good guy, and I like messing around with my office door locked and way too many people pretending they don't notice. But I'd also like to have a beer with you on a Saturday night and hang out with you and your friends. Is that so terrible?"

"I'm an alcoholic. I don't drink beer." Still so difficult to look him in the face, though his eyes were sincere.

"We'll drink pink lemonade then, if that's what you want."

"You don't even know what I drink." His closeness was setting off alarms in her head. Leah had always tried to blame her aversion to romance on her stoic Norweigan heritage. But the truth went deeper than that. Sex was the easiest part of her few, failed relationships, but actual intimacy made her want to jump out of her skin. Leah had attended enough trainings on the importance of parent-child attachment in child development to know that her drug-addicted, dysfuncional parents shared a good part of the blame for her inability to connect to people.

"You drink about five Diet Cokes a day, which you try to hide, along with a bag of M&Ms that are always in your bag." Kemp's knowledge of her vices was not making her feel any more comfortable. "At that Christmas party two years ago when you kissed me you'd had ten Diet Cokes, at least." He winked.

She wanted to punch him in the stomach. "You were so drunk I'm surprised you remember at all. And *you* kissed *me*."

"Oh, I remember. I was drunk enough to finally get up the nerve, that's all."

"What do you mean, *finally*? You had just separated from your wife. The ink was just dry on your divorce last fall." His face drooped as she mentioned his ex-wife and their bitter divorce, and she was annoyed with herself for ruining the moment that was making her squirm just seconds ago.

Down the hall, Olivia woke up and started to fuss. Kemp backed up and gave Leah some breathing room just as Zoe walked in the back door.

"So sorry, guys," Zoe said, rushing past. "Keep talking. We totally can't hear a word of this through the open window right behind you."

Leah's face burned. "You suck, Kemp. Party's over."

He picked up the steaks off the counter and headed back outside. "Oh, no. Party's not over. We haven't even eaten yet," he said over his shoulder. Leah covered her face with her hands and tried to regain some composure.

Olivia came out to the kitchen followed by Zoe, fighting back a grin. "Eat? Eat?" Olivia asked, her hands outstretched for any offering of food.

Kids were such a wonderful distraction. "You bet, sweets. Let's head out and find you a snack. And you tell your mama to get rid of that silly grin." Leah held the door open for both of them.

Olivia pointed at Zoe. "Mama, you got siwwy gwin?"

"Mama's just happy for her friend Leah," Zoe said, scooping up Olivia and patting Leah on the arm. She then leaned in and said under her breath, "Now you don't have to get floor burns from that filthy carpet anymore."

"I hate you." Leah whispered back at Zoe. Bright red, Leah gave up on hiding her embarrassment and followed her friends outside.

As it turned out, Kemp knew very little about grilling. The chicken and steak were both dried out and burned on one if not both sides, and piled unceremoniously on a platter in the middle of the weather-worn picnic table. It was tight for all of them to fit onto Leah's deck, but they managed with Kemp and Leah sitting on camping chairs and everyone else seated around the table. Olivia and Dylan were bellied up between Zoe and Sam, both toddlers covered in strawberries and mangled barbecue potato chips.

"Mmmm, look how black the chicken is," Leah said, holding up a piece of charred meat. "Do you want some, kids? Uncle Kemp has charbroiled a delicious piece of coal for you."

"Hey, this is perfectly cooked if you like it on the done side," Kemp said, pointing to Zoe and Sam. "You should be thankful I'm not giving your kids salmonella."

"Olivia was eating Post-it notes on the way here," Sam said. Hearing her name, Olivia looked up and grinned with strawberries in her teeth. "We've relaxed our standards."

"Good practice for this cardboard," Jake pointed at Sam across the table with his fork.

"Okay, you know what, Sharpie," Kemp said, "it will take you years to become half the grillmaster I am." Everyone laughed at the "Sharpie" comment except for Jake, who turned to Amanda, his beloved and recent fiancée.

"You told them?" Jake face reddened, so Amanda stifled her smile.

"A little . . ." Amanda squinted, bleary-eyed from the wine, and Jake shot Leah a look as she snickered.

Kemp poked Jake with the spatula. "Come on, dude. It's precious . . ."

"Adorable," Zoe declared with a confident smile and wink. She and Leah had actually agreed it was the most embarrassing proposal of all time, but had promised to be kind to his face.

Jake straightened his short frame as tall as it would go. "Well, she said yes, didn't she," he huffed.

"Okay, I haven't heard this story," Sam said, bouncing Dylan on one leg while Olivia crawled under the picnic bench.

"Really?" Zoe said. "I can't believe I haven't told you this one. They got engaged weeks ago."

Jake grimaced, but Amanda wrapped her arms around Jake and grinned. "It's a beautiful story, and I'm proud to tell it."

"That's love, future Mrs. Sharpie." Kemp waggled his eyebrows at her.

Amanda made a face at him, and turned to Sam. "We were staying at the Westin in downtown Minneapolis for the weekend. Gorgeous suite . . . we had a hot tub in the room. We had this amazing dinner and went back to the room for drinks, and uh, *et cetera* . . ." Leah held her napkin up to her mouth to hide her snickering. Amanda glared at her. "And when we got in the hot tub I saw his proposal . . ."

"Tattooed on his chest!" Kemp finished.

"I didn't get a tattoo," Jake protested, his cheeks red but mouth turned up, embarrassed but with enough wine in him to finish the story. "I declared my love and desire to be with Amanda forever . . . on my chest . . . with a marker."

"Permanent marker!" Zoe announced with glee, squeezing Sam's hand. "I really can't believe I didn't tell you this story."

"Maybe you didn't want to make me feel bad since all I did was get down on one knee . . ." Sam grinned.

"And it was lovely," Zoe said, leaning into him.

"Blah blah blah, back to Sharpie," Kemp interrupted. "And he shaved his chest to create a *clean writing surface*, all smooth like a baby's rear end, and ended up giving himself a great big homemade tattoo!" Kemp sat back and drained his beer.

"I do *not* have a tattoo," Jake insisted. "I have a few dots on my chest where the ink sank under my skin where I had razor burn, and it stayed and smeared and . . . yeah, okay fine . . . I have a couple of tiny, smudgy chest tattoos." Amanda leaned over and kissed him on his temple. "Totally worth it."

As daylight faded and her friends laughed and talked and refilled their drinks, Leah sat back and tried to figure out what to do about her resistance to dating Kemp openly. Clearly they had some sort of pull toward each other, and Leah was tired of being single and lonely. Her track record with men was the real problem here. Her jackass of an ex-husband, Rob, was her forgettable first, but they split up a few months after they got married. Getting away from him was Leah's first step toward sobriety, although to be fair to herself, very few women could tolerate that man sober.

After Rob, Leah went through a period of very poor choices, to put the situation mildly. Unfortunately many of those choices could be attributed to things she said, did or purchased (damn that Internet) when drunk. Leah was working overnights at a shelter for teenage girls and waitressing at a rural bar in western Wisconsin. Her waitressing gig usually ended by 9:00 p.m. when the grill closed, and she spent the rest of the evening partying with the patrons, who were usually fellow borderline alcoholics. When she woke up in the cab of a pickup, naked from the waist down, with a huge, hairy middle-aged man draped across her, she knew enough was enough.

Leah never went into treatment, but her mother had been attending AA meetings for years, so one particularly lonely night she went along as a guest. One meeting led to two, and before she knew it she had earned her ninety-day medallion. No one had ever told Leah she couldn't drink again, but it seemed to make sense to quit altogether. That was the AA way.

Most of the time abstaining wasn't a hardship. But when she watched her guests that night drinking beer and wine, laughing and relaxing together, Leah felt something like craving. Or perhaps it was more like longing. After a few beers, they relaxed in a way Leah had never been able to do, and the laughter and buoyant moods were enviable.

The evening faded into night, and Zoe and Sam packed up their kids and headed home. Jake and Amanda helped carry in the dinner dishes and beer bottles. Leah politely asked if they wanted one more, but Jake declined saying he was tired. Amanda winked at Leah, and they made their way home, leaving Leah and Kemp back in the kitchen, alone.

Leah was worried about what to do regarding Kemp, and about when Luke was going to come home, and how she would explain each to the other. She was tired, anxious and a little gloomy despite the festive atmosphere of the night. And she still had no idea what she really wanted from Kemp. But when he gently brushed the hair out of her eyes and smiled down at her, she leaned in to him without another thought. Sleepily they shuffled off to her bedroom like an old married couple, and the sex that night was slow and sweet, leaving Leah breathless. And then terrified.

chapter three

MONDAY MORNINGS at Terrance County Social Services usually involved lingering over cinnamon rolls and coffee in the hallway before taking on the pile of police reports that had come in over the weekend. Leah was relieved to get away from her personal life for eight hours and spend her energy where she felt competent. When she woke up on Sunday morning with Kemp in her bed, her insecurity and ambivalence were there in full force. She just wasn't ready to linger over breakfast and the Sunday paper with him, and she definitely wasn't ready to introduce her criminal, marijuana-dealing brother to her cop boyfriend (if that's really what he was now), so she hustled Kemp out as fast as he would go. He was hurt, but he kissed her, patted her ass, and left without complaint. Luke came home early that evening looking much worse for the wear, but Leah again fought the urge to ask what he had been doing.

Kemp had emailed a copy of the preliminary report he completed on Sunday night. He included an update on the baby's condition: critical but stable. His leg fracture had been surgically set on Sunday, and the swelling in his brain appeared to be under control. The report also included photos, so Leah took a deep breath and forced herself to look for the first time. Little Ben had a cast on his leg up to his hip, and a urinary catheter so he didn't need a diaper. There was an obvious handprint bruise near his ribs on the right side, and one rib was clearly misshapen and out of place. But it was his face that was unbearable. His eyes were swollen shut, and he had two deep, shiny purple black eyes. His head was wrapped and covered in gauze, bits of black hair poking out haphazardly. Leah printed two of the less troubling photos, closed the file on her computer and wished she was back at home.

At their staff meeting, Max started by asking Leah to update them on the investigation with Ben.

"It was a long day," Leah began. "I have some photos, but they're effing awful. The baby's still critical, but he's stable." She passed the photos around the table.

"What's his prognosis?" Roberta asked softly. With the distinction of being at Terrance County longer than anyone else, Roberta admitted that not much upset her anymore. Today she could only glance at the photos and still looked nauseated.

"I don't really know," Leah admitted. "We focused on the investigation on Friday, so I don't know much about how the baby's doing. He was in surgery when we were there, and it was almost easier that way because it kept my head clear for the interviews. I'm planning on going back to the hospital today to see him and talk with the doctor. He has a care conference at two. I'll know more after that."

The normally talkative group was quiet.

"Leah, aren't you going to tell everyone the good part of this story?" Max asked.

"Oh, please give us something to feel good about," Jill said. Leah was confused for a minute until she understood he was talking about their interviews.

Leah avoided Amanda's eyes. "We got a confession from the boyfriend."

"Wow, Leah!" Jill said. "Great job." Roberta patted Leah on the back.

"It was totally Kemper," she admitted.

"Kemp can get just about anything out of anyone," Jill said. Both Amanda and Zoe looked away significantly.

"Was he high, or is he some kind of vicious bastard, or what?" Roberta asked, still reeling, because she rarely swore. "Did he have any explanation for himself?"

"He was drunk," Leah said. She didn't want to go into detail about the possible blackout, the nagging uncertainty about the confession growing in her mind.

"What are they charging him with?" Zoe asked.

"Attempted murder," Amanda said. "Plus first-degree assault and several other things. He's looking at twenty years easily."

"That assumes the baby makes it," Leah said. Heavy sighs around the table.

"You know they'll kick the shit out of him in prison," Jill said, patting Ben's little face and passing the photos back to Leah. The image of Joe in prison getting beaten to a pulp was no consolation, and did nothing to get the images of the baby out of Leah's mind.

"Okay," Zoe said, clasping her hands. "So the plus side is he's stable, his mom didn't do it so she'll be there for him, and the guy who did it is in jail." Zoe, the eternal optimist, always had to find something positive.

"You're absolutely right, Zoe," Max said. "It's not all bad news for little Ben. And children's brains are amazingly resilient, so he may really surprise us." Max collected the printed photos and put them back on Leah's file. "Are you ready for an ongoing worker? I mean, I think it's safe to assume we'll substantiate maltreatment and determine services are needed for Mom, right?"

To substantiate maltreatment meant that their agency officially determined there was enough information to say Joe had harmed Ben.

"We'll substantiate against the boyfriend, but we don't have any allegations against Mom right now. I think we need to talk about that," Leah said. "Joe had no prior history of assault, other than being 'mean' when he drank. Do we think he was a reasonable caregiver to be in charge of Ben all day, every day, or was it neglectful for Mom to leave Joe in charge?"

"Do you know much about Joe's pattern of drinking?" Jill asked. "Was he trashed all the time? Did they have any rules about not drinking when he watched Ben?"

"I didn't ask specific questions," Leah said, growing irritated, "but I will today."

The next order of business was to review the new intakes. The law required that every report needed to be screened according to prescribed guidelines set by the state. If the report met the legal criteria for abuse or neglect, they were required to conduct a less formal assessment or a more formal investigation. There was an educational neglect report for an eight-year-old who had twenty-three unexcused absences. Consensus: It was past the deadline for filing educational neglect reports, so Max would inform the school they would have to monitor the situation themselves and file next year if the problem was still there. Next report involved a sixteen-year-old placed in foster care over the weekend due to an altercation with her mom, during which they both apparently scratched each other's faces, the mom pulled out a tuft of the girl's hair, and the girl tore a hole in the mom's pajamas ("You all have my permission to smack me silly if I ever get into a shoving match with one of my kids, no matter how mouthy they get," Zoe said.) Consensus: Jill would do a family assessment because of the hair-pulling and scratching. The final report was that a family had been reported many times due to the condition of their home, but there was no new information and nothing hazardous to the older children who lived there. Consensus: it didn't meet the criteria for neglect, so it was ruled out.

By the time the group was reviewing ongoing cases that needed input, Leah was mentally checked out. Amanda was talking again about the Chuck Thomas family, the case that had turned her life upside down the previous year. Chuck

Thomas had been sexually abusing his daughter, Rachel, for most of her life, and he had beaten up his son who had threatened to tell.

The Thomas case had been all encompassing for Amanda for months, and, selfishly, Leah had grown tired of hearing about it. Lucky for all of them, the case was drawing to a close, and Amanda was telling them about how Mary Thomas actually shook Amanda's hand at the end of their court hearing last week, thanking her for helping their family. Or what remained of their family. Chuck had a heart attack and died in prison four months after he was sentenced. Kemp had correctly predicted that a narcissist like Chuck Thomas was never going to make it in prison. "One way or another, the universe rights itself in the end," he had said.

"In other words, Amanda owes us cinnamon rolls!" Roberta said, patting Amanda on the back. "Job well done, kiddo."

While they were wrapping up, Max assigned Ben's case to Amanda since she was going to have time after closing the Thomas case. As the investigator on the case, Leah wanted to talk to the doctors and still needed to see Ben before she could close her investigation. Amanda, as the case manager in the ongoing case, would work with Jenny on ensuring she was able to keep Ben safe and address his needs. Both Leah and Amanda were pretty confident Jenny was capable of protecting Ben, but there were some nagging issues. Amanda would work with Jenny to create a case plan that would include the safety issues they needed to address regarding Jenny's care of Ben. Amanda and Leah agreed that, if Jenny knew Joe was frequently intoxicated or high while he took care of Ben, they would need to address the issue with Jenny.

The first appearance in court for Joe was that morning at eleven, so Leah and Amanda decided to go to the hearing, grab some lunch, and head up to the care conference at the hospital. By the time they gathered their files and made it to the courtroom, they were late and had to sneak in the back. Joe looked petrified as the judge read the charges against him. Leah noticed with some degree of relief he had been assigned Steven Grayson for his public defender, so he would have a rigorous defense. Steven made no statements other than to enter a plea of "not guilty" and to request a speedy trial. She also noted that Jenny wasn't there, which was good for Jenny and Ben, but not so good for Joe. The courtroom was empty, so it appeared that he would be facing the charges alone.

After the hearing, they drove through a fast food place and grabbed some sandwiches on their way to Children's Hospital. Amanda drove and Leah navigated, getting confused and flustered in the parking ramp again. By the time they got inside, Leah was a grouch.

"How do you know where you're going?" Leah asked, trying to keep up with Amanda and her damnable long legs.

"Lucy delivered her baby here," Amanda said over her shoulder. "And I remember the PICU."

The Pediatric Intensive Care Unit was hard to forget. Basically one large room with spaces that could be separated by curtains, the beds were mostly filled by children that looked too young for school. She supposed it made sense the children who were injured or sick were the youngest and most vulnerable. Seeing the parents' vacant, aching eyes and the frail bodies wrapped in tubes and wires was almost intolerable. Yet Amanda seemed unfazed.

"If this place doesn't drive a person to drink, I don't know what would," Leah said, gaping at an unconscious toddler with a ventilator tube coming out of his mouth. "Why aren't you as freaked as I am?"

"With my mom sick for so long, I spent more of my adolescence in a hospital than in school," Amanda reminded her. "You just get immune after a while."

They found the main nurses' station and asked for Suni, the hospital social worker assigned to Ben. A moment later a stunning older woman with jet black hair that reached her waist and skin the color of terra cotta greeted them. She led them to a larger meeting room where the care conference was to take place. There were already several doctors or other hospital staff gathered around the table wearing either hospital scrubs or expensive-looking suits.

"Are we still waiting for Mom?" Suni asked the group.

"Baby just came out of surgery," a young blonde with a pile of charts in front of her answered. "She wants to make sure he's settled before she comes in."

"What were they doing today?" Leah asked. Everyone at the table quieted and turned to the new strangers in the group.

"This is Leah and Amanda, CP workers from Terrance County," Suni said. Quiet murmurs and groans around the table.

"I don't know how you two can do your jobs," said an Asian woman in her thirties wearing a black blazer and stethoscope around her neck. "The misery you must see . . ."

Leah was still rattled by the sight of all those children clinging to life. "I guess we could say the same to you."

"Fair enough," Suni said.

"They reset his leg," an older man in scrubs said in answer to her question. "And they had to take his spleen today. Too much bleeding."

There were some murmurs around the table. No one looking too surprised or alarmed at the news that Baby Ben had an organ removed.

"Is he going to be okay?" Leah blurted. "I mean, my God, how does a two-year-old tolerate this much trauma?"

The various medical staff looked at each other. Finally a fortyish woman with long red hair and a face full of freckles answered with some authority: "We think he's going to pull through." Leah exhaled. "But Ben will have a new normal. We think we have the swelling in his brain under control, but we won't know the extent of the brain damage for several days, weeks, or months. We took him off the vent for a few minutes before his surgery this morning, and he did quite well, so he has some good brain functioning. He can function without a spleen, and the rest of his injuries will likely heal with few long-term effects."

The red-haired doctor, Ben's lead physician, took charge of the meeting and went around the room asking for updates from Ben's large medical team. Amanda asked a couple questions, and both she and Leah took notes, trying to understand the medical terminology.

After about fifteen minutes, Jenny entered, and it was amazing what a difference a few days could make. No longer shell-shocked, Jenny looked calm and competent as she sat at the table and took notes with the medical providers. Her face was washed clean of the heavy makeup, and she wore a Vikings sweatshirt and jeans. With two years of nursing school under her belt, Jenny could keep up with the terminology better than Amanda and Leah. She even spoke up to answer a few questions about his IVs and urinary output.

When the meeting was over, Amanda and Leah approached Jenny, and Leah introduced Amanda as their family's new social worker.

"Hey, guys," Jenny said quietly. "They said you need to see Benny today."

"If it's okay. I just need to stop in for a minute, just to say that I saw him face to face," Leah said. "Then I'll be wrapping up my investigation. Amanda will work with you from here."

"You bet," Jenny said and led them back into the main PICU area. Amanda raised her eyebrows at Leah, as if to ask if this was the same mess of a woman she had seen a few days before. Leah shrugged her response.

Jenny stopped at the bed nearest the nurses station. "Here's my baby boy," she said, reaching out and stroking his one visible hand. A blanket covered his legs, and his abdomen was wrapped in a mesh surgical bandage. "He didn't need much time in recovery," Jenny said proudly. "He handles the surgeries really good." The ventilator tube was taped to his little mouth, his head was still wrapped, and the bruises had faded to mottled purplish blobs all over his body. Amanda stepped forward, unflinching, and smiled faintly as she patted his hand. Leah felt like the floor was shifting under her feet. She wanted to punch a wall.

As promised, they only stayed a few minutes, then wished Jenny well. As they unraveled the mystery of their path back to the car, Amanda raved about Jenny.

"She seems like she'll be great to work with. She was so calm, almost peaceful about Ben. And she handled the care conference like a pro. He's lucky his mom is so put together, at least right now. I mean, I get that there are still questions about how we got here, but this is a really good start." Amanda finally noticed Leah's stony silence and stopped talking.

Leah began to feel Amanda's comments were about her somehow, as if she knew Leah could barely function in this place. It took her mood from irritable to pissed off. Amanda tried to engage Leah, but Leah just shrugged her off and kept walking to the parking ramp she couldn't maneuver through without getting lost.

When they finally reached the dumpy county car, Amanda paused before putting the key in the ignition. "Are you okay, Leah? You seem really off."

Probably meant to be supportive, Amanda's calm made Leah feel even more incompetent. Then again, she thought, what didn't push her over the edge these days?

"I'm fine," Leah finally answered. "Let's go. I wanna get back at a decent time."

Amanda started the car and headed out of the ramp (without missing a turn, Leah noted with resentment) and drove straight home. After a few weak attempts at conversation, Amanda gave up talking to her friend. Leah knew her insecurity was making her mean, but it matched how she felt on the inside so she just didn't care. She stared out the window and wondered why the hell she ever thought she wanted to do this job.

chapter four

IT WAS ONLY MONDAY, and Leah was already counting the days to the weekend. The ride home from the hospital never got better. When they got back to the office, Leah muttered something mildly apologetic about being premenstrual, went straight home and fell onto the couch. Her day became even longer when she remembered she had agreed to take her mother grocery shopping.

Beverly Danco gave meaning to the phrase "hard miles." Only fifty-five years old, she carried herself like a haggard Disney villainess. Cigarettes, vodka, marijuana, and a fair amount of LSD in her younger days had carved deep lines in her face and built a hump between her shoulder blades. Abscessing teeth, thinning hair, and permanent gravel in her voice completed the picture of a woman in need of TLC and a makeover. While hard living had taken its toll, the loss of her husband at age forty-five had permanently sucked the color out of Beverly's life. Despite their differences, Beverly and Roger seemed cut from the same cloth. Their similarities helped them forge a bond that probably should have stayed between the two of them. Leah had learned years ago, much too late for her dad's sake, that there was a name for her father's quirkiness, self-absorption, and rigidity: severe Asperger's Syndrome. He was a dear man who couldn't take care of himself and could rarely pull himself out of his obsessions or away from booze long enough to remember he had children.

Together, Roger and Beverly navigated their life in a marijuana-induced, vodka-enhanced haze punctuated by acid trips and Star Wars events. Leah and Luke were dragged all over the country in a beat-up conversion van to attend sci-fi conventions, book signings, or "meet and greets" with the cast members.

Obsessions were a hallmark of Asperger's Syndrome, and Roger Danco's lifelong passion was Jedi Knights. Luke loved their lifestyle, but Leah grew weary of parents who acted like twelve-year-olds. As a child, Leah was hyper-responsible and raised her brother in front of, and with little help from, their distant parents. She babysat Luke in cheap hotel rooms while her parents partied with fellow

George Lucas fans, including her parents' horrible friend Carl. They ate dinners of vending machine candy bars and Cheetos while watching grisly R-rated movies on cable. Their parents would stumble in late in the night, or occasionally the next morning. As those weekends ended, their dad would usually submerge into a depression that lasted until he found the next book signing or convention.

By high school, Leah was tired of being a mom and started to neglect her younger brother as much as their parents did. Luke was bewildered by her sudden abandonment, but Leah was fed up and ignored his pleas and pitiful stares.

Things happened to Luke back then—or at least she suspected they did. Leah couldn't bear to think of what she had seen one night when he was twelve. Usually the memory was pushed so far away she could forget, or at least pretend, that it wasn't even there. But she knew the reason she put up with so much of Luke's crap as an adult was that she never forgave herself for leaving him back then. He was hers to protect, if only because no one else was going to do it, and she had failed.

Leah escaped her parents' dysfunction by creating her own. She started dating her bastard of an ex-husband when they were sixteen. He was a football player with a wicked sense of humor who could barely read. He and Leah fought, got drunk, made up, and drank some more. Their longest breakup began the month before she left for college, and he accused her of cheating on him before she even left town.

Her mediocre grades barely got her into a state college, but she left home with relief and excitement to have, finally, no one to answer to or take care of except herself. With that attitude, she lasted a little over a year. College professors simply weren't willing to pass students who never showed up. Leah dropped out of school and moved to Petersville, a small town outside of Terrance. Defeated and lonely, Leah and her boyfriend reconciled. Her judgment sank even lower when she agreed to marry him so they could sign a joint lease. She cosigned on a truck loan and two credit cards before he banged a waitress, and she beat up his truck Carrie Underwood style and kicked him out. Finalizing their divorce took longer than their marriage lasted. She took a waitressing job to pay back all his debt, and her drinking took a miserable toll.

What happened to her family during those years had never been clear to Leah. One snowy night when she was twenty-four, she received a call from her sobbing brother while she was just finishing a long, lonely shift at work. Dad was gone, he wailed between gasps. He couldn't answer when she asked how it happened, and she never asked again.

Leah drove the twenty miles to her house to find Luke as close to catatonic as she ever cared to see another human being. After hugging her desperately the second she walked in the door, he shut down, and they didn't have a real conversation for months. Their mother was in worse shape than Luke. Beverly was lying in the bed she had shared with her husband and drinking straight vodka, Star Wars movies on a seemingly endless loop on the VCR. This left Leah to contact the funeral home, call their few relatives, and arrange the service. Fourteen people attended Roger Danco's funeral, which consisted of two Bible readings, a song from a CD, and Leah giving a brief but sincere eulogy about her dad's best intentions. Leah, Luke, and Beverly sat in the front row of the funeral home's small chapel, the three of them so paralyzed by emotion they barely spoke or moved, sitting in their hardback chairs like a chain of lonely, stoic islands.

AFTER THE FUNERAL, LEAH RETURNED to her dreadful job and did her best to ignore her family. The calls from Beverly's doctors, which started within days, made that impossible. Less than a week after the funeral, Beverly collapsed at a grocery store and was taken by ambulance to the hospital. She had acute pancreatitis and alcoholic hepatitis. She avoided commitment to a locked treatment facility by checking herself into a nicer (i.e. unlocked) program voluntarily.

Beverly loved treatment, making friends and delving into the issues and struggles that led her to drinking in the first place. Leah and Luke attended a cringeworthy family session during which Beverly sobbed through a lengthy apology for "not being there for them the way a mother should." Luke was tweaking during the entire session, and Leah was weary and nauseated from a wicked hangover, but they forgave their mother. They all hugged and promised to spend some real family time together after Beverly returned home. Leah attended Beverly's graduation and dutifully clapped when she earned her medallion. Beverly was discharged that same day and Leah drove her home, celebrating with ice cream on the way. When Leah left her mom's house, Beverly was smiling through grateful, happy tears.

An hour later, Leah received her first call from Beverly, who was "a little worried" about the noises in the basement. Three hours and fourteen phone calls later, Leah gave up working and went to her mom's house, where she found Beverly locked in her bathroom with a butcher knife, sobbing about the stalker she was certain was in the basement. She had been out of treatment for seven hours and sober for twenty-eight and a half days.

What followed was a series of increasingly anxious and paranoid nights that culminated in a trip to the emergency room where the ER doctor gave Beverly her first shot of Ativan, a "lovely medicine" that Beverly said handled her anxiety for a few hours. And thus began Beverly's cycle of therapy, medications, and hospitalizations as they realized that alcohol and marijuana had been masking a crippling anxiety disorder.

As Leah pulled into her mother's driveway to begin the tedious job of grocery shopping with Beverly Danco, she braced for the lecture she knew was coming. Leah hadn't been to a meeting in months. Her mother was convinced she was on the road back to drinking and was trying to guilt her into coming back. While AA was a lifeline for many people, it had become a source of irritation (add it to the list) and stress for Leah. For one, her mother ended up in tears at almost every meeting, and the melodrama was exhausting. Plus, Leah could not find a single meeting that didn't include at least one former client. Terrance and its surrounding communities were simply not big enough to make AA anonymous for Leah.

"I got ants in the kitchen," Beverly said by way of a greeting. Dressed in a black-and-gold Terrance Warriors hoodie and black fleece pajama pants printed with neon smiley faces, she was on her front step having a smoke while she waited for Leah to pick her up. She waved her cigarette at Leah angrily. "Those pigs downstairs musta brought them with those disgusting, dirty cardboard boxes they had when they moved in." Beverly lived in a shabby eight-plex for adults with significant mental illness.

"Tell the manager," Leah said, through the open car window, "and we'll get some traps, too." She stayed in the car in hopes her mom would climb right in and they would get on their way.

"I don't have money for traps. Those things are at least five dollars each. I'm on a fixed income, you know. I won't be able to buy toilet paper if I have to pay for those things, all because I got pigs for neighbors." Beverly hadn't moved off the front step.

"Are you out of money, Mom?" Leah asked, knowing that her mom was just hinting to make her feel guilty and manipulate her into buying the ant traps.

"I never have money, sweetheart," she said, her eyes cast dramatically downward, still not moving. "That Social Security ain't enough for anyone to live on. You know that."

Leah held back a hundred nasty comments piled on the tip of her tongue. "I can help you out, Mom. Let's just get going."

Beverly crushed out her cigarette as she blew a long cloud above her head. "I forgot my list. Just come in while I get my stuff."

Leah knew staying in the car wouldn't move her mother any faster, and that now she would be drawn into a long process of finding coupons, checking cupboards, and having "one more smoke" before they could leave.

She entered her mother's minimalist apartment, grateful that part of her mental illness was a distinct discomfort with mess and clutter. The counters were bleached, dishes were washed, and her tiny living area was sparse, furnished with a "really good couch" she had found on a curb that she spent the next week cleaning with a toothbrush. Beverly shuffled from one room to the next to gather what she needed, and then she unexpectedly turned on Leah in the kitchen.

"What's going on with your brother?" Beverly had never stopped thinking that Luke was Leah's responsibility.

"I really don't know, Mom. There's always something with Luke."

"Are you looking out for him? He's got problems, you know. He can't help the way God made him." Beverly pulled her graying hair away from her face and secured it with a neon-pink scrunchie, circa 1987, that was too crappy to be full price even at the Dollar Store. Leah dressed for comfort rather than fashion, but she still cringed at the things her mom wore. And she wanted to find the nimrod who started wearing pajama pants in public and punch her in the face, because they were all her mother wore anymore. "Why should I wear uncomfortable clothes?" Beverly said to her once. "Isn't my life hard enough?"

"You're not even listening to me, are you?" Beverly whined. "He's your brother, in case you forgot."

"Yes, Mom, I am listening to you. I got distracted by your glowing pony tail."

"What?" She grabbed her hair. "What're you talking about? Are you making fun of me?"

"Nothing, Mom. Nothing." Leah felt a rare surge of sympathy for her mother. She couldn't help the way God made her, either. "I try to look out for Luke, but he's an adult, and I can't babysit him. He seems like he's . . ." What did he seem like? He had been at her house every night, but stumbled in late and barely spoke to her. He wasn't working and had no visible means of support, yet he had enough money to buy food and get around. He had to be dealing, she knew that, but he hid it well. "He's certainly been worse," she finally said because it was the most reassuring thing she could say that was actually true.

Beverly slumped in relief. "I just don't want him to end up like your dad." Beverly patted her ponytail and started for the front door. "I'm ready."

"What do you mean, 'like Dad'?" Beverly hadn't mentioned their father out loud for months, maybe even years. "You think Luke is going to have a stroke?"

Beverly stopped with her hand on the counter, facing away from Leah. She paused too long. "That's what I meant."

It clearly was not what she meant. She followed her mother outside, choosing her words carefully. "Isn't that what happened to Dad?" she asked. "It was a stroke, right?" Leah and her mother had never had this conversation, but something Luke had said years before had made Leah believe it was a stroke.

Beverly got into the car, pretending she didn't hear the question. Leah climbed in the driver's side, still trying to decide if she wanted to hear the answer.

"Mom."

Beverly turned away, clutching her purse tightly on her lap. Still silent.

Leah shook her head, mostly to herself. It wasn't worth stirring things up with her mom tonight. She let the question drop back into the chasm between them. Leah started the car, and they were on their way.

SIX HOURS LATER, LEAH was in bed staring over Kemp's shoulder at the wall. Shopping with her mother had been fine, and they even had a rare laugh together over a beautiful little baby boy who cooed at them in the checkout line. But something else had settled into her belly, and once again she craved comfort. When she got back home, Leah texted Kemp a vague message, but he took it for the invitation it was. He was at her door in minutes, and she pulled him into her bedroom with barely a word. Kemp happily complied and devoured her. An hour later he was naked and drifting off to sleep with one arm draped across her.

"I'm not good at this," she whispered, almost hoping he was already asleep. The admission was a leap toward a real relationship with Kemp. It made her vulnerable. Naked. As soon as she said the words she wanted to take them back.

"Good at what, babe?" he muttered.

"This . . . dating thing . . ." Leah flushed, ". . . with you."

Kemp popped open one eye. "I'm a good guy," he said, leaning his chin on her shoulder. "You don't need to worry about me being an asshole."

"Yeah, I know you're not going to beat me up or anything, but I'm . . . messed up when it comes to this stuff. The guys I've dated just drift away, no explanation, just gone." Leah was grateful for the dark, feeling like her dad, who couldn't tolerate the intimacy of eye contact. "If we're going to do this, then no lying, no cheating, and you can't disappear."

"I'm a good guy," he repeated wearily. "I don't lie. I sure as hell won't cheat. And I won't disappear." Kemp kissed her shoulder and was asleep seconds later.

LEAH ROLLED OVER TO GET KEMP'S hot breath off her face. He took up a lot of the bed.

Even with all of his reassurance, all she wanted to do now was get away. If she needed any proof that she couldn't handle relationships, here it was—five minutes after taking a step forward into a "real relationship" with Kemp, she wanted to take it all back. He was too much—always wanting to sleep over, waking her up early with a hand on her belly or a kiss on her neck. Messing around with someone like Kemp had been fun and easy, but now he started *liking* her, nuzzling and caressing and making sex into something . . . intimate. It was smothering.

The back door opened and closed, and Leah could hear Luke's heavy footsteps as he stumbled through the kitchen and to the guest bedroom. She thought he sounded drunk, though she couldn't identify what it was about his walk that made her think so. Perhaps it was years of listening to her parents stumble in that taught her what drunk footsteps sounded like.

Leah teetered on the edge of the bed all night, avoiding Kemp's hot, hairy arm that he kept draping across her back. Sliding away every time he tried to nuzzle closer.

> *The little man was growing up just how his uncle had hoped. With an interest in trucks, spaceships and trains, his favorite uncle could easily convince the little man to come to his house and play with his toys . . . so to speak. The analogy made Uncle chuckle.*

chapter five

SATURDAY BROUGHT A NEW KIND of hell called bridesmaid dress shopping. When Jake and Amanda announced their engagement, all pink and happy, Leah was as selflessly thrilled for her friends as she had ever been for anyone. But when Amanda followed the announcement with a nervous request for Leah and Zoe to be her bridesmaids, Leah groaned until Zoe elbowed her and said they would both be honored. Since then Leah had trudged through bridesmaid rituals like she was on a death march.

After their trip to see Ben, tension hovered between Leah and Amanda for days. That is, until Zoe forced Leah to bring Amanda an iced coffee to apologize for being "such a bitch," and Leah promised to be extra pleasant for at least the rest of the week. Amanda reminded her the week didn't end until Sunday, and she expected her to be "sweet as freakin' pie" for their trip to the bridal shop on Saturday.

So they were off to Grand Avenue in St. Paul, where they had an appointment at a relatively modest bridal shop followed by brunch. Amanda and Zoe loved to shop and lunch on Grand any chance they got, but Leah found the neighborhood, with the governor's mansion a block to the north and shops that sold twenty-dollar bars of soap, intimidating and snooty. As her mother would say, "Those people up in the Cities act like their shit don't stink."

"Canon in D" announced Amanda's bridal party—Leah, Zoe, Lucy, and Amanda's soon-to-be mother-in-law Trix Mann—entering the shop. A blonde woman with endless, willowy limbs strode across the shop to greet them with equal parts condescension and boredom. "I'm Barbie," she breathed. Leah fought back a snort.

Trix stepped forward and took Barbie's hand in both of hers.

"Hello, dear." Trix was so petite she spoke into Barbie's bosom. "Amanda already has a dress, but we need to look at bridesmaid dresses today." Barbie nodded and motioned them to a back nook with racks full of pastel silk and chiffon.

Amanda's bridesmaids fanned throughout the store. Leah had met Amanda's tiny friend Lucy a few times. She was perfect maid of honor material—full of energy, sentimental, organized, selfless. Leah felt like Lucy's antithesis—weary, cynical, scattered and selfish. When Amanda asked her to be a bridesmaid, Leah barely caught herself before she said that Amanda must not have that many friends. It was true, but it would have been terribly mean. Leah was finally learning that biting comments seemed funny in her head but weren't amusing out loud. The wounded looks of enough people had taught her that. Fallout from being raised by social misfits was that her own interactions were often stilted and mired with faux pas.

And Leah did like Amanda and enjoyed and truly needed their friendship, so she didn't want to mess it up. When she was growing up, her parents had very few friends, other than her dad's creepy friend, Coolie. Unintentionally, Leah had followed suit through most of her life, unable to maintain friendships for reasons she didn't understand. Things changed when she joined Terrance County Social Services. The job created the need for friendships just by virtue of the required confidentiality. They couldn't talk to anyone but each other about what happened at work, so talk they did. In this context Leah's dark sarcasm was accepted, and for the first time in her life, Leah felt like she had real friends.

This friendship was forcing Leah to shut her mouth and try on taffeta. Leah's wedding had been an afternoon at the courthouse with her parents and his, and supper was the fish fry at the Legion. The asshole got drunk and passed out before they could consummate their doomed union. Clearly there had been no bridesmaids.

"She's thinking either honey gold or persimmon. I think she would really love persimmon, but in the fall it might be a challenge," Mrs. Mann had taken over, and Amanda followed her, looking scared.

"What in the hell is persimmon?" Leah whispered to Zoe.

"Something beautiful that you'll wear without complaint," Zoe said under her breath as they followed Mrs. Mann and Barbie around the shop.

"I know *that*, Mrs. Bossy. I just don't have the foggiest idea what color it is. Kind of bluish?" Barbie led them to a sitting area with leather couches and a low table with several formal wear portfolios. They all sat obediently while Barbie fetched fabric samples.

"I think it's kind of orangey-red," Lucy said as she joined Leah on the couch. Zoe was on the next couch with Amanda, and Mrs. Mann stood with her hands on her hips, happily supervising.

"Oh . . ." Leah said, fighting back a groan. "Orange looks great on everyone. Especially in taffeta." Zoe stepped on her foot. Leah glared back. She was being as nice as she knew how to be under the circumstances. Lucy smiled nervously and picked up a portfolio.

"Don't they serve champagne in these places?" Lucy asked. "Wouldn't a mimosa be wonderful right now?" Amanda's eyes darted to Leah.

"It sounds awesome," Leah admitted. *Don't jump down her throat,* Leah told herself. "But I'm not a drinker. You guys should definitely have one, though." But her tone was so falsely cheerful that even Barbie would know she didn't mean it. Lucy's eyes widened as she looked down.

Barbie returned with about a hundred fabric squares held together with large silver rings.

"I don't see persimmon for fall," Barbie said. She handed a ring of swatches to Amanda. "Those are the 'up and coming' colors for this fall. If you like persimmon then check out the pumpkin, squash, and maize. They are the more *autumnal* versions of the orange family. " Amanda nodded blankly.

"Autumnal? Seriously?" Leah smirked at Zoe, who didn't smile back.

"Shut it," Zoe whispered to Leah. "You know what, Amanda? I think we need to just start looking at some styles, and they can do most of these dresses in any of those colors." Amanda looked relieved. "Leah will try some on."

Leah turned to Zoe slowly. "How generous for my friend, Zoe, to volunteer me without my permission."

"You're a perfect size eight—they'll have all of these in your size," Zoe flashed a plastic grin.

"Well, honey?" Trix said, staring intently at Amanda. For the first time, Leah looked at Amanda and saw how much she was struggling with this day. The only other time Leah had ever seen this look on her face was that incredible day in court when she learned that the judge was her father.

Leah hopped up and held her hands out to Barbie. "Let's get me some maize."

FUN WOULD BE TOO STRONG A WORD, but Leah had to admit the morning got better. They did have every style in her size—strapless, one shoulder, cap sleeves, floor length, cocktail, to the knee. Leah rarely even wore dresses, but on that morning she tried on at least a dozen. They settled on knee length, and they all chose different styles that suited them best. For the color, Amanda deferred to Jake's mom, who must have heard Leah's griping. She agreed that autumnal colors were hard to wear, so she found a shade of bluish-purple they all liked. Mrs. Mann said that any nude pump would do, so shoe shopping was unnecessary.

"I'm treating for brunch," Mrs. Mann announced happily. "Time for mimosas!" She led them to the next block to a bright, crowded restaurant that advertised two-for-one Bloody Marys and mimosas for brunch.

While Mrs. Mann put their name on the hostess's list, Amanda's dark expression returned, and she squinted at Leah.

"I'm sorry. I'll bet you hate this," she whispered as the two of them pulled away from the group.

"I don't hate this," Leah said as sincerely as she could. "I'm just . . . bad at it."

Amanda nodded sadly. "I'm bad at this, too." She eyed Mrs. Mann over the crowd waiting for tables, and kept her voice low. "I'm not sure I even want a wedding. I mean, I want to be married to Jake. I know that. But a wedding? My student loans are so huge I don't have any money, so Jake, his family and Matt are paying for almost all of it. I bought my dress because I just couldn't let them do that, but now my credit card is almost maxed."

"Well, your mother-in-law seems to be enjoying herself," Leah said, watching Mrs. Mann smooth a stray hair from Lucy's ponytail and rub her back.

Amanda heaved a sigh. "This wedding is for her. She's taken care of me and looked out for me for years. Jake and I were ready to go to Cancun and get married on the beach, but when we told her she burst into tears."

"Oh, man, no pressure there."

"It's fine, we'll have a wedding," Amanda sighed. "It's just that I'm not exactly looking forward to it." They both laughed and their table was called.

Everyone ordered mimosas but Leah, who requested a Diet Coke with her eggs Benedict and tried to quash her growing resentment at her friends' drinking around her. She was used to the happy hours and usually was distracted enough with office gossip and appetizers that she could ignore the alcohol. But lately it seemed that alcohol had infused every event, and she was tired of being a good sport about it. Their open drinking around her started years ago at her own insistence that they shouldn't avoid happy hour just because of her. Leah didn't know why it was different, but she wasn't going to change the rules now.

Making matters worse, the drinks arrived and Mrs. Mann asked with no pretense, "How long have you been in recovery, Leah?"

Leah flushed. Amanda and Zoe exchanged looks across the table.

"Um, about ten years ago," Leah said, glancing around the table at the downcast eyes.

"Good for you, hon." Mrs. Mann said.

"Yep." Silence. Lucy took a long sip of mimosa and scrunched her nose at the champagne bubbles.

"It must make you a good social worker. Understanding and such, I'm sure." She went to pick up her drink but pulled her hand away, like she shouldn't talk about Leah's alcoholism while she was having an alcoholic beverage herself. Leah stifled a rude snort.

"Yep," Leah said again. She didn't want to be rude, but she had nothing but snide, sarcastic comments ready to spill out. Mrs. Mann was a doting, affectionate mother, and Leah was falling into her adolescent tendency to mock what she envied.

"This group really enjoys happy hour, though, right? Jakey said there's always a group having margaritas after work. Do you go with them?"

"Sometimes . . ." Leah said with a polite grin. "I really just go for the nachos."

"But you're tiny!" Mrs. Mann said with equal notes of approval and concern. "You must have one of those fast metabolisms."

"Nah, actually I'm bulimic." At that, and the aghast look on Mrs. Mann's face, Amanda choked and almost sprayed mimosa across the table, her nervousness spilling into uncontrollable giggles.

"She's kidding," Zoe said, annoyed, but even she had to relax and smile at Amanda's apoplectic laughing fit.

"Oh . . ." Mrs. Mann patted Lucy on the back again, the only one of the group she could really relate to at this point. "This is usually when my husband would pat my leg and tell me I've said enough."

"No, I've said enough." Leah found herself liking Mrs. Mann despite all the nosiness. "I was just being funny, but sometimes my mouth gets ahead of me."

"You remind me of Amanda," Mrs. Mann said kindly. "You're funny and tough." Out of the corner of her eye, Leah saw Lucy look away from the table.

"And you are too kind. I'm really just a bitch, but most people are too nice to tell me that."

"I'm not," Zoe said, her glare still a warning.

"What a crew you've chosen, Amanda." Mrs. Mann beamed around the table.

"The only three I could get to say yes," Amanda said with her first genuine smile of the day.

THE GROUP SPENT THE REST of the afternoon shopping for centerpieces, favors, candles, and other details. Leah saw Mrs. Mann sign a credit card receipt for $450 at the craft store where they bought an assortment of knick-knacks that would be assembled into "lovely centerpieces like they had in that bridal magazine." At dinnertime, Mrs. Mann said that she needed to get back, and Lucy decided to ride with her to get home to her baby.

"I'm dying for some nachos," Leah said, and the three of them burst out laughing all over again.

"Sam's got the kids at his parents' house, so I'd like to avoid them as long as I can," Zoe's eyes got wide. "His parents, I mean. Not the twins." She sighed. "Let's get some apps before we head back."

They decided on the Green Mill in a southern suburb, rescuing Leah from Grand Avenue. A younger hostess with a huge gap between her front teeth seated them at a booth near the largest television.

"I'm thinking about going off the wagon," Leah blurted as they were seated, not realizing she was going to say it until the words came out.

Amanda and Zoe glanced at each other nervously.

"This whole 'not drinking' thing sucks," she said through their uncomfortable stares. "I never went to treatment. I was never *addicted* to alcohol, and the only real reason I quit was because I was attending meetings with my mom and just got caught up in the whole AA thing." Leah didn't know she had a speech prepared, or that she felt like she had to convince her friends it was the right thing to do.

Amanda and Zoe looked at each other, and Leah knew what was coming before either of them spoke.

"Don't you think—" Amanda began.

"Let me just stop you right there." Irritation and opposition welled up. "I wasn't asking your permission. I was just letting you know."

"I wasn't going to tell you that you couldn't—"

"Hey, ladies!" A lanky red haired waiter came to take their order. "Would you gals like to hear the specials?"

"Nope. We're still deciding, thanks," Zoe said. He nodded and headed to the next table.

"Leah," Zoe started, "you know we can't and won't tell you what to do. Neither of us knew you in your drinking years, and obviously it's not for us to decide anyway." Zoe was playing with her napkin and choosing her words carefully. "Can I just ask what made you decide to start up again?"

Hard to answer that question without sounding needy and dysfunctional. "It's just gotten old, you know? Right, wrong, or otherwise, alcohol is a big part of hanging out, and I'm so sick of not being part of it. I'm not out to get bombed, but I'm really tired of Diet Coke." They all sat quietly for a moment.

"So . . . I don't really know what the supportive friend is supposed to say," Amanda said, running her hands over her ponytail. "Are we supposed to encourage you to do whatever feels right? Are we supposed to be all disapproving and judgey?"

"When is it ever right to be disapproving and judgey?" Zoe asked with a faint smile.

"Maybe when the issue is addiction? Or child abuse? Domestic violence . . ." Amanda faded at Leah's look.

"You're comparing my having a drink to child abuse?" Now Leah was getting mad.

Amanda noticed. "Maybe we don't have to say anything else. Looks like we've wrecked drinking for you already."

Their carrot-topped server returned, leaning over the table close enough that they could see the beads of sweat along his hairline. "You ladies ready to order?"

They all paused too long. Finally Leah motioned to Zoe, who took the lead. "Yeah. Um. I think we decided to share the chicken nachos, and maybe some onion rings, too." She looked up at them both. "Executive decision since we didn't talk about it. I'm starving."

"How about drinks?" Carrot-top asked, distracted by loud laughter at a table near the bar.

"Right . . ." Zoe said slowly.

"I think I'll just have a lemonade," Amanda said decisively, avoiding eye contact with Leah.

"Me too," Zoe said quickly.

Carrot-top nodded. He turned to Leah. "And you?"

She was oppositional enough to order a drink just to make a point. But their show of support for her sobriety ruined any desire she had to jump off the wagon. "Make it three," she said quietly. He nodded absently and sped away. "You guys suck," Leah grumbled, but she said it with affection, stuck on the wagon at least one more day.

chapter six

DURING THE WEEK FOLLOWING their dress shopping, Leah tired of keeping a smile on her face. She finished the investigation paperwork on Baby Ben and tried to let go of the case until the possibility she was needed for the prosecution.

Ben moved out of the ICU two weeks after his last brain surgery. Amanda visited Jenny there every few days to get an update on his condition and to discuss supportive services Ben might need when he eventually went home. Amanda was full of praise for Jenny's newfound commitment to her son. Jenny had acknowledged that she knew Joe was often drunk or high when he cared for Ben, but she was so busy going to school and working to support them she didn't feel like she had any other options. Amanda would work with Jenny to ensure she would always make her son's safety her top priority.

Every time Leah thought about the case, Joe's confession gnawed at her. She, Jake, and Kemp met on July third, a Thursday, to talk about the case, but it was difficult to get Kemp to focus on work. He was hours away from a three-day weekend with a glorious forecast, perfect for taking his new boat out on the river.

"We're going at least ten miles downriver a day," Kemp said, feet up on Jake's desk with his eyes closed. "I'll drop anchor and sleep the day away. Just my boat, my Coors Light, and a cooler full of deer sausage and cheese."

"Not to mention a wicked case of gut rot," Jake grimaced. "Deer sausage and a case of Coors?! It's a good thing you'll be alone."

"Alone? I'm not gonna be alone. Right, babe?" Kemp leaned over and squeezed Leah's knee. Leah's back was pressed up against the wall in Jake's closet-sized office, so she barely had room to flinch.

"Knock it off," Leah scolded, pushing his hand off her knee. "We're here to work on a case. Do you think you can try to focus on something besides your tan?"

"I know you've got a thing about my tan . . . and where it starts and stops . . ." He winked at her.

"You're gross," Leah said, fighting back the grin that always seemed to be there when she was with Kemp.

"Focus, both of you," Jake said, shuffling through the file again. "Did you guys interview both doctors?"

"There are about twelve doctors," Leah said. "The red-haired neurologist seems to be in charge of coordinating Ben's care."

"What do they expect the long-term damage to be?" Jake asked, pushing a tall stack of yellow and green files to the side to make room to write in Ben's already large file.

Kemp shook his head, and the channel in his brain changed back to work. "No one will speculate too much. The kid's two years old. At that age his brain can find ways around the damaged parts."

"Developmentally, he's progressing," Leah said. "So that's a good sign. You might not ever know if a learning disability or behavior issue is related to the brain injury, or if it would have been there all along. But the bruises, the fractured leg and ribs . . . those are clearly abuse injuries, too, and not as subject to interpretation." Leah swallowed the lump in her throat.

"Right," Jake said. "We've got the correct charges filed. It's going to come down to the confession and whether the judge will allow it in the trial. If not, we'll live and die by the circumstantial stuff." Jake clicked his mouse a few times and leaned back to the table behind his desk to take a page off his printer.

"If we leave early enough, we can get a great spot for fireworks all the way down in Jacksport," Kemp said, his gaze stuck on the wall of windows across the main office area. "Eighty-five and sunny all weekend, guys. It's like God's telling us to get the hell outside and appreciate his majesty."

Jake raised his eyebrows. "I didn't know you were such a spiritual guy, Pete Kemper."

"Perfect weather in Minnesota is an act of God." He stood and stretched, his polo coming untucked, revealing a stretch of his deeply tanned hip that finally pulled Leah's focus away from Ben.

Jake and Leah stood, and Jake walked them to the main entrance to the county attorney's office. "You two better think of me when you're on the river and I'm trapped at a crappy park in Mankato with fifty of my mom's cousins."

Jake stood with his hands on his hips, a gesture Leah suspected he used to make him look bigger, especially around the much taller Kemp.

"Dude, you gotta learn how to lie to your family," Kemp said. "You two coulda been out with me and hot stuff on the river." Jake shrugged, and Kemp grinned over his shoulder at Jake and put his arm around Leah and walked back to their offices. Leah stiffened, not okay with even mild PDA at work.

"Drop your arm or I'll break it," she said under her breath, but her voice echoed in the empty marble hallway.

"Harsh." Kemp moved his arm and patted her butt.

"Hey!" She punched him in the ribs and tried to sound mad.

"Ow. Oh, owwww," he wailed and held his ribs. "A social worker beat me. Child protection! Help me!" As they passed the open door to the county tax assessor's office, a sour-faced grandma glared at them like they were making noise in study hall. Kemp straightened up. "Sorry, ma'am," he whispered and flashed his winning smile. She softened and smiled back at charming Pete Kemper.

They went out the back door where Kemp would need to head down the sidewalk to the police department while Leah would cross the street and go back to the social services building. He crossed his arms and grinned down at her, his bravado fading and his face softening with affection. "Why don't you pack a bag and come over tonight?" That smile again.

A flood of something (insecurity? fear?) washed over her, and she needed him to back off. "You can pick me up in the morning," she said, looking over his shoulder because eye contact was too much.

Kemp recoiled a bit and searched her face, but she kept her gaze fixed across the street. "Okay, babe." Subdued. They parted with an impersonal wave, and Leah wanted to kick herself for ruining the mood. Again.

KEMP'S SPIRITS WERE HIGH when he picked up Leah the following morning before nine. Leah was anxious about being trapped with Kemp in a space the size of her bedroom for the next three days. But when she awoke after a few fitful hours of sleep, she vowed to find a way to enjoy herself. If her biggest problem was spending three days on a boat with Kemp, she knew she needed to get a grip.

The weather app on her phone still promised upper eighties and sun every day, so Leah packed bikini tops, t-shirts, swim shorts, running shorts, and one sweatshirt for evening. Kemp was also counting on her ("as the woman" he declared in his most objectifying caveman voice) to pack the food unless she wanted to live on deer sausage all weekend. She scolded him but complied, filling a cooler and two shopping bags with grapes and watermelon slices, bagels, various sandwiches, carrots, cheese and crackers, sunflower seeds, Oreos, and Diet Coke. Kemp promised that, in addition to bringing ample deer sausage from his four-point buck he bagged last fall, he would pick up his own beer. He promised to go easy since the water patrol would be out in full force, looking for people to arrest for boating while intoxicated. Leah wheeled the cooler to his truck and pointed to the other bags for him to bring.

"Nice work, doll," he said, pawing through the bags.

Boating was a big part of Terrance's identity, with the Apple River running through town and separating history from development. Leah and Amanda lived in North Terrance, sometimes called the *old* side of town, and known by all as the *wrong* side of town. While the river divided the town, it was also a great equalizer—fishing boats held together with duct tape mingled with four-bedroom yachts.

Boating was more than a pastime in Terrance; it was a strong thread of the town's fabric. Marinas were tucked in half a dozen corners along the Apple River shoreline in Terrance, and it seemed everyone in town either owned a boat or had friends and family who did. The weekend place to be was on the river, and on this holiday, Leah was happy to be one of them.

The process of launching a boat into the water was an art, one Kemp still had not perfected. He lined up his pickup to prepare to back the boat in, but he kept jack-knifing the boat trailer left and right, nearly causing the trailer to drop off the ramp. He cursed under his breath repeatedly while Leah just watched the process in her side mirror. Finally, when the boat was far enough in the water, he directed Leah to get in the driver's seat while he turned the crank on the trailer and eased the boat into the water. She then drove the pickup and trailer into an extra-long parking spot. He reached his hand out when she approached the boat and she grabbed on, climbed in, and they were off.

Kemp's boat seated eight legally, six comfortably, and there was room to sleep four legally, two comfortably. Leah sized up the seating area at the back and knew it would be hers for the weekend. Kemp stood behind the steering wheel in the mid-section of the boat, like the president of the United States behind his podium. Kemp had a rag tucked in the back pocket of his faded swim trunks, which he pulled out frequently to polish the chrome or wipe down the steering wheel. Leah stretched out across the back seats and found her sunscreen in her bag, rubbing it on her arms and chest.

"My turn," Kemp said, waggling his eyebrows. They were still trolling through a no-wake zone, so the boat was slow moving and easy to control. "Watching girls give themselves a sunscreen rubdown is the hottest thing ever."

"You'd get aroused watching a woman floss," she said. He put his hand to his ear like he couldn't hear her. "You'd get off watching a woman FLOSS!" she yelled.

Two college-age guys trolling in a speed boat next to them hooted and made obscene gestures. "Ooh, floss me, baby!"

Kemp laughed. Leah flipped them off and turned the other way. She was relieved most boaters weren't as obnoxious as those two. Boating culture dictated they give passing boaters a one-handed wave as they crossed each other's wake. Leah had only been on a boat a handful of times, but she'd learned the rules fast.

By the time they passed through the no-wake zone and Kemp could turn up the motor, Leah was starting to relax. The steady spray of river water from the wake kept her from getting too warm. The cushions shifted under her, so she rearranged them until she was comfortable and pulled out a magazine.

River traffic was especially busy, even for a holiday weekend. Boats of all sizes surrounded them, each filled with boisterous, happy people who seemed to know how to enjoy their lives. Leah knew how to screw around, and she knew how to be alone. What she didn't know how to do was be in a relationship, especially with someone like Kemp, who said what he was thinking and showed affection all the time.

They approached a narrower channel. Kemp slowed the engine and sat in the captain's chair. He reached into the cooler behind him and pulled out a beer, still well before noon.

"Cheers, babe," he said, raising his can to her. "You want a Diet Coke or something?" She shook her head. Of course she wanted a beer—bitter, foamy, and cold. She knew that on a day like today, it wouldn't be just one. It would be a great weekend for a steady, happy buzz to keep her mood light. As much as she had insisted that her friends go ahead and have their drinks, she felt a stab of resentment Kemp couldn't go a weekend without his ever-present Coors.

Ahead of them was a slow-moving houseboat full of deeply tanned, college-age girls in bikinis. Leah glanced up at Kemp to see his reaction, but he just looked troubled. .

"Dad?!" A blonde in a yellow two-piece leaned over the back and waved. "Dad!" Leah turned back to Kemp, who held up his hand with a weak smile.

"Hi, sweetheart," he said in a soft voice Leah had never heard. Kemp rarely spoke of his girls, but Leah recognized Annie from her picture on his desk.

The girl nudged her friend. "That's my dad!" A few more girls turned and waved. Kemp's boat could have fit on the back deck of their boat. *Annie must have rich friends*, Leah thought.

"Hi, Annie's dad!"

"Hey, Mr. Kemper!"

Kemp slowed his boat so they were only a dozen yards apart. "So is that your mom, Annie?" Leah wanted to hide under a cushion, but she was stuck, exposed.

"Oh, my God, no!" Annie said with a giggle.

What the hell is that supposed to mean? Leah screamed inside, but instead gave a sardonic grin and waved.

"Who's your friend, Daddio?" Annie smiled at Leah.

Kemp's face went blank. "Where've you been all summer, peanut?"

Annie's smile drooped. "I'm staying at school this summer. You knew that." She turned to her friend and said something they couldn't hear.

Leah looked up at Kemp's sad smile. "I know," he said. "Have a great day on the river, ladies. Stay safe!"

Annie tilted her head and crossed her arms. "Bye, Dad," she said, turning away and heading to the front of her boat.

"Dammit." He took a long swallow of beer and slowed the motor, letting Annie's friend's yacht get further ahead of them.

"You okay?" Leah asked, both annoyed and relieved he didn't introduce her. Kemp shook his head slightly and stared straight ahead. The topic of Kemp's divorce was off limits. She leaned back in her seat and closed her eyes, the only way she could give Kemp some space.

SOMEWHERE AROUND 2:00 that afternoon they pulled up near a popular sandbar. Kemp dropped the anchor, jumped out and waded onto the beach. Cottonwood trees lined the river on both sides, and the cottonwood fluff dropped from the trees gathered at the shore. It left a cottony sludge on the shoreline and around Kemp's ankles as he waded through it. He walked back to a shady area to empty his bladder instead of using the onboard toilet. Leah hadn't peed in the woods since her drinking days. Even with the tiny toilet on board, she told Kemp she would wait until they docked for dinner.

At least ten other boats had docked along the sandbar, and kids were everywhere—little ones building sandcastles, boys throwing a football, teenage girls lying in a row suntanning. Pure joy.

Kemp's gloom from seeing his daughter was gone. He wandered across the beach, stopping to chat with an older man and woman sitting on beach chairs. Mr. Popular seemed to know everyone in Terrance and for miles in every direction from town.

Leah had never told Kemp, but she remembered him from high school. She would have been about ten when he was seventeen, and she knew him from the swimming pool where she spent most of her summers. A daily pool rat, Leah knew all the lifeguards and had figured out who was dating whom. Kemp was the deeply tanned lifeguard with white-blond, chlorine-damaged hair who all the little girls loved. During the breaks when the swimmers had to clear the pool and crowded along the perimeter to dunk their feet, Kemp showed off with huge cannonballs that drenched all the kids huddled around the deep end. He was also the lifeguard who got handsy with the older girls in bikinis. A few of them smacked him and pushed him away, but most played along, flirting and teasing back. Kemp was the first boy Leah had really noticed.

Over twenty-five years later, she was the object of his affection. Popular Pete Kemper worked every room like a politician without an office, just for the fun of it. Leah laid back and closed her eyes. Once Kemp started talking he could be there for a while.

The gentle rocking of the anchored boat lulled her into a half sleep, so the splash of cold, greenish river water over her perch shocked her system and sent her scrambling to the wet, sandy boat's floor.

"You son of a . . ." she caught herself, remembering there were a lot of people within earshot. She leaned over the edge of the boat and found Kemp grinning at her, treading water a few feet past where they were anchored.

"Come on in!" he huffed.

"No, you schmuck." He pushed another wave of water at her and did a somersault, showing off his hairy legs and terrible somersault form. He came up with his hair slicked back, revealing his growing forehead. Yet she could still see that blue-eyed, flirty lifeguard from years ago that made girls fawn. Leah sat back, wringing out her damp shorts, and watching as he floated further into the boat traffic, nearly getting hit by a couple of white-haired fisherman in a short aluminum boat. She could hear Kemp's laughter while the men glared. A wave of affection for him made her cheeks flush. He caught her watching him and winked as he treaded water. Finally he swam with perfect form back to the shore, picked up his t-shirt and slides, and waded to the boat.

Leah tidied their small living area, picking up wrappers and dumping Kemp's warm, half-empty beer in the river.

"Hey! That's alcohol abuse!" He hoisted a hairy leg over the side of the boat and climbed in, dripping all over their cooler and the back seats. He pulled a faded beach towel out of a bin and rubbed it over his sopping hair.

"I can't even think about all the bacteria and biowaste you must be covered in right now," Leah said. "That river is pure filth." Kemp sat back in his captain's chair and Leah leaned forward, pulled an unidentifiable chunk of blackish goo out of his hair, and tossed it over the side with a grimace.

"You were teasing me all morning with that hot little bod of yours. Don't you think I had to cool off?" He threw the towel in back and pulled up the anchor.

Leah sat back on her perch, turning away to hide her smile. Kemp stowed the anchor and leaned a knee on the cushion next to her. "It's okay to smile, sweetheart. This is supposed to be fun, you know."

"I am having fun!" she snapped.

"You don't know how to relax, sweets. Just let those shoulders down and enjoy the sun, the water, and the sexy company." When she was about to protest, he slid his hand under her hair, pulled her close, and kissed her. He pulled away and put his forehead against hers, so close she could see his pupils dilate as he gazed at her. "Mellow out, sweetheart."

Leah was momentarily paralyzed, but feeling returned along with her attitude. "Bite me. I can relax just fine."

Kemp pulled back and held his hands up in surrender. "Just want you to have a good time." He sat back in his throne, started the engine, and they were off.

LEAH ONLY MADE IT A FEW more hours before nature called, and she insisted on a real bathroom. They docked at a restaurant on the Wisconsin side of the river called Crabby Dan's. The floors, tables, chairs and even the walls were coated in an inch of clear shellac to protect from the flooding that happened every few years. In the flood of 1997, Crabby Dan's could have been a total loss from the floodwaters that made it as high as the bar. But Dan had good flood insurance, so he rebuilt the restaurant to withstand a typhoon. His famous Juicy Lucys had been enough to help the business survive the recession, too.

Kemp found them a spot at the bar while Leah raced to the restroom. She had dozed since their last stop, so she shouldn't have been surprised to find she looked sunburned, puffy and groggy in the dingy restroom mirror. She splashed cold water on her face and tried to tidy up her wild hair.

Back in the restaurant, she found Kemp seated at the bar chatting with a group of college-age guys who looked scorched and pickled. He hopped up when she got back and motioned for her to sit.

"Nice, Kemper." A tall chubby guy in neon green swimtrunks and a shredded Minnesota Gophers t-shirt nodded his approval at Leah.

"Thanks, Goldie," Leah said looking him up and down. "Who are these drunk young men, Kemp?"

Kemp clapped Goldie on the back. "This is Trey Heartz. He graduated high school with my Annie. He's playing receiver for the UW-Eau Claire Blugolds!"

"Really? Why aren't you wearing a Blugold shirt? What the hell's a Blugold, anyway?"

Troy shrugged his beefy shoulders. "Your girlfriend is dumping on me, Kemp."

"Yeah, she does that," he answered, pulling a long swallow of MGD light, never explaining the mystery of the Blugold. Eventually the college guys stumbled back to the dock, leaving Leah and Kemp to order burgers and eat at the bar. Watching the bartender and waitresses fly around the restaurant swarming with toasted boaters reminded Leah of her drinking days. Most of the time she thought of her waitressing years and cringed, but there were fun times, too. Times when it felt like a big party, and she was the host.

Kemp finished his burger in about four bites and ordered a second beer. "So Annie's grown up into quite a bombshell," Leah said, feeling brave.

A frown flashed across his face. "What the hell kind of comment is that about my nineteen-year-old daughter?"

Leah shrugged. "Just curious. You never mention her, so . . ."

"You want me to cut to the chase?" Kemp pushed his plate away and leaned on his elbows, staring at her. "Annie covered for her mom. She knew about the affair and lied to me more than once about what her mom was doing. When the shit hit the fan, Annie fell apart. It wasn't her fault, but we never really got past it."

"Yuck." Leah wished she could take back the question.

"Yeah, 'yuck' doesn't begin to describe it." He glanced at Leah for a second before he took a swig. Leah reached over and patted his arm. It was a stupid, grandmotherly gesture, but real intimacy was as foreign to her as modesty was to Kemp. "We still have a ways to go to get to our fireworks spot, so we better head out soon." Kemp drained his beer and grabbed the last of her fries. He didn't pat her ass as usual, but grabbed her hand instead. His was warm and a little sweaty. Leah was pretty sure the last person who held her hand was her dad. The memory stabbed her in the gut, and she involuntarily squeezed his hand harder.

DUSK IN MINNESOTA—stagnant, thick air filled with barbecue smoke, mosquitoes, and sweat. River traffic was slow as boats wound around each other, maneuvering for prime fireworks viewing spots. They had only headed another mile or so downriver before they got to an area outside of river traffic near a large campground famous for its fireworks display. Leah went below deck and retrieved her sweatshirt. Kemp was quiet, focused on parking and anchoring. His boat was more small than large, and they were flanked by a couple of personal yachts that each could have slept a dozen people. Behind them, a family crammed in an aluminum fishing boat bickered over bug spray.

Dropping the anchor with a satisfying *ploop*, Kemp took a seat next to Leah as the fireworks started further in the distance than expected. She was ready to tease him for anchoring so far away, but his quiet made her pause. He slid his arm around her and pulled her close enough for her to smell Old Spice and the onions on his breath. Then he kissed her against the exploding night sky. And the gentle way that popular Pete Kemper held her face and touched her hair put tears in her eyes that stayed all night.

chapter seven

IN THE WEEKS AFTER the long Independence Day weekend, the temperature rose. Amanda's patience for her future mother-in-law, her coworkers, and her fiancé dropped.

"I'm pretty sure this wedding is the biggest mistake I've ever made," Amanda announced as they left their staff meeting on a morning in late July so humid the windows were dripping with condensation. "You know the reason brides wear long white dresses is because it makes them look 'virginal.'"

"Everyone knows that, kid," Jill said, finishing the last sips of the largest coffee sold at Caribou and carrying out a plate that formerly contained decadent white-chocolate oatmeal cookies.

"Kid? Really?" Amanda glared at Jill. "If I decide not to get married that day, someone could just throw me into a volcano, the other traditional time a woman wears a long white dress."

"If you want, I'll wear a long white dress, too," Roberta said. "Maybe we could all wear our old wedding dresses."

"Yeah, super idea. I just had twins. I'm sure mine will just zip right up." Zoe groaned.

"Do you get to say you 'just had twins'? They're two years old!" Amanda said a bit nastily.

Zoe shrugged her off.

An image flashed through Leah's head of Kemp in a tux and her walking up the aisle in a white dress. Her face flushed, and she sped back into her cube before anyone noticed. Her phone had been buzzing at her throughout the staff meeting. She had a text. Finally alone at her desk, she checked it. Kemp—*Let's do it in your shower tonight, hot stuff.* An embarrassed giggle escaped as Max walked in to her office. He pretended not to notice.

"Here are those two files." He handed her two thin files from the reports she had been assigned—a flea-infested garbage house and a two-year-old who had been placed in crisis foster care after both parents were arrested for a mutual, drunk domestic assault.

Leah nodded, flustered from Kemp's sexting and feeling like Max could read her mind.

"How are things going for you lately?" Max asked, dropping into the chair by her desk.

"I'm good." For the first time in a while she really looked at her boss. He looked exhausted, perhaps sad. "How about you?"

He looked up suddenly. "Why do you ask? Does it show?"

Leah tried to be casual. "You look tired, maybe bummed out or something."

"My wife moved out." He leaned on Leah's desk, avoiding eye contact, words spilling out despite Leah wishing they wouldn't. "She left last weekend. Said she needed to figure things out. There's another guy . . ." He blinked fast, and Leah realized in horror her boss might cry, right there in her cube. She was probably the least sympathetic person at the agency, so she couldn't understand why he would spill his guts to her.

"That sucks, Max. I'm sorry." There were no other words. She considered saying something cruel about his gorgeous wife, but she wasn't sure Max was ready for that. "Who has Jade?" Jade was the couple's two-year-old daughter.

"Mostly me," Max said, relief in his eyes. "Christine says she needs some space to figure out what to do next. I don't know how a mother could be torn between that son of a bitch and her daughter, but I guess Christine isn't the mother I thought." Leah cringed inwardly, wondering who the son of a bitch was. She tried to hide her uneasiness.

"I'm glad she's with you," Leah said, hoping to end the painful subject and move on. "Do you need anything from me, or any of us? Have you told people yet?" Leah looked up at the wall of her cube and wondered if Jill was at her desk, listening. Sound carried.

"I just told you now. That's all I've been able to spit out so far." She and Max just didn't have this kind of relationship. Leah was acutely uncomfortable. He was still staring straight ahead.

"Should I tell people or just keep it quiet? Either way is fine. I just want to know what you want me to do, boss." The word snapped him back to attention. He cleared his throat and shook his head.

"I'm sorry, Leah. This was very unprofessional of me. Very sorry. Let's just forget the whole conversation." He stood suddenly and straightened his khakis. "Let me know if you need anything else before you start those two assessments."

As Max backed away awkwardly, Leah's phone buzzed with a new text. *So are you gonna wash my back tonight?*

Max and Christine had always looked incredibly happy, and their daughter seemed to complete their idyllic life. Things weren't always as they seemed.

Leah put her phone back in her purse. Perhaps she would respond to Kemp's proposition later.

THINKING SHE COULD JUST "stop by" and check on the garbage house was the first of many mistakes that sweaty afternoon. The home was north of the river, but miles away from Leah's house, as far on the edge of town as it could be while still in Terrance city limits. While they had screened in the report for assessment, Leah assumed it would be routine—mistake number two of the day. The decaying cat on the sidewalk leading up to the dilapidated home should have been a clue this was more than a typical garbage house.

Cindy House was a young woman who had lived in rural Terrance County her entire life. Her parents had been there all of their lives, living in a 100-year-old house that looked like it would tip over in a strong wind.

When Leah knocked, she heard a full five minutes of scuffling and chaos behind the door. Cindy had four children ranging in age from eight years old to six months. The reporter who called in the concern refused to give his name, so oftentimes those reports were viewed with a bit more scrutiny. However, this reporter had given a great deal of specific information that added credibility.

Finally, Cindy—heavy, dull, and delayed—opened the door and allowed Leah inside. Her kids were nowhere to be seen.

Leah had been to dozens of garbage houses in her years at Terrance County, and most of them involved a ten-minute walk-through and a serious conversation about what needed to change, but that was it. This was the kind of home that made the evening news. Leah made it as far as the entryway before she knew she needed an officer. The children were going to be removed.

The odor was assaultive: sour, like ammonia, feces, and filth. Mounds of overfull, spilling garbage bags filled the entryway, and Leah had to back away from the swarming flies—both the typical ones and tiny fruit flies that had overtaken a pungent, decaying watermelon shell. Clothes, dozens of shoes, and toys filled the living room off the entryway so that a person could barely walk.

But it was the colony of bats, at least a hundred of them, hanging from the rafters in the dark hallway that stopped her cold. Most were still, their claws hooked into exposed beams in the ceiling. A few were moving, exercising their wings or winding their heads around. When she tore her eyes away from those tiny flying rats, Leah noticed the piles of guano—bat feces—along the hallway floor. Guano was highly toxic to humans, and Leah knew from her training on pestilence that cleaning it up required full haz-mat gear. These children needed to be removed. Immediately.

"Holy effing bat crap. Sweet Jesus." Leah's stomach rolled, and she held her hand under her nose to try to keep the smell from penetrating her nostrils. She had dealt with mice, cockroaches, and bedbugs at various times in her career. But *holy hell* . . . bats?!

"Yeah . . ." Cindy said helplessly.

Short and quite heavy, with thin black hair barely covering her thick head, Cindy wore a gray t-shirt that bared a strip of her ample, pasty belly and pink sweatpants that dragged on the ground, the edges frayed and black with sludge.

"Cindy, where are your kids?" Cindy dragged her hand under her nose, and Leah grimaced at the sheen of mucus on the back of her hand. Cindy shrugged and motioned toward the back of the house. Through the hall of bats and bat shit.

Tears had already welled up in Leah's eyes from the ammonia and threatened to fall. Leah wasn't one to be scared of mice, bugs, or snakes, but somehow attaching wings to a little pest transformed it into something terrifying. Yet she had no choice but to walk through the hallway.

"All right, Cindy, I'm going to go back there and check on your kids. You need to come with me. You have four kids, right?"

"Um . . . yeah."

Leah pulled her file out of her bag and turned to the intake sheet. "Tommi Jane, Brittany, Gloria, and Chet? Chet is the baby, right?"

Cindy's face split into a wide smile that revealed about eight teeth that looked like they were covered in mashed potatoes. "He's a sweetie."

Leah nodded. "I need to call someone from my office, and then we're going back there." She was stalling. She dialed Kemp's direct line, but he didn't answer. "Call me ASAP," she left on his answering machine. With a last-ditch effort, Leah texted Kemp, *Call my office, find out where I am and get out here. Worst garbage house ever.*

She set the phone back in her bag and took a heavy breath in resignation. "What do the bats do when you walk by them?"

"Bats?" Cindy asked blankly.

Leah wondered if Cindy was more delayed than she thought. How in the world had Cindy raised her children this long without child protection involvement?

"Yes, Cindy. The bats. What's going to happen when we walk by them? Are they all going to start moving?"

"Oh, them. Nah, they don't usually bother you at the daytime. My daddy says there's a hole through the rafters so they fly outside a lot. He put up a blanket by that hallway to keep them away, but then it fell down . . ." On the other side of the hallway lay a gray army blanket. Past the blanket must be the kids' bedrooms.

On cue, the baby wailed and Cindy padded her way through the hallway from hell, stepping on bat shit in her bare feet. As she said, most of the bats stayed motionless. Only a few shuddered or shifted.

With an impulse she didn't know was there, Leah held her binder over her head and followed as quickly as she could. Cindy led them to a room just past the hallway where all four kids lay on a large, filthy bed. The oldest, Tommi Jane, was curled up on some pillows with the baby on her lap, and was reading a library book. The middle girls, Brittany and Gloria, were eating macaroni and cheese out of a pan with their hands, both girls covered in cheesy sauce up to their elbows. The kids were filthy, but not in imminent danger in the bedroom.

Leah stepped out of the room and moved toward a corner that appeared to be batless while she called sheriff's dispatch. "This is Leah Danco from human services. I need an officer to come out to a house with me to put kids on a hold. I'd like you to find Pete Kemper if you could. Otherwise, I'll take whoever can get here fast." Leah gave the address and hung up.

"Cindy," Leah began, "please step in the hallway with me for a minute." Cindy blandly followed. "We need to have you guys stay somewhere else for a while. This house isn't safe to live in."

"What's wrong with my house?" Cindy asked, her face darkening.

"Well, the bats are a big problem. Bats carry very serious diseases." The thought passed through Leah's mind that one of the kids could already have been bitten. Rabies is always fatal after symptoms started. "Have your kids been feeling okay? Any health problems?"

Cindy turned and looked at her kids in the bedroom. "Nah. I don't think so. They're good." Cindy wiped her nose again, leaving a long trail across her arm. "We all got sore throats a lot. Bad tonsils, my daddy says."

It also could be that your noses and throats are irritated from the very strong smell of urine in your home. Leah's throat was already starting to burn. Pretty soon she was going to have to hold a tissue in front of her nose. "Cindy, do you have anywhere else you could stay?" While talking with Cindy, Leah was wrestling in her head about what to do. Could these kids go with their mom and stay with a friend, or did the kids need to go to foster care so that another adult could meet their needs? Their job was to try to keep families together whenever possible.

Cindy shrugged. "We could go to my auntie's. She lives in that trailer up the hill."

"Is she your only relative?" Placement with relatives was always preferable over foster care.

"Uh. Kind of. My daddy passed at Christmas time. My mamma's gone. My auntie gots a lotta cats and her house is kinda messy." *Dear God, if Cindy thinks her house is messy then it must be condemnable. But then, the piles of guano in this house are pretty clear evidence this house is condemnable, too.*

Leah decided she wanted the kids to go to foster care for now, and they could continue to look for relatives. At this point, it was more important to get the kids cleaned up and to the doctor, and the way Cindy was describing her family, it wasn't clear her relatives could make that happen.

"What about the kids' father?"

Cindy just stared.

"Cindy," Leah began, a horrible suspicion arising in her head. "Who's the father of your children?"

Cindy shrugged. "Daddy says it ain't important who the daddy is. We don't worry about daddies around here."

Leah cringed. "Cindy, have you ever had a boyfriend?"

Cindy started to giggle. "Boyfriend? I got boys who like me."

"Cindy, do you know who is the father of your kids?"

"Huh?" Cindy looked genuinely confused.

"All right, Cindy." Leah abandoned those questions for now. She would have to talk to Cindy again, next time with tape rolling. "Here's the deal. We need to have your kids stay somewhere else for a while. And I need your help to talk to them about it and not scare them. Can you do that?" Leah checked her phone. Still no call or text from Kemp. She needed that officer to come soon to put a hold on the kids. Social workers did not have the authority to remove kids on their own, despite public perception that social workers were baby snatchers.

Cindy's lower lip stuck out, and she looked like she was going to cry. "They ain't never been away from me," she whined.

"I understand," Leah said, her patience thinning by the second. "But they'll need to stay somewhere else for a few days. This is very serious. Your house is dangerous, and we need to make sure your kids are safe and healthy." At that moment, proving her case, a bat swooped between them, an inch from Leah's nose. Leah ducked and screeched, maddening tears welling in her eyes.

Cindy waved at the air where the bat had swooped and sniffed loudly. "Fine," she humphed. "Do I gotta pack clothes and stuff?"

"Yes, just pack enough for a couple days, and we'll figure it out from there."

Cindy shuffled around her house grabbing clothes off of piles in the living room floor and stuffing them into a brown paper bag that had been sitting on the kitchen counter. Leah stood in the doorway of the room watching the kids and keeping an eye on Cindy. Tommi Jane calmly bounced the baby on her lap, holding his pacifier in his mouth. Brittany and Gloria finished their mac and cheese and licked their hands, wrists, and arms. Leah watched, feeling she should probably intervene, but her tolerance for ick had reached its max.

Finally there was a "cop knock" at the door. Cindy didn't notice, methodically putting piles of clothes in the paper bag. Leah eyed the door, but the only way to reach it was through the hallway of doom.

"Come in," Leah yelped.

A uniformed officer, stocky and in his mid to late forties, came in the house and made a quick survey, immediately focusing on the hallway ceiling. "Are those *bats?*"

Leah nodded. "The kids are back here. Let's get everybody outside, and we can regroup."

But regrouping is not what occurred.

When she looked back on the day later, this conversation was the last thing Leah could remember.

LEAH AWOKE ON HER COUCH wearing hospital scrubs. Splintering headache. Her face felt . . . wrong. Leah sat up a few inches and touched her cheek gingerly. It was swollen to the size of a baseball. Her head felt muffled, and a surge of panic was ready to break through.

"What the hell . . . ?" The words came out garbled, her tongue thick.

Amanda was on Leah's loveseat and set down the magazine she was paging through. "Hey, there," she said, like she was talking to a three-year-old. "How're you doing?"

Leah squinted at her. "Wha's happ'ning?"

Amanda grimaced before she could rearrange her face into a smile. "Do you remember anything?" Leah strained to move her head side to side, but even the slow movements adding to the pounding. "The doctor said you have a concussion, but you'll be just fine in a few days."

Leah squinted in confusion, her head heavy with fog and sedation. "At that house?" Vague pictures slid in and out of her head . . . the house . . . piles of clothes . . . the hallway . . .

"Yeah . . . there was an . . . incident," Amanda said reluctantly.

Leah's body shuddered in a visceral reaction she couldn't grasp. She stared past her friend out the living room bay window. It was night. What could have been so horrible that she blacked out and lost most of the day?

Amanda looked worried and dismissed Leah's questions, encouraging her to rest. When Leah finally demanded some "goddamn answers," Amanda relented.

"Well, okay." Amanda took a breath and looked like she was about to tell Leah she had a few months to live. "The cop talked to Max about it after they got you to the ER. Apparently, there were a lot of bats inside the house. The report never mentioned bats. I went back and looked," Amanda said apologetically. "Somehow the bats got disrupted and started to scatter." Amanda paused and looked like she didn't want to continue.

Leah, who had frozen still, waved her hand to tell her to keep talking. As Amanda told the story, Leah glazed over in a post-traumatic-stress reaction that kept the memory away.

Amanda spoke fast. "A couple of the bats went toward you and you kind of panicked. You ran, hit a low beam, and blacked out. The cop called an ambulance, and they took you to the ER. You got some meds that made you groggy, but you walked out of the ER with me a couple hours ago. But they said you might not remember . . ."

Leah absently patted her hair and touched the goose egg on her cheek.

"Rabies shots," Amanda said grimacing. "One of them scratched you and they didn't know if you got bit, so they had to give you a rabies shot in the area of the scratches. It made you swell up . . . a little."

Leah nodded for several minutes, unable to process. She looked around her house, but it was dark, cold, and quiet. Not wanting to deal with any of it, Leah rolled over and pulled the blanket back up over her ear. Her cheek burned, her stomach ached, her head throbbed. Yet the main thought that ran through her head was what Kemp would say, and why he wasn't there, laughing in his easy way, as he should have been the one taking care of her.

chapter eight

IT WAS A WEIRD, but legitimate, workers comp claim, and Leah was given two weeks off, with pay.

Leah spent the first couple days in uncomfortable, medicated silence, mostly staring out the window in a daze and patting the shrinking mass on her cheek. At first it looked like there was a golf ball underneath her skin, and her cheek was bright red and shiny with the skin stretched over the site of the scratch. Within a few days the fog and confusion dissipated, as did the lump on her face. Leah was left with a persistent pain in her head and face, and a very bad mood.

Luke sat with her most days, forcing Leah to introduce him to her friends. On her second day home, Zoe brought over a huge pot of wild rice soup, and Luke and Zoe had a lively conversation about the Vikings and football during the Dennis Green coaching era. Amanda also came or called every day, bringing food, magazines, DVDs and wedding chatter.

But mostly, Luke and Leah hung out together. It reminded both of them of the many nights they had spent in hotel rooms together while their parents got drunk and tried to get autographs from "Jedis." During those first days, she could tell herself Kemp was working, busy, or distracted. She felt ugly and diseased, so it was almost easier he wasn't there.

But after five days, she ran out of excuses for him and had to admit he was just blowing her off. It was inexcusable—ignoring her when she was hurt after pursuing her for so long. Making a show of wanting to date her, except when she wouldn't be available to mess around. Zoe and Amanda had each asked about him exactly once, and Leah's fury ensured that they never asked again. Her mood went from irritable to nasty.

While two weeks of sitting on the couch—interrupted only briefly by a few more trips to the doctors for more rabies shots—made Leah crazy, it was Luke's lifestyle, and he loved the company. When Leah's headache finally subsided enough to tolerate the television, Luke set them up with a mountain of junkfood and a marathon of superhero movies, starting with the original *Superman*.

"This makes me crazy." Luke, cross-legged on the couch in a grungy sweatshirt and ancient jeans, motioned at the television. "Superman turns back time by flying around the earth and making it turn the opposite way." Luke swallowed a mouthful of trail mix. "There are so many things wrong with it that it makes my head hurt."

"*That's* the problem you have with this movie?" Leah asked as she licked Cheetos dust off her fingers, dressed in the same beat-up sweatshirt and frayed yoga pants she had worn for two days. "You can accept that this guy manifests superhuman strength after flying lightyears away from his planet as a baby in a little space pod, but spinning the earth backward is your limit."

"It's the physics of it. There's just no way." Luke took a swig of Red Bull that Leah eyed longingly. The AA community frowned on energy drinks, and Leah loved, yet avoided, them.

"You're smart, Luke." Leah threw a Cheeto at him. "Why can't you find some way to use your powers for good?"

"How do you know I'm not?" Luke asked with an offended pout.

"Because you're here with me on a Tuesday afternoon. You clearly have nowhere to be, and as far as I can tell you don't even have a job."

Luke slumped. "Well, that was just mean."

"Actually it was a compliment. You are smart. That's what I said."

"You took a shot at me for not having a job," Luke whined.

"You don't have a job, loser. I'm just speaking the truth."

Luke slumped further.

"Here's the deal, little brother. You waste your brain sitting around your dumpy house, or being here with me, when you could be doing something way more productive and actually have a life." Leah dipped her Cheeto in salsa and shoved the whole thing in her mouth to emphasize her point.

"Hey! I have a life. Back the hell off." Luke finished his Red Bull and almost threw it on the floor out of habit until Leah gave him a scorching look.

"I'm brutally honest because you're my brother, and I've been on this couch for days. This feels like I'm finally doing something constructive."

"Being mean?"

"Fixing your shitty life."

"Bully." Luke sat back and glared at Superman as he pulled Lois Lane out of the rubble of an earthquake.

"Luke, are you dealing?" Leah blurted. She sat up and brushed bright orange crumbs off the Twins insignia on her sweatshirt.

His face gave him away. "What? Dealing . . . ?"

"Oh, my God, Luke, you *are* dealing." Leah covered her face with her hands. "Do you understand, at all, what I do for a living? You could get me in so much trouble if you do any business from my house."

"I'm not stupid, Leah. I'd never do that to you." Luke got up and headed for the bathroom. "But it doesn't matter because I'm not dealing," he muttered.

Leah shifted and the infernal headache returned. On the TV, Lois Lane came back to life.

DARKNESS FELL AFTER 9:00. They had shifted to *Spiderman* because the later *Superman* sequels were so stupid, Luke declared.

"Peter Parker is such a weak character," Luke said, washing his hot wings down with a can of Miller Genuine Draft. "I know it's supposed to be his deal, but it just makes him pathetic."

All through their dinner of garbage food, Leah's irritation grew. It didn't help that Luke had brought all that beer in her house.

"Maybe he's doing the best he can," she said. "Maybe what *Peter Parker* really needs is to figure out what he wants to do with his life and get on with it."

Luke set down the wing in his hand and glared. "Why can't you leave it alone?"

She met his glare. "Because you've been living with me for a month, which makes your crap my business."

"Then I'll leave," he snapped. "Goddammit, Leah. Why ya gotta do that?" His eyes were bleary after at least five MGDs.

"Have you noticed that you are never beerless?" Leah continued.

Luke threw his hands in the air. "You are just on my ass tonight, aren't you? Well, you know what? You wouldn't like me without it. My brain doesn't work right." He motioned to his head with sauce-covered fingers.

"What are you talking about?"

Luke's face drooped. "I'm crazy, sister princess. Without a doubt."

He looked so damaged. Leah leaned forward, pushed down her rage and tried to find some compassion. She couldn't look at him when she spoke. "It's just you and me, Luke. Mom is half gone if she's ever even really been there at all. It's just us, and I don't want you to piss your life away." Her face throbbed and her stomach ached. And her heart hurt, too.

Luke deflated. He slurped buffalo sauce off his thumb. "I'm trying to get some shit figured out," he admitted.

Leah nodded but didn't ask. Didn't want to know. He was trying, and with Luke, that was enough for now.

ON DAY TEN, LUKE asked about her "cop boyfriend." They had both finally tired of TV and were sitting on the deck pondering their dinner.

"He stopped yesterday," Leah said, unwilling to add details.

"Where was I? Did he wait until I was gone?" Luke asked, hoisting his feet up on the picnic table.

The thought hadn't occurred to Leah. "I don't know. He didn't stay long." Kemp had appeared at her door the previous evening. He didn't make eye contact, knowing he'd made a fatal mistake by staying away for so long. He hid behind roses Leah refused to touch. She just stared, his affection, gift, and distant attitude adding to her anger.

"Hey, babe." He just stood there with a stupid look on his face. No explanation. No apology. Kemp tried to take a step forward inside her house, but Leah stood her ground. She wanted to scream at him for being the asshole he promised not to be. She wanted to smack herself for caring.

"You need to go," Leah had snapped. Kemp stepped back, his face unreadable. Leah didn't want any problems with him or any drama at work, so she tried to force the anger out of her voice. "I can't do this . . . whatever we were doing. It's not a big deal. It's fine. But we work together and need to leave it at that."

Kemp's face drooped, and he nodded and looked away. "Sorry, babe," he muttered, and he turned and left. And that was that.

"So, are you gonna marry the dude?" Luke asked, bringing her back to the present. He swatted a bug on his neck. They weren't going to last outside long on a muggy July evening with mosquitoes in full force.

"Shut up." Images of Kemp in a tux maddeningly flashed through her head. She was done with him, so the last thing she needed to think about was him in wedding attire. She hated herself for being such a girl.

"Seriously. Do you like him?" Luke was staring out into the yard, ever-present beer in his hand, condensation from the cold can dripping down his wrist.

"Seriously. Shut it. We had a fling. Now it's done. It's none of your damn business."

"That's a yes." Luke said softly. Not teasing, just honest.

Leah couldn't conjure much of a protest. Her brother knew her. "I work with him. We had a thing for a while, but it's over." Leah stood and patted Luke on the back. "I'm going to bed." It was Friday evening, and she was due back at work on Monday. She was ready for a routine—to be busy and useful instead of lying on her couch like a slug.

But her weeks of convalescence had shown her a few things. Her friends were her friends, visiting and texting and bringing food almost daily. Her brother was her only real family, making Leah his responsibility and taking care of her the best he could. And Kemp was exactly who she thought he was. Absent. He had pursued her, pushy and insistent. Charming and funny. But ultimately when she needed him—and damn, she had no intention of needing him or anyone—he wasn't there.

So that was that. Her fling with Kemp was over, and the most infuriating part was that she allowed this relationship in the first place. Anger settled into her belly, the only emotion that made sense.

A FEW HOURS LATER at Terrance County Sheriff's Department, Pete Kemper closed his laptop and sat in the dark in his cluttered office. They had taken a major step forward in the biggest case of his life. It was actually his second chance at the same big case, the one that fell apart on his watch the first time around, and this time it had to be right. Three states and the feds were involved. No room for error.

Once again this job and having any sort of personal life were incompatible. He had slept on the floor of his office the last two days and couldn't help but think about the floor burns he and Leah had given each other on that grubby carpet.

Leah. She wasn't going to forgive him.

After this final interview, he finished his part of the criminal complaint and forwarded it to the federal investigator for review. Hopefully it would lead to arrest. Other officers would make the arrest, if it occurred, so there was nothing left for him to do. He dragged himself out of his desk chair, snapped off the light and headed out to the parking lot. His star witness, who had insisted on midnight interviews, was leaning against the side of the building finishing a smoke.

"Night, Kemper," he said, waving his cigarette.

"Night, Luke," Kemp said as he got into his truck. Two weeks of interviews put them on a first-name basis. And the only way to avoid lying to Leah's face about the ongoing contact Kemp had been having with her brother, the star witness in this case of a lifetime, was to stay away from her. Luke told Kemp there was a chance she would get over it. But Kemp knew better. He knew that he and Leah were done.

chapter nine

THE ROUTINE WAS DIFFERENT that Monday morning when Leah returned to work. For one, Leah had to start her day at a meeting with the county's human resource rep and attorney. She signed some paperwork agreeing not to sue the county for any present or future consequences of "the incident." It was hard not to laugh at their discomfort as they struggled to talk about what happened without actually saying the words "bat" or "rabies."

After the meeting, Max and Leah walked back to the human services building, enjoying what was going to be the only tolerable time in the early August day. Her iPhone told her another ninety-plus-degree day lay ahead with stifling humidity.

"So are you really feeling better?" Max asked as they waited for a line of cars to pass at the intersection by the main government building.

"Yeah. My headache was gone in a couple days. It was those shots that hurt like hell." They hustled across the street at a break in traffic. "But I'm going to need therapy for all the dreams I'm having that end with me foaming at the mouth and someone shooting me to put me out of my misery."

"Therapy is part of the deal," Max said quickly.

"What?" Leah stopped, hands on her hips. "I'm not going to therapy."

Max stopped with her. "It's just a one-time thing. Well, maybe a three- or four-time thing. You know, it's part of the liability issue."

"It's not happening, Max." Her anger was building. Not helpful when she was trying to make the case that she wasn't impacted by The Incident.

"Well . . . I don't really know if they can make you go, but it could be a condition of your return to work."

Leah snorted and resumed walking the last sidewalk up to their building. "Then we're fine, because I'm already back. Are you going to send me home?" Leah knew that Max was still the boss, and she knew enough not to outwardly challenge him. He could be passively challenged with the same result anyway.

Max tilted his head while he considered his next move. "No. I'm not sending you home." They arrived at the front door, and he held the handle for a moment. "But you need to see someone. At least once." Leah glared at the back of his head. She could tell he was smiling, probably because he finally had the chance to send her to therapy, and God knew she'd needed it for years.

They were greeted by the perpetually cheerful Maddie.

"Leah!" Maddie announced. "So good to see you!"

Leah gave her a thin smile. "Thanks. It's, uh, good to be back."

"You're such a liar," Jill said, her work tote over her shoulder and weighed down with files. "It's good to see you, though." Jill patted Leah on the arm and Leah recoiled a bit, not realizing until that moment that she was still a little jumpy.

"Where are you heading?" Leah asked, stepping back but trying to be friendly and conversational.

"I'm going to that conference in Duluth this week." Jill grinned. "I'm sure it'll be a rigorous week for me, but I'll muddle through."

"Oh, yeah, don't wear yourself out spending a week in a hotel room by yourself," Leah said with a fake smile. "So that means I'll be doing all the investigations for the week. Awesome."

Jill shook her head. "I think he's going to have Roberta do as much as possible."

Leah's irritation swelled. "Do I look like I can't do my job?"

Jill looked up from her bag where she was organizing her files and forced a fake smile. "You look great! Gotta go. Have a good week!" Jill hustled out the door.

Leah wasn't completely back to normal, even just in appearance. The shots were supposed to keep the rabies from "taking hold." The swelling had subsided in her cheek, but she still didn't look quite right. Luke told her she looked tired, but Amanda and Zoe would only say that she looked "so great!" Their false cheer was equally helpful and annoying.

Leah made her way to her cube, where she found some kind of Barbie doll on her desk wearing black leather and a mask: Batgirl. Hilarious.

"Oh, look at the funny prank my sensitive coworkers have played on me," Leah announced in a monotone. "It's Batgirl. Just like me. How witty and clever." At least they weren't tiptoeing around her.

Roberta came around to her cube. "Welcome back, hon," she said, giving Leah a squeeze. Leah flinched again at being touched, but Roberta pretended not to notice. "We missed you."

That was the thing about this place. Even with all the stress and chaos, her work gave her something that she had experienced so little in her life—belonging.

THEIR STAFF MEETING had a late start. Everyone was distracted by Leah's return, and by the requisite cinnamon rolls that accompanied any celebration at Terrance County. Abby's Bakery made the famous rolls that were light and fluffy, rich and decadent. Zoe had picked a still-warm batch, so the fragrant sugar and spice made it hard to think about anything other than the spirals of dough they were all devouring.

Leah hadn't worn anything but yoga pants since the incident, so she had learned getting dressed that morning that her convalescence had another consequence: weight gain. She managed to avoid eating a roll for about ninety seconds, until the oozing cream cheese frosting was too much to resist.

"So what did I miss?" Leah asked, licking a blob of frosting off her finger.

Amanda shrugged. "Really nothing. Rumor has it Barb Cloud is dating, but it's an election year so she won't say a word."

"Somebody sat on one of the sinks in the women's restrooms and it broke off the wall," Roberta added. "That whole corner of the building flooded. The downstairs folks got to leave before their equipment shorted."

"Yeah, and no one said a word to us. As usual." Jackie said, unraveling her cinnamon roll and taking small, happy bites.

"Sorry," Max said, not picking up the sarcasm. "I didn't know, either." He was still gloomy and humorless, which meant his wife still wasn't living at home.

"So, no one did any work in the last two weeks?" Leah asked.

"Eh, work is work," Zoe said. "We told you the important stuff."

Leah unconsciously touched her still swollen and hardened cheek. "So what happened with those kids at that . . . the house?"

Jackie shrugged. "I've got the case. It's pretty amazing, actually. The kids were so dirty Gracie said their bathwater turned black." Gracie was the experienced, gentle, miracle-working foster grandma who took all four kids. "Turns out the two-year-old's brown hair was actually light blonde after it was washed."

"Blech," Amanda said. "Poor baby."

"I know, right?" Jackie said, wrinkling her nose. "But here's the thing. The kids are mellow and well behaved, and their mom does okay with them. I mean, other than the whole garbage house thing."

"That's a pretty big thing," Leah snapped back.

"Well, yeah. And there's the whole paternity issue. It's almost like Mom doesn't get what I'm talking about when I ask who the dad is." Jackie scribbled on her notebook. "I'm pretty sure she's just being manipulative because she doesn't want to tell me. It's hard to tell for sure. Part of me wonders if she really doesn't get it."

"So maybe saying she does okay is a bit of an overstatement," Leah said. It sounded as bitchy as it felt. So far she wasn't convincing anyone she didn't need therapy.

Jackie nodded carefully. "Good point." Leah and Jackie liked each other but were the two people on the staff most likely to disagree. Jackie could be as blunt as Leah. Depending on the day, that could make their staff meetings tense. Plus Jackie's life was a bit of a mess. She had her son when she was sixteen. He was now thirteen with very unstable diabetes. Max was patient with Jackie's endless absences—a single mom, she needed her insurance and had no one to help take care of her son most of the time. It felt unusual to have her in their staff meeting.

"So what's on the agenda today?" Zoe asked, smoothing over the tension. Max was staring into space. Zoe tapped the table in front of him gently. "Looks like you have a big pile there," Zoe said. He jumped.

"Yep, lots of intakes." He looked at his pile and then at Leah with worry. "Jill's out this week, so Roberta is going to take a few investigations." Roberta patted Leah on the back, one of the few people who could get away with the gesture.

Max reviewed the reports from over the weekend: a newborn baby tested positive for heroin, a fifteen-year-old was placed in crisis foster care after he and his dad got into a scuffle, and a toddler came back from a visit with his dad with a handprint on his cheek. Leah grimaced before she could stop herself. Child protection was so gritty, a detail she always forgot when she was away from work for a while. Leah had no desire to deal with any of those messes.

"Why don't you give me the mom and baby in the hospital," Jackie said. "I can do the assessment and get started working with her." Max nodded and wrote her name on the file.

"I can take the two-year-old and the teenager. I'm really quiet this week." Roberta reached for the files as Max wrote her name on them.

Leah reminded herself not to sound huffy before she spoke. "Excuse me, guys, but what am I going to do all week if you take all the new cases?"

"Well," Zoe began with false cheer. "I know we'd all love a few extra days to catch up and clean up our paperwork."

"My paperwork is fine." Leah looked over at Max who was back to staring at the wall. "Max. Seriously. You need to give me some work to do."

Max started to answer when Maddie popped her head in the door. "The PD needs Leah," she said uneasily.

"Now?" Max asked. Out of the corner of her eye Leah saw Zoe look at Amanda with concern.

Maddie nodded. "Rick Jordan called. Said they need Leah to do an interview right away." They all turned to Leah, who stood with a triumphant smile.

"Well, there you go. I'm outta here." Leah stood before Max or anyone else could object.

"Leah . . ." Zoe pleaded, "wait a second."

"Guys," Leah said, turning around to look at the faces of her worried coworkers and friends. "I have been home, bored out of my mind for the past two weeks. I'm rested. I'm not traumatized. I'm *fine*, and I need to work." Leah grabbed her calendar and her coffee. "I'll check in soon." Leah walked out and stopped at Maddie's desk for the written message: *Interview at Pete Kemper's office at 10:00 a.m.*

It hadn't occurred to her that the interview would be with Kemp. She was ready to work. She just wasn't ready to face Kemp.

TERRANCE COUNTY SHERIFF'S DEPARTMENT and Terrance Police Department shared one of the few modern buildings in downtown Terrance. The sleek, three-story glass-and-stone building was the pride of the county but loathed by those who thought it interfered with Terrance's historic beauty. City police officers and investigators were officed in the basement, and the sheriff's deputies on the upper two floors. Leah went to the reception area and punched in her code to get in the security doors.

The last time Leah had been in the building, she and Kemp had "celebrated" their victory getting Joe to confess to beating Baby Ben. Leah had forgotten to ask for the update on Ben and made a mental note to ask when she got back to the office. Chief Investigator Gordy Hoffbrau met her in the waiting area outside the interview rooms and motioned her to the observation room connected to the soft interview room.

"Thanks for coming," Gordy said without his usual joviality. Like most of the cops, his humor was harsh and profane, a necessary defense in law enforcement. More so for Gordy, because of his multiple health issues. "There's no way this little girl could be interviewed by a man."

Leah followed Gordy into the observation room where Jake, Barb Cloud, Kemp, Rick Jordan, and two uniformed officers were already discussing the case. Rick and Kemp took chairs on opposite sides of the table, which was fitting. Rick was shooting up the ranks at the Terrance PD, and that scared the hell out of Kemp.

"I don't think the time's right," Rick was insisting. "The kid hasn't even had a full night's sleep."

"You need to do an interview today," Barb Cloud, county attorney said. She was the ranking authority in the room, thus the discussion ended. "It's a public safety issue. This girl was found half naked and unconscious on a gravel road. We need to try to find out what happened to her, and get whoever did this picked up as soon as we possibly can."

"Half naked?" Leah asked. "Unconscious? What the hell happened?"

Rick reviewed what they knew: Fourteen-year-old Annika West was found at 12:49 a.m. by uniformed officers after her mother, a single parent, made a report Annika was missing. She was a teenager, so initially the situation was treated as a potential runaway, although her mom had insisted there was no way she would run away. Annika would be in ninth grade in the fall, was a conference champion swimmer, a straight-A student, and a gifted pianist. Annika did not break rules.

All the squads on duty were looking for Annika, and two officers had gone to the places she could be—friends' homes, the library, McDonalds. They had found her by accident in North Terrance when a new officer took a back road to get back downtown from the residential area where several of her friends lived. He saw a figure on the road and thought it was too big to be a deer. As he got closer he could see the glint off the reflective strip on her running shorts . . . that were bunched around her ankles. When he got closer and saw the blood stains and bruises on her hands and around her fingernails (defensive injuries), he checked her vitals but didn't move her. The officer covered her in a blanket and held her quivering hand until back-up officers and an ambulance came.

The ER report indicated Annika had been violently sexually assaulted. She had marks around her neck and broken blood vessels on her face from being choked. Annika was semi-conscious during her exam in the ER and was admitted to the hospital for the night. But her mother had checked her out early that morning, thinking she would recover better at home. Her mother had agreed to bring her to the police station because she said she was also desperate to know what had happened. Annika hadn't spoken a word since she was found.

"We just need to get basic information," Barb said. "We may need to do multiple interviews with her, depending on the degree of trauma." Barb looked up at Leah. "Obviously she's not going to want to give a description of the suspect. And she may have just blocked the whole thing. You're going to have to think like a cop on this one, Leah. We don't have any information: no motive, no suspects, no witnesses, nothing. This could be a serious public safety risk if we can't figure out who this guy is. People are going to panic fast."

Leah tried to summon some of her old swagger. She was one of the best interviewers in the county, but she still felt shaky and lost. And having Kemp in the room, staring at her with big, worried eyes didn't help her confidence. His constant gaze left her more confused.

But then she looked at Jake, who raised his eyebrows in question—was she up to this? Leah nodded at Jake's unspoken query and focused on Annika, who needed Leah to pull herself together. Jake smiled grimly in a show of support.

Their plan was for Leah to go very slowly and get basic information. They would go as far as Annika could tolerate, and Leah had the group's permission to end the interview at any point she thought Annika had had enough. Leah glanced over at Kemp one more time, but he was absorbed in the report. She forced herself to look away and focus on the interview ahead.

ANNIKA WAS A WISP OF A GIRL—blonde, translucent skin, frail. In a long-sleeved t-shirt and heavy black sweatpants, she swam in her clothes. Her eyes were wide and blank. Leah wondered if she had been sedated at the hospital, because it was like Annika was looking through her. She was emotionless. Blank.

Leah escorted her into the soft interview room. Square, not more than ten by ten feet, it was fully wired for sound with a video camera hidden in a glass orb on the ceiling. Annika slipped into the room without her mother almost too easily. It was preferable to interview her alone, but they were also prepared to allow Annika a support person in the room. Annika shrugged off the offer and went directly to the sofa. A one-way mirror was at Leah's back, allowing the staff in the observation room to see the victim's face during the interview. A small phone on a stand next to the chair let anyone with questions call the room and tell Leah what to ask. Leah sat on a chair near the couch. She pushed an easel and paper to the corner, out of the way.

Annika shifted gingerly. Leah's heart sank, recognizing that Annika must still be in pain where the abuser penetrated her so violently. She hoped the video had started rolling so the future jury could see this child was hurting.

Determination settled into Leah's gut. She was not going to let go until she found answers, justice, and peace for this little girl.

With the camera rolling, Leah strayed from the typical interview protocol. Instead of introducing herself, explaining why they were there, and starting her inquiry, Leah sat with Annika in silence. Annika stared at the wall, breathing shallow and fast. Leah took deep, measured breaths, hoping Annika would follow and start to relax. Leah looked at Annika with serious eyes.

"This room was built to interview kids," Leah said softly. Annika's light-blue eyes shifted to Leah. "We're way inside the police station, and there are two sets of locked doors, so it's just us and the cops in this whole building. Very secure." Annika didn't move.

"I'm a social worker. My name is Leah. My job is to talk to kids and teenagers." Leah took another deep breath and let it out slowly. Annika followed and pulled in a deeper breath and exhaled. Leah leaned forward and rested her elbows on her knees. "You're in charge here today. When you say we're done talking for the day, we'll stop." Annika eyed the door. Leah knew she was out on a limb giving Annika all the power to end the interview from the very beginning. She went on an instinct that Annika wanted to talk, and she wanted her to feel safe.

"Are you going to be in high school this fall?" Leah asked. Leah wanted to see if Annika would answer any questions at all. Annika gave a short nod. Promising.

"What kind of activities are you into?" Again, Leah already knew the answers but wanted to get a word, any word, out of her.

Several seconds passed, then a whisper. "Swimming."

"Swimming is intense," Leah said, pulling everything she could remember about competitive swimming. "You're in the water for hours and hours, cold and wet all the time . . ." Leah could see Annika was listening and possibly even commiserating a bit. "Which events do you swim?" Leah kept her eyes averted, still hoping for a whole sentence.

"Butterfly," Annika said, her voice scratchy. She cleared her throat and tried again. "And backstroke."

"Awesome. Good for you. Butterfly's tough. You must be very strong."

Annika shrugged.

"Do you practice in the summer?"

Annika shifted again, tears popping into her eyes. Leah was trying not to look at the handprint bruises on Annika's neck. "That's where I was."

Leah cringed, forgetting that Annika failed to come home after evening swim practice. Leah had no intention of talking about the incident this early in the interview. "Right. Sunday practice, huh?"

"That's when the pool's open."

"I suppose you have to take it when you can get it."

Annika was studying her hands, as if noticing the scratches and bruises for the first time. "I like Sunday practices. The coaches usually make it easier. Then we play games or have diving contests."

Leah nodded and smiled. "Nice they let you play sometimes. Sports can get so intense."

Annika's mouth turned up a bit. "I'm pretty intense. I like to work hard."

"So . . ." Leah considered for a second, then decided to go for it. "What time did practice get done last night?" Establishing a timeline.

Annika shrank, knowing the real interview was starting. But she kept eye contact with Leah. "About eight o'clock. It was starting to get dark." Annika held Leah's gaze for a moment. Leah felt she was telling her she could keep going. Leah asked a few questions about who was at practice, who watched her leave, and what route she usually took home. Annika answered everything, her eyes occasionally darting to the two-way mirror.

"So you took the back way home . . ." They were getting close to when Annika must have been jumped.

Annika took a breath and braced herself. She looked at her hands as she spoke, the words eeking out in tight whispers. "He pushed my bike down. Grabbed me by the neck from behind." She motioned with her hands, showing how his hands went around her neck. Her eyes were glassy again.

"He grabbed you from behind . . ." Leah said, repeating the words for the tape, keeping the conversation moving.

"He's pulling my hair . . . hands over my mouth and my eyes . . . ." Annika's voice dropped, barely perceptible, her breath fast and choppy. She had switched to present tense, which meant she was reliving the assault. Leah looked at the mirror, wishing she could make eye contact with Kemp in their silent communication to decide if it was time to end. If Annika was reliving the assault, then this interview had to be over soon.

"Annika." Leah spoke her name a bit louder, trying to get the girl's attention and bring her out of the flashback. Annika flinched and looked up sharply, her eyes still unfocused. "Do you think we've done enough for today? We could come back another day and talk more."

Annika's eyes snapped into focus on Leah. "No. I want to keep going."

"Are you sure?"

Annika slid away again, her face slack. "I don't remember much more than that anyway. He pushed me off my bike. Grabbed my neck, covered my face with something . . . then . . . I don't know . . . it got dark. There was a bad smell, and I got really woozy. That's all I know. I woke up in the hospital."

"Okay," Leah said. "I still would like to ask a few more questions. You may know more than you think. I'm trying to get details about what happened, and it might be hard to try to remember. So if it gets too hard, let me know."

Annika nodded.

"When you went down on your bike, you said 'he pushed me'? Was it obvious from the beginning it was a guy?"

Annika squinted. "He was big and bulky. Strong. And, I guess he smelled like a guy."

"What does a guy smell like?" Leah asked.

"He smelled like my uncle, actually. Like car grease or something. And smoke, and kind of spicy. I saw a sleeve, too. Dark flannel. His arms were not huge but not skinny either." Her words spilled out. "He wore a mask."

Important detail. "A mask? What kind of mask?"

Annika grimaced at the memory. "A winter mask. Like for skiing. It was black or navy, and it had some kind of patch on the side."

"What kind of patch?" Leah was picturing different types of masks.

Annika closed her eyes. "Maybe a sports team? I don't really know."

"Okay, so he had a mask. Did he say anything?"

"No, not really. Just grunted. It seemed like he was in a hurry."

"Why do you think that?"

Annika put her hands down and looked at Leah. "I guess it just seemed that way." Annika let out a big deep breath and sat back in her chair, her eyes glassy again. Leah tried to ask a few more questions but Annika shrugged, clearly done for the day. It wasn't ideal to do more than one interview, but the victim's well being had to come first, and Annika clearly couldn't do any more. Annika had retreated far inside of herself. Dissociation was a powerful trauma response, protecting the victim from seeing or feeling too much. Leah recognized the sleepy, vacant look in Annika's eyes and ached for the girl.

Leah stood and thanked Annika for her time. Annika agreed to come back another day if they had more questions. She got up and gasped in pain, tears welling in her eyes.

"Let's find your mom, hon," Leah said. Despite her pain, Annika left the interview room looking stronger than she did when they started. Leah felt the opposite—weak, tired, and heavy with this young girl's trauma. Annika's mom stroked her hair, and they headed for their car.

It wasn't enough information to create a sketch or to conduct much of an investigation. Leah didn't really listen as she sat in the observation room, watching the investigative team hash out next steps. They agreed Annika had probably been drugged, so they would be sending her back to the clinic for a full toxicology screen. More trauma for Annika.

Leah was once again distracted by the pain playing out right in front of her—Annika's post traumatic stress, the disappointment and guilt of not getting any real answers that would help, her own neediness morphing into anger. All of it was choking out any ability to think like a professional.

And to top it off, something was sticking from that interview. Something Annika said. It was significant that a detail had adhered. It was that detail, and what it meant, that would soon blow Leah's life apart.

The game was changing. The little man wasn't little anymore, and it took a little more juice to make things happen. Uncle took charge, though. He changed the game, enhanced it really, and the little man followed the way Uncle knew he would: Compliant. Sexy. Thirteen.

chapter ten

Hey, lady! Should we meet for coffee at the regular place tomorrow? I can get away around 9. Hope it was a great week. Miss you.

The text on Leah's phone was from a number she didn't recognize and wasn't in her contacts. It must have been sent inadvertently. Disappointing. Coffee with someone, anyone, if she was being really honest, would have been nice.

The week ended with reports, casenotes, and voicemail messages she chose to ignore. After Annika's interview, Max kept her away from anything of substance—translation: any fun cases. Leah craved a tangle with a verbally abusive stepdad or a bully of a mom she could argue with, respectfully and professionally, of course. Every once in a while a parent went on the attack, and Leah savored the chance to yell back and blow off a little steam. Zoe could diffuse any parent with a combination of listening and validation, and was so skilled Max thought she should work for the UN. But sometimes a bully needed an in-kind response, and Leah was the best at handling them. Not everyone agreed with her approach, but Leah knew how to keep herself from crossing any lines.

Without any jerks needing to be handled, Leah's pent-up frustration had nowhere to go. Zoe had thrown together an impromptu engagement party at her house for Amanda and Jacob, and Leah was afraid she would get bitchy and either embarrass herself or perhaps make the perpetually weepy Lucy cry. Zoe must have sensed this, because she wouldn't let Leah help with the details.

"Seriously, all you need to do is come with your shiny smile, and maybe an hors d'ourve if you insist." Closing time had finally arrived, and Zoe switched off the light by their cubes as they headed for the back door.

Leah shrugged. "Who's coming to this thing, anyway?"

Zoe held open the outside back door, and they were overcome by a wave of soggy air. Early August heat wave. "Oh, it's so gross out here," Zoe said. "Nobody will want to be outside."

"Maybe you can push your guests out to your deck with a fan." Leah pulled her frizzy, hair dye-damaged hair into a ponytail before her neck got too sweaty. "Now tell me who'll be there."

Zoe reached her minivan and paused with her hand on the door. "Mostly county people, plus Lucy and William. And, yes, Leah, I invited Kemp. Is that going to be a problem?"

Leah scowled. "You're awfully pissy with me lately."

Zoe stared at Leah. "I love you, but you're pissy, yourself. We've been pretty much avoiding you around here."

Leah frowned, knowing it was true.

"Are you ever going to tell us what happened with you and Kemp?"

"There's nothing to tell," Leah sighed. "He was never my 'boyfriend.' We weren't anything. All we ever did together was blow off some steam. I guess I need to find a new outlet," Leah added with a wry smile.

"You two were more than that," Zoe said. "Tell yourself whatever you want, but your real friends know the truth."

"Yeah, well, good for you." Leah didn't bother to argue with Zoe, but would have denied it to anyone else.

"What I really want to know is if you're ever going to let yourself have a serious relationship." Zoe wiped the sweat already dripping into her eyes. "In all the years we've worked together, you've been a fiercely loyal and hilarious friend, and a prickly bitch to any man who tries to get near you."

As always, Zoe spoke a piercing truth impossible to ignore. "Men suck. Relationships suck," Leah wiped her forehead. "Pass on both."

"I love you, but–"

"You know what," Leah interrupted. "Even I know 'I love you' isn't supposed to be followed by the word 'but.'"

Zoe nodded and brushed her still perfectly shiny, straight hair out of her eyes. "Fair enough, girlfriend. My house at six o'clock. Please try to leave the attitude at home."

Leah's hair had tightened into a ball of fuzz in her ponytail. "I'll be there early just for the A/C."

J & G'S WAS LEAH'S OLD LIQUOR STORE. Joe and Glen both knew Leah by name, as they probably knew many heavy drinkers in town. Leah pulled her Subaru in the lot three days before but never got out of her car. The following day, Leah went in and wandered the short aisles for forty-five minutes before the questioning glares of some new employee irritated her into leaving.

But on that Friday, after a long week, and in anticipation of a social event with coworkers, friends, and goddamn Pete Kemper, Leah's car seemed to drive itself to J & G's. Glen was working the till and greeted her like an old friend and without judgment, as if telling her he trusted her to make her own decisions.

Leah left with a bottle of Jameson's whiskey and a cloud of guilt so thick it was stifling. She drove home and set the whiskey on the counter, opening and closing it twice, pouring a glass, then dumping it down the sink. Leah took a shower and dressed in a tank top and denim cutoffs. She found herself back at the kitchen counter in a staredown with Mr. Jameson.

She was chasing that old feeling—the boost, the confidence, the hope—that came with a few drinks. Leah didn't miss the shakes and the gloom that came with the hangover, and she certainly didn't crave the humiliation on the morning after she went home with some townie creep.

The drunk euphoria had enabled her to forge a bond with those losers. But that bond had to be artificial, because as of this day Leah couldn't remember a single one of her old drinking buddies' names. Even their faces were foggy and distorted. Zoe was right—unless she was doing an investigation, Leah didn't know how to connect with people.

But what she did know was that Pete Kemper made her feel needy, jerked around, and pathetic. That had to end. He was distant now, proof Leah had learned to keep men away as if they were opposing magnets.

A muffler-less truck pulled up, and a car door slammed. Luke was home. She grabbed for the whiskey and tried to hide it like a criminal, but Luke was too quick. All she could do was leave it on the counter and pretend it wasn't hers.

"Oh, sister princess, did you get me a bottle of Jameson? " Luke asked as the back door banged shut behind him. His eyes lit up at the expensive bottle of booze that he wouldn't and couldn't buy for himself.

"Does that sound like something I would do?" She guarded the bottle like a dog protecting a bone. While she didn't want to admit it was hers, she sure as hell wasn't going to let him have it.

"Probably not, meanie," he slurred.

Leah looked closely at his face. "You're high, asshole." As she said it, the sweet, spiciness of recently smoked weed wafted over her.

Luke stared, his reflexes too slow to respond.

"Dammit, Luke, get out of here and go to bed."

He started to protest, but Leah grabbed the whiskey and her keys and headed out the door.

EVERY TIME LEAH DROVE to Zoe's house, she remembered, as she passed expansive lawns and sprawling homes, that Zoe was rich. Not just well-off, upper middle class, but genuinely wealthy. Zoe's dad was an orthopedic surgeon at Mayo Clinic, which would have been enough, but her mom, a dermatologist, had invented some kind of skin tool thingy (the details never seemed to stick), and they became millionaires. Zoe's parents died within weeks of each other just after Zoe and Sam were married and left Zoe, their only heir, a millionaire.

Other than their home, however, Zoe and Sam didn't live like they were wealthy. Zoe tended to ignore their money. She was already working at the county when Leah started eight years ago. An only child, Zoe was adopted by her well respected, doting parents in their early forties and spent her childhood with adults, so she learned early to talk to anyone. Zoe never explained why she wanted to be a social worker, or really why she worked at all. It was a touchy subject to imply that a mom shouldn't work if she didn't have to.

Leah pulled into the circular driveway by the door, but then kept driving and parked near the street. Easy getaway.

The whiskey was on the floor in the backseat. She left it there, not wanting to deal with Zoe's reaction. And not wanting Zoe's guests to drink it.

SAM WAS VACUUMING, the twins were eating an early dinner at the breakfast bar in the kitchen, and Zoe was unwrapping catered hors d'oeuvres. Zoe nodded her greeting and told Leah to put her sweatshirt away and help set up outside. Leah wandered into the living room to the wall of windows overlooking the rolling bluffs of the Apple River valley. Gnats and mosquitoes skipped throughout the glossy carpet of soft grass. Lawn games and tiki torches lined the yard along the back perimeter. The left side of the yard was a mess as they had just broken ground on an in-ground pool, but an ample hot tub was uncovered, steaming, and ready for the party. Lucy and William were setting up a makeshift bar by the hot tub, with a punch bowl and large colored buckets full of ice and beer or soda.

Lucy . . . sigh.

From the first time Amanda introduced them, Lucy and Leah never seemed to hit it off. And William was so hyper-protective of Lucy he didn't seem to like Leah, either. Leah let herself out the sliding glass door onto the enormous, multi-level back deck. As she headed down the stairs, she tried to plant a smile on her face.

"Hey, guys!" Leah said with a plastic grin.

William and Lucy looked up from the cups they were stacking, and Leah swore she saw a grimace cross Lucy's face before she smiled politely back.

"Hey, there." Lucy said into the punch.

"Need any help?" Leah asked.

William shrugged. "I think it looks pretty good," he said, waving his arms around the yard. "All that's left is for us to test out the punch." Will poured a glass and held it out to Leah.

Lucy shook her head at William, but he didn't notice. Leah ignored her disapproving eyes. Leah accepted the cup and had a swallow. Syrupy sweet: orange juice, pineapple juice, and Malibu rum were all she could detect. It tasted like summer.

"I thought you . . ." Lucy trailed off.

"It was just a taste," Leah said, almost feeling euphoric from that tiny sip. Her hand, working before she even gave it a thought, tipped the cup and poured the punch out onto the lawn. "See? All gone."

Will looked back and forth between the two of them. Lucy gave a weak nod. "It's actually a little sweet for my tastes, so I'll probably stick to beer," Will said, grabbing a Corona and raising his eyebrows to Leah, asking if she wanted one. Lucy's eyes got wide.

"No thanks," Leah said through her gritted teeth and false grin.

Will nodded. "How about a game of beanbags before everyone gets here? I'll take you both on."

Lucy backed away. "You two go ahead," she said quickly. "I'm going to head inside and check on Javier," their adorable one-year-old.

"Then it's you and me, Leah. Prepare to lose," Will said as he headed to the beanbag game and tossed her the blue bags. Leah relaxed. Maybe Will didn't dislike her as much as she thought.

THE PARTY WAS IN FULL SWING by 8:00, and many of the guests were feeling their booze by 9:00. Most people were on the deck or in the yard, where white lights were strung around the deck railings and from tree to tree, with Chinese lanterns hanging from lower branches. The sky glowed pink in the west where the sun had just set, and the night sky was clear with a few winking stars.

Both Amanda and Jake had punch glasses in their hand that someone was always refilling, so they had become sloppy and affectionate. They made their way through the guests with Jake's arm perpetually resting on Amanda's shoulder, kissing every chance they got.

Kemp had set up camp near the bar, and couldn't be anything but the life of the party. Surrounded by cops and attorneys, all eyes were on Kemp as he shared war stories from his uniformed cop days. Wearing a Bruce Springsteen concert t-shirt and khaki shorts, he actually had a beer in each hand. Even from her hiding place across the lawn, Leah could see the tan lines across his temples from sunglasses. He must have been spending a lot of time on his boat, which brought back their July Fourth weekend together. The memory was warm, sharp and sad.

Leah found Jackie up on the deck, but they could only visit for a minute until Jackie said she had to get home to check on her son. So Leah wandered, avoiding Jake and Amanda, avoiding Lucy and her disapproval of the sip of punch, and trying to dodge Kemp at all costs.

"Hey!" Zoe popped up behind the twins' swingset and gave Leah a hug. "So far you haven't been a bitch at all. Good for you!"

"Gee, thanks," Leah said. "Is that Barb Cloud over there?" She motioned to the group playing a heated game of beanbags.

"I think so. I saw her talking to Jill. A lot." Zoe grinned and raised her eyebrows.

"That's nice. Any sign of Barb's mystery guy?"

Zoe stared at Leah. "No. But she's talking to Jill a lot. *If* you know what I mean."

Leah looked back at the group, where Barb and Jill were on the same beanbag team, sparkling all over each other.

"Huh!" Leah finally said. "Didn't see that coming."

"I think we need to keep it to ourselves until after Barb is re-elected. Not because anybody cares, but you know how private Barb is."

"Got it," Leah said, as Zoe chugged the last of her punch. "Hey, I want next game," Zoe yelled, running toward the group and leaving Leah alone again.

It was fully dark outside now, and Leah kept wandering, Diet Coke in hand. She found Max and his daughter, Jade, drawing with sidewalk chalk on the back patio under the deck.

"Hey, guys," Leah said, grabbing a piece of chalk and sitting next to Jade. "I like your picture." Jade was covered in pastel chalk dust, and looked as though she had tried to color her left leg blue.

"Look who wants to be like Cookie Monster." Max said with a tired, affectionate grin.

"*Girl* Cookie Monster!" Jade corrected, coating the back of her left hand in pink chalk.

"Of course." Leah wrote J-A-D-E on the cement. "I think your car is going to be a pink-and-blue mess when you head home."

Max shrugged. "Christine is picking her up soon," he said. "I'm not so worried about her car."

Leah nodded. She had been wondering how they were doing, but his gloom seemed to answer that question. She finally found someone whose mood matched her own. They watched Jade scribble on the cement and herself.

"We better get you packed up, snuggle bug," Max said, starting to brush her off.

"Noooooooo!" she wailed, backing away from Max. "I wanna stay at the party!"

Leah helped them gather their stuff while Jade whimpered and whined, and they went inside where it was bright and quiet. She watched through the front window as Max loaded Jade in Christine's car and backed away as Christine drove off. He looked defeated and heartbroken, a cautionary tale about the hazards of marriage and expecting that it would last forever.

Leah wandered to the kitchen and refilled food trays, pondering how soon she could leave without hearing about it later.

When did parties become so miserable? Leah had attended many county functions over the years and usually stayed all night. What's more, she used to enjoy it. Was it when she and Kemp started dating that everything got so messy? The dating part wasn't so bad, but the expectations were the problem. Other than her disastrous marriage, Leah was never one for long-term relationships. She screwed around a fair amount in her drinking days, and was mostly celibate when she went back to college. She started at the county when she was twenty-seven, dating here and there, but never letting it get far. By the time Kemp made his first real advance two years ago, it had somehow been almost five years since she had sex, and refusing was pretty much impossible.

Leah still squirmed when she thought about their first time together. A few weeks after their kiss at the Christmas party, they got assigned to a difficult investigation—a dad had spanked his six-year-old so hard that he wouldn't sit in his desk in kindergarten. Back at Kemp's office, Leah was shaken, both from the brutality of the abuse and the fury unleashed on them by the dad. When Kemp put his hand on Leah's shoulder and said she had done well, she softened. His hand moved behind her neck and pulled her into a kiss, and before either of them knew it, they were up against the wall, on the desk, and finally on the floor.

When they had finished (Leah thought she could have blacked out at one point—no one should go five years without sex), Leah was ready to jump up and go running out the door, but Kemp made a joke and they both dissolved into giggles. After a few moments, their nakedness in his office just got weird. She found her khakis in the corner, cringed at her tired old underwear, and put herself back together the best she could. As she headed back to her office, Kemp patted her ass and thanked her for a fun time. She felt trampy, the way she did in her old drinking days, and confused about what that meant for both of them.

But Leah had felt other things, too—exhilaration, desirability, a little less lonely. In fact, she was so overrun with emotion that she followed her typical pattern and backed away from him. They were all business for months after their first tryst, friendly but awkward. The next time they found themselves wrapping up an investigation in Kemp's office after hours, Leah couldn't look at him for fear he would read her mind. Thankfully he did, slowly closing the door, kneeling next to her chair, and pulling her into a kiss that led them back down that sweaty road they would travel many times together in the next few years.

Through the open kitchen window, Kemp's chortles rose above the soft roar of conversation and laughter and startled Leah out of her uncomfortable memory. Kemp was impossible to get away from or ignore. Thankfully, it was nearly 10:00, and Leah thought she may finally be able to go home.

But the laughter started coming closer to the house, and then suddenly the crowd was inside. Many of the cops and attorneys were involved in a training exercise at

6:00 the next morning, so most of the group was heading home. Leah smiled and chatted and waved, her teeth clenched and her face tight. She grabbed her sweatshirt and keys and almost had made her escape when Amanda caught her arm.

"Oh, no you don't," Amanda said, swaying slightly. "We're all getting in the hot tub."

"Count me out," Leah said as politely as she could.

"Wedding party in the hot tub." Jake said, bleary eyed. He looked like he would probably pass out soon. "No exceptions."

ZOE HAD A DRAWER FULL of bikinis and told Leah to grab whatever she wanted. Leah stood over that drawer a long time. Zoe was taller and at least two cup sizes bigger than Leah, but at least that meant the top would keep her covered. Leah changed quickly and ran out back, hoping she could get in before anyone else. Unfortunately, as she hustled down the deck stairs in a black bikini and wrapped in a bath towel, she interrupted Jake and Amanda in a clutch in the hot tub.

"Aw, geez, you guys," Leah said as loud as she could from as far away as possible. "I'm not getting in until you two are on opposite sides."

Amanda giggled and Jake yanked his hand out of her bikini top.

"Seriously. I know you're the happy couple and everything, but gag!" Leah dropped her towel and lowered herself in the corner of the tub.

Jake grinned at Leah. "Your ponytail is so curly it looks like a poodle tail." Amanda and Jake thought this was hysterical.

Ornery and sober, she had no patience for teasing. "Jake, if you let your hair get any longer, you'll look like Peter Brady."

"Who?" Jake asked, his foot bumping into Leah's as he tried to play footsie with Amanda.

"Do you really not know the Brady Bunch? Are you twelve?" Leah kicked him in the shin.

"He's gonna be twenty-seven in a few weeks," Zoe yelled from the top of the deck, slurring. "Oooh, I should cannon ball right on top of you guys!"

"Don't even joke about it," Sam muttered, coming down the steps with a baby monitor in his hand. He was quiet by nature, but rarely this grouchy.

"Sheesh, crabby," Zoe said. She followed him down the stairs and plopped herself in the hot tub, splashing everyone and spilling water over the sides. Sam rolled his eyes and sank into a deck chair.

Sam's irritation only added to Leah's desire to go home. It was a gorgeous summer night that reminded Leah of a tradition she had with her dad. On warm nights like this, she and her dad would sit in the backyard, ignoring the trash and van parts littering the yard, and look for constellations. It was one of her only good childhood memories: drinking root beer and slapping mosquitoes with her dad pointing at the Big Dipper and the North Star in the summer night sky. A rare surge of nostalgia brought tears to her eyes. It did not help when Kemp slid into the hot tub, his familiar hairy thighs brushing against her. With five of them in the eight person hot tub it was getting crowded and the water was spilling over the sides. Kemp had to rest his arm across the edge of the hot tub, just brushing against her back.

"Great party, Zoe. Can't wait until the pool is done," Kemp said.

Leah tuned to glare at Kemp. Did he really think he was part of their little group now?

Lucy and Will came down the stairs together, still dressed and looking disheveled. "We're just going to stick our feet in for a few minutes. We need to get baby home," Will said.

"Oh, my God, you guys totally just did it!" Amanda bellowed.

"Amanda!" Lucy cringed.

"No worries," Jake said. "You're with friends." Lucy's eyes darted to Leah, who forced an encouraging smile. The group sat for a few moments enjoying the quiet after a noisy party. The songful chirp of the mosquitoes and the distant, warm breeze epitomized summer in Minnesota.

"So it's less than two months 'til the big day . . ." Zoe said. "Are you ready?"

"I have no idea," Amanda said. Jake slid his hands up through Amanda's hair, a frisky grin on his face. "Jake's mom is doing everything."

"She never had a real wedding," Jake said, still nuzzling Amanda's neck. "And my sisters had their own ideas for their weddings. This is her chance to do it the way she wants."

"Uh huh," Amanda said, pulling away from Jake's octopus arms. "Total control. Everything *she* wants for *our* wedding."

"You brides are psycho," Kemp said, shifting in his seat and rubbing up closer to Leah.

"Hey!" Amanda splashed Kemp in the face. "Do I look psycho to you?

"You always have, babe. The bride thing just gives your crazy a happy glow."

"Watch it, Kemper," Jake said, woozy from the heat. "Thass my woman you're talking 'bout. Don't make me fight you."

"Settle down, Sharpie," Kemp said, making Jake shrink down in the water so his self-administered tattoos weren't showing. Everyone laughed, including Leah. She leaned her head back to see the Big Dipper, remembering her dad teaching her to follow the handle to the North Star. He was troubled in so many ways, but when they were staring at the sky they could connect. Leah wondered if her dad was somehow part of that sky, still a presence in her life. Crazy childhood or not, his absence hurt.

Kemp's hand on her knee disrupted her thoughts. She turned to glare at him, expecting his drunken, lecherous grin. Instead he looked at her with a melancholy smile that matched her mood. It would be so easy to rest her head on his shoulder and let him back in.

But Pete Kemper was all about goofing off and keeping it light, and a part of her that she wished wasn't there wanted more from him. It scared the hell out of her to need someone like that, especially someone whose track record showed he would let her down. It was a set-up she couldn't allow.

Leah stood and stepped out of the hot tub. "I'm going to head out, guys." Sam, absorbed in his phone, wordlessly got up from the table so she could find her towel. Lucy and William got up, too, followed by Kemp, and finally Jake and Amanda followed.

"Party's over already?" Zoe whined. "It's early!"

"Let's go, Zoe." Whatever was going on between Sam and Zoe was still unresolved. Sam was cold to his wife all night, but she seemed not to notice. The group wearily made their way upstairs and back inside, where everyone scattered to find their clothes and get dressed before heading home.

"Can I use your bathroom again?" Leah asked Zoe.

"Sure!" Zoe yelped, dripping all over the living room carpet.

"Shhh!" Sam ordered. "Three sleeping kids in this house, remember?" Zoe turned to face her husband who had been barking at her all night.

"Yes, Sam. I know." Zoe finally caught on that his mood was directed at her. Leah headed to the bathroom to avoid their tension.

Zoe and Sam's bedroom was palatial yet cozy, decorated in silver and dusty purple. The bathroom was bigger than Leah's bedroom at home. She changed quickly and set the swimsuit on the edge of the bathtub. Leah went back out through the bedroom where Sam was sitting on the bed, still messing with his phone. He set his phone down just as Leah's buzzed in her purse. Leah retrieved her phone and found that she had three messages from that same mystery number that texted her earlier in the week:

She's driving me crazy with this party. More attention on her guests than her family. Haven't heard back from you. Are we still on for tomorrow? I would love to see you, the first text read.

Everyone is hot tubbing now. These people are never going to leave.

They're finally leaving. Thank God. I'm just going to show up at Coffee House tomorrow and hope you're there.

It took a moment to understand. She stood dumbly in the doorway of Sam and Zoe's bedroom, and finally looked up at Sam. These messages were from him, complaining about his wife, arranging to meet someone else. Leah stared at him until he looked up at her.

"Heading home?" he hinted.

Leah looked at him an uncomfortable moment too long. She couldn't find words, especially with Zoe in the other room. She turned and walked down the hallway in silence, then paused and went back to the bedroom, where Sam was checking his phone again.

"Sorry we stayed so late, Sam," Leah said, her words clipped. "You're such a good sport letting all these county people take over your house. And your hot tub."

Sam looked up at her with a flash of irritation. "That's okay," he said.

"Is it okay?" Leah and Sam stared at each other, Sam searching Leah's face. He finally broke eye contact.

"Sure it is," he said, a glimmer of the Sam she knew showing through. "I'm just a little tired tonight."

"Hmmm. Any plans this weekend?" Leah still stared, her anger on her friend's behalf growing.

Sam's eyes widened. "Not really . . . no . . ." He looked uneasy but defiant.

"So you'll just be staying home tomorrow morning, right, Sam?"

Bam. Leah hit her mark. Sam's mouth dropped, and he stammered. She walked up to him and stopped just inches from his face. Years of confronting clients made it easier than it should have been to face off with her friend's husband. "I don't know what you're doing, but it ends now. Do you hear me?"

To Leah's surprise, tears welled up in Sam's eyes. "I haven't done anything, Leah. Nothing." Sam looked serious and sad. "I love my wife. And I miss her . . ."

Leah didn't know what he meant, and didn't want to know any more than that. His tears slowed her anger. "Keep it that way." Leah turned and walked away, leaving Sam slumped on that great big bed by himself.

LEAH WAS ALMOST HOME when her phone rang. She wanted to call Zoe but couldn't find the words, not wanting to have to keep this intimate information about her friend, but not wanting to share it either. She had punched in Zoe's number once, but didn't press send. Her phone was still in her hands, so she jumped when it rang.

"Is this Leah Danco?"

"It could be. Who's calling?" Leah forgot to check the caller ID, but it could be sheriff's dispatch looking for a social worker to manage a crisis. No thank you.

"Hennepin County Medical Center. We have a Beverly Danco here. Are you her daughter, Leah Danco?"

Leah's stomach dropped. "Yes."

chapter eleven

MOST OF THE TIME generalized anxiety disorder just made everyday life harder. It turned sore throats into leukemia and a forgotten phone call into a tragic accident. In Beverly Danco's mind, her children had died a hundred times in any number of horrific ways. But something had happened that night that turned excessive worry into active hallucinations. Beverly thought there was someone in her apartment. When she couldn't reach her kids, she took a $300 cab ride to Minneapolis to get away from the intruder, refusing to allow the cab driver to leave because she saw the mystery man at every stop. The frustrated cabbie finally drove to Hennepin County Medical Center and left Beverly there, where she hid under a plastic chair in the ER waiting area. The ER doctor gave her a heavy dose of Ativan, but there were no beds on their psych unit, so all they could do was have a family member pick her up.

Leah arrived at HCMC shortly after 1:00 a.m., and had her groggy mother back in her car within half an hour. Beverly was calm and irritated at first, but then dissolved into pitiful, drugged tears.

"I'm sssssuch a burrrrden. Oh, I'm ssssss0 sssssssorry, sweetheart. I ruin everything." Beverly was sobbing into the sleeve of her neon-green hooded sweatshirt, which topped off her hot pink sweatpants studded with black hearts. Leah wanted to say that the only thing she was upset about was that outfit. How did anyone let a woman in her fifties buy those clothes?

Leah could barely keep her eyes open, even with the two Diet Cokes she bought from the hospital vending machine. When they pulled into Beverly's driveway, Beverly was snoring loudly. Leah parked and sat for a moment, trying to summon the energy to gather up her mom and go inside.

Hallucinations. Her mother had not hallucinated since she first quit drinking. It seemed unlikely that this started out of nowhere. Perhaps her mother quit taking her meds, or started drinking again. The ER doctor told her she needed to get in to see her psychiatrist ASAP. Leah felt like a selfish brat because all she could think was that she did not have the time or energy for this.

Leah got out of her car and went to the passenger side, opened the door and patted her mom's arm.

"Let's go, Mom. We're at your house." Beverly didn't move. The night was still so warm condensation clouded the windows from the muggy air. "Mom!" Leah picked up her arm. It flopped down. There would be no waking her.

Leah stood and considered her options. She could leave her mother in the car and let her sleep, but Leah would probably have to sleep there, too, or she risked her mother waking up and wandering. If she was still hallucinating, she might run or hide or who knows what else.

Leah texted Luke: *Mom freaked out and went to the hospital. We're back at her house. I need your help. Get over here now.*

This night was never going to end. With resignation, Leah sat on the back of her car and stared at the sky. The moon had shifted—or really the earth kept turning so the moon appeared in a different place in the sky. Her dad explained it all to her one night when they went out to watch the harvest moon emerge low and huge on the horizon, and then rise and shrink as the night went on. He made it sound like magic. Leah thought it was a sign not to trust what she saw. She remembered when she found Orion's belt with three stars in a row. Like a Jedi toolbelt, her dad had said. She wondered what other people talked about with their parents. Sports . . . politics . . . religion . . . ? Her dad's obsession was such a part of their childhood she couldn't imagine a world without his fanatical knowledge of Star Wars. It was his religion.

A pickup with a bumper that nearly dragged on the ground pulled up on the street and parked in front of her mother's house. Luke climbed out. "Hey, sis. Mom's freakin' again, huh?"

"You don't have enough 'Driving after Revocation' tickets already?" she asked. "How are you ever going to get your license back if you keep driving without one?"

Luke threw his hands up. "Hey, do you want me here or not?"

Fair enough. "Fine. Let's just get her inside." Leah led Luke to the passenger side of her car, where they opened the door and stared at Beverly, head back, mouth hanging open, snoring loudly.

Luke turned back to Leah with a snort. "What the hell is she wearing?"

Leah giggled out of pure exhaustion. "Don't get me started on Beverly Danco's wardrobe." Luke reached across her, unbuckled her seatbelt, and awkwardly picked up his mother like a child. Leah ran ahead of him and opened the front door. They made their way to her bedroom, with out-of-shape Luke grunting and panting all the way.

"Are you staying?" Luke asked when they were back in the living room.

Leah shrugged. "I suppose one of us should stay, at least tonight."

"We can both stay," Luke said. "I'll go get some wings and beer."

"Gross, Luke. I'm not eating wings at two o-clock in the morning. This isn't a slumber party. I'm going to bed."

"You're such a party pooper." Luke started rifling around the kitchen for food, and then grabbed a plastic package. "Ramen!"

Leah found a blanket and a pillow and flopped on the couch. Luke could take the recliner or the floor. She expected to crash immediately, but the Diet Cokes had finally kicked in and all she could do was stare at the ceiling. Luke banged around in the kitchen a few minutes, and then came back to the living room with a steaming bowl of ten-cent noodles.

"So what's new, sis? Wanna watch a movie?"

"I want to sleep, Luke." But then a thought occurred to Leah and she sat up on one arm. "Actually, I have a question. How did Dad actually die?"

Luke recoiled. "Huh? Why're you asking about him?" Luke got very interested in his noodles.

"Come on, Luke. What's the deal? What do you know, and why don't I know?"

Luke shrugged. "You were gone. It was just us, and it was messed up back then."

"It was always messed up." Leah sat up and squinted through the dark at Luke, who was avoiding eye contact.

"No, it got really bad after you left. Dad was pickled drunk all the time, and they were taking shitloads of pills and dropping acid, too. Everybody was just out of it." Luke stuffed his mouth full of ramen.

"Why didn't anybody tell me?"

"Tell you what? You were doing your own thing, and you were pretty drunk yourself those days." Harsh but true.

Leah tried to remember the time she spent with her family when she was in college, or after she dropped out. But Luke was right—that was the height of her drinking days and her family was far from her mind. Everything was fuzzy for her, too.

Luke set his bowl down and leaned back in his chair. "After you moved out, Dad got worse. Mom got mad. And I stayed away as much as I could. A whole bunch of shit went down all at once, and then Dad did it."

"Did what?" Leah leaned forward.

"Offed himself." Luke said sleepily. He pushed the recliner back and closed his eyes.

"*Offed himself?!*" Leah yelped and Luke jumped. "What the hell . . . ?"

Luke opened one eye. "You didn't know that?"

"Son of a bitch, Luke. No I didn't know that." Leah was reeling. Suicide? Tears filled her eyes at her dad's pain. "Why would he do that?"

"Because our family's fucked up." Luke's eyes were closed, arms were crossed. He was done talking. Tears dampened the stiff throw pillow on the cheap couch that smelled of plastic and dandruff shampoo. Her heart was thudding with too much caffeine and sadness. Eventually she drifted off wondering if her dad really wanted to die, or if he had a fleeting moment of regret as he faded away.

LEAH AWOKE A FEW HOURS later with a searing pain in her neck from sleeping at an awkward angle. She sat up and stretched, the plastic sofa cushions crackling and shifting. The recliner was empty—Luke was gone. The jarring memory of her conversation with him settled back on her. She thought of her dad's pathetic memorial service with the handful of people attending. Leah cringed at the memory of her mother sobbing over the cheap urn. Her dad's friend, Coolie, was a sticky presence during the entire service, trying to step up and take care of Luke, his hand on Luke's back most of the day. She shuddered at her memories of Coolie and Luke.

Ugh—Coolie. He had been a constant presence in their lives. He had known Beverly and Roger since well before Leah was born, and he acted like he had more of a place in their home than Luke and Leah. He went to every convention, usually sleeping in his dilapidated van. Whenever Coolie was around, Leah complained to Luke, but Luke would just pretend Coolie didn't exist.

Beverly shifted in her bed and moaned softly. Leah willed her mother to go back to sleep, hoping for a few hours of peace before they had to talk about what her mom needed from her next. Apparently she needed more help, and there were case managers for this. Leah could bring her mom to the office and have an adult mental health social worker help her mom figure out medication, therapy, and support. Perhaps that was the real task for the day—convincing her mom to let someone else help her.

The crackling couch got the best of her, so Leah gave up on sleep and decided to make coffee and breakfast. Put her mom in a good mood so she didn't feel like Leah was abandoning her. Leah threw together a buttermilk coffee cake and cut up some grapefruit, and still her mom slept. She cleaned the kitchen and the bathroom even though they were spotless, and her mom slept some more.

At 10:00 a.m. Leah made sure her mom was still breathing. Leah looked around the bedroom at the obsessive order—socks folded in neat rows in a drawer, bandanas draped over hangers from light to dark. Leah peeked in her mom's jewelry box and found what she didn't want to find—loose weed in a baggie, a few fat joints rolled and ready, and a variety of clips and pipes. In the section of the box where rings would usually be set between spongy rolls of velvet, she found pills. A rainbow of pills carefully laid out in rows by color, shape and size. Quite an extensive stash for someone who had supposedly "taken the cure." Perhaps this was why her meds weren't working for her.

Leah picked up the biggest joint and sniffed. Weed had never been her drug of choice, but there was still a twinge of temptation.

"Are you after my stash?" Beverly's voice was husky.

Leah jumped and turned to find her mother sitting up in bed, still in her neon sweats, her graying hair sticking up on one side and matted to her head on the other.

"No, Mother. I don't want your weed."

"Good." She pulled herself out of bed and went to the bathroom. Leah used the opportunity to open a few drawers and look for additional contraband. Nothing.

Leah went to the kitchen and set out breakfast. "Come out here and have some coffee cake, Mom," she yelled.

There was a flush and Beverly shuffled to the kitchen. "I'm not hungry." Leah sat at the tiny kitchen table and motioned to her mom to sit, too. Beverly shrugged and sat, her usual melodrama gone. At least today her meds were working, or the extra Ativan was keeping her calm.

"So what are your plans today?" Leah asked as she pushed a plate of coffee cake toward her mom.

"Meeting." Beverly took a sip of coffee and frowned into her cup. "This ain't very strong."

"Sorry," Leah said. "I still don't drink it so I don't really know how to make it."

Beverly set down her cup and looked at Leah. "You should come with me."

Leah groaned. "Aw geez, Mom. I don't want to go to a meeting."

"I'm sure you don't," Beverly said, patting her hair down and straightening her neon sweatshirt. "But I want to go. I need you to drive me, and I hope you'll stay."

It had been months, possibly even years since Leah attended a meeting, but this wasn't a day she felt like she could say no to her mom. "Fine. But you have to put on normal clothes."

"There's nothing wrong with my clothes," Beverly muttered, indignant. "I bought them in the *junior* section at Wal-Mart so you know they're fashionable."

There was no arguing with that logic.

THIRTY MINUTES LATER they were on their way to downtown Terrance. Leah was unable to talk her mom out of a sweatshirt with a cartoon old lady holding up two bowling balls with the caption, "I like big balls."

The meetings were, ironically, held in a worn-down meeting room above a bar. Several people were huddled outside the back entrance smoking.

"Bev!" A fortyish short, round woman with chins rolling down her chest and thin blonde hair wrapped her arms around Beverly's waist and hugged tight.

"Hi, Maggie!" Beverly melted into her friend's hug while Leah stood back holding a bottle of Diet Coke and wishing she could go home already. Maggie and Bev went inside arm in arm while Leah followed behind, climbing the stairs covered in years of filth and duct tape.

Three fans pushed damp, stale air around the meeting room. Nine or ten men in their sixties and seventies were settling into folding chairs while a few stragglers trickled in. Beverly, Maggie and Leah were the only women. Leah had never been to this particular AA meeting because it was known as the old men's group. And because she hated AA.

A man with one good eye and one empty, caved-in socket started the meeting. The group stood to recite the serenity prayer, then One Eye asked for check-ins.

"I'm 180 days sober!" Maggie belted out. Bev put her hands to her cheeks and smiled, tears in her eyes. "I'm just so happy," Maggie sang. "I've almost got the loan to buy the bakery, and then my dream will finally come true. I feel like I've found myself."

Leah stifled a groan. Sharing personal business and feelings. There were so many reasons to hate AA.

"I'm having a hard time," Beverly said when her turn came. "I don't want to get into the details, but . . . well, there's a reason I need my daughter here with me today." The group turned their attention to Leah. She waved briefly and checked the clock. Six minutes had passed.

A few of the men starting talking about the process of change and that relapse was part of recovery. Leah expected her mother to admit her marijuana and pill use, but she didn't. Instead Beverly enthusiastically went along with the conversation, refilling her coffee twice and alternating between laughter and tears. Finally the hour ended, and Leah and Beverly were almost out the door when Maggie grabbed their hands.

"Please stop by the bakery with me. I'm meeting the realtor there. I'd love for you to see it."

"Of course," Beverly promised, glancing at Leah and motioning that it would only be five minutes. The bakery was a few doors down from the bar, and the realtor was waiting and let them right in before scurrying off. It was a small space but could work quite well for a new bakery.

"It's amazing!" Beverly squeaked. "I can see you making cupcakes behind that counter."

"I know." Maggie grinned. "I'm so happy. Education just wasn't for me. I couldn't stand taking charge of all those kids who didn't want to take responsibility for themselves. It led to my relapse."

"She used to teach 'problem kids' at the high school," Beverly explained to Leah. "They went on adventures . . . climbing rocks and hiking and other dangerous things with naughty teenagers. You know it's just too hard on a person to be around that all the time, right, honey?"

"I've been at my job for the past nine years."

"I was at mine for five," Maggie brushed her wispy hair out of her eyes as Leah thought that some of this sounded familiar. Amanda worked with those kids at the high school last year, so Leah wondered if she might know Maggie. "Former army brat, then I spent a whole lotta years getting high and drunk. I thought education was the way out."

"But it led to her relapse," Beverly said ominously.

"And butter and sugar were my way home," Maggie squealed, and she and Beverly cackled together. Maggie didn't seem to mind that she was carrying about fifty extra pounds of butter and sugar around her waist.

Beverly and Maggie finally hugged again and Leah convinced her mom they needed to get back home. Beverly chatted all the way back about what an amazing baker Maggie was, and how they were such close friends. Leah resisted the urge to say that she had never mentioned her before, but stopped herself. If Beverly had a friend, that meant someone else could go to her rescue besides Leah. She should be encouraging this friendship with everything she had.

When they got back to the house there was an old pickup in the driveway. "Hmmm," Beverly hummed in a high voice. "Looks like Carl stopped over."

"Oh, God, Mom. Not Coolie."

"You need to be nice to your uncle," Beverly said, checking her hair in the mirror.

"He is *not* my uncle." Leah parked in the street. Beverly got out, but Leah took an extra moment before dealing with the dreaded Coolie. He was a big part of those family secrets Leah avoided thinking about.

Leah finally dragged herself out of the car and went inside. Somehow Coolie had already let himself in. Leah left her purse by the front door and tried to head straight for the kitchen, but Coolie was impossible to ignore.

"Hey, kid." He was perched on the recliner, his filthy bare feet up on the footrest. Her mother was on the couch looking a bit too sparkly and smiley.

"Uh huh." She was being rude, but he'd earned it. Leah went into the kitchen and scrounged around the cupboards, but her mom had almost no food, and the coffee cake from the morning looked heavy and unappealing. She was starving and running out of patience and tolerance for her mother and all the craziness that came with her.

Beverly and Coolie giggled, and a familiar smell wafted in the kitchen.

Leah went out to the living room in time to see her mother taking a hit off a fat joint. "Oh, my God, Mother! Didn't you just come from AA?" Coolie leaned back in the chair with a contented grin, showing his yellowed, grimy teeth. Neither was listening, both sliding into a stoned haze. "Please don't do this while I'm here."

Coolie laughed. Leah snapped around to glare at him.

Beverly peered at Leah through half-closed eyes. "Oh, sweetheart . . ."

Leah grabbed her purse. "It looks like you're fine, Mother. I can see you're in very capable hands, so I'm heading home."

Leah pulled the door shut as Coolie slurred, "She's such an uptight . . ."

LEAH SLAMMED HER CAR DOOR, setting off a headache that had been threatening all day. The whiskey in the backseat taunted her as she drove away. It gurgled at her while she drove through Dairy Queen and ordered a chicken strip basket and a large hot fudge sundae. And it rolled and rumbled and banged around her back seat all the way home, proving to her that this bottle of whiskey was tough, and it wasn't going anywhere.

The little man was speaking up again. Making demands. Expecting something in return. Uncle had a choice to make . . . pacify or dominate. But Uncle had to face the reality that he didn't hold all the cards anymore. Fortunately there was a way to meet both of their needs, so the game changed. And the little man learned to love that, too.

chapter twelve

MONDAY MORNING, with its routine and purpose, was a welcome distraction from Leah's stupid life. She spent Saturday night watching *Cheers* reruns and piling more food on top of the Dairy Queen stress binge she consumed on the way back from her mom's. On Sunday she ran six miles, cleaned her house from top to bottom, and then made a huge mess reorganizing her kitchen cupboards and baking (and inhaling) apple mini muffins.

But that flurry of activity wasn't enough to turn off the questions playing on an endless loop in her head—why would her dad commit suicide, and why didn't anyone tell her? When her worries weren't enough, her thoughts drifted to Pete Kemper and all the ways she missed him, needed him, and hated herself for it.

So Monday was a relief.

When she fired up her computer, she found an email waiting from Max: *Jackie's son is in kidney failure and needs to start dialysis. She has requested at least a month off, possibly more. Let's meet ASAP and distribute her cases.*

The group collected in their meeting room ten minutes later. Max had a stack of green files that needed attention in the next several days. Roberta, Amanda and Zoe each took three and Jill took one, barely allowing Leah to get a word in.

"So that leaves . . . Cindy House." Max looked up at the piles Roberta and Zoe had in front of them.

"I'll take it," Jill volunteered, but Max frowned.

"We have four new investigations waiting already," Max said. "I don't think you can take that many—"

"I've got it," Leah said. "No problem. Cindy and I already know each other."

"That's okay," Amanda spoke up. "I totally have room for Cindy."

"You don't have room for Cindy," Leah snapped. "You're a big bunch of do-gooders and I appreciate it. Sort of. But knock it off. I'm fine, but if you don't let me work I'll go crazy." Leah rarely took cases for ongoing management, but she welcomed the variety and the challenge.

Max nodded. "Fine," he said, and turned to Leah, "but you and I are not finished with our discussion about your other . . . appointment."

Therapy. "Yeah, yeah, sure, Max. Whatever."

Max glared at Leah and moved on with the meeting.

Zoe raised her eyebrows at Leah. She leaned over and wrote: *He wants me to go to therapy* on the edge of Zoe's notebook.

That's a good idea, Zoe wrote back.

Why do you hate me? Leah wrote, and then scribbled away their conversation. Zoe patted Leah's arm and smiled.

LEAH RETRIEVED CINDY'S FILE from the mess on Jackie's desk. Papers slid out of the file and onto the floor, which Leah scooped up and shoved back into the file. Jackie's paperwork was a perpetual disaster.

Paperwork was the bane of a social worker's existence, and Leah hated it as much as anyone. Every case required extensive documentation, including a description of every meeting, phone call, home visit, and letter. Risk and safety assessments need to be filled out at the beginning of each case and periodically throughout. Then there were the court reports, referral letters, and social histories, each requiring hours of planning, research, writing, and editing.

Every worker managed workload stressors differently. Zoe was meticulous and thorough, and usually took a few nights a week to write up casenotes after the twins went to bed to stay caught up. Amanda was new enough to dot every I and cross every T, which meant she'd usually fall behind and then pull a few long, late nights just to meet deadlines. Leah had learned to write the minimum legally required to be part of a case file, and not a word more. And Jackie's cases were a lawsuit waiting to happen. It wasn't entirely Jackie's, or anyone else's, fault. The paperwork requirements in child protection were impossible to meet without working fifty-plus hours per week.

So it was of no surprise to Leah the Cindy House case file told her nothing about what was happening in the case. She read the plan, which included a psychological and parenting evaluation that would not bode well for Cindy. She was also required to complete parent education, as recommended by hers and the children's therapist. She needed to locate safe, affordable housing and demonstrate she could maintain a safe home. And she needed to participate in the children's therapy and visit the kids at least three times per week.

Post-it notes littered the file and gave most of the updates. It appeared, through Jackie's cryptic shorthand, that Cindy never missed a visit with her kids, but she had trouble doing just about everything else on her plan. The notes from the visitation supervisor showed that Cindy could play with and nurture her children, but as soon as she had to do anything else—change a diaper, prepare a snack, take one of them to the bathroom—things fell apart.

Cindy was living at a women's shelter, and Leah would need to visit her there soon. *At least I won't have to go to the bat cave again*, Leah thought with relief. The case would hinge on whether the parenting evaluation showed Cindy had the capacity to parent safely, and what services and support she'd need to get there.

Glad to have a purpose since Max still avoided giving her investigations, Leah headed out to Gracie and Lars' foster home to meet with Cindy's kids. Gracie and Lars were foster care legends in Terrance County, having taken in over thirty children, and even adopted four in their younger days. Former foster kids were always going back to visit, knowing they were welcome there forever.

Leah pulled into their trailer court and parked in front of Gracie's flower garden. Gracie met her at the door with a hug, kiss, and plate of warm scones.

"Good morning, sweetheart." Gracie wiped a smudge of her peachy lipstick off Leah's cheek. "Come in and have breakfast with us." Leah stepped inside Gracie's wonderland of collectables that made weary children feel like they had entered a dollhouse. Two of Cindy's daughters, Brittany and Gloria, were sitting at the breakfast table eating scones with strawberries and yogurt. Baby Chet was smearing cereal on his high chair tray while Lars chuckled softly and kept spooning in cereal when the baby would take it.

Leah slid into a chair next to Lars, who gave her a nod and a wink. Leah had heard fewer than twenty words come out of Lars since she met him early in her career, but still felt like she knew him. Leah looked around the table at the fresh-faced, pink-cheeked children and felt she was seeing them for the first time. The last time she saw Brittany and Gloria they were up to their armpits in mac and cheese.

"Tea or coffee, darling?" Gracie had a hand on each of the girls' backs, and they both leaned into her. So many of the children who went into foster care were hyper and anxious, but a few days in Gracie and Lars' home tended to soothe all but the most challenging kids.

"Tea if it's no trouble," Leah said. What she really wanted was a Diet Coke, but Gracie wouldn't have any soda in her home, and she knew better than to decline.

Gloria finished her yogurt and set her spoon by her plate. "I be all done, Gammie."

Gracie leaned over to kiss Gloria's forehead. "Yes, sweetheart. Come up here and let me get you cleaned up." Gloria, a three-year-old with light-blue eyes rimmed with fluttery dark eyelashes, scooted off her chair holding out her slimy, yogurt-coated hands. Gracie gently wiped down the hands and face of the beaming little girl, who then trotted off to the living room and dumped out a bin of plastic horses.

"Ho-sie!" Brittany squealed and wriggled down from the table. Gracie followed behind and mopped yogurt off of Brittany's thick fingers and round cheeks. The girls divided the horses and immersed themselves into their play, the woven rug turned equine pasture.

Gracie came back around the table and sat next to Leah, setting her soft wrinkled hand on Leah's and giving them a squeeze. "These are some of the most soft-hearted, gentle children we have ever had. So often the little dears you bring to us are wild and busy. Brittany can barely talk, and neither of them is toilet trained, but we're working on it. And that Tommi Jane is smart as a whip! She's at the library right now because we don't have enough books to keep her busy."

Leah took in this information but didn't know what to say. These kids were mellow, respectful, and well-mannered . . . all signs of good parenting. How was that possible in that house of horrors? But Leah had also learned in her years of social work that many families were deeply complex and impossible to characterize.

Leah slid the file out of her bag and started to sort through the mess. "What did Jackie have set up for visits with Mom?"

Gracie shook her head and folded her hands in front of her lips. "Three times per week. The visits break my heart," she said. "All four of those kids climb up in Mom's lap and hold on tight. That makes Mom cry, so then the kids cry, so there they sit on the sofa together and sob their little hearts out. The first time they cried like that I had to go in my room and do some quilting while Lars sat out here with them. It just broke my heart to see them clutch each other like that. We figured out that when their mama leaves, we need to go to the park so they have something else to think about. Otherwise we're just pulling them off of their mama's lap, and that's not good for anyone."

None of this was fitting into Leah's memory of the bleak family living in the dilapidated, bat-infested farmhouse. "Do the kids seem traumatized?"

"I'm sorry to say this, sweetheart, because I know you did what you had to do, but I think the real trauma for them was being taken away from their mama." Leah looked over at the girls arranging horses around the rug and whispering whinneys at each other.

"They aren't traumatized by the precautionary rabies shots?" Leah fought to keep the tone out of her question as Baby Chet sputtered cereal all over the tray of his high chair. Gracie popped up and started wiping him off while Lars brought his bowl and spoon to the sink.

"The shots are hard now that they know what's coming," Gracie said. "And I think the medicine stings their little arms." Gracie unhooked the tray off the high chair and Lars lifted the baby out of the chair and onto his lap. The two of them worked in silent cooperation and seemed to anticipate the others' moves without a word. Leah had never seen a couple who were so interconnected that it was hard to think about the two of them ever existing on their own.

"What about this one?" Leah asking, tickling Chet's toes. He squirmed and smiled and laid back against Lars's solid chest.

"He seems to be doing the best, actually. But Grandpa Lars has always had the touch with babies." Gracie squeezed Lars's shoulder and the corners of his mouth turned up, pushing his glasses up with his cheeks.

Leah left her notebook at the table and wandered to the rug, sitting next to Brittany. Leah picked up a worn plastic horse the size of her palm.

"I love horses," Leah said, making hers gallop next to Brittany's, who was delighted to have someone else to play with. Brittany made her horse nuzzle Leah's horse, knocking their heads together. Leah looked up to see Gloria staring at her, holding her horse in mid-air. When they made eye contact, Gloria dropped her horse and scurried to Gracie, burying her face in Gracie's lap.

That had to mean that Gloria remembered Leah, and the memory triggered fear. Brittany jumped when her sister sniffled, and then Brittany ran to Gracie and patted her sister, her face contorting with fear like her sister's.

Gracie patted both girls and smiled at Leah with kindness and apology.

"I'm sure you did what you had to do . . ."

"Of course I did!" Leah snapped. Lars looked up from his chair and held Leah's eyes for a second until she dropped hers. "You didn't see the house," Leah said in a tone of which Lars would approve. "There was no choice."

"I know, honey." Gracie patted both girls on the back one more time and pointed at their horses. Brittany toddled back to the carpet pasture while Gloria sat on the floor between Gracie's feet and sucked her thumb. "What's going to happen to them?" Gracie whispered.

Leah watched Brittany and her horsies, Gloria at Gracie's feet stroking her slippers while she sucked her thumb, Chet nearly asleep on Lars's lap. Figuring out what was going to happen to these children was Leah's job, and at this point she had no answer. She didn't want to accept the strengths or acknowledge the hope there with Cindy and her kids. It was easier to stay mad and blame Cindy for Leah's two-week unplanned leave, the lingering headaches from the concussion, and the persistent nightmares that kept ending with her foaming at the mouth like a rabid dog. So maybe Max was right about her needing therapy after all. Leah dropped the file back in her bag, waved at the kids and hustled out to her car, leaving the tangled mess of the Cindy House case behind.

LEAH TOOK THE LONG WAY back to the office on Central Avenue, the winding road that followed the river through town. Terrance was a popular weekend destination for Minnesotans looking for a quick escape. The bike path that followed Central Avenue was often populated with tourists. A young couple walked slowly, pointing out landmarks and sipping large, indulgent coffees.

Leah hated them.

That annoyingly happy couple didn't know Cindy House, and they didn't have to fix her life. She was sure as they watched seagulls over the river they didn't have the subconscious fear Leah had that one of them would swoop into her face. And those stupid people certainly didn't have Annika—her terrified eyes and trauma-soaked words running through their heads in the middle of the night and before opening their eyes in the morning.

Leah took an extra loop around downtown to clear her head, wishing she could go for a run because it seemed to dissolve work stress better than anything. She settled for inhaling a bag of half-melted M&Ms before she forced herself to go back to work in time for Joe's pretrial hearing.

Leah wasn't ready to face her desk, so she texted Amanda and asked her to come outside so they could walk to court together. While neither of them had a formal role at the hearing, they both wanted to see what would happen next. Joe's public defender wasn't talking to Jake, so he couldn't be sure, but Jake sensed Joe might back away from his confession. Kemper and the other investigators had some thin evidence connecting Joe to the crime, but Jake was the first to admit that much of their evidence could be attributed simply to Joe living in the home.

On their way into the building, they passed Amanda's dad, Matt, the former judge turned tax attorney. Matt and Amanda looked like father and daughter, both with tall athletic builds and the same dark-blond hair. Amanda had told Leah how disconcerting it was to look into stranger's eyes and see her own.

"Hey there," Matt said with a stiff smile and big eyes. "Hi, Leah." He held up his arm like he wanted to pat Amanda on the back, and then pulled his hand back.

Amanda nodded, shifting and crossing her arms in front of her. "Hi. What brings you here?"

"Work," Matt said, nodding too enthusiastically. "How about you?"

"Yep. Work." Leah noticed Amanda didn't, perhaps couldn't, make eye contact.

Painful pause. Matt and Amanda looked past each other. Then Matt finally said, "Okay . . . have a good day." Matt kept walking down the stairs and to his Lexus SUV.

"That was weird," Leah said under her breath. "I thought things were getting more comfortable with him." Amanda met her father for the first time when she was twenty-four, and they were struggling to create a relationship out of nothing.

"It's this damn wedding." Amanda exhaled heavily. "He put in a bunch of money. I think it bothers his wife. I can just tell she's weirded out by the whole situation because she's barely nice to me. When I see Matt, he never brings his family, even though he's said before he wants me to get to know his boys. I think Tina just can't handle it."

"Are you going to have him walk you down the aisle?" Leah asked as they climbed the marble stairs.

Amanda shuddered. "I almost break into hives just thinking about it. I don't want to be escorted down the aisle. I don't want to wear a white dress. I don't want a wedding!" Amanda caught herself yelling and lowered her voice. "We were going to go to the Bahamas and get married on the beach," she said with such longing that it almost brought tears to Leah's eyes. "I love Trix. I really do. But keeping her happy isn't worth this."

"Yeesh," Leah said. "Do you want to back out? You still could."

They arrived at the top floor of the courthouse and paused before they got to the bailiff's desk. "I tried to talk to Jake about it. He doesn't get how much I don't want to do this. We have the last deposits to put down this week, so if we're going to back out we need to do it right away."

Leah was ready to ask something else when Jenny approached them.

"Hi, Leah." Jenny looked different than the first time they had met. Her makeup was soft, and she had a sense of maturity and calm. "It's weird to be here. I've barely left the hospital since it happened. The hospital can become your whole world, you know."

"Yeah." Amanda smiled wryly. "I know."

"How's he doing?" Leah asked. "Did that last surgery go okay?

"The swelling in his brain has gone way down. His vision is better than they thought *and* he's going to be bearing weight soon." Jenny beamed. Mothers usually bragged about how smart and advanced their kids are, but bearing weight and reduced brain swelling felt just as miraculous.

"So is he going home soon?" Leah asked.

"Oh, gosh, no," Jenny said. "They think he'll be there for a few more weeks. Then he'll have to go to full-time rehab for a couple months."

"Wow." Jenny was matter of fact, but Leah's stomach churned with anger, grief, and responsibility. The bailiff indicated that the judge would be on the bench soon, so Jenny headed back to her seat by the bailiff's desk.

"I'll check in when court's done," Amanda said. Jenny nodded and smiled.

Obviously late but unconcerned, Steven Grayson, gorgeous public defender, came up the stairs and checked in at the bailiff desk. The rumor was Steven could bench press 300 pounds. Joe followed him, looking like he could barely bench press thirty. Joe's grandmother had posted the $10,000 cash bond on the $100,000 bail, so he was out of jail. With short hair, jacket and tie, and a clean shave, Joe looked responsible, respectable, and defiant. Steven put his hand on Joe's back and led him to a small conference room.

Both Leah and Amanda gawked as Steven closed the conference room door. "Do we have any idea if Steven has any lawyer-type skills?" Leah whispered. "Or is he just dumb and beautiful?"

"Jake says he's one of those people who gets away with everything, not just because he's Brad Pitt but because he's a Boy Scout. Just the nicest guy ever," Amanda replied under her breath. "So his briefs are late and he still doesn't really know criminal law, but it never matters. Even Jake thinks he's hot."

Leah nodded. "Jake's got good taste."

"Thank you." Amanda grinned and motioned toward the room where Joe and Steven had just shut the door. "Joe looks good. Steven seems to be giving him good advice so far."

"Yeah." The insecurity about Joe's confession came back, especially seeing him so put-together and defiant. "What does Jenny say?" Amanda had been meeting with Jenny and Ben weekly at the hospital.

"Jenny's freaking amazing," Amanda said. "She doesn't think about Joe, or at least she says she doesn't. Her priority is Ben. She says whatever happens with Joe is what needs to happen."

Jake came up the stairs with Kemper, who wore a gray jacket and a purple tie. Kemp looked like a dog forced into a sweater—like he could squirm and scratch until that button-down shirt was in shreds. He had to be testifying in the pretrial hearing. Leah regretted coming to court as soon as she saw that tie. Kemp smiled at her briefly before following Jake into a conference room, and Leah got a whiff of that damnable Old Spice cologne.

Amanda watched Leah's forlorn gaze. "You guys are being so stupid," Amanda said. "What happened between you and Kemp that messed you up?"

Leah couldn't find the words to explain how Kemp's absence and her neediness ruined everything. He did exactly what he said he wouldn't do—he disappeared. And she did what she never intended to do—she cared.

"I . . . he . . . it was nothing . . ." Joe's case was called, interrupting Leah's stammering. Amanda and Leah stared at each other for a long moment, with Leah breaking eye contact first. Amanda decided to let her comments go, and they filed into the largest courtroom and sat in one of the back benches.

Jake informed Judge Nancy O'Toole, who expected nothing but formality and decorum in the court room, that they had reached an agreement about the dates for the trial. Joe sat up very straight, hands on the table in front of him, eyes red and tearful. Jenny was on the opposite side of the court room taking notes, looking serious and calm.

"Your honor, the defense has a motion to introduce," Steven said easily, smoothing his jacket as he stood behind the heavy, antique attorney's table. Judge O'Toole nodded. "We are requesting that the interview on June 12 be thrown out because my client's fifth amendment rights were violated." Kemp was sitting in the front row behind Jake, and at the words "fifth amendment," his head snapped up.

Turns out gorgeous Steven was kind of an ass. Jake was caught off guard by the motion and gaped at Steven as he spoke.

"Come on, Jake," Amanda whispered. Leah kept her eyes on Kemp, who sat motionless. Before the interview that day, Kemp and Jake had agreed that Kemp was going to do a "soft Miranda," which essentially was a less formal version of the "You have the right to remain silent" speech that put most criminals on guard and shut them up.

Steven gestured behind him where Kemp was sitting, making his point that much more personal. "The investigator in this case has been disciplined in the past for failing to read the Miranda warning to suspects. He failed to do a sufficient Miranda warning with my client as well."

"What?!" Kemp snapped audibly.

Jake reached behind his chair and motioned for Kemp to be quiet.

"Permission to approach?" Steven asked with a sincere half smile Leah wanted to slap off that beautiful face.

"Granted," the judge said curtly. Steven set a packet on the table in front of Jake, who had yet to speak, and brought one to the clerk of courts.

"When would you like a response, Your Honor?" Jake asked, finding his voice, calm and businesslike.

"Two weeks," the judge said without looking at a calendar or consulting with anyone.

"Your Honor," Steven began again. "If the Court does not dismiss the charges, my client would like to invoke his right for a speedy trial. We propose October 2."

Amanda shook her head as Jake said, "That's fine, Your Honor."

"Are you kidding me?" Amanda whispered too loudly. Jake flinched, obviously hearing his fiancée's reaction to scheduling a trial five days before their wedding.

Leah was still watching Kemp, staring straight ahead, stone faced. The judge set the trial, and the attorneys discussed a few details before court was adjourned.

They rose as Judge O'Toole left. Jake turned around and found his fiancée glaring and his friend seething.

Leah grabbed Amanda's arm. "Let's let them work. You can kill him later."

Amanda spun around and left the courtroom. "This wedding is off. When he's in trial he works sixteen hours a day. He can't possibly expect me to do all this planning by myself."

"You're just looking for any excuse to cancel your big wedding," Leah said, trying to keep up with Amanda's long legs.

Amanda flew down the stairs. "Damn right I am. I'm not even sure I want to marry such a dumbass." Leah laughed, and Amanda spun around halfway down the stairs. "You think this is funny?" Leah had never seen Amanda's face so red.

"It's a little funny," Leah said as gently as she knew how. "Let's go get cinnamon rolls for lunch."

"So I can smear it all over his face?" Slightly calmer.

"It'd be a crime to waste that frosting," Leah said as they reached the door.

"True," Amanda said, pulling in a deep sigh. "I'll have to find some other way to punish him."

"You're creative," Leah said. "I'm sure you'll think of something."

THE MAGIC OF CINNAMON dough and cream cheese frosting had settled Amanda's bridal fury. They were just finishing at the bakery when Leah's cell phone buzzed.

I need you, the text from Kemp said.

"What?" Amanda asked Leah, who had stopped in the middle of the doorway.

Leah looked up, trying to process. "Kemp, uh, needs me."

"Why? What does that mean?" Amanda asked. "Do you think he's upset about the motion to dismiss the case? What was that all about, anyway?"

Leah walked out of the bakery and sat on a bench outside. The air was thick, the sky gray and overcast. A summer thunderstorm was on its way.

"I don't know." Leah cringed at how his words paralyzed her.

Another buzz. *How soon can you get here?*

"Wow. He really needs you," Amanda said. "What do you think's going on?"

"It might be about the hearing today," Leah said, holding her phone to her lips in an unconscious gesture Amanda did not miss. "The Miranda warning is a big deal with Kemp. It's the thing that got him in trouble all those years ago."

"I've never heard that full story," Amanda said, gently pulling her friend from the bench. "All I know is he got in trouble and will never get promoted because of it."

"It's more that they won't promote him into anything administrative," Leah said, walking quickly up the steep sidewalk away from downtown and toward the county buildings. "They seem to decide internally who they want to move up, so he's the one who gets the opportunities. When Kemp messed up, Gordy Hoffbrau started getting the good jobs."

Amanda grimaced. "Gordy—ugh. Jake thinks he's the best, funniest guy ever. I just don't like him."

"Every female I know reacts that way to Gordy," Leah said "I actually feel kinda bad for the guy. He's got some chronic disease so he looks like he's in pain all the time, his eczema's out of control, and he can barely breathe from COPD or whatever he has. But the guys think he's great, and he knows his stuff. I've heard he's the obvious choice for sheriff."

"And he stares at my boobs every chance he gets."

Leah nodded. "Yeah, but to be fair, you're so tall and he's so short that your boobs are at his eye level. You've got a nice rack. It's really a compliment . . ."

Amanda snorted. Leah's phone buzzed again.

"Yeah, yeah, Kemp. Keep your panties on."

"Wow. He's not fooling around." Amanda grinned.

Leah texted back. *I'm on my way.*

THE ENTRYWAY TO THE SHERIFF'S department was bright and inviting by design, which was ironic since it was also the entrance to the county jail. Leah was composing a casual opening line when she arrived at the entryway and found Annika hunched under her mom's protective arm. Leah's first thought was that she hoped they didn't need anything right away so she could talk to Kemp in private first. Then the reality of the situation settled on her, and Kemp's "need" for her became obvious. And professional.

"Hey, Annika," Leah said, keeping her tone light, hiding her humiliation at the thought that Kemp was interested in anything other than another interview of Annika. "You look better, kiddo." And she did. The cloud of trauma had dissipated. Her face wasn't as gray, her eyes less dull, but they were fixed on the floor. Annika's mother, Pam, had her hand on Annika's back, where it had been attached since the assault.

"Hi." Annika was polite and sweet and devastated. Her eyes didn't meet Leah's.

The door buzzer beeped. Kemp came out. Leah could see the remaining anger from court in the set of his shoulders and the dark line of his brow, but he had his game face on for Annika. "Hi there, folks. Come on in."

Leah, Pam, and Annika followed Kemp through the security doors and into a conference room.

"Let's get Leah up to speed," Kemp said after they all sat down. "Annika's therapist, Bonnie Ackers, called because Annika has some new details to share, and she's ready to do another interview." Annika stared at the table.

"And you want to do this today?" Leah leaned toward Annika and asked. Annika finally met Leah's eyes and nodded.

THE TAPE WAS RUNNING and Kemp, Jake, and Gordy were in the observation room.

Leah watched Annika, who was looking around the room and kept glancing back at the two-way mirror.

"How have the last few weeks been for you?" Leah asked. Annika seemed to move more comfortably, so she hoped that meant she had healed from the physical trauma.

Annika shrugged. "Okay. Bonnie is nice."

"Good," Leah said. "I've worked with other kids who really like her." Annika nodded in silence. "How's swimming?"

"The doctor said I can't swim for six weeks," Annika said to the table. "I mostly just stay home. My mom's there with me most of the time."

"That's tough," Leah said, wanting to find the bastard who did this and kill him herself. She needed to push her anger away and try to focus. Annika's vulnerability was gut wrenching.

"He took my ID." Annika blurted. "My school ID."

A trophy. Leah could picture Kemp and Gordy in the observation room reacting to the prospect their offender took a trophy. It put the crime on a different level and all but guaranteed this guy would strike again. They would need to plan quickly to keep the details under wraps while taking precautions to protect the public and avoid panic. A reporter from the *St. Paul Pioneer Press* had been following the case.

So far the articles were brief and buried on page three of the local section, but that was more attention than Terrance usually got in the metro newspaper.

"So, the guy who assaulted you took your ID," Leah repeated for the camera, and ultimately for the jury. "How do you know that?"

"He ripped it off my neck. My housekey and ID were on a lanyard. I had it around my neck when I left swim practice." Annika stared at the wall. This time instead of reliving the trauma she had dissociated, shut down and separated herself from her emotions. Her words were matter of fact, distant, and cool.

Leah absorbed this, trying to fill in this detail from what she remembered from the previous interview. "When did he do that?"

"After he pushed me down."

They sat quietly a moment. Leah wished she could have spoken with Bonnie to prepare better for the interview. Annika had seemed so ready to talk in the waiting area, but when the questions started, Annika went away.

"Annika, did he say anything to you when he took it?" Trying to cull details.

Annika shook her head. "He never talked. He, like, grunted and stuff but never said any words."

"Which direction did he go?" They had never established where he might have gone next, if he was in a car, or if he just ran.

Annika shrugged. "I don't know. Maybe I passed out. It all just went dark after that, and I woke up in the hospital."

Leah debated what to do next. They needed more details. She didn't do a typical interview the first time because Annika was so traumatized. "Annika. I have more questions. I want to know if you feel ready to answer them today. In investigations, we need as much information as possible. Can you do more questions today?"

Annika slumped on the stiff, institutional sofa, and ran her hands over her face, pushing her wispy blonde hair back. Her eyes were hazel but looked almost yellow in the light, and the color intensified as her eyes filled with tears that threatened but never fell.

Leah wished she could still do her job if she withdrew the question, but she couldn't. Annika's answer came out in a defeated huff of air. "Okay."

LEAH SLOWLY TOOK ANNIKA through what she remembered of the assault. They drew a map of the street, and Annika put an X where the guy had jumped her.

It matched the cop's report of where Annika was found. They weren't questioning what she had said, but it was always good when details matched.

"He must have tackled me off my bike. I have a bad bruise on my right hip from falling on the handlebars. I rolled, and he was there."

"What did he do when he first got to you?" Leah asked.

Annika's shoulders slumped. "I was on the ground and my hands were all scraped up from falling. I was trying to get up when there were hands on me—big, rough hands. On the back of my neck. He flipped me over, grabbed at my shorts and got them off. He did it. Hard." Annika was far away now, and was speaking as if she were describing a movie playing in front of her, but her words were cold and flat. As she spoke, she rubbed her left forearm with her right hand, and Leah noticed some scratches on her arms.

"When you say he did it . . ." Leah asked quietly.

Annika's eyes shifted to Leah in a rare moment of eye contact. Their eyes locked and Annika seemed to be pleading with Leah to understand so she didn't have to say it.

"He . . . hurt me . . ." Silent tears ran down her face, her expression wooden, but her eyes giving away the pain. She wasn't going to be able to talk much longer.

"What did he hurt you with? How did he hurt you?" They were awful questions Leah wanted to take back. But they were the right questions, needed to establish that a rape occurred.

Annika's breathing intensified, her chest heaving, her chin quaking now. "His hand on my . . . my private . . ." Trauma overtook Annika's body like a giant crashing wave. She curled into herself on that unyielding couch and sobbed uncontrollably. The camera in the ceiling recorded every wail while Leah sat idly by, still an investigator, paralyzed by her role. She let the camera capture the sight of lost innocence consumed by blinding fear and incomprehensible trauma.

chapter thirteen

AUGUST DRONED ON. Tension was everywhere. Jake and Amanda joylessly slogged through wedding plans. Zoe and Sam awkwardly avoided the friction between them. And Leah and Kemp completed a couple investigations together that ended in Leah running out of the police station so they didn't have to spend a second longer than she needed in the place where they had carnal knowledge of each other.

The staggering August heat wave made everything worse. Even breathing the air, thick with humidity and mosquitoes, added to the pressure that seemed to be everywhere Leah went.

In the weeks that followed the second interview with Annika, the Terrance County Police Department walked the line between investigating a heinous crime and trying not to scare the shit out of the public.

Kemp was the lead investigator, and became the outward face of the ineptitude of the department. Every day they fielded calls from county commissioners, school principals, and a whole lot of citizens wondering why they hadn't found the rapist. People asking if they really understood how terrified the people of Terrance were about having this man on the loose.

"Yeah, I understand," Kemp told Barb Cloud at their latest consult meeting on this case. Barb, Jake, Gordy, Kemp, and Leah gathered around Barb's desk, which was much more disheveled than usual. Barb had been getting daily calls as well, and the stress on her was showing.

"Why don't we know more?" Barb asked, pointing her pen at Kemp. "I don't think you have a scrap more of information than you did the day we started this investigation." Barb's newly colored and highlighted hair was distracting Leah from her angry questioning. Jill had finally acknowledged, just to Leah and Zoe, that she and Barb had been seeing each other for months, but they had no intention of going public. It had been fascinating to watch Barb's transformation from frumpy to fabulous, and even more so because only a few of them knew of her new girlfriend's impeccable taste and influence.

"We do have more questioning in the neighborhood," Kemp said. "We've gotten some good stuff from those interviews." He looked rough. The circles under his eyes were deep and dark, and his khakis were so wrinkled, it looked like he may have slept in them.

"That's right, goddammit," Gordy Hoffbrau bellowed and shifted painfully in his seat. Leah had no problem with colorful language, but Gordy seemed to mean what he said when he cursed, like he really did want to damn someone to hell .

Barb rolled her eyes and scowled at Gordy. "Like what?"

"We've gotten a lot from the neighbors. You can't act like we're just sitting on our asses, Barb." Gordy huffed and adjusted his bulletproof vest which compressed his ample girth and and made it even harder for him to breathe. The lack of air added to the purplish cast already there from his flaring, scaly rash.

"The neighbors told you they saw a guy in dark clothes running through their yard. I could have told you someone was going to be running away after raping this poor girl." Barb glared.

"We've got tread marks from an athletic shoe right by the scene, and then again way back in the woods by those yards. It's probably our perp's shoe." Kemp added, sounding so desperate Leah felt sorry for him.

"Uh huh. The athletic shoe of undeterminable brand in a men's size nine to twelve." Barb said. She was in a nasty mood. "Should we start shaking down all the men in the area who wear athletic shoes?"

"The initial tox screen is back," Kemp continued, ignoring her snarky comment about the shoes. "It didn't flag any of the typical stuff, but we sent it for further analysis at the Bureau of Criminal Apprehension. She talked about a bad smell, so we're thinking he used ether."

Gordy nodded vigorously. "He's right, Barb." Gordy had extensive knowledge of chemistry and drugs from his own research on his disease. "It would knock her out so she wouldn't or couldn't fight back, and it'd explain why she went dark."

"Trauma would explain those things, too," Barb snapped.

"I still think we need to focus on motive so we can narrow the pool of who we're looking for. Get a profile . . ." Kemp spoke a little louder than necessary. He had been saying for a while that he wanted a chance to interview Annika himself, but the rest of the team was uneasy with another interview. "This girl was followed, and I think it's because the perp knew her somehow. It doesn't feel random. Either she was chosen, or the perp is using her to send a message."

Jake leaned forward, his face blank. "You've been saying that for a while, but why her? You haven't culled any information to advance that theory other than your gut feeling." Which Jake didn't seem to trust.

Kemp turned to face Jake, who was avoiding eye contact. "Oh, really," he said.

"Yes. Really," Barb said. "Your theory doesn't get us anywhere. Your evidence doesn't get us anywhere. We need to call in the BCA investigators." Bureau of Criminal Apprehension—the state agency which provided investigative support to local agencies. Kemp's face went dark.

"That's bullshit," Gordy said. "Using the BCA lab is fine. But we don't need any more investigators. They can't do anything for us on this."

Barb stood up and leaned in toward Gordy. "It is necessary for us to call in help when we don't have any leads. And you need to get over your turfy bullshit and realize the priority for all of us is to find this guy." Barb gathered her notebook and flounced out the door, her trendy new pumps clicking on the marble floor. The group sat in pouty silence.

Kemp turned to Jake. "Thanks for the support, *friend*." Jake didn't look up from the table. Kemp stood abruptly, knocking over his chair, and stomped out of the room, leaving Jake, Leah, and Gordy at the table.

Gordy sighed and pushed his bulk away from the table. "Kemp was a lot better at this when he was getting laid." Gordy eyed Leah.

"Excuse me?" Leah glared at Gordy and flushed.

"I'm just sayin' . . ." Gordy said as he shuffled out of the room.

"Holy sexual harassment!" Leah said. "Did you hear that?"

Jake shook his head at Leah. "Kemp isn't doing so good," he said. Leah had been all business on their last two investigations so they didn't have to talk about it, but she couldn't help but notice and agree that he was in tough shape.

"You mean he's messing up the investigation?" Leah asked.

Jake shrugged. "It's not that he's messing it up, exactly. It's that he's just messed up. We haven't had any breaks at all, and he feels responsible. Gordy's really been staying close to him. Everyone is worried."

"Worried how?" Leah asked. "What does that mean?"

"The Miranda rights issue the defense brought up in Joe's case isn't going away," Jake said. "There are differing opinions on a soft Miranda warning, and what constitutes enough of a warning to make it constitutional. I think what Kemp did was enough, but we're going to get bogged down in this." Jake ran his hands through his curly hair and made it stick up all over his head, and Leah had the random thought that Amanda would want him to get a haircut before the wedding. "This issue pushes all of his buttons because it's what almost got him fired and lost a huge case a few years ago."

"What was the deal with that?" Leah asked. Kemp's "big mistake" with the Miranda had been discussed for years, but Leah never knew the full story.

"It was before my time, but apparently Kemp didn't do a Miranda. I mean, he says he did," Jake said quickly, keeping his face neutral but giving away his skepticism. "But there was no evidence of it on the tape, and the Miranda warning form got 'lost.'"

Leah thought back on all the interviews she had seen Kemp do during the past seven years. He always read the suspects their rights. "I've never seen him miss a step," she said.

"Me neither. But I didn't work with him before this happened, so I don't know how it was back then." Jake closed his notebook. "Anyway, you might want to check in with Kemp. He's not talking to anyone else, but he might talk to you."

"Nah," Leah said. "Kemp and I didn't have that kind of relationship."

"I think you did." Leah looked up and Jake held her eyes. "He was pretty nuts about you. Still is." Leah's heart thudded hard.

"What do you want me to say, Jake? It's weird between us now. I wouldn't know what to say to him."

"Could you just check in with him anyway? See if he's okay?" They both stood and headed for the door of the county attorney's conference room.

"I suppose," Leah said. "I'll call him or something."

"Thanks. And please call my future wife, too. She's so sick of this wedding I'm afraid she's going to leave me at the altar." He said it with a grim smile, but it looked like wedding stress was getting to them both.

"You know she doesn't want this wedding, don't you?" Leah blurted.

Jake stopped walking and looked at Leah. A skinny guy in squeaky hiking boots from the county assessor's office passed them and nodded at Jake. Jake lowered his voice. "What's she said?"

"That she doesn't want a big wedding, Jake. She never has." It wasn't her place to tell him, but the words just flew out.

Jake looked sick. "Why does this bother her so much? My mom is handling everything. All she has to do is show up."

Leah crossed her arms and glared at him. "Do you know any women who would be happy about the fact that all they have to do is 'show up' at their own wedding? It's supposed to be the bride's big day. Instead it's your mom's big day."

"Oh, my God." Jake said, slapping his forehead. "I never thought of it that way. What am I supposed to do now? Everything is paid for. My mom will die if we call it off now."

"I think you illustrated the problem right there, big guy." Leah said. "You're worried about pissing off your mom, and in the process you've pissed off your bride."

Jake closed his eyes. "Why didn't she say anything?"

"I think she tried." Leah started walking again, and Jake followed slowly behind. "Sorry, Jake. Didn't mean to wreck your day."

"Yeah, well . . ." They reached the main entrance to the county attorney's offices. Jake put his hand on the door and then stopped and turned to Leah. "We were talking about Kemp. Go see him."

Leah kept walking. "I will."

THE WALK FROM THE COUNTY attorney's offices to her office was short, but Leah dragged her feet, even though more time in the humidity meant her hair would be wild the rest of the day. Leah didn't want to call Kemp, and didn't know what to say. But she was concerned, too, so she forced herself to take out her phone and dial his cell.

"Kemper," he answered on the first ring.

"Hey, Kemp." Now what? She had no plan of what to say, so there was an awkward pause. "H-how's it going?"

"Shitty. Obviously. Weren't you paying attention in our meeting?"

"I'm sorry. It's not your fault. Everybody's part of this investigation. Not just you—"

"Who told you to call me?" Kemp interrupted.

"Huh? " Stalling. "What? Why do you say that?"

"Because you haven't called me in a month. Because Jake and Gordy and pretty much everybody thinks I'm losing it. I'm getting to be the head case of the county. But it's not surprising, is it? I can't freaking believe I'm defending myself on the Miranda again." His voice always carried, and Leah hoped his door was closed.

"I'm sorry," Leah said. "I was there and I know you did the Miranda. It was soft, but it was there."

"I did it eight years ago, too," he said sullenly. "Things get messed up."

Back to awkward silence. She really should have thought this through.

"So . . . you wanna come over and screw around in my office?" She could hear his grin through the stress and fatigue.

"Nope." But she couldn't help smiling and was glad he wasn't there to see it. "Have a good day, Kemp."

"Thanks for calling, babe."

He could still make her heart race.

BUSINESS, SO TO SPEAK, was slow on this particular day in the child protection world. It was a welcome change, but boring. Leah wandered over to Jill's desk, where she found Jill texting.

"There's a chance my boys may kill each other by the time school starts. And they all have it coming," Jill said, dropping her phone in her Coach purse. "Adam needs a ride somewhere every day, and his brothers find a way to be gone every time. I just texted Scotty and told him to get his butt home and give his brother a ride to the weight room, or I'll sell his car for scrap metal."

Leah laughed, always enjoying Jill's tales of raising three teenage boys who fought like dogs and ate their weight in food every day. "Sounds like an idle threat."

"Absolutely it is. If I had to go back to driving around all three of them I would have to quit my job, and subsequently lose my mind." Jill sat back in her chair and rubbed her eyes with the heels of her hands. "And I'm bored. Are you working on anything right now?"

"Not really," Leah said, dropping into the chair in front of her desk. "I mean, yeah, I have eight to ten reports I need to finalize, but I'm pacing myself."

"Tell me about the rape case. Maybe I can figure it out for you." Jill said, sliding her basket of toys across her desk. The toys were a good distraction for the nervous kids who didn't want to talk. Leah, as always, went for the silly putty.

"I don't know what to tell you. This sweet girl was grabbed off her bike and violently raped on the side of the road." Leah smashed the silly putty on Jill's desk calendar blotter, picking up the word "August." "It's a nightmare anywhere, but especially in a little town like Terrence."

Jill pulled a koosh ball out of the basket and rolled it around. "How is it possible that nobody saw anything? Was the guy hiding in the bushes?"

"It's a pretty remote area, way on the edge of town," Leah said, repeating the conversation she had heard over and over when the team discussed the case.

"How did the guy know she was coming? Is somebody just going to hide out there until the next person rides by?" Jill shook her head. "It doesn't feel random."

"Kemp doesn't think so either," Leah said, rolling the silly putty in a ball and bouncing it on the desk. "He thinks there's a reason this girl was chosen, or some other reason that it happened. There's something big we're missing."

"The whole thing scares the shit out of me." Jill shuddered and tossed the ball to Leah. "New topic—how's the trial with the guy who beat up Baby Ben?"

"There's another mess for you," Leah said. "Kemp's in trouble on that one, too. They say he didn't do a Miranda, or enough of one. So the guy's attorney, Mr. Beautiful, attacked Kemp on that issue and Jake is spending his time defending him instead of prosecuting the case."

"Wow," Jill said. "There's a theme developing: Kemp's falling apart. He did better when he was hooking up with you," Jill wagged her eyebrows at Leah.

"Man, I could sue the county for hostile work environment and win a million dollars" Leah said, throwing the koosh ball back at Jill. "Gordy said the same thing. It's not my fault if Kemp needs a woman."

"No, it's not your fault," Jill said. "But it wouldn't hurt you to do something about it, would it?"

"Depends on your definition of hurt," Leah said, harsher than she intended.

"Fair enough." Jill said. "You guys were good together. It was nice to see you with someone."

"Well, that makes me sound pathetic," Leah said.

"Since you started at the county, I have never known you to date," Jill said. "I was starting to wonder what was going on with you, and then finally you and Kemp started hooking up. What was that, two years ago?"

"Oh, my God, how did you know about that?" Leah looked over her shoulder to see if anyone heard.

"Oh, honey," Jill said with a smile. "You didn't actually think that was a secret, did you? You were screwing a cop in his office."

"*After work hours*," Leah hissed, and then thought back to one tense, sweaty lunch hour. "Mostly."

"The cop shop never closes. There is always someone in that building. You know that." Jill smiled and patted Leah's arm. "Everyone just played it cool because Kemp told them to."

"You have got to be kidding me." Leah was horrified, a maddening blush spreading across her face.

"It was such a relief when you actually started dating. Well, for that ten minutes, or however long you let him make a respectable woman out of you."

Leah glared. "You're lucky I like you."

"All I'm saying is you have a great big fence around you, keeping most people away. I'm glad you let Kemp penetrate your walls." She giggled. "So to speak."

"You're gross." Leah waved her middle finger at her friend. "Maybe everyone should mind their own business."

"Just wanna see you happy, my friend," Jill said.

"Barb looks awfully happy," Leah said, finally finding a way to change the subject. And stylish, too." Leah grinned. "You worked your magic."

Jill looked for eavesdroppers over Leah's shoulder in the hallway, and then dropped her voice. "It's so much more fun to makeover a girl."

"So I have to ask–" Leah said.

"No, you don't," Jill said. "I know exactly where you're going with this."

"How do you know that?"

Jill sighed and smiled politely. "How could I be with a woman after being married for twenty years?" She raised her eyebrows. "Right?"

"Okay, yeah, right."

Jill shrugged. "It's just one of those things that's hard to know at the time. You grow up thinking girls are supposed to like guys, so I just went with it. I really liked Marty and being married was fine."

"Fine?" Leah laughed. "What a fairy tale."

"Well, yeah, exactly. It was just so blah. No spark. Nothing clicked. We stayed married so long because Marty's nice, and because he travels so much for work that we weren't together a whole lot. Then a couple years ago I started working with Barb on a case." Jill's face lit up at the memory. "It was like I finally figured out what everyone was talking about."

"That explains you," Leah said. "What about Barb? Wasn't she married, too?"

"Barb was married a long time ago right out of law school, and divorced two years later."

"So you and Barb just started hooking up?"

Jill threw the koosh ball at Leah. "I think you have me confused with you," Jill pointed at Leah. "No, we didn't just start hooking up. We started spending time together and one thing led to another. I still feel bad about Marty and how vicious it got in the end. He was cheating, I was horrible, and neither one of us had the stomach to just end it."

Leah sat back in her chair and looked up at the ceiling. "I think you and Barb might be the only happy couple I know. It seems like everyone falls apart eventually."

"What are you talking about? Amanda's getting married. Zoe and Sam are great. Max's situation is a mess, but I still think he and Christine will be okay."

Amanda and Jake were fighting all the time. Zoe and Sam had something awful coming between them. Max was separated and nearing divorce. Her own parents had a ridiculous marriage. And she and Kemp had fizzled less than a month into their attempt to be more than a tension release for each other. Leah had no faith or trust in anything but friendship.

THE END OF THE WORKDAY finally arrived.

Who's up for happy hour? she texted to Amanda and Zoe. In less than a minute she received a *hell yes* from Zoe, who had been home for the past two days with her feverish, sneezing twins.

Ten minutes later, Leah had a table at Las Margaritas, toward the back since she passed a family she had completed an investigation on a few months ago.

"Hola, señiorita," her waitress said with a tired smile.

"Hola," Leah said, distracted by the plastic table tent that displayed the happy hour specials.

"Margarita? Corona? Well drink? It's two for one until six o'clock." The waitress had long black hair tied back in a low ponytail, and a heart tattoo on the back of her neck.

"Two margaritas. I'm waiting on a friend," Leah blurted.

"Lime, strawberry, raspberry . . ."

Every second she had to think about it was a second she had to change her mind. "Lime for both." Her waitress gave a pert nod and trotted off. Leah's heart started to beat faster with the guilt. Zoe would hassle her about the drink; there was no way around that.

The drinks arrived—large plastic glasses with ample salt on the rims. Leah loved tequila in her drinking days, especially margaritas. At the last few work happy hours Leah had ordered virgin margaritas, which left her full, nauseated, and pissed off.

Leah glanced around at the restaurant full of strangers. She took a nervous sip. No one disapproved. Her eyes and throat burned in warning, but she took another long swallow and her face warmed. The restaurant was raucous with relieved, Friday night laughter and tonight Leah was just another one of the crowd.

"Hey there!" Zoe screeched and slid into her chair. "I soaked myself in hand sanitizer before I left. Poor Dylan has a double ear infection and pink eye, and I think Olivia could be getting pneumonia!"

"Poor kiddos," Leah said, stupidly wrapping her hand around her glass like she could hide it.

Zoe pointed at the glass in front of her. "Mine? Good," she said and took a healthy swallow. "Thanks, hon." Leah nodded. Zoe's eye caught Leah's unhidden beverage. "What're you drinking?"

"Same as usual." Zoe looked away. Leah would have preferred hassling to the distracted silence that followed. Leah took another long, icy swallow. Finally Zoe spoke up, but the new topic was worse.

"Sam has been so weird lately," Zoe said, playing with the salt on her already half-empty glass. "Half the time he's pissy, and the other half he's just morose. And he won't talk to me. He seems so unhappy right now, and I don't know why."

Decision time. Leah had uncharacteristically kept her mouth shut because she could never figure out how to bring it up. And if she was really honest with herself, she was focused on her problems these days. But a few more gulps of the margarita, definitely not virgin, brought a wave of that old, dangerous liquid courage.

"Yeah . . . about that. I think Sam has something . . . going on with someone."

Zoe, who had been chewing on a chunk of ice, choked and sputtered. "What?!"

Oh boy, that came out wrong. Leah waved her hands, regretting the tequila jumbling her thoughts. "I mean, I don't think he's done anything. Nothing like that."

"How in the hell do you know what he's done or hasn't done?" Zoe's eyes filled and her chin quaked. "What are you talking about, Leah?"

The only way out of this disaster now was the full story. "The night of your party for Jake and Amanda—" she began.

"My party? That was weeks ago." Her voice was getting higher and squeaky, and the couple at the next table glanced over.

"Yeah." Leah rubbed her hands on her legs and could barely make eye contact. "Please just let me get this out." Zoe nodded and choked back a sob. "I got some text messages, one of them from earlier in the week. I thought they were sent to me by mistake so I just ignored them."

"What did they say?" Zoe blurted. They were complaints about Zoe and her friends and plans to meet. Nothing that a wife wants to hear about her husband.

"Um, they were just, like, boring stuff. Nothing I remember or that even stands out." Leah let herself look at Zoe for a moment, who seemed willing to accept that answer. Leah exhaled, not knowing that she had been holding her breath.

"Why do you think they were from Sam? Why did they go to you? This doesn't make sense."

Leah took a breath, fighting through the tequila fog, hoping she could do a better job finding words. "It was the timing of the messages that made me realize they were from him. When I went to change clothes before I went home, I used your bathroom. You remember how he was on his phone a lot that night. And he was a little crabby . . ."

Zoe squinted at the memory. "He's crabby all the time lately. But, yeah, that's about when I started to notice it."

"I'd gotten three messages that night, and they were talking about a party. The third one came just as I was walking out of your bedroom. He had just sent a message. I heard the little message whooshing sound as I walked by him. Then my phone buzzed, and I had another mystery message. It said something about everyone finally getting out of the hot tub. I figured it had to be him."

Zoe took a big swig and finished her margarita. She waved two fingers at the waitress breezing by and asked for two more. "That might have been him," Zoe said. "Your number's probably in his phone because it's also in mine. But you don't know for sure. If he was just complaining about the party, that's not so bad."

It was Sam's guilty look that confirmed it for Leah, but perhaps Zoe didn't need that much information.

"You're right, I'm not 100 percent sure. There was also a message about 'seeing' someone the next day. Meeting her, I guess I assumed it was a her, for coffee. But when I got that last text from him, I sort of . . . confronted him."

Zoe's eyes popped up and she met Leah's, sitting very still.

"He swore he hadn't done anything. And I believe him," Leah said. "But he looked . . . guilty."

Zoe's tears were back. "What am I going to do? This is so unlike him. We barely even fight."

"I know you don't–"

"And when were you going to tell me?" Zoe snapped. "Seriously, Leah, what is with you lately?"

In a moment of poor timing, their waitress returned. "Two Cuervo margs."

"Wait, no," Zoe said, and then paused, looking at the drinks, and then at Leah. "Hers is nonalcoholic." Zoe looked up at Leah and held her eyes. "Right?"

The waitress awkwardly looked at the drinks in her hands. "Uh . . ."

"No," Leah said, holding her friend's gaze.

Zoe looked away. "Why am I not surprised?"

KEMP'S OFFICE WAS DARK as usual, the building mostly emptied out for the evening. He sat across from his star witness. They were both somber, discouraged.

"So the feds are out?" Luke asked.

"For now," Kemp said, rubbing his balding head with his hands. "It didn't come together enough for the federal prosecutor, so they're not willing to charge at it this time. We could keep working on some type of local charge for possession. Right now it's your word against his, but we could set up a controlled buy . . ."

Luke shook his head wildly. "No no no. I told you he needs to go away for a long time or I'm not talking. He'll mess me up for this. It only works if he gets ten to twenty."

"I know, Luke." Kemp leaned back in his chair with his hands over his face.

Luke closed his eyes and considered, his hands shaking. Then he abruptly sat up, looked at Kemp and exhaled the weight of a secret held for decades. "Actually, there's something else that could put him away."

Kemp sat up. "I'm listening."

> *Uncle made a mistake. He had been sloppy and stupid, and now he needed to solve his problem. Really, he needed to eliminate it. Uncle had spent too many years apologizing, pretending, hiding. Being afraid to defend what was his. To do what needed to be done. This time, he would not hesitate. He was smart, and he had a plan.*

chapter fourteen

THE WORST DAY OF LEAH'S life didn't start that way. It was a regular Tuesday in many ways. She poured herself cereal for breakfast, but was out of milk, so she left the bowl on the counter and picked up a muffin on the way to work. When she walked by Max's office, he called for her to come in.

"Hey, Leah," Max said, passing her a report. "Annika's in the hospital."

Leah's heart dropped. The report indicated that Annika had overdosed on Tylenol and was found by her mother several minutes after she passed out, so luckily there would likely be no permanent liver damage. Annika was in the psychiatric hospital in Rochester, and her mother was asking for help from social services.

"I want you to go down since you know the family," Max said. "And we'll have Amanda go along to offer mental health case management." While Amanda usually worked just with child protection clients, she also worked with some children and adolescents with mental health issues who needed additional support.

Thirty minutes later Leah and Amanda were on their way. Amanda was surly, even more so since they had to take county car #5, a stripped down economy car that felt like it would shimmy apart when they drove over fifty miles per hour.

"So . . . how are the wedding plans going?" Leah asked, trying to get a conversation out of her normally chatty friend.

"Terrible." Amanda didn't take her eyes off the road. "Or maybe I should just ask you, since you know so much about me and what I want."

Uh oh. "Jake said something? I'm sorry." Her big mouth got her in trouble again.

"I hate this wedding, right? I never wanted this, right?" Amanda shook her head. "I wish you could learn to keep your mouth shut sometimes. This wedding was my decision. I thought I was just venting to my friend about how much it sucks. It's not your place to tell my fiancé anything." Amanda neared tears, rare for her.

"I'm sorry," Leah said again. "I'm such a shit. I'll call Jake and tell him it was all me."

"You will do nothing," Amanda snapped. "Just leave it alone."

They drove in silence down Highway 52 toward Rochester, cornfields flanking the busy four-lane highway that connected the Twin Cities with the Mayo Clinic. Leah tried to get conversation going a few more times, but Amanda was sulking.

By the time they pulled into the psychiatric unit of the hospital, Leah was as irritated as Amanda was angry. Maybe she had overstepped, but it was the truth. Everyone was so afraid of being honest. Sometimes the truth just spilled out of her.

They parked underground and followed a tunnel to an elevator that brought them to the fourth floor, which held the adolescent psychiatric wing. They stepped off the elevator and were greeted by a female security guard barely five feet tall, but who had the frame of a body builder.

In many ways, psychiatric units look the same as other hospital units—centrally located nurses' stations, quiet hallways, nondescript rooms. But the locked doors and security procedures were a constant reminder the residents on the fourth floor weren't allowed to leave.

Annika's mother, Pam, was sitting in a lounge area just outside of the secure entrance, red-eyed and pale.

"Hello, Pam," Leah said quietly. She was rolling a tattered magazine across her lap and jumped when she heard her name. "This is Amanda. She's another worker from my office. We're here to check in and support you and Annika."

Pam forced a polite smile but then the tears started. "I miss my girl," Pam said, wiping her eyes and shredding her tissue. They had found a table in a family waiting room outside the unit, which was good because Pam was in no shape to visit her fragile daughter quite yet. "I was trying to be strong. I *was* strong, until she started all the talk about dying." She held the tattered tissue to her nose while tears spilled down her cheeks. "She just got tired of the flashbacks. She's afraid all the time . . ."

Amanda patted Pam's hand. Again Leah was jealous of Amanda's ability to tolerate other's emotions. While most people ran away from pain, Amanda could sit with it without being dragged down. Leah usually turned clinical or became neutral and shut down. "So what do you think led to her overdose?" Amanda asked.

Pam blew her nose and shook her head. "She hasn't slept a full night since it happened. She's jumpy. Twitchy. I have to lie with her for an hour and help her relax and fall asleep, but every night she wakes up, sometimes around three, sometimes closer to five. It's the worst when she wakes up an hour after she falls asleep, because those are the nights both of us are up all night."

"Have you tried having her sleep in your room with you?" Amanda asked gently.

Pam tilted her head at Amanda. "She's been in my room ever since it happened," she snapped. Then she caught herself and started to apologize, but Amanda waved her off. "She would never be able to sleep in her room. I went back to work two weeks ago, and she spends every day at my parents' house. If they didn't live in town, I'd have to find someone to come stay with her. She can't be alone for more than a couple minutes before she's in full-blown panic."

"I'm so sorry she's going through this," Leah said. It was all there was to say.

Pam turned to face Leah. "So what's it going to take to figure out who did this? Why aren't there posters around town? Why aren't there more news stories, more cops on the street? If I didn't know better, I'd think no one in this town gives a damn about what happened to my daughter." Pam's voice shook as she got the last words out.

"I promise you a lot of people care very much about what happened, and are working extremely hard to find the man who did this." Leah understood Pam's anger and couldn't defend the lack of progress, but she wanted to defend Kemp.

"When are they going to find him?" Pam said, her voice catching. "When? I need my daughter to feel safe before she just gives up!" And then she dissolved into sobs, her head dropping to her chest. Amanda looked up at Leah, who shook her head and shrugged. Amanda patted Pam's hand and let her cry. Leah wanted to take out her phone and call Kemp. She didn't know what else to do for Pam but ask him for an update so she could tell Pam something . . . give her some glimmer of hope.

Amanda hopped up and found a box of tissues at another table and brought it back. Pam took several, blew her nose, and let out a heavy sigh.

"I'm sorry," Pam whispered. "This has been such a nightmare."

"Don't be sorry," Leah said. "This *is* a nightmare, and we need to find him. We *will* find him."

"We want to help you and Annika now," Amanda said. "People are amazingly resilient. I have all the faith in the world she'll be okay. "

Pam stared at Amanda as if she was willing those words to be true.

"Maybe one of the things they can do here is give her a med to help her sleep," Leah offered. "Fatigue makes everything worse."

"I'm afraid to let her have anything after the meds she got in the emergency room. She was so knocked out from that supposedly mild sedative I'm afraid they'll turn her into a zombie."

"What did they give her?" Amanda asked.

"Ativan. They said it was a small dose to help her sleep. But it seemed like much more than that, because she was so groggy for days."

"Trauma can do that," Leah said. "Sometimes kids sleep a lot, and others are unable to sleep, and they look even worse."

"It just seemed like more than that," Pam said. "Her eyes, her voice. Everything looked altered. But I don't know." Pam's eyes filled again. "Maybe that's just how people look when they've been so violently . . ." Her head dropped, and the tears resumed.

"Pam . . ." Leah didn't know if she was supposed to share this detail, but it felt like she deserved to know. "Officer Kemper thinks the guy may have . . . drugged her somehow . . ." Amanda's head snapped around, and she stared at Leah in disbelief. Pam held her head in her hands like she was afraid of what would happen if she let go.

It took another cup of coffee and some small talk about the high school sports, but eventually Pam was able to pull herself together. They went to the entrance of the adolescent unit and loaded their purses, bags, and cell phones in lockers outside the doors, keeping their IDs and notebooks. Pam rang the bell by the door, identified themselves, and a nurse buzzed them in.

Leah had visited the adolescent unit in Rochester a handful of times in her career, and always had the same uncomfortable reaction—it could have been her. The kids on the psychiatric unit often had seriously dysfunctional families, or they may have developed significant mental illness. Both could be true for Leah. How she escaped their fate was a mystery, and it made her feel grateful and guilty. As they waited in a meeting room for Annika, they watched a frail nine-year-old walk the hall in stocking feet, pale from stress, tears from his last meltdown still on his cheeks.

Pam was studying the patient board on the wall behind the nurse's station. The patients were designated by initials, and the comments by Annika's initials indicated she was still on one-to-one supervision—meaning she was at high risk for self harm.

When Annika finally arrived, Pam wrapped her daughter in a hug. Annika's arms hung limply by her sides while her mother held on, rubbing her back like she could soothe the fear and pain out of her.

Finally they sat at the table, Pam's hand still on Annika's back. Annika wore yoga pants that hung loosely on her thighs and a thick sweatshirt—heavy layers that coated her like armor.

"Hi, again," Leah said. "I'm sorry you're having such a hard time right now, kiddo."

Annika blinked at Leah and Amanda like she wasn't sure who they were. Then, softly: "Did you find him yet?"

Leah sank into her chair, wishing she could bring the investigators to this room and feel the weight of Annika's pain. "No, honey. Not yet."

Amanda leaned forward. "Hi, Annika, I'm Amanda." Leah felt a flash of irritation Amanda interjected herself in the conversation already. Leah intended to introduce them when Annika was comfortable.

"Hi." Annika was still polite, a shred of the innocent little girl that remained.

"How's the food here?" Amanda asked.

"I don't know," Annika said. "I can't eat." Annika's bony hands were folded in front of her, fingernails shredded and bloody.

"We've heard you're very bright," Amanda said. "Top of your class, huh?"

Pam nodded and actually let out a tiny smile. "She's amazing. Talented, beautiful, smart. She has everything. Everything."

Annika's face remained blank, and they all sat, unsure what to say next. Annika was nowhere near being ready to leave the hospital. Leah somehow thought that a night in the hospital and a visit from them would restore her.

"Can I tell you something, Annika?" Amanda sat forward in her chair. "When bad things happen, you might feel damaged. Like you'll never be whole again." Annika nodded slightly and looked at Amanda. "But here's the thing. The incident . . . assault . . . it's over. You're safe now. And even though your mind's kind of stuck, and it feels like it keeps happening, it's not. It's *over*, and you *survived* because you're strong. It can all go up from here."

Annika's head tilted slightly.

"You can learn to fight it off. That feeling. It'll always be with you, but it's not happening anymore. You can fight it off and go on with your life." Leah looked at her friend, who knew of what she spoke.

"I'm so tired," Annika whispered, melting into her mother's arms. Pam held her baby and rocked gently. Annika relaxed for the first time in a month, and fell asleep.

THEIR RIDE BACK WAS SUBDUED, the argument and the stress of the day still hovering between them. Leah couldn't get the picture of Annika's face out of her mind. Annika wanted to die. *Tried* to die because of what this man did to her.

"I think you really helped her," Leah finally said as they reached the valley at the edge of town.

"My heart's just breaking for her," Amanda said. "I hope she gets some peace."

"It makes me feel like a schmuck for complaining about anything in my life."

"Yeah, yeah, I know." Amanda sighed. "If my biggest problem is that my wonderful fiancé and his generous mother want to give me a beautiful wedding, I need to shut my mouth."

Leah wasn't intending to hint, but it was a fair point.

"So, they think he drugged her? Oh, my God, can this get any worse?"

Leah shook her head. "I don't see how it could."

"Are they making any progress on finding this guy?" Amanda asked.

Once again, she felt the need to defend Kemp. "They're working really hard. They are. It was such a random crime and Annika can't provide any description, so they're stuck. But it's not like they aren't trying."

"Of course they're trying," Amanda said. "I never said they weren't. I asked if they are getting anywhere. Do they have any leads, or ideas, or even guesses?"

"I don't think so," Leah said, trying to calm her defensive beast. "At the last meeting, everything blew up in Kemp's face. I think Barb would have fired him if she could have. The BCA is coming in to help, which pisses off Kemp. But he also knows they need help."

"You know, I thought Gordy would be getting the heat instead of Kemp. Isn't Gordy head of investigations?" Amanda turned into their parking lot and pulled into a space designated for county cars.

Leah considered for a moment. "They put Kemp in charge of this one."

Amanda nodded. "Makes sense, I guess. I hear Gordy's not doing well lately. What's wrong with him, again?"

"M.S. Or maybe lupus. I can't remember for sure. It's whatever gives you chronic pain, makes it so you can't breathe and gives you eczema."

"I'd feel worse for him if he weren't such a creep," Amanda said. They both climbed out the car and used the back employee entrance into their building.

Back at her desk, Leah checked her cell and found a voicemail message from earlier in the day. It was from Luke.

"Hey, sis, I gotta talk to you. I did somethin' and I needa tell ya . . . aw, shit. I'm sorry. I hope you won't hate me." The message cut off. Luke's words were slurred, his voice thick with weed and remorse. She was too exhausted and sad to even consider what Luke might have done this time.

THE MELANCHOLY MOOD stuck all day, and by the time 4:30 arrived Leah shut down her computer and moped to her car. When she got home she dropped her keys by her back door, pulled on some running clothes and went out for a long, hilly run to try to burn off the day.

After four miles, Leah was dying of thirst so she ran the last block as fast as she could, all the way up her driveway, into her house and straight to the shower. She blasted herself with water as cold as she could stand, then got dressed, leaving her hair to dry on its own into a blonde brillo pad. She chugged a tall glass of water and tried to catch her breath.

Four miles apparently wasn't enough to get Annika off her mind. Prisoners of war might have the look Annika did. Or children in Africa who lived in huts and spent their lives evading warlords and malaria. But their little town in sleepy Minnesota wasn't supposed to hold this kind of danger for teenage girls who liked to swim and were always on the Honor Roll. Annika needed her safety back, and Leah felt it was her job to get it for her. Leah grabbed her keys and headed to Kemp's house, hoping she could do something to push the case a little further.

Kemp owned a turn-of-the-century, three-story home in a historic neighborhood near downtown—a perpetual fixer-upper. During one of their early trysts she noticed a strip of gray paint across his thigh. When the sex was over and they were trying to reassemble themselves, she teased him about needing a shower and he explained he was always painting and could never get it all off.

Leah found his gray house with the leaning, tattered porch and pulled into the driveway. Before she could second-guess herself, she trotted up the driveway and knocked on the door.

In the ninety seconds it took for Kemp to answer the door, the worry and anger of the day were taking over again. Kemp opened the door to find Leah clenching her jaw and her fists.

"What needs to happen to find the guy? The rapist. What do we need to do?" Her voice trembled.

Kemp wearily leaned against the doorway, unable to hide his pleasure at having Leah at his house. "You wanna piece of me, too?" he asked with a sad, tired grin. "I'm meeting the BCA team tonight to work on profiling. We came up with some new directions—"

"Annika tried to kill herself." Leah choked on the words.

Kemp closed his eyes and rubbed his hands over his hair. "Is she okay?"

Leah pictured her gray face and the way her arms hung when her mom hugged her. "She's so broken, Kemp."

Kemp ran his hand down Leah's arm to her hand, and then held her hand tightly. "Kids are stronger than we think. Stronger than adults, for sure." Leah held on, comforted by the small, intimate gesture. "She's gonna be okay."

"You don't know that." Still holding on.

"Are you okay, babe? Is it all getting to you?" It would have been so easy to make a joke. Or even better, to run her hand up his arm, push him in the house and fall back into old habits. But her worry for Annika, for Baby Ben, and even for herself felt bigger than something that could be shoved away. She felt responsible for everyone, and she was failing them all.

Leah's silent shrug was answer. Kemp squeezed her hand. She pulled away.

"We'll figure it out," Kemp said, and Leah nodded as she headed back to her car and away from him having accomplished nothing at all.

KEMP WATCHED HER DRIVE AWAY, and then pulled out his phone and dialed the same number he had been calling all week.

"Have you told your sister anything yet?"

Luke groaned. "Kemper? Goddamn dude, 'm workin' on it."

Kemp's blood pressure rose. "Are you stoned? I thought we agreed you were going to lay off the shit. Off of everything. Those pills'll scramble your brain."

"I gotta lot going on right now, and I'm all sick in the head. 'S not a good time to jus' quit . . ."

Kemp's patience was fading fast. "Did you tell Leah?"

"I dunno. Sorta, I guess." Luke's words were so slurred it was hard to understand anything.

"Luke! Your sister needs you to step up."

"Aw, God, Kemper . . ."

Kemp hung up and closed his eyes. Everything he touched was a disaster.

IN LATE AUGUST, the sunset arrived before 8:00 p.m. A stunning harvest moon hung low and orange, and the heat of the day dissolved as soon as the sun went down. The air had an edge as the fickle Minnesota summer was retreating like it had given up for the season. Houses were silhouetted as dark, boxy shadows, and a few stars twinkled. It was so clear the ethereal cloud of the Milky Way galaxy was visible. Leah remembered how excited her dad was when they could see the Milky Way—he said it always meant good things. On nights like that he'd hold her hand, able to tolerate closeness as long as they were both looking up. Leah was overwhelmed. She felt small. Defeated, she drove to the only place that had ever felt like home.

As Leah locked her house for the night, Luke's call came back to her. She needed to let go of Annika tonight, so she turned to her own life. Leah listened again to his garbled message, trying to discern some meaning. He said he messed up. Nothing new there. He hoped she would forgive him, he said. She always seemed to, proof that biology clouded most judgment and common sense.

Agitation, layered on top of her gloom, was making her feel sick. Leah paced her living room, wondering what Luke meant. Wondering where the hell he was, and how he spent his time. She never asked about his coming and going, but just allowed him to use her home like a free hotel, with no questions or obligations. She felt stepped on, mistreated. And angry.

Her pacing brought her into the hallway and past the guest room, his space in her home. The hollow old door was closed tightly, as usual. Leah paced and stared at that door. Her door, in her house. She put her hand on the knob, paused, considered, withdrew, then opened the door before she could stop herself.

The sour funk of dirty clothes combined with the spicy musk of weed to create an infuriating stink. Unacceptable.

Privacy be damned, this was her house. She started cleaning. Leah grabbed the garbage can from the corner and piled the convenience store sandwich wrappers, discarded rolling papers, and soda bottles into it. The can was soon overflowing. Her anger grew as she found many of her nicer dishes, her grill lighter, and her hairbrush among his belongings. On the dresser was an old cigar box. Inside she found about a dozen assorted pill bottles with the names scratched off and a baggie with a few marijuana buds. Her disgust grew. She yanked open the closet door. A mountain of grubby t-shirts and jeans spilled onto the floor. She grimaced as she pulled out all the clothes, deciding to wash them just to get rid of the smell. At least this was one area of her life that she could grab a little control.

Her hand brushed it first when she reached the bottom of the closet. She didn't give it a thought, and kept scrounging for dirty socks. But it could have been karma that made her fingers slide by the smooth plastic again.

The worst day of her life, so far, felt only like a dull ache—a haunting abuse case, bickering with a friend, a cloud of loneliness that wouldn't dissipate. But behind that ache a sense of foreboding had started when she interviewed Annika. A detail had tickled in the back of her mind from that interview, and her subconscious wouldn't let it go.

When Leah's heart started to beat harder at something so insignificant as a piece of plastic, she should have known it was more. But she couldn't have ever known or guessed how much more.

She couldn't have known, in those last few seconds before everything in her life collapsed, until she pulled out the plastic rectangle, and was met by the same eyes she had looked into earlier that day. Leah had never seen those eyes look so unburdened, innocent, and light.

It was Annika, smiling a joyful, eighth-grade smile. It was Annika's ID. And it was in Luke's closet.

HYPERVENTILATING, LEAH TRIED to summon an explanation that would make this not mean what it had to mean. But then she looked down at her other hand, still clutching a scrap of black fleece. She knew instantly that it was the detail that had been nagging her since the interview—a ski mask with a logo of the Minnesota Wild. She recognized it at once as Luke's and as the mask that Annika described her attacker wearing.

A sob escaped Leah's throat, her thoughts scrambled and insane. She backed out of the closet, out of his room, stopping only for her purse and her keys, before she ran to her car and screeched away from her home . . . which was now a crime scene. Leah made one phone call to sheriff's dispatch, informing them of what they would find.

And then Leah drove desperately over the county line to Apple Falls, where she somehow checked into the first hotel she could find. She took her bottle of Jameson whiskey out of its place in her backseat, into the hotel room and poured it down her throat, hoping to take herself into oblivion.

chapter fifteen

COURTROOMS WERE USUALLY COLD. Despite the polished wood, high ceilings, and regal atmosphere, the cold was a reminder that court was not a welcoming place. Rights were respected and honored, but other than the ever-present box of tissues at the defendant's table, comfort was in short supply.

Attorneys, however, love the courtroom. It was their stage, their place to demonstrate, publicly, they were the best at what they did. Prosecutors and defense lawyers alike felt they were on the correct side of the law. Whether they were protecting the public or preserving the Constitution, Jake had often remarked that despite lawyer jokes, most attorneys believed in the nobility of their profession.

On the day Luke Danco appeared for his detention hearing for first degree criminal sexual conduct, Jake felt many things, but noble was not one of them.

When Jake received the call the night before, he had been asleep in a chair in their living room, and in his half-conscious fog he didn't understand Kemp's ranting. Instead, the words *brother* and *rapist* got jumbled in with a lot of cursing. Then it did sink in, and Jake did the cursing. He shot out of his chair and threw on some clothes, while Amanda followed him around the house asking what was going on. Jake wasn't supposed to tell his fiancée about a confidential investigation until there was an arrest and the matter became public knowledge, but Jake had given up on that a long time ago. While he had his limits, Amanda still knew more than she should about Jake's cases.

But this time, he had to keep it all to himself, especially since he didn't know where Leah was or what she knew. It would be impossible for Amanda to withhold the information from her friend, and Jake couldn't risk compromising the investigation. So Jake apologized but told her he couldn't tell her what was going on. The look on his face told her enough.

THE SEARCH AT LEAH'S HOUSE had lasted all night. Officers combed the entire house for evidence that connected Luke to the crime. Kemp supervised, his head pounding, as they turned Luke's bedroom upside down, putting the student ID and face mask into evidence. They marked and cataloged every item in Luke's closet, including the pills, a collection of marijuana pipes, the baggie with marijuana buds left in it, barely enough to come up with a charge for drug possession. But this was recorded, too, as they would need every shred of evidence.

Kemp's headache was a sledgehammer on his skull by the time they got to Leah's bedroom. Kemp's stone-cold face set the tone in the room, and he only allowed two officers he trusted most to enter. He knew it had to be done, but it was still infuriating to watch the officers open every drawer, rifling through her underwear and workout clothes. They emptied a box of condoms in her bedside stand to ensure there was no contraband in the box. There wasn't, Kemp knew, as he had purchased the box himself before one of their last times together. He noticed with relief that most of them were still in the box.

After midnight, two BCA technicians arrived. With thorough professionalism they set about looking for hair and fiber evidence. They removed and labeled hairs from every room, hairbrush, and sink drain. They crawled on their hands and knees inspecting the carpet with black lights, spending most of their time in that closet.

Kemp and Jake had their first argument of the night at about 2:00 a.m. Jake was at his office putting together the criminal complaint and needed the update on the evidence. As Kemp described what they were finding through clenched teeth, Jake told Kemp he really shouldn't be there.

"This is my goddamn case. My mess to clean up. What am I supposed to say—that I'm in love with the suspect's sister, so I can't work it?"

"Whoa, buddy, you're what . . . ?" Jake asked.

"Whatever. You heard me. You can't expect me to get off this case."

"That's exactly what you are supposed to do," Jake said. "Hell, Kemp, none of us should be on this case. Barb and I will have to talk about getting a change of venue in the morning. In the meantime, we don't need to give them any ammunition to say this case is contaminated.

"Like the Miranda case, huh, Jake?" Kemp said. "You getting tired of defending a dirty cop?"

"Knock it off, Kemp. If you were using your head you'd know I'm right."

Kemp hung up, the first of many times he would anger his coworkers in the coming days. At 5:00 a.m., when the BCA left and the local officers were finishing up, Kemp turned his focus back to Leah. Kemp tried to call and text several times, but her phone seemed to be turned off.

It wasn't until after everyone left that fatigue and his temper got the best of him. He went into Leah's room, where her drawers were dumped out and most of her clothing had been piled on her bed. Boxes in the closet had been emptied, and her scant jewelry box had actually been taken into evidence because of two small boxes they could not open. He tried her number again as the first glimmers of sunlight pierced the blinds in her room. Hearing her chipper voice on the voicemail broke something inside of him, and he swung around and punched the wall, hearing the crunch as several bones in his wrist broke.

APPEARANCES FOR THE "IN CUSTODIES" were at 11:00 a.m. Kemp left the emergency room with a cast from his fingertips to just below his elbow and had to run to his car to get there in time. The doctor had wanted to give some time for the swelling to go down before he casted it, but Kemp flashed his badge and assured the doctor this was going to be his one and only trip to the clinic, so he needed to take care of everything right then.

Jake and Barb Cloud were together at the prosecutor's table, and Tom Backerson, another county attorney with extensive trial experience, was sitting behind them. The courtroom was full, and Kemp recognized the victim's mother, Pam, sitting in the second row accompanied by a similar-looking woman who must have been her sister.

Amanda and Zoe were sitting in the back row, both looking ill. Kemp made eye contact with Amanda and mouthed: *Did you find her?* Amanda shook her head.

"All rise," the senior bailiff announced. Judge Manuel Guerrero—late thirties, polished dresser—took the bench. While the rumor used to be that affirmative action got such a young attorney a judgeship, people only had to hear his encyclopedic knowledge of the law to know he earned his job.

Judge Guerrero took his seat as Luke was led into the courtroom, shackled, and in the lime-green prison scrubs distinctive to Terrance County. He took his seat next to Steven Grayson, public defender.

"This is the case of the state vs. Lucas Bo . . . Bob-a- . . . Bob-a-f . . ." Judge Guerrero looked up questioningly.

"Your Honor, I believe it's 'Bobafett,'" Barb Cloud said. Boba Fett, a character from Star Wars. Kemp shook his head. Leah had always said her parents were a little off.

Judge Guerrero nodded. "The case of the state vs. Lucas, ehem, Bobafett Danco." He had the attorneys state their names and whom they were representing for the court record. The issue of bail was discussed at length, with Barb Cloud asking for half a million in bail because of the risk Mr. Danco posed to the community. Luke's attorney described the state's evidence as "highly circumstantial" and they did not have anything linking Mr. Danco to the "supposed evidence" found in the room in his sister's home.

Kemp knew the evidence was thin—Annika's ID in Luke's room wasn't a slam dunk, but the lack of alibi and the ski mask and ID were enough for Barb to agree that they could arrest him. Luke lawyered up immediately. Wisely. Grayson told Jake he would not allow his client to be interviewed, so they had to prosecute based on what they had. When the prosecuting team met this morning, Barb warned them they needed to do better, and Gordy had sworn to her now that they knew who they were looking at, they would tighten up the case. Kemp tried to offer suggestions to Gordy, but he put up his hand and shrugged Kemp off.

The debate in court continued while Kemp's hand throbbed, the Tylenol he was given at the clinic barely heading off the pain since he had refused to take anything stronger. Kemp studied Luke. He wondered if people looked at Luke and saw a monster. Kemp didn't know what he saw anymore.

"I'M SO SCARED. There's still no sign of her." Amanda was on the phone with Lucy as she and Zoe were walking back to the office from the hearing. "Her brother got $250,000 in bail. Everyone in the room was looking at him like he was the devil. I can't imagine what it'd be like to be related to a suspected rapist. What a nightmare."

Amanda listened to Lucy for a minute and then said okay and hung up.

"Lucy said she's going to drive around and look for her car," Amanda said.

"We'll have to file a missing person's report soon." Zoe's voice shook. "Even though it still won't have been twenty-four hours, having your only brother arrested for a vicious rape has to count as an extenuating circumstance."

"She wouldn't do anything crazy." Amanda declared. "She just needs space. You know how she is."

Zoe grabbed Amanda's arm and they stopped. "She's drinking."

Amanda winced. "How do you know?"

"When we went out for drinks the other night, she had a margarita. I was so mad at her about the whole Sam situation I couldn't say anything."

"Oh, God, this is scary." They were quiet for a second, lost in worry. "Are things any better with Sam?" Amanda asked.

Zoe shrugged with tears in her eyes. "He just keeps saying he didn't do anything, but I can't get him to explain who she is, or what's going on between us. All he will say is that he was never going to do anything with her, but he's lonely. I thought we were fine . . ." She crossed her arms and took a big breath, trying to compose herself. "I can't think about this right now. We need to find Leah."

They picked up the pace and hustled into their building. "I'm telling Max we're going to look for her. There's no way that I can sit at my desk today."

Max was all in favor of Zoe and Amanda looking for Leah, so they shut down their computers for the day and met at Zoe's car, a Lexus SUV that was much more comfortable than Amanda's aging Honda.

Amanda and Zoe drove all afternoon, up and down every street in Terrance with no luck–through Leah's older neighborhood and the new developments, along the river walk and around downtown, including an unprecedented stop at Abby's Bakery without buying a thing ("Ugh–food looks terrible," Zoe said, and Amanda agreed). Zoe called Leah's mom and asked for Leah, but when she said Leah hadn't answered her calls in days, Zoe mumbled and hung up. By late afternoon Zoe was too upset to drive, so they gave up and went back to the office to finally report their friend as missing.

Uncle had done something horrible, by conventional standards, anyway, although he didn't feel horrible. The funeral wasn't even sad. Sure, he would miss all those weekends with his friend. The beers in the backyard. The camaraderie. But there was a deeper truth he would admit only to himself. He felt strong and alive for the first time in his life. And there was no going back now.

chapter sixteen

ALCOHOLICS ANONYMOUS TEACHES THAT ALCOHOL magnifies feelings already present. Happy people feel happier, and if there is sadness it grows, often exponentially. It takes a whole lot of alcohol to push past the emotions to get to the fog.

Leah still wasn't sure if she actually slept. She laid in bed on top of the covers in a two-queen room that reeked of carpet cleaner and dirt. The bottle of whiskey sat between her legs, the symbolism glaring. The night passed with infomercials, burning swallows of booze, and pockets of fitful sleep, dissociation, or whatever it was. The guilt, the shame, and her responsibility for what Luke had done wouldn't go away no matter how much she drank. Her stomach churned as the family secret—an incident she had witnessed with Luke when he was about twelve—played in her mind over and over. She had protected it, and ultimately dismissed it, for so long it was all but forgotten, but in light of this new arrest it had to mean more. It was unbearable, so Leah drank and drank, pushing that memory back into the darkest corner of her mind.

When the room starting getting lighter as the sun came up, Leah thought of food. The Apple Falls Super 8 had a sad continental breakfast of stale donuts and a community jug of orange juice. Stumbling drunk and reeking of liquor, Leah lost count of how many times she stumbled through the breakfast area to collect her mini plate of donuts and dixie cup of OJ. Donuts were the ideal drinking food that created a fatty, dense base to coat her stomach. Leah knew it was the only food she would get for a while, so she stocked up.

BY THE TIME *JEOPARDY* CAME ON, several mangled donut pieces were demolished on a plate next to her, but the bottle was dry. Leah's throat and stomach burned from a swirl of alcohol, bile, and acidic grief that could only be neutralized by more booze.

Blinking hard, Leah looked around the room for the first time. Nothing would stay in focus. Beige plastic curtains were pulled tight over a double window with a view of the parking lot and highway leading into Apple Falls. A sliver of sunlight glowed with the orangey haze of late afternoon.

When Leah stood, her stomach rolled and lurched, her doughy breakfast threatening to reemerge. She wove her way to the bathroom and squinted at herself in the mirror.

Frightening.

Her hair was matted and limp, tracks of crusted mascara streaked down her cheeks. She had foggy eyes and her mouth hung limp and colorless. She needed more liquor, but there was no one to call to bring it. Enough sense remained that she knew she could not drive.

So she was trapped, alone in a hotel room, with nothing but her aching heart and the charred remains of an already mediocre life. She had kept it away for almost a day, but now there was nothing left to protect her from the overwhelming cascade of grief and rage. Leah sunk to the cold tile of the bathroom floor engulfed by sobs.

KEMP AND JAKE SAT ACROSS from Barb Cloud's ample desk, the only three left in the office as it was getting dark.

"So how close were you to charging him?" Barb asked, tapping a pencil on her desk.

"We had Luke's statement," Jake said wearily. "But it was complicated. A few corroborating facts, and if we could get a search warrant we could have potentially gotten some good evidence. We were within the statute because it was crim sex. The last incident was about six years ago."

"So Luke was molested for years by this 'uncle.' The man who eventually became his dealer. *The* dealer, Carl Vole, you've been after your entire career." Barb said, raising her eyebrows. "Right, Kemper?" Her voice held judgment, but in light of their current situation he was in no position to get defensive. Barb shuffled through the file. "And he was ready to talk?"

"He gave a long statement, but it was short on details," Kemp admitted. "His whole life's a fog. He started using when he was about twelve. The episodes with the uncle are woven in somehow. The kid barely knows what happened himself."

"So, yeah . . . we hadn't decided what to do about the charges," Jake said. "The goal was to get him arrested on the crim sex, hoping that a search warrant would lead to more evidence at his house, and then we would get enough to nail him on the dealing charges, too. And now in light of Luke being charged with crim sex himself, it almost adds credence to his story, even though it makes charging Carl pretty much impossible."

Kemp crossed his arms. "I still can't believe this. Luke's always seemed harmless. Low-level dealer, but that's it. Harmless."

"Obviously you misjudged him," Barb snapped at Kemp, and then turned back to Jake.

"So on our case against Danco . . . I reviewed the transcripts with the victim, and it doesn't look like we're going to get a lot more detail from her. Do you think she knows anything more?"

"She was hospitalized last weekend. Suicidal," Kemp said. He flashed back to Leah's tearful visit to his home twenty-four hours ago. How could it have been only twenty-four hours? "I think we're going to have to go the therapy route with her and see if details come as she gets stronger."

"I talked to Hoffbrau about going after Danco and getting the wheres and whens from the night of the assault, " Barb said. Kemp flinched hearing the name "Danco" until he realized she was talking about Luke, not Leah. "Grayson's considering whether we can talk to him now. We need a hard interview at him to pin down those last twenty-four hours, and then we need to get to everyone in this guy's life."

"Yeah, I know," Kemp said. He had been thinking about how to question Luke after they had been collaborating for weeks, and who else he would need to interview.

Jake bit his lip. "It's not your interview, man." Jake said quietly. "Rick Jordan is going to do it."

Kemp sat back in his chair. "So when did this get decided?"

"We were talking this afternoon after court. Gordy said Rick just got back from some advanced interrogation training. He's in a good spot to go hard after Luke."

Kemp knew Jake was right. After spending multiple evenings with Luke and considering he was Leah's brother, he was in no position to interrogate him. But after thirty-six sleepless hours, his nerves were frazzled and his thinking was off.

"That's just great," he said. "I suppose you don't want to leave it to the local flunkie." Kemp didn't finish college the first time around—he was partying too much and lost his financial aid because his GPA was so low. Even though he sailed through his two-year law enforcement degree program a few years later, his dad called him "Flunkie" for years. Kemp didn't even know he was holding on to that one.

"All right, I've had enough." Barb pointed with her pencil at Kemp's nose. "I'm going to put this in terms you can understand. You had an indiscreet sexual relationship with the suspect's sister for years, you were collaborating with the suspect on a case, and most of all, your monstrous ego is casting a shadow over everything you touch. So, yes, Investigator Kemper, your unbiased, well-trained colleague is taking the case. Grow the hell up and back off."

Jake was looking at the floor, the guilt on his face revealing he agreed with Barb.

"Fine." Kemp stood up and fought the urge to shove the chair into Barb's giant desk. He headed toward the door. "I guess I'm done here." He was almost out the door when he stopped and turned around to share a detail that had been bothering him. "Luke doesn't wear athletic shoes."

"What?" Barb asked.

"We had footprints in the area of the assault. Running shoes. It had been raining earlier, so they were pretty fresh, and we think it's better than fifty-fifty they belong to our perp. I've never seen Luke in running shoes; it's always boots. There were no running shoes in his closet or in his room, and he was picked up in boots."

Barb stared at Kemp for a second, and then tilted her head. "Fair point."

Jake looked down to hide his smile. This was the Kemp he had been waiting for.

chapter seventeen

EVERYTHING HURT. Her throat was on fire, her eyes would barely open. Her neck throbbed from sleeping at such a crazy angle on the cold floor. The room was stuffy, and she reeked of whiskey, donuts, and tears. And nothing had changed. Her brother was still an accused, vicious rapist.

Leah had no idea how to face anyone at the county, and her heart ached at the prospect of dealing with Pam and Annika. But the shame of waking up on the floor of a cheap hotel was enough to tell her this self-destruction had to end, so she forced herself to move.

Leah pulled herself off the rock hard tile floor of the bathroom, reached over and turned on the shower. Her head throbbed with hangover and hunger, so she stripped off her booze-soaked clothes and stood in the shower, surprised her tears were gone. She lingered under the lukewarm, weak spray until she was ready to get out and figure out what to do next.

The sharp knocking at the door actually hurt, adding to the pulsing behind her eyes. The last knock had come from housekeeping trying to clean her room yesterday. Leah was pretty sure she slurred "Go away" with enough force to scare away anyone on the other side of the door.

"Leah?" A familiar voice—small and soft and probably judging. Familiar voices were not welcome right now, so Leah didn't answer. "Leah. I heard you in there. Please just let me in for a minute. Everyone is so worried about you."

Leah sat on the edge of the bed wrapped in a towel, hair dripping down her back, and stared at the wall until the knocking resumed, sharp and insistent. It was the "cop knock" she had heard so many times on the job.

"Leah Danco? Apple Falls PD here to do a welfare check."

Dammit. Leah groaned and dragged herself off the bed. She stood by the door. "Yes. I'm here and I'm fine. I don't need anything."

"Terrance PD wants me to eyeball you, ma'am. Please open the door."

"Terrance PD can bite me. I'm fine. I haven't broken any laws, and I'm not opening the door." Leah looked through the peephole and saw a uniformed officer accompanied by a petite woman with dark hair and eyes and a furrowed expression. Lucy.

"Leah, please. Just let me talk to you for a minute. If you don't let me in, Zoe and Amanda will come over here and break down the door. Or Jake will probably get some kind of search warrant. Or Kemp will just shoot the door knob right off. Seriously, Leah, no one is going to back off until we know you're okay."

A sob caught in her throat. There was no way she could be okay. But Lucy was right, so she opened the door and allowed her to come inside. The officer looked her over and then looked away. "Let me know if you need anything," he said more to Lucy, the sane one, than to Leah.

Lucy slid through the doorway and gave Leah, still wrapped in a towel, a quick onceover. Leah went back to her bed and sat down. "Don't say it. I know I'm a mess."

"Oh, Leah, anyone in your situation would be a mess," Lucy said, sitting on the corner of the other rumpled bed. "I think I'd have started driving until I got to a place that had never heard of Terrance, Minnesota."

Leah leaned back on the plastic headboard with a pained smile. "That would have been a better idea than the Apple Falls Super 8."

"Leah, would you like to hide out at my house for a day or two and just regroup?" Lucy asked. "I'll make you some decent food and you can watch old movies or read or just sleep."

"No . . . I couldn't . . ." It was hard to muster a protest when hunkering down at Lucy's house was better than any option Leah had considered.

"Yeah, you could," Lucy said with uncharacteristic pushiness. She popped up. "I have a gym bag in my car with some clothes that'll fit you, I'm sure. You can get dressed and we'll head to my house."

Leah couldn't find an argument, so Lucy took over. Leah went in the bathroom and tried to rearrange herself into something presentable while Lucy got her gym bag out of the car, and then Leah dressed in Lucy's t-shirt and running shorts that mostly fit but were a bit snug across the hips. They were in Lucy's car in a matter of minutes and drove across town to Lucy and William's home, a newer split level with a sprawling yard. Leah made it up the stairs and into the guest bedroom before overwhelming fatigue took over and she was in bed and asleep.

WHEN SHE WOKE UP, Leah was momentarily confused. It felt like afternoon. She could barely remember the trek to Lucy's house and wasn't sure where she was. But when it all came back, she felt empty but calm. The rest must have done her good.

Leah followed the noise and smell of food and stopped short of the dining area and kitchen, where Zoe and Amanda were standing in the kitchen helping Lucy fry vegetables and shred lettuce. So much for hiding out.

They all noticed Leah at once. Zoe bounded across the room and devoured Leah in a hug, which Leah returned with a stiff pat on her back. Zoe wouldn't let go. Leah glared at Lucy over Zoe's shoulder.

"I know, and I'm so sorry," Lucy said with an apologetic smile. "I said you could hide here. I told them you were okay and needed space, but they wouldn't listen."

"That's because she doesn't need space from us," Amanda declared, setting the lettuce on the counter and squeezing Leah's arm.

Leah withdrew herself from Zoe's tearful, smothering hug. "It's fine," Leah said. "These two have no boundaries, so you shouldn't be surprised."

"You got that right," Zoe said. "Now let's find you a toothbrush before your breath knocks us all over."

TEN MINUTES LATER they gathered in the living room with full plates of fajitas.

"Where's your baby?" Leah asked, unable to remember his name, climbing over toys and settling into a leather recliner in front of the fireplace. The room was a study in eclectic decorating and defined their priorities—a painting of Jesus surrounded by children was displayed prominently on the wall, surrounded by two prayer candles. Another wall was covered in framed photos of the baby. The rest of the walls in the house were empty—"no time to figure out what to put up," Lucy said. The group had managed to avoid conversation while they were cooking, but now silence was settling in, and Leah was hoping to keep it light.

"Will came home from work early and took Javi to his parents' house, so they're getting their grandparent time." Lucy settled onto the couch next to Zoe. "Being the first grandchild on both sides makes him way too popular."

"He won't be the first grandchild for long . . ." Amanda said, raising her eyebrows.

Lucy's face fell. "My eighteen-year-old sister's pregnant," Lucy shared with a sigh. "Family drama."

"Yeah . . ." Leah said slowly. "I get family drama."

Amanda cringed.

"Well . . . okay. Let's get it over with," Leah said, looking around the room at her friends, who were avoiding eye contact. "What do you busybodies need to say to me?"

Nervous glances all around.

"Okay, I'll start," Leah said, forcing a mimicking smile even though it felt foreign to smile. "We're just *so worried* about you, Leah, and about your relapse, and how you're handling the . . . uhhhh . . . *situation* with your brother . . ."

"You're mocking us because we're worried about you?" Zoe said, unable to mask her irritation. "Really?"

Leah drooped, the grief threatening to take over again. Lucy leaned forward, ready to reach out for Leah's hand and comfort her.

Amanda shook her head. "She's mocking us to make us mad and push us away, so we don't have to talk about her disastrous life." Amanda sat back and took a big bite of chicken while Lucy turned to glare at her. "I mean, I'm honestly expecting a Lifetime movie producer to show up at your door begging to tell your story."

Zoe tilted her head a moment, and then jumped in. "You're one hot mess." Zoe got up, leaned over Leah's chair and gave her an awkward hug. "We love you, hon." Zoe grabbed her plate and went to the kitchen for seconds.

Tears slid down her cheeks and splatted on her plate. "Dammit," Leah whispered. "Apparently I'm a crier now. That's just great. I can't stand criers."

Lucy stuck her chin out in a rare moment of attitude. "Yeah, well, we criers don't want you on our side, either. You scare the hell out of people like us." Amanda raised her eyebrows and grinned at her friend.

Leah smiled at Lucy, taken with that golden feeling of connecting with a new friend. Somehow her friends knew the best thing they could do to smooth over the awkwardness was harass her.

"Okay, now for one more moment of truth," Zoe said, back on the couch. She pointed at Leah with a tortilla chip. "You smell like holy hell. One shower is not enough to wash away that wicked hangover funk."

Leah reached over and crushed the chip in Zoe's hand. "Ha freaking ha," she said. But her heart was a little lighter with gratitude for true friendship.

LEAH WAS BACK IN BED in a few hours. It was a work night, so Amanda and Zoe headed back early. Zoe hugged Leah and gave her a look like she was ready to say more. Amanda grabbed Zoe by the shoulder and dragged her out before she could lecture or cry. Handsome William and adorable Javi came home, and Leah watched them maneuver their evening routine. She backed out of the room and let them have their family time.

The guest bed was lumpy, and Leah was sad. It wasn't soul crushing anymore, but it was almost worse because it felt permanent. Luke could never just be her brother any more. He was the worst kind of human, and she couldn't help feeling that viciousness meant something about her, too. But it was the memory, and what that memory meant about Luke, that haunted her sleep and stoked her guilt. She was supposed to be Luke's protector, and she had failed.

Leah stared at the wall and waited for sleep to come. But she couldn't let go, so sleep evaded her, and there was no comfort to be found.

The little man went away. His father was gone, and so the little man—well, almost a man himself now—had slipped into a haze that made all the old games impossible. All Uncle could do now was change the game. Anything to keep the little man close.

chapter eighteen

LEAH LEFT LUCY'S HOUSE on Saturday evening. She even surprised herself by staying two days, but Lucy was right—her house was far enough away it felt hidden, and sanctuary was what Leah needed. But by Saturday, she could see William wanted his wife back, so she packed her minimal belongings into a plastic Target bag, hugged her friend, and made the lonely drive home. She needed the rest, because on Sunday it was time to face her mother.

Lucy had encouraged her to call her mom on Saturday afternoon. "She probably knows and is worried sick about you," Lucy had said. But Lucy, who didn't understand the nature and isolation of mental illness, was wrong. Beverly Danco had gone about her days of AA meetings, coupon clipping, and daytime TV like normal until Leah called on Saturday afternoon and demolished her world.

It didn't help that Leah wasn't prepared and blurted most of the story in all of its unvarnished horror. Beverly was silent at first, then the moaning started. Then the wailing, and finally a full-fledged, dramatic scream. Lucy heard it all, shaking her head with her hands on her forehead, mouthing, "I'm so sorry," over and over. She helped Leah come up with a lie to buy her one more night before she had to face her mom. Beverly had begged Leah to come over immediately, but Leah said she was in Wisconsin at a meeting and would be back early Sunday morning, promising to drive straight to her mother's home then. Beverly agreed to take an Ativan and go to sleep.

On Sunday morning when Leah finally knocked on her mom's door, she should have known who would answer. There was no way Beverly would have spent the night alone.

"Hey, kid," Coolie said, opening the door and then stepping away, scratching himself under his grubby t-shirt. The sound of his nails raking through his graying chest hair sent shivers down Leah's spine and made her long for the Apple Falls Super 8 and a fresh bottle of whiskey.

Leah found her mom in her bedroom clutching a decades-old hot water bottle with a washcloth over her eyes. She wanted to be mad that her mom was being dramatic, but her friends had been nothing but kind and supportive during her own meltdown. The universe required Leah to do the same for her mom.

Leah sat on the edge of the bed. "Mom?"

"Princess?" Beverly asked in a voice on the edge of hysteria. "Are you really there?"

"Yes, Mom. I'm here." Leah pushed away her irritation and took Beverly's hand and held tight, starting a cascade of sobbing.

"I just don't . . . I don't . . . understand . . ." Sniveling, whimpering.

"I know, Mom. I don't understand, either. It's awful."

Beverly pushed herself up on her elbow, her nose running and dripping onto her sweatshirt—navy blue with a silkscreen of dogs wearing tutus and the caption *bitches be crazy*. "So what do we need to do next? How do we get him out of there?"

Leah stared at her mom, who was clenching her teeth to hold back more tears. "Get him out of jail?" Leah asked.

"Of course! He has been falsely accused of a terrible crime! Horrible! We can't just abandon him." She pulled a tissue out of a box by her head and swiped it under her nose. "You have friends over there. What have they said? Are they working on getting him out?"

Coolie stood in the doorway of her bedroom and smacked his lips and huffed. "Bev . . ."

"I swear to God, Carl, if you say one more word—"

Coolie put his hands up. "I didn't say anything . . . Jeez."

Well, there was a thought. In all the horror and insanity of the last few days, what had never occurred to Leah was that Luke could be innocent. *Innocent*. Was it even possible?

Beverly sat up and straightened her shirt, blew her nose, and smoothed her matted, graying hair around her head. "How much money do you have? My Social Security comes next week, so between the both of us we could probably find a real smart lawyer."

"I don't really have a lot of extra money, Mom, and neither do you," Leah said firmly. "I'm sure he had an attorney assigned to him already."

"Well, you can find out, can't you?" Beverly heaved herself out of bed and went across the room to her jewelry box where Leah knew she kept her stash of pills and weed. Bev opened the box, considered for a second, and then snapped it shut. "No," she whispered, fighting back another wave of tears. "Luke needs me to be clear right now." The irony that Luke's arrest had driven Leah to drink while it pushed Beverly toward sobriety was not lost on Leah.

"I can ask my coworkers what's going on with his trial," Leah said.

Beverly turned to face Leah, the strain of it all weighing Beverly's face down and settling onto her shoulders like a thick shawl. "When will he have to go to court?" Beverly's chin crumpled as she seemed to picture her son in a courtroom.

"He's already had his first appearance. He won't appear again for a couple weeks."

Beverly nodded, went to her closet and pulled out a clean sweatsuit. "It'll just take me a minute to get dressed, and then we can go." She headed for her bathroom with newfound strength.

"Where are we going?" Leah asked, afraid to hear the answer.

"To see your brother, of course," Beverly said. "Carl said the jail visiting hours are one o'clock to five on Sundays."

Of course Coolie would know the jail visiting hours. "Um, Mom? I'll drive you there, but I'm not going to visit Luke."

Beverly turned with a hand to her throat and gasped. "What?" She shook her head. "No. You have to visit your brother. The Dancos stick together!" The Dancos . . . Leah's stomach rolled as she realized what her name would become in this town. Everyone would know that Luke Danco was the violent rapist who had been feared by the entire town for weeks. Leah pictured herself using a credit card, giving her name at a restaurant, filling a prescription. She imagined the look of recognition, disgust, or horror on some cashier's face when he read Leah's name.

Beverly shuffled off to her tiny, sparse bathroom, leaving Leah and Coolie alone. Leah glanced at Coolie, and for one uncomfortable moment their eyes connected. It reminded Leah of leaning over the side of Kemp's boat and looking down into the river, where beyond the murky surface there were things she never wanted to know.

THE TERRANCE COUNTY DETENTION center was in a recently gutted and renovated section of an eighty-year-old government building. With only thirty cells, the jail was usually full, and inmates complained of the cramped cells, the malfunctioning plumbing, and the ever-present stink of sewer gas from ancient pipes. Occasionally Leah had to visit clients at the jail, which involved guards scanning her through multiple doors and escorting her down barren hallways to an eight-foot-by-eight-foot meeting room where the inmates had to be cuffed while they spoke with her.

Visiting inmates as a regular citizen, however, involved a different set of procedures. This time she was not staff, thus was not granted the privilege of conducting business deep in the bowels of the detention center. Instead, Leah and her mother had to present their IDs and fill out a form indicating that they understood their conversations would be monitored and could be audio and videotaped. Beverly, in a velour sweatsuit of muted gray with a silkscreen of a soldier, was quiet, her mouth set in a line of grim determination and defiance. Leah had to admit that, after her initial breakdown, Beverly had found her strength for her son.

Leah avoided eye contact with the guard who escorted them to the visitor's room. They sat in a tiny brick room, painted institutional white, with blinding fluorescent lighting. A thick rectangle of glass between their room and the inmate's room was all that separated incarceration from freedom. Two heavy black telephones, circa 1950, sat on each side of the counter by the glass.

A beefy jailer escorted Luke to his seat in the room across from them. He dropped into the chair and slumped over the countertop in front of him, forehead on his knotted fists.

Leah and Beverly looked at each other for a moment, mute with worry.

Beverly leaned in and tapped the glass with her ragged nails. "Luke? Honey?"

Luke huffed and pulled back. He said something unintelligible and then dropped his head again. After days of soul-crushing sorrow, Luke's selfish disregard for their visit stoked a hostile fire in Leah's gut.

"Luke!" Leah banged on the glass, and then caught herself when she remembered there were rules against it. She picked up the phone and barked into the receiver. "Luke!" She could hear her muffled voice on the other side of the glass, but he didn't move. "Hey! Dammit, Luke! We came here to support you!" Beverly patted Leah's arm, trying to shush her, but nodded in agreement.

Luke, still slumped with his head on his hand, pulled the phone off the receiver and held it to his ear. Leah held the phone out so her mother could hear.

Then Luke finally looked up at them, which made Leah wish he didn't. His face was gray. Empty. And vacant . . . a ghost of her brother. Beverly gasped and she reached out and petted the glass. "Oh, darling . . ."

"Don't visit me," he grumbled. "I don't know you." He looked directly at Leah when he said it, and suddenly she was grateful for the glass between them.

"I didn't want to," Leah snapped, her own anger stirring the abundance of bitter acid that had been pouring into her stomach for the past five days. His eyes slid away but focused on nothing.

"Oh, now, you two, no fighting. We need to stick together. We Dancos always do. It's always been us against the world." Here was the drama Leah had been waiting for, as if *they* were the ones on the righteous end of this battle.

"*We're* not in anything together," Luke muttered, glancing at Leah again. "You need to leave." He stood and slumped against the door, his head heavy.

"Luke, no!" Beverly wailed. "You aren't alone! We're here for you no matter what, and we're gonna find a way to prove your innocence." Luke was standing by the door, hands shackled to his waist. His head snapped back at the word innocence, and his eyes rolled back for a second. Then the jailer was there, opening the door and escorting Luke back to his cell. And Beverly dissolved into loud, wailing sobs.

chapter nineteen

AFTER THE TECTONIC SHIFT in her life, going back to work felt at once comforting and impossible. Leah took a long time to get dressed that morning, slowed by the discovery of Luke's clothes mingled with hers in the dryer. It felt like a death, losing her brother to his unbearable crime. The reminders of Luke around her house ripped open the wound every time she turned around. Even his favorite ice cream in the freezer–strawberry, the usual choice of little girls and grandmas–knocked the wind out of her. When Leah looked for toaster waffles for breakfast, that pastel pink carton had positioned itself in her way, so Leah snatched it and tossed it in the sink. That unleashed a fury of Luke-cleansing, so she stomped around the house gathering his smelly workboots, his denim jacket, and all of his toiletries. She piled everything on his bed and slammed the door.

With dripping wet hair, Leah slid on the sandals closest to the back door, grabbed her keys and purse and ran for her car like she was evading a predator. She drove through McDonalds and ordered a sausage muffin that she inhaled in five bites and the largest Diet Coke money could buy. As she walked up the steps to her building, she was greeted by a new poster warning of the hazards of giant sodas. It took all of her energy not to hurl her delicious Diet Coke at the freckle-faced poster girl gazing at her carton of skim milk.

Maddie greeted Leah at the reception desk with an anxious frown and a lingering hug. "It's gonna be okay, girl," Maddie whispered in her ear. With parents who were known as Terrance's "gentle dentists," Maddie grew up with privilege and joy. Leah usually enjoyed Maddie, but her pitying hug made Leah want to push her down. Not a good start to the day.

The day took an even more serious downturn when Max met her in the hallway and asked her to join him in his office. His look should have warned her, but she chose to ignore the ominous set of his jaw and the anxious curl of his shoulders.

"What's up, Max?" she asked with as light of a tone as she was capable.

He sat on the edge of his desk looking especially like Barack on a casual day in the White House. "How are you, Leah?"

"Fine, Max."

Max rubbed his hands together, shifting and squirming. He was a great boss, supportive and smart, but he was also a shy introvert at heart, and sometimes he couldn't get his words out. "Leah." He began again.

"Max." Leah's heart sped up as she finally recognized that she was in trouble. She had missed work for three days without calling in because she was on a bender in a hotel room. "Just say what you need to say."

He closed his eyes. "I need to put you on disciplinary probation."

Leah let the words wash over her. While she wasn't fired yet, it was a step toward dismissal. Max looked sick, which hurt more than anything. "Okay," she said, avoiding his eyes. "I get it."

Max pulled himself off the desk, fell into his chair, and slid a blue form across the desk. "Probation Plan" was printed on the top in bold type, followed by several lines of instructions.

1. *The Employee will complete a chemical use evaluation and follow all recommendations*
2. *The Employee will attend at least 6 sessions of individual therapy.*
3. *The Employee will be removed from all case-related duty until her therapist determines that she is fit for client interaction.*
4. *After returning to case related duties, the Employee will have weekly supervision meetings to review job performance.*
5. *Failure to make satisfactory progress on this plan will result in termination.*

Leah clenched her jaw to hold back the career-ending tirade ready to fly out of her mouth.

"I know," Max said, rubbing his hands across his hair. "I'm sorry, Leah. This was out of my hands."

Leah looked up and squinted. "What does that mean?"

Max considered for a moment. "Leah, I'm going to be completely honest with you because that's the kind of person you are, and that's what you deserve." Leah nodded. "This situation with your brother is terribly tragic and painful for you. I fully recognize that. But it's also a mess for us. This was your case, Leah."

"Do you really think you have to remind me of that?" Leah snapped. "Do you think I didn't know?"

"Of course," Max said. "But I know how much you care about the kids on your caseload. And realize, please, that this trial could fall apart because of suspected or perceived improprieties on the part of Social Services."

"*Improprieties?*"

"This was your investigation, and it took a long time for law enforcement to make an arrest–"

"Are you freaking kidding me?" Leah spat, and then caught herself again because he was her boss, a fact she kept forgetting. "How can that have anything to do with me?"

"None of it has anything to do with you, but it's going to become all about you. It was *your* interview and *your* investigation. *Your brother* was arrested after the evidence was found in *your* house when *you* turned him in." After he put it that way, Luke's anger during their jail visit yesterday made sense. Luke thought it was about her, too.

Max let out an exhausted huff. "You are all over this, and there are a hundred ways for people to suspect that this investigation was improper."

"So you are trumping up a way to get me away from this case? And any case?"

Max glared. "We don't have to trump up anything. That's the thing, Leah. You left me no choice. You missed three days work without calling in because you were intoxicated in a hotel room. No one could find you. You made our department's situation ten times worse. I had to do some fast talking for you to keep your job."

Leah felt she left her body for a moment, an unconscious act of self-preservation that kept her from screaming obscenities that would have gotten her fired. Instead she was disoriented, almost dissociative, and couldn't find any words at all.

Max handed Leah a pen, and Leah signed the probation plan. He gave her a copy of it and a scheduling card for her first therapy appointment later that day.

"What am I supposed to do until then?" she asked in a monotone she had never heard from herself before.

"We need all the outdated adoption files scanned and catalogued," Max said, with painful false cheer. "Brian from IT can set you up down there–"

"In the basement?" Leah interrupted.

"Uh, yes, the basement file room," he said, still chipper, all business now.

Relegated to the basement. It seemed about right.

PROVING HOW MUCH TROUBLE she had to be in, Max had found a way for her to start therapy later that day. The Peaceful River Counseling Center was located in an office building on Riverfront Street. The counseling center took up half the second floor, and the waiting area had a whole wall of windows overlooking the Apple River.

Leah sat in a chair by a set of shelves full of educational toys. A woman in her twenties sat across the room texting while her four-year-old son ripped the pages out of a Dr. Seuss book. Leah had resigned herself to sitting through her six mandatory appointments, looking as normal as possible, and that would be that.

The first wrench in that plan showed itself when her smoking-hot therapist walked out and announced her name: "Leah D.?" He was rugged, broad shouldered, and had a permanent grin, which he flashed at Leah as she stood to greet him. "Hello," he said and he shook her hand. "I'm Nick Rhodes." His hand was warm, his handshake strong, and Leah was glad no one but the receptionist could see how red her face was.

She followed him back to his office, which was covered with photos of Nick scaling mountains, whitewater rafting, swimming with dolphins. His hair was white-blond in the photos, his bare chest tan, washboard abs . . . good lord. Maybe it was the trauma of the last week, but she was exhausted and had completely lost her ability to cover her adolescent, hormonal reaction. Nick motioned for her to sit on one of the deep-brown, overstuffed leather chairs. Leah sat across from Nick and his startling blue eyes.

"So, Leah, I just need to review some data privacy forms with you, get your signature on some consents, that type of thing." He shuffled through a stack of papers.

"Oh, I know all about data privacy," Leah said with a stupid giggle, the first of any kind that had left her lips since Luke's arrest. "I do this all the time."

"You go over client's rights?"

"Yep. Social work, you know . . ."

Nick nodded. "Of course. I saw that in the referral material."

Leah cringed. "Ha. Referrals. Usually I'm the one sending out this information."

Nick smiled kindly, the toothy kind of grin he might give his grandmother. They reviewed the forms and then Nick put them in a manila file and sat back in his chair.

"So how does this go?" Leah asked. "I've got work to get back to."

"Do you?" Nick asked, his tone implying that he knew exactly what kind of work was waiting for her back at Terrance County. He sat back and smiled, crossing his legs with quad muscles that bulged through his rather tight jeans. "Well, this was a personnel referral. We're supposed to do some testing, talk about the relapse, and make treatment recommendations." He was maddeningly blunt as he pulled some other forms out of his file.

"Huh," Leah said, eyeing his new paperwork. "Is that what you can usually get done in six appointments?"

"Well, I guess it takes as long as it takes," Nick answered, becoming less endearing by the minute.

"Well I don't have time for any more than is absolutely required." She recrossed her legs and clamped her hands tightly, fighting the tone out of her voice.

Nick held his hands in the air. "We just met each other. I really can't evaluate how long it will take. At least not yet."

His chippy attitude was ticking her off, but everything had that effect on her these days. "I'm sorry, Nick. I know this isn't your fault, but it'll be a cold day in hell before I do more than the required six sessions. I'll take care of it with my boss." She attempted a smile that came across like she was baring her teeth.

"Hmmm," Nick said, making a note on his file.

He was "handling" her, which made her want to smack him. "'Hmmmm' what?"

He set his notebook down and patronized her with his grin again. "Leah, I'm sure this is not where you want to be right now. But you are in a job where you have contact with very vulnerable people, and you are in a rather . . . vulnerable position yourself. I need to do an evaluation, and to do it properly I need three to five sessions, and then there could be more sessions from there. You have to follow laws all the time. I'm sure you can understand."

"Yep, I can understand, *Nick*." She said with too much attitude. Leah reined herself in and found a softer voice. "But I don't want to waste your time. Or mine. What's the point of all those meetings anyway? I'm *fine*."

"Thanks for your concern for my time," Nick said, tilting his head like Oprah during a "very special" interview. "I appreciate that. But this is my job, so I don't want you to worry about how much time we spend together. My focus is on you."

"Well, whatever then," she snapped. Nick was never going to let her off the hook, so she was going to have to take care of the issue with Max. At least their discussion had used up a few minutes. "Let's just get this done."

"That's the spirit!" Nick held her gaze a moment too long. Leah looked away. "So I'd like to start with some questions about you . . . Who is Leah?"

Leah couldn't believe she found this idiot attractive less than five minutes ago.

She bared her teeth again. "Leah is a social worker with a messed-up family who made a mistake with a bottle of whiskey. And, well, here we are, with you asking probing questions and me counting the minutes until I can get out of here."

"Hmmm," Nick said, making another note in his file, probably something about mood swings. "Was that really a probing question?"

"All personal questions are probing," she said with an irritated sigh.

"Really? You don't like to talk about yourself? Some people love to talk about themselves."

"Not me."

"Hmmm."

Oh, God, this is getting annoying. Nick squinted out the window, pondering his next question. Leah let the silence sit between them. Silence was a great way to get the fifty minutes over with.

"So . . . bats, huh?" Apparently Max had made a very thorough referral. Leah took a deep breath for the first time in their session and told herself to quit reacting or she would never be done with therapy.

"Yep. Bats." Leah raised her eyebrows at him. *Next question?*

"That had to be pretty awful. A lot of people don't like bats."

"I don't like them near my *head*," Leah said, biting off her words. She couldn't actually remember them flying toward her, but she was told that was what happened. She couldn't recall any of the incident, which was disconcerting, but she hadn't let herself think about it.

"I don't think anyone would," Nick said. "How traumatic."

"Uh huh." Nick squinted at her. Leah suspected she was getting on his nerves just a bit, which improved her mood.

"Do you think about the incident a lot?"

It seemed unwise to discuss the bat dreams that had been making her leap out of her bed. And she really didn't want to share that her last dream included her dad watching the bats swarm around her until he turned and wandered away from her, slowly dissolving into a pile of dust. "Nah," Leah said with a tone so light she surprised herself. More mood swings. "It was a bad day at work, that's for sure. But it got me a two-week vacation, so I can't complain. Why are we talking about that whole thing, anyway?"

"We're here to deal with whatever might have lead to your relapse so we can get the support you need to stay sober and get back to work." Nick was making some notes in her file and paused for a second. "And to be honest, I thought it might be easier to start with the bats."

"Well, that sure is a bad sign when getting swarmed by flock of bats is the least of the traumas in your life." She planted a smile on her face and figured she had wrapped up the session nicely.

"Hmmm," Nick said, holding eye contact with her until she looked away again.

"So, anything else?" Leah asked, hands on her thighs, ready to hop up and end this awkward hour.

Nick chuckled. "It's only been ten minutes, Leah."

Leah gritted her teeth.

"How about if we get started on that testing," Nick said, apparently giving up on conversation. He set her up in a small room adjacent to his office with a couple of written tests designed to identify signs of an ongoing mental health disorder.

Leah was expected to spend the next ninety minutes answering whether she *never, occasionally, sometimes, frequently* or *always* had experiences like: "At times I have fits of laughing & crying that I cannot control" and "My soul sometimes leaves my body." Leah answered most questions with never or occasionally and understood a little better why her clients were so angry with their social workers. When she got to "Evil spirits possess me at times," she broke into a fit of uncontrollable, hysterical giggles. Tears spilled onto her computer form, smudging the sheet full of dots she was filling with her Number 2 pencil. At the item, "I have a cough most of the time" Leah's laughter inexplicably morphed into coughing, which only made her laugh harder at her descent into madness.

When finally dismissed, it was nearly 4:00. Leah was exhausted. An already horrible day, the worst part was that she was still fighting the urge to buy more whiskey. Leah drove straight home, threw her keys on the counter and went to bed.

> *Little man was an ass. He used his uncle for his own gain, thinking he was hot shit, but he was just a cog in the wheel. Little man was selfish. Always taking, and never playing anymore. But Uncle had found a new game, and it was time to find some new players.*

chapter twenty

BASEMENT DUTY, AS LEAH came to call it, fit her life as it was. Closed files were kept in a dungeon-like room in a lower level corner of the 100-year-old social services building. With sweating pipes and stone floors, Leah wanted to bring the general public on a tour of that room just to refute any suspicions of government overspending in Terrance County. To create "office space," someone had laid a swatch of old carpet across half of the room, dragged in a beat-up desk from the fifties, and set up a lamp that cast a bluish glow to complete a prison-like feeling.

Leah's new office also had its own odor of musty paper, damp iron, and a faint cloud of sewer gas, which merged into a stink that matched her shame. The days took on a new dreary routine, with Leah heading straight for her gulag every morning without visiting her coworkers (or were they former coworkers now?). Every morning she bought the biggest Diet Coke available at the local gas station and made herself a buffet of hard candy, chocolate, and some token fruit to prove she hadn't completely given up. She had a recovering addict's craving of sugar, so she always kept a variety of sweets close by. Plus it was impossible to focus on the tedium without the distraction of a treat every few minutes, much like the pigeon in a Skinner box pecking for a pellet of food.

The job involved taking apart thick files and scanning each section page by page. Then on her computer she dragged and clicked the files into a digital filing system that would be the case's permanent storage. Other files simply needed to be shredded because they had completed the required time for retaining files. It was tedious work, but it wasn't mindless. If Leah stopped paying attention, she found herself putting electronic files in the wrong areas and creating messes that she had to backtrack and redo.

Within a few days she found a rhythm with the work, and discovered the hours passed more quickly when she read snippets of the files she was scanning and shredding. She read about a stepdad molesting his teenage daughters, a prostitute giving birth to a crack-addicted baby, and file after file of kids with slap marks on their faces or bruises shaped like belt buckles on their young bottoms. It was cathartic to shred each file after she had read and scanned it, like she was somehow undoing the wrongs, destroying the evidence, and helping the victims move on.

After shredding a particularly heinous garbage house case, Leah remembered with surprise that it was Friday. Many of her coworkers enjoyed going out for lunch on Fridays, lingering over iced teas in the summer and heavy-flavored coffees in the winter. She felt unworthy to join them, so she ate wheat thins and junior mints at her desk alone while imagining Zoe having a Caesar salad and Amanda ordering a cheeseburger and fries like she did when she was stressed.

The afternoon brought educational neglect, sibling sexual abuse, and chronic meth addiction. Leah read the entire report of the meth mom's quest to get new teeth and her kids back, in that order. She succeeded at the first, failed at the second.

Leah began to see her job with an outsider's eyes. The soupy, tragic mélange of trauma, narcissism, and loss felt like it filled the room with its own stench. Leah had spent years tolerating people's cringes and grimaces when they learned what she did for a living. "Child protection," they would say with a shudder. "How terrible." Now the shuddering was her own.

It was nearly 3:00 p.m. when Leah pulled out what she decided would be her last file of the week. It was thin, so she would work slowly and make it last. But when she saw the names, Leah's stomach dropped.

Perpetrator: April Danscher

Victim: Amanda Danscher

Leah glanced up at the door, afraid she would get caught. She closed the file and pressed hard with both hands, like that gesture could keep her friend's secrets inside. It was her job to shred this file. To read it felt wrong.

Leah opened the file and peeked at the first page with identifying information, noting with surprise that the Danscher's address was listed as the Grafton homeless shelter.

Since her history had been so dramatically exposed last year in court, Amanda had been opening up more about her past. When Amanda and Leah visited a family in a shelter in the tiny town of Grafton, Amanda shared that she had actually lived there a few different times when she was growing up. They had always been poor, Amanda had said, but there were times her mother could barely function and they would eventually end up in the shelter.

But even though Amanda had been more upfront about her painful childhood, reading the case file about an investigation into Amanda's family was different—more personal and invasive.

With all that moral discomfort, Leah thought it should have taken longer than thirty seconds before her curiosity compelled her hand to open the file.

Cathy Phillps called to express concern about fourteen-year-old Amanda Danscher, who is a ninth grader at Apple Falls High School. Amanda maintains A's and B's despite what her teachers call a choatic lifestyle with little supervision or support. Amanda and her mother are currently staying at the Grafton shelter. Staff are very concerned because Amanda recently disclosed that her mother was diagnosed with stage three ovarian cancer, and it does not appear there are any family members who can support Amanda and her mother. Furthermore, Ms. Phillips is aware there is a history of substantiated neglect. Ms. Phillips is hoping a social worker can be assigned to the family to offer support. A review of past records confirms neglect was substantiated against April Danscher when her mother's boyfriend used and possessed items used for the manufacture of methamphetamine in Amanda's presence. This case was staffed with the child protection unit and it was determined that, while it does not rise to the level of a child protection intervention at this time, a social worker will contact the family under the child welfare program.
–This worker spoke with April Danscher, who said she did not need any help "from the government" and Amanda could take care of her "just fine." This case will close. –Roberta

Leah closed the file, wishing she could close yet another can of worms she had just opened. Amanda had probably lived in a meth lab. She had never shared or acknowledged that she had experienced actual maltreatment. Leah knew her own life could have warranted social services involvement. But Amanda's actually did.

It was Leah's job to shred this file, but Leah sat, her hands still resting on the cool, smooth cover. The file was deceptively neat, its twenty or thirty pages carefully stacked, hole-punched, and clipped into labeled sections. What an oxymoron to the mess that lay inside.

Leah tucked the file in between two adoption files that had to be kept permanently. It didn't feel right to shred Amanda's file, but she wasn't ready to do anything else about it, either. Leah gathered her piles of treats, snapped off the lights, and left.

A FEW HEAVY SPRINKLES splatted on her car, but weren't enough to flush away the milky streaks of splattered bugs adhered to her windshield. It had been a terrible day ending a miserable week, but the worst was yet to come. As part of the insulting chemical use evaluation for her probation plan, she agreed to attend AA at least once a week. The week was ending, and the choice was to allow AA to ruin her weekend or just to get the dreaded hour over with.

Killing two birds with one stone, she decided to attend the meeting with her mom. Not only did it allow her credit for seeing her mom, but she could pretend she was just accompanying her mom instead of attending because she had to. Leah pulled into her mom's apartment complex and steeled herself against the crazy that was about to come. Coolie was sitting on Beverly's front step in a mustard yellow bathrobe hanging open to reveal a dingy undershirt and threadbare boxer shorts. He nodded at Leah and shifted, causing the fly of his boxers to hang open and give her a shadowy view of his withered junk. She stayed in her car and forced her face to stay neutral, refusing to react to his favorite old trick. Another memory of Luke and Coolie flashed through her head, but she pushed it away. She was too exhausted to go there today.

"Carl?" Beverly flung the front door open, almost knocking him off the step. "Carl, is it raining? Where's my umbrella?" Coolie ignored her, reached inside his boxers to rearrange, and left his hand there. Leah's stomach churned.

Leah rolled down her window, refusing to get out and hoping it would help her mom feel rushed. "It's just sprinkling, Mom. Let's get going."

"No," Beverly said, disappearing back inside her house. "I don't want to get soaked." Leah's head dropped. This could take half an hour, and the last person Leah wanted to be stuck with was the horrible Coolie. He unhanded himself and pulled a package of cigarettes and a lighter out of his robe pocket.

"Wanna smoke, kid?" He didn't make eye contact.

"You're always here lately." It was a statement, not a question.

Coolie shrugged. He lit his cigarette and took a long drag, exhaling trails of smoke through his nose like a dragon in a cartoon. With wonderful timing, Beverly opened the door right into Coolie's back, spilling ashes down the inside of his naked, hairy, repugnant thighs. He leapt and swore, and Leah hid her first real smile in weeks.

"Okay, let's go."

"Aw geez, Mom, seriously?" Leah moaned as Beverly stepped around Coolie, still slapping ashes off his legs. Beverly had wrapped herself in a blaze orange plastic hunter's poncho that hung to her knees. "I'll drop you off right in front of the Legion. You'll only be outside for two seconds."

Beverly rearranged the hood of the poncho to cover her face so only her nose and mouth were visible, and started her germaphobe's rant: "Viruses, bacterial meningitis, bird flu, legionnaire's disease, influenza A, B, and C—"

"Never mind. Sorry. Wear whatever you want." Leah knew she had to cut her off quickly. Once her anxiety took hold, the path to panic, hysteria, and extra Xanax was fast and straight. "Do you think Maggie will be there tonight?"

Beverly held the hood tight around her face and half-walked, half-ran to Leah's car. When they were both seated, Beverly ran a soggy tissue over her face and down her hands and fingertips. "No," she finally answered. "Maggie is very busy with the bakery, but we're going there to sample some of her sandwiches after the meeting."

Leah hadn't told her mom about her episode with the whiskey (as Leah had been calling it in her mind), so her official reason for going to AA was "job stress." But spending the evening with her mother and the ever-bubbly, always odd Maggie brought its own kind of stress.

Leah stopped in front of the American Legion bar and double parked in front of a row of pickups to allow Beverly to get out right by the door to the meeting.

"I can't get out here." Beverly's voice was muffled by the shuffling of the enormous plastic poncho/tarp covering most of her body.

"Why?"

"Because I don't want to spend the rest of my life in a wheelchair."

Leah bit back her argument that there were no cars around them and she could easily have made it to the curb. She drove around the block twice, finally edging into a parallel parking spot while Beverly gasped and grimaced with fear that Leah was going to hit the cars around them or the curb. By the time they made it inside, Leah had to force herself to bypass the bar and continue toward the meeting.

Once again, Leah was silent during the entire meeting. The group was large for a Friday night, equal numbers of men and women, most of whom were in their fifties and sixties. Leah watched Cheyenne, a defeated, damaged-looking woman in her forties who was sitting near the coffee. Her face sagged, her eyes were glazed and empty, and her voice was so full of smoke and gravel that when she spoke it sounded like she was choking. Cheyenne gripped the hand of the grandmotherly woman next to her as she described her eleventh day in a row without alcohol, a feat she had not accomplished since she was ten.

When they finally muttered the closing serenity prayer, Leah practically ran for the door, but, as always, Beverly wanted to linger and visit. Cheyenne and Beverly hugged and cried and hugged again. Leah stood by the door fighting the look of disgust off her face.

"Leah Danco, right?" Leah flinched at the sound of her name, especially her last name, at Alcoholics *Anonymous*. She turned to find a familiar face, but her gut told her it wasn't in a good way.

"Just Leah. Remember the whole 'Bill W.' thing?"

"Ooooh, yeah, right. Sorry, Leah." The woman was young and petite, and the corners of her mouth turned down, making her look like she was sad all the time. Leah nodded and tried to step away but the woman persisted. "Do you remember me?"

"Not really. No. Sorry. I'm not good with faces."

"Micah Glasby. You took me away from my parents eight years ago after my stepdad beat the hell out of me." Sadly, Leah still wasn't sure she remembered.

An older man who had relapsed after his wife died turned and put an arm around Micah. "Is this her?"

Micah leaned into the man and nodded. "She's the one."

The man pulled Leah into a terribly awkward three-way hug with Micah. "You saved this little girl's life," he breathed into Leah's ear.

"Oh," Beverly squealed, pushing her way through the folding chairs to join the group hug. "This is so beautiful! I knew all along Micah's savior had to be you. I just knew it!"

"Okay, folks," Leah pulled away abruptly. "We really need to get going . . ."

"I respected your privacy! Do you hear that, hon? I never told anyone that you might have been Micah's social worker." Beverly pulled a small package of tissues out of her purse and handed them to the huggers.

"Are you a social worker?" Cheyenne asked, her face darkening, the room growing quiet.

"Oh. That was the other reason I was respecting your privacy." Beverly's eyes widened, and Leah looked at Cheyenne again, remembering her face but nothing else.

Leah glared at her mother. "We need to leave." Beverly's tried to pout, but Leah held her gaze until Beverly's shoulders dropped, and she followed her daughter back to the street. Leah threw the door open and was ready to run to the car she had to park on the next block, but the rain was coming down in sheets.

"Come on, hon. We can sneak all the way down to Maggie's shop under the canopies." Beverly wrapped her poncho around her shoulders and tightly over her head.

In reality, rainwater poured down to the sidewalk between canopies, so they were still soaked when they arrived at the indulgently named "Maggie's Bakery". Leah cringed at the amateurish painted board that looked like a nine-year-old's sign for a lemonade stand. A paper that said "Opening Soon" was secured to the door with packing tape.

"Hello hello!" Beverly announced and threw open the door. Leah flinched at her mother's squeal and wondered how and why her voice raised a full octave whenever she was with her AA friends. The bakery was still in shambles, with painting supplies strewn about, a dilapidated bakery case against one wall, and a card table and two chairs in the middle of the room covered in paper dishes. Maggie popped up and ambled around the counter so coated in flour she looked like she was ready for the deep fryer.

"Bevvie!" They hugged and giggled and hugged again until they looked like they were both covered in paste. "Look at us! We're making batter with your water and all my flour. I should get some sugar and we'd have doughnuts!" It wasn't funny enough to justify their peals of laughter, and Leah was ready to tell them so when Maggie pulled back and dramatically downshifted. "Oh, it feels good to laugh a little bit through all of this suffering, doesn't it?" Beverly's smile collapsed, and she was back in tears.

"All I do is cry and go to meetings," Beverly sniffed. Maggie held out a chair for her at the lone table, sweeping the paper tableware onto the floor with her stubby arms.

"I know. I know. These trials and tribulations make us strong," Maggie said, rubbing Beverly's back.

Leah wondered what her mother and her friends would say to each other if they weren't allowed to speak in clichés.

Maggie finally turned around and acknowledged Leah. "Come sit, Leah dear," Maggie held her arms out to Leah for a hug, but Leah blocked Maggie's hug with her shoulder and slid into the chair next to Beverly. "Yes. Good! Sit! I'm so excited to feed my first customers." Leah was equally starved and afraid.

Maggie slipped behind the counter and through the doorway to the kitchen with surprising speed and returned with two styrofoam plates. "Here's my special ham and cheese on toast." Maggie clapped and stood over them, looking back and forth between Leah and Beverly.

"Is that raisin toast?" Beverly asked. "Fancy."

Leah took a careful bite. Not terrible. Not great. A little strange with the raisins. But she was hungry enough that she ate the whole thing, which Maggie took as a great compliment. She brought out "homemade" chicken noodle soup that tasted like canned broth and noodles, and then followed with bowls of tomato soup she admitted was from a can but wanted their opinion about whether it was good enough to serve. It was getting dark when Leah said as politely as she could that she was tired and ready to go home.

Maggie followed them to the door and handed them a bakery bag filled with assorted cookies. "One of these days I'm going to bring treats for everyone at the meeting. Everyone works so hard, we deserve some treats, too."

"I think we would all enjoy that." Beverly was smiling, and Leah thought they would actually make it home without drama.

But then Maggie had to ask, "So, have you seen your son?" And with that, Beverly collapsed into Maggie's arms.

"He hates us!" Beverly wailed into Maggie's shoulder. "I've been trying to tell myself he's just sad, or scared, and he doesn't really hate his own mother." Maggie and Beverly held each other and rocked like two seventh graders slow dancing. It was so awkward Leah pulled out her phone and pretended to read an important message.

"Oh, darling." Maggie withdrew herself from Beverly's hug and led her back to the table. "Now, Leah," she began, turning and trying to grab Leah's hands, which Leah kept curled around her phone until Maggie quit trying to touch her. "You are part of that whole system. What's your plan with Luke? What are they telling you?"

Beverly looked up with hopeful eyes. "Yes, hon. What are they telling you?"

"They're telling me to go to the basement," she sighed. "Come on, Mother. We need to go now."

"Go to the basement?" Maggie said. "What does that mean? Are they trying to shut you up? " Maggie stood back with her hands on her thick hips. "False accusations and employee abuse!" she proclaimed. "Bevvie, I think it's time for you to get a family lawyer!"

"Yes!" Beverly announced. "Finally, we're going to do something. Carl says I should just let him go, but he doesn't understand what it is to be a mother. Princess, let's get a lawyer!"

"He *has* a lawyer." Leah rubbed her temples where it felt like a giant set of pliers had been squeezing her skull for the past week.

"No, not one of those. Carl said those public lawyers don't have a clue." Beverly blew her nose with a napkin. "But we can't afford a real lawyer. Even if I sold some of Roger's Star Wars figures, and I'd do it for my boy, it wouldn't be enough."

"Then we'll start a defense fund," Maggie declared.

Beverly gasped. "That's it! A defense fund! We can save him."

Maggie sat down next to Beverly and pulled a pen out of her apron. "We could do a benefit, too. I think Scooty's band would play for free, and we could sell sloppy joes."

"Dina makes those wonderful sloppy joes with the chicken and rice soup!" Beverly beamed. "And it would help get her mind off her last relapse."

"Right!" Maggie announced. "Everyone can benefit from Luke's benefit!"

"That's what we should call it! The Luke Danco Everyone Can Benefit Benefit!" Beverly rubbed her hands together. "We can make some posters . . ."

But then something broke inside Leah. "Are you two out of your fucking minds?" Beverly flinched at Leah's cursing and Maggie's mouth hung open, her hands up in mid-gesture. "You want to have a benefit to raise money for an *accused rapist*. Do you even understand what is happening here?" Leah clutched her head with both hands and tried to squeeze the headache and insanity out.

"I think we all understand," Maggie said in a measured voice she probably used on her former students when they were in the middle of an outburst.

"I don't think you do," Leah said, knowing she was amping up to a level she would probably regret later. "This innocent little girl was violently raped so badly by a sociopath that she needed medical care. *Stitches*. Someone did this to her just for sport. And we know that because he took a 'trophy.' He took her student ID, and God only knows what he was doing with that afterward." Leah clasped her hands together and forced herself to take a step back and calm down. But the words kept coming. "Luke had her student ID. He had the trophy, and they probably did DNA testing on it, and they will probably find that little girl's DNA. And that will be that. He will get convicted and go to Stillwater prison forever, and she will try to patch up her shattered life." The memory of Annika during that morning interview brought up a sob, so Leah turned away and tried to breathe.

Beverly and Maggie were still and silent, Maggie breathing so hard through her nose there was a faint whistle when she exhaled. Leah tried to stuff all that emotion, but she still felt like a volcano spilling lava. Nothing would come back in.

"Well." Beverly's voice was oddly strong. "Someday you'll have children, God willing. And you'll learn a mother knows what her child might do, and what he ain't ever gonna do." Beverly hopped up and banged her hand on the table. "My boy didn't do this, and you should know that too, princess. You're his sister, and should know that Luke never hurt anyone."

Luke had been selling weed, and who knows what else, for years, and he assaulted his one and only girlfriend two year ago after she crashed his motorcycle. He had been raised by drug-addicted, mentally ill parents. The truth was that Leah didn't know what Luke was capable of anymore. But what she had learned about herself was that her loyalty was with Annika, and it both restored her faith in herself and made her feel like she had just lost her brother for good.

The game was new. The players were better. And there was no more coaxing or plying to get what he wanted. He had the power, and they would dance for him.

chapter twenty-one

AUGUST COOLED INTO SEPTEMBER, usually a delightful month in Minnesota. Most days a high breeze rustled the trees, with comfortably warm days and sweatshirt weather by evening. Autumn was short in Minnesota since the first snowfall often arrived in late October, so those glorious, sunny fall days were treasured. With Jake and Amanda's wedding only weeks away, the sunny days were spent planning with some urgency, but Zoe also insisted it was time to party.

Lucy and Zoe had planned a bachelorette party opposite Jake's bachelor party, which had been headed up by Lucy's husband William, Kemp, and some of the county attorneys. Since everyone was a little afraid of Leah and her tenuous sobriety, she had been on the periphery of party plans. When the big day arrived, Leah made up an excuse to avoid going to Lucy's to assemble almonds and mints into tiny mesh bags for wedding favors. Instead she walked in circles at her house, avoiding the cinnamon schnapps, a leftover from Christmas a decade before, knowing that anyone who drank decade-old cinnamon schnapps had to be a hopeless alcoholic. Obsessing about the schnapps . . . she didn't know what that made her.

Leah had just pulled in to Zoe's sprawling driveway when she got a text from Lucy, asking for the fifth time if it was truly okay to go barhopping. Leah texted back, *Knock it off. It's a party,* and then followed with a row of smiley faced emojis to convey her tone was fun, not bitchy and bitter. Leah knew Lucy was still anxious about their newly formed friendship, and she seemed to be terrified of pushing Leah back off the wagon. But it was a bachelorette party, and Leah said the first four times Lucy had asked that there was no way they were going to have it without alcohol just because of her. Lucy, Zoe, Leah, and Jake's two sisters, who were both pregnant and wouldn't be attending, had chipped in for the bus, and there would be close to twenty of them partying all night. She checked her makeup (for some stupid reason she put on mascara and was regretting it already) and headed inside.

"I'm sorry, I think it's going to be too weird to party with Barb Cloud," Zoe said as she drained her glass. Lucy poured her another margarita from the blender pitcher. "Holy God, Lucy. Your margaritas are to die for. How did you learn to do this?"

Lucy's eyes darted to Leah, who was sitting at the counter and had just grabbed her requisite Diet Coke. "It's my heritage, chica," she said with a wink.

"Bring some of that heritage over here," Amanda grinned. Lucy was blending as fast as they could drink them and started another pitcher. It was just the bridal party so far, and Amanda was almost slurring already.

Leah had spent her Saturday telling herself that she was going to be a friendly, fun, sober bridesmaid, but she had been at this party for all of four minutes and wanted to either get drunk or go home. And doing both sounded even better. Zoe slid into the bar stool next to Leah and rested her head on Leah's shoulder.

"Aw, geez, are you drunk already?" Leah asked with a saccharine smile.

Zoe wrapped her arms around Leah and squeezed hard. "I love you." Leah closed her eyes and smiled for real. "This is going to be fun. I promise."

The guests trickled in, everyone in a raucous mood. Zoe was blasting a country playlist she had made especially for the night. Maddie the receptionist arrived wearing a spandex halter top, micro miniskirt and four-inch wedge heels. Unsteady and strangely tall, Maddie wobbled in behind Roberta and Jackie, whose son was staying with her mother so she could get a night out. The three of them gratefully accepted tequila shots with salt and lime, and they licked, drank, sucked, and hooted for joy.

Barb Cloud and Jill arrived holding hands, and Leah couldn't keep herself from staring. Barb was nearly fifty and had always been a polished but bland politician. Jill was a hockey mom with an eye for style but never used to take the time. Since Jill and Barb started dating, they had evolved into a stunning power couple, their happiness stoking the glow. Jill was wearing a black halter maxi dress with beaded silver earrings, and her hair was effortlessly piled on her head. Barb wore perfectly cut dark jeans that had to cost several hundred dollars with a black tank top and black patent peep-toe heels. Dressing up for Leah meant a coat of mascara, and she hadn't considered wearing anything other than jeans and v-neck t-shirt. Even worse, her usually frizzy hair had seized into a brittle blonde pompom around her head. She felt like a buffoon.

Amanda was radiant in a strapless silver cocktail dress and sky-high heels. "My husband-to-be is five-foot-seven. This was my only chance to wear heels!" she announced. Zoe tapped on her wine glass with a fork and got the group's attention.

"Maddie is circulating with glasses so we can toast our beautiful bride before we head out," Zoe announced. She and Lucy stood on either side of Amanda in front of the fireplace, and Leah felt a surge of jealousy standing in the back of the room next to the ficus tree. As the other bridesmaid, she belonged up in front of the group, but they seemed to have planned the entire night without her.

"Here, hon." Maddie had a tray of crystal shot glasses filled with clear alcohol, except for the one that had some kind of dark liquid. "Diet Coke, just for you!" Maddie squeezed Leah's hand and kept moving through the group. She was well intentioned but patronizing. Leah wanted to dump her drink in the ficus.

Lucy held her glass in the air: "To my dearest friend Amanda, who taught me how to be strong." Lucy's eyes glistened and she beamed at her friend.

"Boo!" Leah blurted. "This is a bachelorette party! Bottoms up! *L'chaim*! Let's party!" It sounded funny in her head, but the stunned silence of the group showed her she went too far. Zoe's eyes flashed a warning before she stepped in.

"Thank you, bridesmaid and party girl Leah!" Zoe announced, holding her glass out. "To Amanda!"

"Amanda!" they echoed and drank. Leah held her glass out and then shot the ounce of Diet Coke, desperately wishing she could just go home.

BARB CLOUD HAD HER FIFTH shot of the night at Crabby Bill's, the bar Leah and Kemp went to during their July Fourth boat trip. The only evidence of her intoxication was the slight upturn of the right corner of her mouth, especially when Jill put her arm around her. The group overtook two long tables by the dance floor, and Leah found herself seated between Maddie and Jill.

"It's not that I've never loved anyone before," Jill slurred, her hair wild around her pink cheeks. "But it's just that it's this crazy, intense, totally real thing now. I thought I loved my husband. At least in the beginning . . ."

"Jilly, is this really the time to talk about the collapse of your marriage?" Leah asked. Her mood had improved only slightly in a room full of drunkards.

"It's a great time to talk about how much I adore my girlfriend!" Jill's eyes sparkled.

"I've never felt that way about anyone." Leah said it under her breath, knowing it consciously for the first time the moment she said it.

"You were screwing Kemp for months. He's hot! Why don't you love him?" Jill caught Barb's eye across the table and winked at her. Barb gave a slight nod and half grin.

"I don't think I know how," Leah muttered to herself, slumping in her chair.

The DJ started playing "Paradise by the Dashboard Light" by Meatloaf. Their table cleared of everyone but Leah and Barb. The group made a circle around Amanda, who had been getting free drinks all night and looked woozy. Barb got up and made her way around the table to sit by Leah.

"Hi, Leah." Barb kept her eyes on the dance floor, where Jill was jumping, singing, and sweaty.

"Yo."

"How are you doing?" Leah looked sideways at Barb. They were not friends. Barb was not friends with anyone at the county, but now that she was Jill's girlfriend she seemed to want into the group.

"I'm fine." It was a complete lie, but as she had been reminded more than once that night, it was a party.

"You can't be fine," Barb said. "You're faking it, and not very well."

Leah turned to face Barb. "You shouldn't even talk to me. You're prosecuting my brother. This could backfire on you in a hundred ways."

Barb folded her hands in front of her face. "We work in a small town in a small county in a small state. I'm at a party, and I'm chatting with a coworker. I can talk to you."

"Is he guilty?" Leah blurted. The words hung in the air, and Barb exhaled hard.

"People always think the law is black and white. That guilty and not guilty are the only two options."

"Way to dodge the question, counselor," Leah said, leaning right into Barb's ear to be heard over the music. The group on the dance floor sang along as Ellen Foley belted out to Meatloaf: "*Stop right there! I've got to know right now . . .*"

"You know, every generation thinks they invented this song," Barb said. "It came out when I was in high school, and my prom date could sing the whole thing. All eight minutes. All my classmates gathered around him and cheered him on. He dropped to his knees by the end." Barb pulled a long swallow of her beer. "That's when I knew I liked girls."

Leah laughed out loud. "Where did you go to high school?"

"I went to a small private Catholic school in the middle of Wisconsin. The nuns were furious about the prom and did everything they could to stop it, but we were like the kids in *Footloose* and wouldn't be defeated."

"My prom date was my ex-husband. I wish someone would have warned High School Leah about the epic proportions of that mistake," Leah sat back and finished her third Diet Coke of the night. "Maybe I should give girls a try. I seem to have terrible taste in men."

"No, you don't," Barb said, turning to look at Leah. "Pete Kemper is a good guy when he's not being an arrogant ass. What happened with you two?"

The song ended and their group swarmed the table, grinning and sweaty.

"Oh, my God, I need water," Amanda said, falling into her chair. Lucy hopped up and went to the bar, returning with a pitcher of water and a stack of plastic cups.

Jill downed a glass of water and sat on the other side of Barb. "Fix my hair? I was so cute a few hours ago and now I'm a disaster." Barb pulled the pins out of Jill's hair and rearranged it into a high ponytail, patting Jill's back softly when she was done. The simple, intimate gesture brought tears to Leah's eyes.

Zoe sat on Leah's lap, sloppy and sweaty. "Come dance with us!" Then she gasped. "Are you crying? What happened?" Leah shook her head. Barb turned back to Leah.

"Leah and I are guarding our stuff," Barb announced. "You gals go ahead." Zoe began to protest until an old Backstreet Boys song came on. They all squealed again.

"I loooooved Kevin!" Zoe announced, and the table cleared, leaving Barb and Leah and a pile of purses.

"Kemp is a good guy," Barb repeated.

Leah shook her head. "I'm destined for the single life," she said, trying to sound light.

"No, you're not. I used to tell myself I was going to be single forever, but the truth was I didn't want to take a chance on anyone."

Leah let herself say what she had been thinking for weeks, or really for most of her life. "Relationships aren't worth it. They never work. Or at least not for me."

"Come on, Leah . . ."

"No. I'm serious. Look around. Max and Kristine are splitting. Amanda's going nuts with the wedding plans and she's not even married yet. Zoe and Sam are having trouble," Leah caught herself before she said too much.

Barb shook her head. "Amanda and Jake are wonderful together. Zoe and Sam will get it figured out. Relationships are messy and they go up and down, but that doesn't mean they're not worth it."

"No offense, Barb, but this is coming from the woman who was mostly single for the first fifty years of her life."

Barb raised her eyebrows. "That's all you know."

They sat without talking for a moment, watching their friends singing nineties ballads arm in arm.

"Did he do it, Barb?"

"We evaluate every case and weigh the evidence—" Barb said.

"I'm not your constituent. I want to know what *you* think." Leah sat with her arms crossed, aware of how afraid she was of Barb's answer.

Barb paused. "Yes. I think he probably did it." She looked away.

Leah tilted her head. "Probably? What does that mean?"

Barb's face darkened, realizing she slipped. "I mean that I'm not a judge or a jury, and I wasn't there. But we had more than enough to charge him. You know how this works." Barb reached for her water and downed the whole glass.

"Yeah, I know how it works."

A slow song started, and the crowd scattered again. The dockside door opened near the back of the bar and let in a crowd, and suddenly they heard a squeal: "Jakey!" Leah could see through the crowd that Jake and his bachelor party had descended on the dance floor, drunk and scooping up women to dance with. Leah felt a hand on her back and got a whiff of Old Spice and sweaty man.

"Wanna dance, babe?"

Leah was ready to say no, and probably should have. But Gordy Hoffbrau dropped his ample girth in the chair across from Leah, and then Toby Jones, the uber-annoying legal assistant from the county attorney's office, sat next to her. Toby said something about the strip club they just left, and Leah hopped up.

"Let's go, Kemper."

He raised his eyebrows. "Hey, I wasn't expecting you to be so eager. Nice." Kemp's hands found Leah's hips and pulled her close. Still in his cast, Leah could feel the hard plaster pressing on her hipbone.

"Not eager. Just trying to avoid Hoffbrau and Toby." Leah couldn't make eye contact with him and was trying to keep some distance between the two of them. They had never danced before, let alone slow danced.

"I'll take it." His well-worn Bon Jovi concert t-shirt was warm, damp with sweat and sticking to his back.

"How were the strippers?" Leah asked, trying to keep her voice light.

"Hard miles on those gals. I think I've investigated at least a couple of them." He was several inches taller than Leah, but she was still close enough to see that his bottom teeth were crooked. She had never noticed before.

"Don't act like you weren't into it. I'm sure you were buying lap dances for everyone." He also had a scar under his chin. In all the times they had been together, had she never looked at him up close? She felt like she was seeing him for the first time.

"Oh, I was all ready to be into it, and I did buy Jake his lap dance. But you know how the girls start out with g-strings or something and then take it all off?"

"I've never been to strip club, so no."

"Seriously?" he pulled back to look at her face.

"Women don't go to strip clubs, Kemp."

"Sure they do! There's always a few chicks in there." Leah shook her head and Kemp continued with a grin. "Well, anyway, the girls start out wearing something and pretty soon they're bare-ass naked."

"I would assume that's how it goes, yes."

"These girls were shaved bare. Completely bare, like a little girl," Kemp grimaced. "All I could think of was all the pedophiles I work with, and that dad a few years ago who made his daughters shave completely bare down there. Remember that case? This Brazilian waxing shit has just got to end. Seeing that totally wrecked my night."

"Yeah, well, I bet it didn't wreck anyone else's." Looking around the dance floor, Lucy and Will were nuzzling, and Jake was sloppy kissing Amanda while she giggled hysterically.

"Jake is such a Boy Scout. Most dudes love a good lap dance, just to get their juices flowing."

"You are such a pig."

"I'm not a pig. I'm a guy," Kemp said, pulling her closer. "But Jake just wasn't into it. We were gonna keep going to clubs all night, but all he wanted to do was find you girls."

"You don't think that's kind of sweet?" Leah said, trying to make herself feel happy for her friend when all she felt was jealous and sad.

"All I'm saying is there's nothing wrong with a little strip club action every once in a while. It keeps things interesting." Leah didn't know what else to say and was distracted by Zoe and Sam, who were dancing a little stiffly, but close. A truce?

"So should I ask how you're doing?" Kemp said quietly. This was the first time they had been together since Luke was arrested.

"No." The song ended. Leah pulled away and went back to the table. Jake and Amanda were standing by the table, Jake's hand on her back to steady her. Lucy was sitting on Will's lap with her eyes closed, half asleep. Zoe and Sam returned to the table, where much of their group looked like they were ready for bed.

"How about we head back to our house for some food," Sam offered, and the most of the group, not accustomed to large amounts of alcohol or late nights, nodded in relief.

LEAH, KEMP, SAM, AND JILL took over in the kitchen. Kemp cracked eggs as well as he could with one arm in a cast. Jill chopped vegetables, ham, and cheese while Sam made omelets, and Leah found an electric skillet and made hash browns and bacon.

Several members of the group declined breakfast and were getting rides home from the party bus driver, so it was mostly county employees plus Will and Lucy who stayed at Zoe's house. Zoe was offering beer and liquor, but most of the remaining guests took water.

Leah noted that Barb Cloud and Gordy Hoffbrau were sitting near the fireplace and seemed to be wrapped up in an intense conversation. Leah studied the two of them: she was polished while he was disheveled; she was attractive while he was unappealing, his eyes small and set deep in his pasty face. They were both highly intelligent—Barb flew through law school and was on her way to a judgeship—Gordy was a master computer programmer and did most of the IT work for law enforcement just because he could.

Leah knew Barb and Gordy were talking about work, and assumed it had to be about Luke. She eyed Kemp, who was focused on his cutting board and wouldn't try to stop her. The next chance she got, Leah grabbed a finished omelet on a plate and walked directly over to Barb and Gordy.

"We can't count on the DNA," Barb was saying, fully back into work mode, which was an odd contrast to her tank top and party hair.

"I've got four guys doing interviews all day long," Gordy said. "Nobody saw anything that day, and—"

Barb noticed Leah and held up her hand. "Hi, Leah." Gordy's head snapped around. Leah was sure she saw an angry look before he nodded his hello.

Leah went back to the kitchen and straight to Kemp.

"I want to talk to you," she said under her breath. Jill looked up from her cutting board and back and forth between the two of them. Kemp looked at Leah's face for a moment, then followed her to the guest bathroom barely large enough for the two of them.

"Everyone's gonna know what we're doing in here, toots." He wagged his eyebrows at her.

"Tell me everything you know about Luke's case," she blurted, not knowing she was going to lay it on the line until the words came out of her mouth.

Kemp's face fell. "I'm off the case. They've got Jordan doing it now. Gordy won't even let them talk about it in front of me." He avoided her eyes.

"What aren't you telling me?"

Kemp chewed on his lip, hands on his hips, and looked down. Leah stared at him, not breaking her gaze or letting him off the hook.

"There's a lot about your brother you probably don't know," he finally said. "He's involved with some real assholes, but he was trying to get out. And then I don't know what happened."

"Are you telling me you were investigating Luke?" Leah clenched her jaw to hold back tears of fury.

"I'm telling you I can't tell you anything," Kemp said. "I'm so sorry about Luke. I really am. But if I gave you inside information about police investigations Luke might use in his defense, I'd get fired on the spot. You know that."

Leah deflated, and she was helpless against her tears now. Kemp reached out for her, but she put up her arm so he couldn't hold her. He ran his hand down her arm and squeezed her hand, but his familiar gesture only made her feel worse.

"What the hell am I supposed to do?" she asked, pulling some toilet paper off the roll and leaning back against the door to wipe her eyes and blow her nose.

"Do you think he did it?" Kemp asked.

Leah looked up at the ceiling, tears that wouldn't stop still running down her face. "I don't know." She shook her head. "The obvious answer should be, 'of course not.' But, God, if that DNA comes back and shows it's him, I don't know what I'll do."

Kemp frowned. "Maybe you just need to get some space from all of this. Just take some time off and get out of town."

"Maybe." Leah ran her hands over her face.

"Why aren't you working on any cases right now?" Kemp asked.

"Don't act like you don't know," Leah blew her nose, and then pointed at him. "With the way things get around in this county, I know you know."

"I've heard you had a few too many cocktails," he said with his stupid grin.

"Not funny."

"I know, babe. I'm sorry." Kemp squinted. "You looking for something to work on?"

Leah looked at Kemp. "What are you talking about?"

"I want to take another look at the case with Ben."

chapter twenty-two

FROM THE SECOND SHE AGREED to go to Kemp's house and revisit the Baby Ben case, Leah questioned her judgment. She was on probation, she told him, and wasn't allowed to work on cases. He asked if she had been *specifically* told not to work on any cases, or just that she wasn't getting assigned any new cases. Leah couldn't remember.

"Do you want to ask permission now or forgiveness later?" he asked. Through the bathroom door they could both hear the party-goers finding their second wind after getting some food.

"I want the chance to ask forgiveness and not just get fired on the spot," Leah replied. But if Luke was convicted of raping her client, Leah couldn't see a future at Terrance County. The realization was terrifying and freeing, so they slipped past their friends, who were just starting a poker game, and Leah drove them to Kemp's house.

Kemp explained his concerns on the way. Once he got past his ego, Kemp admitted the confession bothered him, too. He reviewed the evidence and realized they had almost nothing that tied him to the crime except the lack of evidence pointing to anyone else. At his house, Kemp brought Leah to the dining room table, where he had laid out most of the case file.

But Kemp was drunk, and they both were exhausted. After a few minutes they lost steam and Leah suggested they sleep on it.

When Leah awoke the next morning on Kemp's couch (she had adamantly refused his bed, so he stumbled away disappointed), she knew she had to be the only party-goer without a wicked hangover. That was a definite plus to staying on the wagon. Not to mention the fact she probably wouldn't have slept on the couch if she had been drinking. The thought sent a wave of mixed emotions through her, and she wondered again why she agreed to go to this.

Leah looked around the living room that she had only seen from the front door and understood why, in all of these years as coworkers, and whatever else they were for those few weeks, they never went to Kemp's house.

Older homes in Terrance were often well-maintained treasures, with beautiful woodwork and interesting architecture inside and out. But Kemp's house was still a work in progress, and was just old. The walls were painted a sophisticated gray, but paint cans still sat on a dropcloth in the corner. The handrailing on the staircase was half sanded, piles of dust below the bottom half of the stairs. It was an analogy for Kemp's life—great potential, but kind of a mess.

Just after 9:00 a.m. while Leah was sure Kemp was still snoring in his bed, Leah sat at the table and started shuffling through papers. Two other investigators had interviewed neighbors, and a few of them knew Joe to be an "okay guy" who would play catch with Ben in the yard. Other than occasional fights, Joe and Jenny seemed to be a "normal" couple. Kemp had highlighted Joe's statement about not remembering anything from the previous night, and his eventual confession.

"Hey, babe." Kemp came around the corner from his bedroom and went straight for the kitchen sink. "Aw, shit, my head hurts. I probably didn't need that last pitcher of Ol' Mil." He gulped a large glass of water, and went to the refrigerator and pulled out three hardboiled eggs he started peeling on the counter.

"Gross," Leah said. "Don't you have any real food?"

"Nah." He shoved an entire egg in his mouth. He reached into a cabinet and tossed her a protein bar.

"So, bottom line on this case," Leah said, tearing into the bar. "If Joe didn't do this, who did?"

Kemp moaned, "Can't I eat first?"

"You can talk and eat at the same time. I've seen you do it before."

"Fine," he said, cracking into a second egg. "I've got a theory. But I'm not ready to tell you yet."

"What?" She looked up at and pointed her page at him. "I'm not messing around with this. If you want my help, you better start talking."

He set his egg down in mid-bite. "Please just trust me."

"You expect me to trust you when you won't talk to me? I'm standing here in last night's clothes because you asked for help." Leah felt worse when she looked down at the Diet Coke stain and guacamole crusted down the front of her t-shirt.

"I know. You look hot."

Leah slammed the papers down on the table and headed for the door. Kemp jumped up and stood in front of Leah to stop her. "I'm sorry. I'm sorry. Please don't leave."

"Then quit wasting my time," Leah said.

"Okay, here's the thing. I'm wondering if you'll help me interview Ben's mom again."

Leah squinted. "What? Why?'

"Because I think we're missing something," Kemp admitted. "And I can't interview Joe or Ben, so the next best person is her."

Leah crossed her arms and sat back in her chair. "How do I know what to ask her if you won't tell me what's going on?"

"We're just fishing right now," Kemp said. "We need background. I want to figure out how Joe spent his time, because the guy didn't work. He had to be doing something all day besides taking care of the kid."

Leah folded her hands on her head and considered his offer. "I guess I can go with you," she finally said, feeling that little prickle of excitement that used to come before big interviews. "But you're buying me breakfast first."

Kemp smiled that big-man-on-campus smile. "That's the least I can do."

BREAKFAST EVOLVED INTO an ordeal that started with dropping Kemp off at Jake's to pick up his truck, and Leah stopping at home to shower and change. Kemp followed Leah to her house and made himself at home on the couch. Leah lingered in the shower, remembering his text messages earlier in the summer offering to come over and wash her back. He was good for laughs, and for a moment she wished she could go back to the days when they were both able to keep it light and fun.

"I'm better off alone," she told her showerhead. She crossed the hall to her bedroom wrapped in a towel and caught a glance of Kemp sitting on her couch staring out the window. Ready to harass him for his vacant stare, she remembered her nakedness and kept walking.

"You should have another barbecue," Kemp said as she returned to the living room, her frizz triumphantly tamed with copious amounts of conditioner.

"A barbecue?" It took a second to remember the night he showed up for dinner, and stayed. Leah blushed as she remembered how Kemp cornered her in the kitchen and told her he wanted to "go steady." His wistful smile said he remembered, too. Before he could say anything stupid, Leah grabbed her purse and headed out. Kemp's offer to buy breakfast turned into fast food lunch eaten in the car. They made the familiar drive to St. Paul Children's Hospital, where Ben was now a patient on the rehab wing.

Kemp parked, and they meandered through beige hallways until they finally found the rehab wing. Kemp had called ahead. Jenny was expecting them, so they were ushered through the security doors and back to a conference room near Ben's room. Jenny met them at the door and followed them to the room with two vinyl couches and an overstuffed rocking chair.

"Thanks for letting us barge in like this," Kemp said.

"It's fine," Jenny sighed, sinking into the recliner. Jenny's hair was pulled back into a small ponytail at the nape of her neck, and she wore a forest-green-and-red Minnesota Wild jersey and blue jeans.

"How's he doing?" Leah asked, taking the seat closest to Jenny. "We haven't gotten an update for a while."

Jenny looked away and her chin shook, a marked difference from the calm and peaceful Jenny who had been in court just a few weeks ago. "He still can't walk. It's everything . . . his balance, the bone isn't setting . . . they may send us home pretty soon because he's not progressing like they had hoped. This may be as good as it gets."

Kemp and Leah looked at each other. "I'm sorry," Kemp said. "That's really tough."

"Yeah," Jenny said. "It is."

Leah felt like a manipulative bully for trying to interview her on what was obviously a hard day. She told herself it was for Ben. "Jenny? Are you okay with our being here?"

Jenny shrugged. "I really don't know."

Leah nodded. Honesty was good. "We don't want to add to your stress. If you want us to leave, we'll go."

Jenny looked at her hands, rubbing them together rhythmically. "No," she finally said. "You can stay."

"Thank you, Jenny," Kemp said, his smooth DJ voice returning. "We would like to talk about Joe." Jenny's face darkened, and she looked up at the ceiling blinking back tears. Kemp and Leah exchanged glances.

Jenny looked back at them with tears running down her face. "They're gonna call me as a witness in his trial. Both the prosecutor and Joe's lawyer. I tried to tell them to leave me out of this, but they won't." Jenny reached for a tissue and wiped her eyes and blew her nose. "They both interviewed me for a long time.

I don't know what they were waiting for me to say, but neither one of them seemed happy."

Kemp leaned forward, elbows on his knees. "This case is complicated, and things don't seem to fit together. What we're looking for is a picture of what happened, and usually when you're working a case the evidence you gather comes together in a picture that fits like a puzzle. Good cases have enough pieces filled in that you get a pretty accurate picture of what happened. In this case, it feels like we have about four puzzle pieces when we need a hundred."

"I hate it when you call him a case," Jenny said bitterly. "Your case is my whole life."

"I'm really sorry," Leah said. "You're right. He's not a case. He's your son. He's also part of our job. We're trying to do our jobs so no one else can get hurt the way Ben got hurt."

"I know." She heaved a deep sigh and leaned back in her chair. "What do you want to know?"

Kemp pulled out his pocket recorder. "I would like to record this conversation. Is that okay with you?" Jenny shrugged uneasily but didn't protest, so Kemp took that as a yes. He set it on the table between them and pushed the record button.

"I can't believe this is my life now," Jenny said. "I've never been involved in anything like this, and now I'm in the middle of a big, public court case." She looked up at Leah. "Do you know what I mean?"

Leah wondered if Jenny was being rhetorical or if she knew about Leah's "situation."

Kemp jumped in before Leah had to answer. "We want to try to understand Joe better. Who he is as a person. How he used to spend his time. That kind of thing."

Tears welled up again. "I thought he was a good guy, but what do I know? He was home most of the time. He took care of Benny while I was at work and school. They were buddies. Benny loved him."

"I'm sure he did," Kemp said. "And you told us before that he was a little rough with Ben sometimes."

"Kind of," Jenny said. "Like he'd grab his arm too hard and stuff. But seriously, I did that, too. I mean, nothing that would hurt him or even leave a bruise or red mark or anything." Leah and Kemp both nodded their understanding. "Joe was good with him."

"Are you in contact with Joe?" Kemp asked, and Leah knew she was asking to judge if Jenny was going to be honest. This was easily verified, and Kemp probably already knew the answer even though Leah didn't.

Jenny looked worried. "Yeah . . . I visited him a few times. I thought you knew that."

"I haven't checked for a while," Kemp answered. Leah still couldn't tell if he knew more than he was saying, but Jenny seemed to accept that answer. They were silent and hoped Jenny would elaborate, but she didn't seem to want to talk about their conversations.

Kemp moved on. "So . . . he didn't work . . . what did he do for money?"

Jenny scrunched her face. "What do you mean?"

"Well, most people need to work to pay their bills," Kemp explained. "How did he pay his bills?"

"I paid everything," Jenny said matter of factly.

"Really?" Leah asked. "Rent, utilities, phone bills . . . everything?"

Jenny considered for a moment. "I guess not everything. He paid for his phone because we're not on the same plan. And he buys food a lot." She looked past Leah like she was trying to remember something.

"So where does that money come from?" Leah asked.

Jenny's eyes darted back and forth between Kemp and Leah. They both held her gaze expectantly. "If I tell you something, can I get in trouble, too?" Leah's heart beat faster as she looked at Kemp. He lifted his shoulders, and Leah could tell he was pondering his answer carefully.

"It would depend on what you have to say, to be honest." Kemp began. "But I can tell you that people who are honest and come to us with information do much better than people who are 'caught' for their crimes."

Jenny shook her head quickly. "No no no. I didn't actually do anything, but . . . I knew about it. I want to get a real nursing job if me and Benny can ever get back to a normal life after all of this."

"It's pretty hard to know whether you could be in trouble without knowing what we're talking about," Leah said. From the corner of her eye she could see Kemp give her a warning look not to shut Jenny down. Leah ignored him because it was the truth, and she didn't have a lot of energy to play games.

"I'm pretty sure he was selling weed. A lot of it. And heavier stuff, too." Jenny blurted, avoiding their eyes. "I don't want to get in trouble myself. I never really saw anything, but I knew. We fought about it. And the thing is, he wanted out. He was talking to his brother and trying to get out." Leah didn't find this news earth shattering, but Kemp's whole demeanor changed.

"Jenny." Kemp leaned forward with such intensity that Leah gave him a look telling him to settle down. But Kemp was completely focused on Jenny. "We need you tell us everything you know about Joe's dealing."

Jenny pulled back, her eyes wide and scared. "Is this going to affect my nursing license?" Kemp started to shake his head, but Leah interrupted him.

"It's hard to know how it could affect it," Leah said slowly. "Social workers have licenses, too, and there are some strange things that can get us in trouble. If he was dealing or using around Ben, then that could be a child protection issue if you knew about it and didn't intervene. I'm guessing child protection issues can be a problem for your license, right?" Jenny nodded. "But the truth is, there's going to be so much scrutiny on Joe that this is going to come out one way or another. My experience has always been that if you are straight up with what you know, you'll fare much better than if we find out later."

Jenny seemed to accept this answer, and she shrank, ashamed. "I knew he had to be dealing because he had money. He wouldn't tell me much . . . maybe he was trying to protect me? But he told me he was going to make changes and get his life on track."

"Okay, that's good," Kemp said, his voice higher and faster than usual. "Can you tell me, Jenny, what kinds of things made you think he was dealing? Please be as specific as you can."

Jenny considered. "A lot of little things, I guess. He smoked it in his car every night after Ben went to bed. He used to leave the house for fifteen minutes here and there to 'drop something off.' Um . . . oh . . . He kept a bunch of stuff locked in a box in the closet in our room."

"What kind of box?" Kemp asked for the information he would need for a search warrant.

"It's like this silver lock box you can get at Wal-Mart. But you're not going to be able to open it. I don't know the combination. He would never tell me."

"There are ways we can get around that," Kemp said. "Keep going, Jenny, this is very helpful. What else did you see?"

"Lots of people at our house," Jenny said, but then corrected herself. "Not a lot of people, I guess. But the same seedy people. I just hated it. He had his buddies who would play *Call of Duty* at our house, and that was fine. But then he had these other scumbags who would come over. They would go into the bedroom for ten minutes and then leave."

"Names?" Kemp asked quickly.

"Oh, you know," she said with a wave of her hand. "There are never any normal names. There's one big, fat guy that Joe called Tits because the guy should have worn a bra. J-Pod was another one. Badger, Coolie . . ."

Leah's breath caught, and she made a noise somewhere between a cough and a gasp. Kemp looked over at Leah, his eyes full of question and warning. "Could you identify any of these people?" Kemp asked.

Leah looked back and forth between the two of them. It had become obvious the conversation had taken a significant turn. "I think so," she said slowly. "Why?"

Kemp eyed the recorder. "Jenny, it's important for us to investigate this crime from all angles. We need all the information we can possibly get, and the people Joe was associating with are part of that." It was an answer for the jury, and Jenny seemed smart enough to know there was more to it than that.

"I could identify them," she said again. Kemp nodded, and was processing his next steps. "Anything else we need to know about Joe?"

"I don't know," Jenny said. "I can't think of anything, but I really don't know."

"That concludes our interview at 13:20 hours," he mumbled for the recorder, and then turned it off. "Jenny." Kemp leaned forward, his hands outstretched. "What do you think happened to Ben? Put aside the investigation and what everyone else thinks, and what you think you're supposed to say. What does your gut tell you?"

Jenny shook her head, and her eyes were clear. "That Joe would never hurt Ben like this," she answered without hesitation. "But I've thought about this a lot. And he was the only one there, so he had to have done it, right? He used to smoke after Ben went to bed, and I was gone, so he didn't get the chance to smoke. Maybe he was tweaking . . ." Jenny choked back a sob and recomposed herself. It looked like she had a lot of experience fighting off tears because her face went blank again in seconds. She pulled in a heavy breath and let it out in a huff. "He had to be messed up somehow. Who knows what he could have done if he was messed up?"

Kemp nodded. "Fair enough, Jenny." He stood. Jenny and Leah stood up, too. "Thank you for your time. I hope Ben keeps recovering. He didn't deserve this."

Jenny shook her head and her tears started again. "No. He didn't."

Jenny agreed to show them to Ben's room briefly so they could see him. They followed Jenny in what seemed to be a circle through crazy-making gray hallways until they reached his room. Ben was in bed with no one else in the room. When he saw his mother he reached his arms out toward her, and she laid on the edge of the bed and stroked his hair. He didn't speak, but rested his head on her shoulder and petted her hair. He wore a t-shirt and pajama pants, and the braces on his legs made them look oddly thick when the rest of his body was so small. He was sedate for a two-year-old, but that was probably from all the medication.

Ben was broken but healing, vulnerable but strong. Seeing such strength in a two-year-old was unbearable. But inspiring.

LEAH WAS PREOCCUPIED and distant as she followed Kemp through the maze. He was on his phone scrolling through emails. When they reached the empty elevator bay for the parking ramps, he stopped and turned to Leah.

"You recognized a name back there, didn't you?" Kemp put his arm up on the wall in front of her so she couldn't get past.

Leah stopped in front of him, her head swimming as she was still trying to grasp the significance of what she had heard from Jenny. "What aren't you telling me?"

Kemp clenched his jaw. "I told you, you need to trust me right now. I can't explain everything."

"Well, let me know when you're ready to fill me in, and then we can talk." Leah shoved his arm away and pushed the button for level D of the parking ramp. Kemp pulled away and walked around the elevator bay with his hands clasped on top of his head until the elevator arrived.

They found the car and rode back to town in silence. Leah stared out the window, surrounded by aging buildings she called "skyscrapers" when she was young and visited "the Cities." Kemp took Interstate 94 east out of downtown St. Paul and eventually turned southward, winding through suburbs filled with restaurant chains and big box stores. Finally they were driving through cornfields and cow pastures. Terrance was a town with its own identity, far enough away from the metro not to be considered a suburb. But sometimes Terrance felt like an island, isolated from the outside world but deeply interconnected within itself. In Terrance, neighbors knew each other's business, and it was impossible to get away from the past.

Her mind wandered further, and Leah thought of Coolie. She couldn't remember a time when she didn't hate her Uncle Coolie. He was a fixture in their home, but he was open with his disdain for Leah, and neither parent ever came to her defense. He mocked her frizzy hair, the way her belly protruded, and how she couldn't say her Rs. Beverly would pretend she couldn't hear him, and her dad would sometimes laugh along for a while, eventually telling him to "cool it" when Leah left the room in tears when she was young, and when she told him to "fuck off" when she was older. Leah's language was the only thing that seemed to get a rise out of Beverly, never the verbal abuse.

Leah was twelve years old before she understood what her parents and Coolie were doing with the funny looking glass lamps and the sawed-off metal pipe cigarettes. Leah's way to cope was to leave, but Luke always seemed to be in the thick of it, sitting on one of their laps while they got high. Luke's addiction probably started when he was a toddler, giggling in a haze of marijuana smoke, playing with Star Wars figures. Coolie didn't work, so he would be at their house all hours of the day. He was a babysitter for Luke when Leah was in school and both parents were engaged in their occasional, and always failed, attempts to hold a job. She shuddered at the thought of all that time Coolie had alone with Luke.

As they pulled into town, Leah pondered the meaning of Jenny and Joe knowing Coolie. With his ever-present supply of marijauna, and who knows what else, and his lack of employment, ever, it was suddenly obvious Coolie was dealing. Leah felt stupid she didn't figure it out long ago.

If Joe had associations with Coolie, it probably meant that Joe was dealing, too, or at least that Coolie was Joe's dealer. Kemp seemed to think that was significant, but Kemp also wasn't talking.

They wound through the updated sections of town, past the busy downtown area, and then over the railroad tracks and into Leah's older neighborhood. Most of the time she didn't give her neighborhood a thought, but today it was another reminder she wasn't so different from the families they investigated. Joe and Jenny lived blocks from Leah in a tiny, rundown rambler just like her own. Kemp pulled into her driveway, killed the engine and looked over at Leah with his arms wrapped around the steering wheel.

"I'm sorry I can't say more." He did look sorry, which stirred up a confusing array of emotions in her.

"Why did you want me to come along?" She was so confused that she didn't want to look at him, so she stared out at her yellowed, neglected lawn. Another failure.

"I don't know . . ." he said. "I wasn't sure what we'd get from her, so I wanted to be prepared for anything. And, I guess, I wanted a witness."

Leah exhaled and leaned back in the seat. "But you won't even tell me what I witnessed." Her anger crumbled, leaving behind smothering fatigue.

"If you don't know, then I definitely can't tell you," Kemp said, the sympathy back in his voice.

"I hate my life," Leah breathed, and climbed out of the car. She didn't see Kemp reaching for her and then pulling his hand back, as if he thought better of it.

KEMP WATCHED LEAH go inside, and then pulled out his cell and dialed a number.

"Yeah?" Jake answered.

"I wanna talk to you." Kemp said as he backed out of Leah's driveway with one hand on the steering wheel. "I have a theory."

"Never a good thing," Jake said.

"Shut it," Kemp said. "Listen to me. I think we're looking this case all wrong."

"Which one?" Jake asked. "Joe? Or Luke?"

"Both."

chapter twenty-three

LEAH WALKED INTO the Terrance County Social Services building on Monday morning to find her coworkers gathered in a clump around Max trying to plead her pathetic case.

"How long is Leah going to have to stay in the basement?" Zoe whined. As soon as Leah heard her name, she pulled back and hovered in the entryway, out of sight.

"Seriously." That was Amanda. "It's like she's in time-out. It's humiliating."

"You know I can't talk about this with you gals," Max said so softly Leah could barely hear him.

"At least let us know when she can get back to work," Jill said. Leah cringed as she realized most of the staff were there. "I can't do all the investigations forever."

"I know. We may need to get a temp in here—"

"What?!" Roberta groaned. "A temp? How long do you plan on leaving her down there?"

Leah's stomach rolled at the word "temp."She couldn't stand it anymore, so she walked down the hall with as much dignity as she could muster.

"Hey, Leah!" Zoe squeaked. Amanda avoided eye contact, Roberta still looked livid, and Max gave her a sad smile.

Leah tossed her purse under her desk and grabbed her notebook and a handful of M&Ms from the ever-present bag in her top drawer. Then she turned back to her painfully silent coworkers. "Yes, I heard everything you guys said. Yes, I feel like I'm in time-out. And yes, I probably deserved it. Max, I assume I'll be grounded until I finish my therapy, right?"

Max's mouth fell open. "Uh . . . you know I can't . . ."

"I don't care if these guys know you sent me to therapy. I want them to know when I can work again." Leah dumped the rest of the M&Ms in her mouth and stared at Max, waiting for an answer. They all looked at Max.

"At least three more sessions," he finally answered. "Three weeks, as long as you are doing well."

"Staying sober, you mean," she interrupted. Max nodded.

"So after Amanda's wedding. When she's on her honeymoon, we'll have Leah back." Zoe grinned. "That's good news!"

"Just peachy," Leah said, heading back down the hall. "Assuming I don't get tanked at the wedding."

"Not funny!" Amanda yelled after her.

THE MORNING CRAWLED BY. Leah didn't even bother trying to do her "work." The interview with Jenny was tumbling around in her head, and she was trying to make some sense out of the whole picture. Coolie was connected to both Joe and Luke—and both were in jail now. Both charged with violent crimes. Both probable dealers and frequent users. Were they just a cautionary tale about the dangers of addiction? Were they set up? Falsely accused?

Or was she just desperate and unwilling to accept the truth?

When noon finally arrived, she shut down her computer and went out the back employee exit feeling like a paroled inmate, blinded and confused by the sunlight and freedom. She walked to Abby's Bakery and sat at a corner table by herself, her back to the entrance so she didn't have to talk to anyone, and inhaled an entire giant cinnamon roll. Then she roamed through downtown and the riverwalk, picking at the second roll she bought for later until it was a mound of naked bread she dumped in the garbage on her way to therapy.

A lanky black woman with shoulder-grazing braids walked out of Nick's office just as Leah was walking in. "Leah Danco," she announced. The woman stood to her full height and looked down on Leah. The name suddenly came to her: Aileen Washington, another client whose children Leah had removed and never returned. Why wouldn't she run into yet another angry client?

"Hello." Leah sat in a chair, leaning away and hoping that would end it.

"Were your ears burning?" Aileen crossed her arms and glared.

"No, Aileen," Leah sighed.

"I just need you to know," Aileen began, "that I've spent the past five years in college, earning my degree in social work, so I can someday be a social worker. I want to help people. I want to change the system, and the world!" Her chin shook, but her voice grew louder as she warmed into a speech she had clearly rehearsed and finally had her chance to perform. "But I won't be a social worker anything like you. I'll give people second chances, especially people who are addicted to crack trying to turn their lives around, and I will . . ."

Leah tuned out the melodrama, now remembering Aileen was found strung out in an actual gutter near Main Street in Terrance. After a protracted court battle, she went to treatment but bombed out immediately. She remembered thinking how smart Aileen was, and how she could have done so much. She was happy to see her success and would have told Aileen that if she hadn't been so bitchy. Leah watched Nick through the sliver of open door. He sat cross-legged in his tall-backed recliner, his hands turned palm up resting on his knees, eyes closed. *What a friggin' flake.*

". . . and I hope you never forget what you see from me here today. That I have triumphed over the tragedy you brought to my life, and I'll use my suffering to help others." Aileen took a deep breath in and exhaled slowly, as she had clearly been trained to do, until her face calmed and cleared.

"Good luck to you," Leah said blandly, but she meant it. Aileen's eyes bulged for a minute, and then she turned and huffed away.

"Hello, Leah," Nick stood in his doorway, looking refreshed and annoying as ever in gray cargo pants, tan sperrys with no socks and a loose linen shirt. "Come on in." Leah entered Nick's office with an exaggerated cough.

"Are you burning incense in here?" Leah asked as she took the same spot on the couch she had sat in the week before.

"I was smudging," Nick explained. "Many American Indians burn sage and then use the smoke to cleanse themselves, or a room, or any space that needs healing."

"I know what smudging is," Leah said, recalling with fondness the time a client had shared the ritual with her. "I didn't know you had Native American heritage."

"Oh, I don't," Nick said lightly.

"Of course you don't," Leah sighed.

"I just like the ritual." He gave her a toothy smile and moved to the chair across from her. "How was your week?"

"Lovely. I just found out this morning my sentence has been cut in half," Leah said.

"Sentence?"

"I only have to do three sessions with you now." She bared all her teeth back at him.

"Therapy is a sentence, huh?" Nick said mildly.

"Darn right," Leah said, and then sat and watched him smile and blink. Leah could win any staredown, and it would probably use up some time. A full minute passed, and Leah was sure she saw a glimmer of irritation in his eyes before he spoke up again.

"So, Leah. What would you like to work on while we're here together?"

"Knock it off," Leah snapped. "I'm here by force, and we're not going to pretend otherwise."

"Charming." Nick leaned back and took a thin, manila file off his desk. "Would you like to hear about your testing?"

Leah's eyes lit up in spite of herself. Psychological evaluations were a cornerstone of child protection social work, and being on the receiving end was insulting and intimidating but ultimately fascinating. "Sure," she said, with effort to keep her voice even. Nick pulled several pages out of the file and leaned over to share the papers with Leah.

"I gave you the MMPI and the Millon for starters. Both are standardized evaluation tools that look for both serious mental illness such as depression and bipolar disorder, as well as what we call personality disorders, which are more about daily interpersonal functioning. I also did a quick and dirty evaluation of your intellectual functioning, and I did a couple of measures that look at addictive behavior."

"I know all this already," Leah huffed. He gave her a look a second longer than necessary, and then shuffled through the paperwork and showed her a bar graph that showed many short bars and one tall bar. Each bar only had initials for labels, so she couldn't figure out what the bars meant.

"This is your MMPI raw data—the actual scores from each test. I usually don't go over raw data with my clients, but I want to show you this to make a point. Each of these bars represent a different scale measured by the test, such as tendency toward depression, addiction . . . you get the idea."

"And it looks like I only have one tendency area," Leah said triumphantly.

"Nope." He smiled and crossed his legs. "The only elevated bar is the validity scale. You invalidated the test so this data is basically useless." Whether or not he intended it that way, Leah took it as an accusation.

"Or maybe I'm just completely sane, big guy. Ever think of that?"

He raised his eyebrows. "The validity scale gets flagged when you try to give socially proper answers on basic things. Like saying you never lied, or never get angry."

Leah sat back in her chair and crossed her arms. "Maybe those things are true. Maybe I am always completely honest and even tempered."

"Impossible. You're an addict." Leah clenched a fist and almost punched him in the leg, but she didn't want to illustrate his point. "Moving on." He brought up the next sheet with a few more bar graphs with bars that were mostly short but a few were longer. Leah didn't like the look of this one. "This shows the results of your Millon. Shall I read?"

"Isn't that why you took it out?" Leah asked through clenched teeth.

"Yep." Nick pushed his sunbleached bangs out of his eyes. "This individual tries to present a confident appearance but is actually insecure, anxious and lonely. This person may often be surly and sarcastic or even hostile, but these are usually defenses to keep people away because this individual does not trust people and sees the world as a dangerous place. Prone to outbursts, this person may also struggle with deep sadness. Because of difficulty with coping and relationships, individuals with this profile are often at high risk for chemical abuse." Nick paused and laid the page on his lap. "Reactions so far?"

"Nope," Leah said, feeling her pulse rise. She attempted to squelch her anger.

"Nope? You don't have any reaction? Really?" Nick craned his neck around to look Leah in the face while they were still sitting side by side. "Do you think any of this sounds like you?"

"Nope."

"Huh," Nick said, with so much infuriating false cheer that Leah was picturing herself extracting his teeth with pliers, one by one. "Cuz I think they nailed you."

"Fuck you." She said it softly so he couldn't call it an outburst. Leah popped up and went to the window to hide the flush in her cheeks and the tears in her eyes.

"I'm sorry if I offended you," Nick said quietly. "I was just trying to see if we could get at some real emotion." Leah didn't move. "I know you don't want to be here, but you're in a helluva miserable bind, and I think anyone would be struggling to cope. Max is worried about you and doesn't want you to fall apart, both for you and for the agency. He's just looking out for you." Her tears wouldn't stop, but Leah wasn't going to give Nick the satisfaction, so she stayed firmly planted against the window. His office had a gorgeous view of the river that sparkled in its slow migration. Leah longed to be back on Kemp's boat, aching for a time when her biggest problem was tolerating Kemp trying to be her boyfriend.

"It would be a great day to be on the river," Leah said, more to herself. The September sun was still strong enough to keep the river's chill away for a few more weeks. Leah could almost feel herself back on the boat, rocking away the afternoon anchored near the sandbar.

"That it would," Nick agreed. "Do you have a boat?"

"Kemp does." She regretted the answer and all that it implied, but her exhaustion won and she couldn't keep up the anger or defenses any longer. A distant part of her brain wondered how Nick had managed to break her—maybe his sage drugged her somehow? She didn't want to believe she was that vulnerable to his mind games.

Leah brought her arm up and wiped her tears away with the sleeve of her cardigan, and went back to her chair as casually as she could. Nick had the good sense to avert his eyes and not acknowledge her tears. Nick had already pushed his chair back across from hers, so they were facing each other again.

"So, Leah," Nick said. "I really don't want to torture you with therapy that you clearly hate, so let's get to the nitty gritty of this drinking stuff. Can we do that?"

"You can ask. I may or may not answer." She stared at her knees, focused on a stray pen mark on the left knee of her tired, old khakis.

"I can accept that." Nick leaned forward and held out three fingers. "I've been thinking about you a lot, Leah, and I have three questions I'd like you to mull over: One—why did you buy the whiskey in the first place? Two—why didn't you drink it right away? And three—why did you drink the whole bottle after you turned your brother in?"

Leah gaped at him. "How in the hell do you know all that?"

"Max told me. He said your friends pieced it all together. They all knew you had a bottle of whiskey in your car."

Leah wanted to be irritated again, but she was too tired for that. "Well, I can answer all three right now. One, I bought it because I was sick and tired of always being the sober one in the room. Two, I didn't drink it because of pure AA guilt and shame. And three, I downed that whole thing because I didn't want to deal with any of Luke's shit. I gotta tell you, Nick, these are pretty basic questions with obvious answers."

Nick leaned back in his chair with his eyes closed, and he stayed that way for so long Leah wondered if he had dozed off. But then he pulled his head up and looked at her again. "My guess, and I could be wrong about this, is that we need to focus more on what led you to *buy* the bottle instead of what led you to *drink* it. Because I think Luke's arrest was the excuse you had been looking for to fall off the wagon."

"And I think that's psychobabble bullshit," Leah snapped, pleased that a bit of her feistiness had found its way back.

Nick closed his notebook, and Leah noted with deep relief that their session was coming to an end. "One more issue for you to ponder," he said, and they both stood up facing each other. "Do you think Luke did it?" They locked eyes and neither of them moved. Leah could see on his face that he knew her answer. She hated Nick for knowing, and she hated herself for giving up on her only brother.

KEMP AND JAKE HAD been cooped up in Jake's office arguing most of the afternoon, and Jake was getting tired. They were supposed to be reviewing the investigation into Ben's assault, but Kemp kept going back to his theory: Carl had a problem with Joe so he went in Joe's house, beat up Ben, and framed Joe for it. And he knew Luke was snitching on him, so he raped Annika and planted the evidence in Leah's house.

Jake was having none of it.

"You know what? We're done here. I need to put my energy into this trial." Jake closed his laptop, disconnected it and slid it into his bag to bring home for another long night of work. "Your theory is complete speculation—insanity really—and you can't even back it up."

Kemp sat back in his chair, almost hitting his head on the wall. "We can barely back up the charges against Joe! What the hell, Jake? Don't you think you have a responsibility—"

"Dammit, Kemp! Take a step back here for a second." Jake sat up as tall in his chair as he could. "How does an idiot like Carl get in and out of Joe's house without a shred of evidence? How does he assault Annika with no one seeing a thing? The guy is sixty years old and could barely walk across a parking lot without getting winded."

"That's why he drugged Annika! She would've overpowered him. He had to."

"I already told you there was nothing on her tox screen . . ." Jake was struggling to keep calm while Kemp was getting more animated.

"Ether is in and out that fast and you know it. They didn't test her until the next morning."

Jake sighed heavily. "And you think he snuck into Joe's house, knocked Joe out somehow, beat up the kid, and left?"

"Exactly," Kemp nodded.

Jake stood and put his laptop bag over his shoulder. "You've been going after this guy for so long you're ready to see just about anything."

"I see what's there." Kemp stood in front of the door and wouldn't let Jake through. "What's it going to take for you to get me that search warrant?"

"Something else that connects him," he sighed. "You need actual evidence, not a hunch." Jake tried to get around him, but Kemp stood his ground.

"I know you think I'm effed up on this."

Jake glared up at his much taller friend, his voice softening. "I think you're effed up in general. And the judge is going to make his ruling on the Miranda garbage, and I think we'll be fine. The case against Joe's weak. Everyone knows it. I wish you were spending your time bolstering our actual case instead of chasing your white whale."

Kemp moved aside. "Yeah, but at least the guy got the whale in the end."

Jake let out a sardonic chuckle. "Okay, buddy, we'll go with that." Jake shook his head as he walked ponderously out of the county attorney's office.

Kemp threw his arms in the air. "He does get the whale, right? What the hell kind of story would it be if he didn't?"

Toby Jones, the legal assistant no one could stand, shook his head in disgust. "No. He doesn't get the whale. Don't you read? Everyone dies but 'Ish and the fish.'"

"I don't know what the hell that means," Kemp muttered. "But I'm getting this asshole."

TERRANCE COUNTY DETENTION CENTER was unusually empty, so the inmates were allowed extra time in the common areas to watch television. On that dreary evening, many of the current detainees were happy to enjoy *Monday Night Football*—or at least they appreciated the opportunity to howl and groan and yell. They cheered and high-fived when a running back for the Cardinals was hit so hard he was immediately unconscious—socially sanctioned violence was quite an outlet.

Luke sat with his back against the wall in the corner of the common area. It had been a hellish few weeks. Without weed, booze, or sunlight, he was a shell of himself—hollow eyed, anxious, angry. There was no escape from the game without booze or dope. Scenes ran through his mind, one after another, without reprieve. At night it was unbearable—the smells of the jail were too close to what he experienced during the game. Many nights he cried, as quietly as he could, until the thug from two cells down yelled for the "bawling candyass to shut the fuck up."

Chewing holes in his lime-green scrubs calmed him for a while, until he learned that chewing on his hands was better. Pain was soothing. He gnawed on the spot between his thumb and forefinger of each hand until he was raw and bloody, and then he moved to his wrists and forearms.

The detention deputies must have told the jail nurse, because he was delivered to her one morning a few days prior to *Monday Night Football*. She had snapped on latex gloves and examined the raw, bloody welts up and down his arms and hands. "Xanax," she muttered, and Luke had felt a glimmer of hope for the first time since he was yanked.

Xanax injections (to avoid any chance of cheeking and sharing the pills) did a few things for Luke. The nightmares—flashbacks, really—went away. The images that seemed to swim in front of his face shrunk and grew fuzzy. And his pounding heart steadied and didn't feel like it was trying to break through his chest wall any longer.

But Xanax created a new problem in the form of vivid auditory and visual hallucinations. "Back off, man," jailers reported they heard from Luke several times each shift.

That evening as the Cowboys were walloping the Cardinals, Luke's banter escalated. But when Luke dropped the lime-green prison scrub trousers to the floor, held his flaccid penis in his hand and started yelling, "you wanna piece of me too, Dad?" Luke earned himself an escort to his cell and a loss of all privileges.

"You want me to settle down?" Luke screeched, sweat running down his forehead, mingling with his tears and dripping off his nose and chin. "Get him to leave me alone."

"Your dad ain't here," the jailer named Garret muttered under his breath.

It wasn't clear if Luke was angry at the comment or if he thought he had finally gotten the chance to get some revenge. Either way, Luke let out a yelp and charged Garret, a wiry punk of a jailer who had been on the edge of getting fired for years. He didn't see Luke coming, so he didn't have a chance to put his hands out or block his fall. Garret landed on his face and spit two teeth out, blood gushing down his chin. Before the other jailer could stop him, Garrett hopped up, grabbed Luke by the neck and pounded on his face until his nose was pouring blood like a faucet. The other inmates who witnessed the fight all said the same thing—as soon as Garret started punching, Luke went limp. It was like the life went out of him, and he just wanted this to be the end.

THE CALL CAME JUST after Leah had sat down in front of the TV with six Oreos and a caffeine-free Diet Coke since it was after ten and she wanted to go to bed soon.

"Is this Leah Danco?"

"Who's asking?"

"Terrance County Detention Deputy Dexter Owens. Leah Danco is listed as the emergency contact for Luke Danco." Leah's heart dropped. The deputy explained that Luke's nose and several teeth had been broken in a jail fight. She stared at her glass, knowing she wasn't going to sleep that night no matter what she drank. "Ma'am?"

"Yes. What?" Leah said, her voice wooden.

"I'm required to notify his emergency contact of any serious incidents. Do you have any questions?"

"No." She turned off her phone and slid it away from her on the end table. She didn't touch her Oreos. Didn't allow herself to move, knowing that if she did she would go straight for the car to buy herself a new bottle of whiskey.

The new game . . . it was complicated. Always a new problem to solve. But Uncle wasn't afraid to solve problems . . . his way.

chapter twenty-four

LEAH WAS PRETTY SURE she didn't sleep at all that night. Even with Netflix distracting her with *Grey's Anatomy*, she couldn't stop thinking about Luke. Wondering if he was in pain, and if anyone tried to help him. Thinking the universe was evening the score.

At 5:00 a.m. she gave up on sleep and dragged herself out of bed feeling shaky and sick. Facing another day in the basement was nearly unbearable, but being in her house wasn't any better. She ate three bowls of Rice Chex and watched TV until she was numb again, and when she couldn't put it off any longer she headed back to work.

But then the unexpected happened: Max caught Leah at her desk and relieved her of basement duty. Finally something to feel good about.

"Okay, Leah." Max leaned against her desk holding a file. "We've hit the wall with reports, and we just can't spare you any longer. I'm counting on your word that you will maintain your sobriety and continue to attend therapy while we get you back to work." Leah nodded, but Max still looked uneasy. A reprieve—was it really going to be this easy to get back to work? "You're going to have to get ready for the court hearing on Cindy House."

"Real work?" Leah couldn't hold back a smile. "I promise to keep my crazy under control.

"I never said you were crazy."

"You never said I wasn't." Leah touched her cheek. The smile on her face felt so foreign she had to see if it was still there. Max handed her the file, and she accepted it like a treasured gift.

"I'm still not giving you investigations," he warned. "And Amanda's going with you."

"You really want to spare two workers?" Leah opened the file and paged through the case notes. "Never mind, I don't care. Let's go!" Amanda popped up from her cube a few sections away from Leah.

"You betcha," Amanda said. She grabbed her bag and grimaced at the keys for car #5, the hatchback with shocks so bad that riding in it felt like galloping on a horse. "We have to take #5," she moaned dramatically for Max's sake.

They found the car parked behind the building and ventured south to the tiny town of Grafton. When the Grafton High School closed due to school consolidation in the 1990s, a local nonprofit bought the building for a dollar and renovated it into a shelter for homeless women and children.

"My mom and I stayed here a few different times," Amanda said in her "no big deal" voice that was too high and chippy to be genuine. Leah already knew Amanda had lived there from her file, which was hidden until Leah could figure out a way to tell Amanda about it.

Leah knew she should either say something about the file or bring it back and shred it. She did neither. Leah pondered what a case file for her own life would say. How many times could her parents have been reported to social services? Leah tried to picture Roberta knocking at the door, followed by her mother yelling and her father pacing because nothing good ever came from someone coming to the front door. Luke probably would have answered. But she was pretty sure none of them would have talked. Living with her parents was bad, but they would have all assumed whatever a social worker could do would have been worse.

"Does it bother you to have a more messed-up life than half of the families we work with?" Leah blurted, surprising herself by saying what had been in her head since Luke was arrested. Leah hadn't registered how awful that sounded until she saw Amanda's face crumple. "Wait. Let me try that again." Amanda nodded, avoiding eye contact, and Leah mentally kicked herself for being so insensitive, again. "I'm just saying . . . you and I both grew up with, ya know, a crazy family situation."

"I am aware." Amanda stared straight ahead.

"So does it bother you?"

Amanda exhaled heavily. "I can't believe you care about that stuff."

Leah stared out the window. "Are you saying you don't?"

"It could make you crazy if you care what people think—"

"That's not what I mean." Leah turned back toward Amanda. "I don't give a shit what other people think. "

"Liar," Amanda shot back.

"Okay, I mostly don't give a shit about what people think. But what I'm talking about is how it feels. Inside. To know your life is crazier than the people you're supposed to be helping."

They rode in silence a moment, bobbing and bouncing in miserable car #5.

"I like to think it helps me understand the families we work with," Amanda finally answered. "I don't judge. Or at least I try not to. And I'm grateful for basic things I never had. So, I got through it, and my past made me the person I am today."

"Yeah that's a nice little meme," she snapped. "But that's not how it feels." Leah choked on the last word.

"Luke is messed up, but that's not a reflection on you." Amanda was scolding in her tone, but Leah ignored her, wishing she hadn't broached the topic at all. She couldn't tell her friend it really was her fault. That her actions, or actually her failure to act on her brother's behalf several years ago, made her quite responsible. Leah had been running from that reality since Luke had been arrested, proving denial could only work for so long. Leah pushed the memories away, again.

WHEN THEY PULLED INTO THE SHELTER, Amanda parked and brought their cheap carnival ride in car #5 to an end. Amanda briefed Leah on Cindy's case—the kids were still doing great with Grace and Lars. Quiet and respectful, the kids seemed charming to everyone who met them. The younger kids were still developmentally behind their peers, especially in communicating, but they were catching up. But every time they visited their mother, all four kids still sobbed until they were pathetic little messes. Cindy would rock and hold them until the tears stopped, but Tommi Jane, the oldest, was often inconsolable.

"Okay . . . so the kids look pretty good," Leah knew she either needed to be open to Cindy's strengths or she needed to transfer the case. Her own bias wasn't fair to anyone. "I know that means she must have done something right. But all that crying could be about trauma, too."

"Going into foster care was traumatic for all of them, and Tommi Jane's therapist said that part of it was about isolation," Amanda said, leaning on the steering wheel. "These kids go to that tiny little Lutheran School on the highway. Other than that they're home or at the library. And Brittany has signs of chronic histoplasmosis—"

"Histo-what?"

"It's a disease people can get from bat guano."

"Well, no shit!" Leah said. "This has to be the weirdest case ever. At least is she getting her stuff done from the case plan?" Leah asked, dragging the already-heavy file out of the backseat and slamming the door with a rusty creak. "How's Cindy's psych eval?"

"You know," Amanda said getting out of the car and wading through piles of crispy leaves from a maple tree. "She has dependent personality features, so she's barely able to make a decision on her own. Her dad basically raised the kids, and when he died last winter things went downhill in a hurry. That's why we hadn't heard of them. And she has no insight at all—she doesn't get what the big deal was. But the kicker is her IQ."

"Sixty-five?" Leah guessed.

"Fifty-eight full scale—sixty-nine performance, forty-four verbal. Dr. Jonas said he rechecked the results because the split between the two scales was so huge."

They had reached the front door of the run down building and stood in front of a faded sign that read *Grafton Shelter for Women and Children*. "So, she's done parenting," Leah said with finality.

"By herself, anyway. We'll have to see if she's got a relative who could take them all in—the kids and Mom. That's the conversation we need to start with her today." Amanda looked grim.

"So good to be back at work," Leah sighed.

CINDY HOUSE LOOKED DIFFERENT. In a clean pink polo and black knit pants with her hair washed and combed, Cindy looked like an average person Leah might pass in the grocery store parking lot. Leah's memory had distorted Cindy into a cartoon—clownlike and crazy. But she wasn't either—she was just ordinary. Perhaps that would help Leah's nightmares stop.

"It's good to see you again, Cindy," Leah said with a smile that felt so fake she thought it might break her face.

"Hi." Cindy dropped herself into a rust-and-brown floral couch, circa 1977, while Leah and Amanda sat across from her on mismatched recliners, same era. They were the only ones in the community room of the shelter since most of the residents were on an outing with the shelter staff.

"Do you remember me, Cindy? I was at your house the day the kids moved to Grace and Lars's house. Then Jackie worked with you briefly, but she had to quit to take care of her son. I was assigned to take over, but I . . . had to . . . attend to some things." Amanda looked at the floor. "So Amanda worked with you. But now I'm back, and I'll go back to being your full-time case manager. Kind of chaotic, I know. But I'll be working with you from now on."

"I know you," Cindy said. "You're the screamer." A terrible image flashed through Leah's mind—arms waving madly, blurry figures swooping, her own terror and screeching. Leah's head snapped back for a second, and she shook her head to lose the image.

"How was your visit yesterday?" Amanda asked, noticing Leah's face and trying to bring her back to the conversation.

"Okay," Cindy said, pulling her polo to cover her Buddha belly. "Tommi Jane ain't ever gonna stop crying until we all go back home together."

"Cindy, remember we talked about this," Amanda said gently but firmly. "No one's ever going to live in that home again. It was so dangerous that people aren't allowed to live there."

"My house ain't dangerous," Cindy grunted, but she didn't want to argue so the subject dropped. "I seen that guy."

"Dr. Jonas?"

Cindy shrugged. "He had them funny blocks, and he was wearing yellow pants. Like a woman." Amanda and Leah smiled. Dr. Jonas was well into his sixties and known for his colorful style—Leah thought of him as Mr. Rogers in technicolor. But Cindy didn't share their enthusiasm for him. "My daddy used to say it's not right for a man to look like that, wearing woman clothes."

"I'm sure they were men's clothes," Leah said. "He just likes to be flashy."

"Did he talk to you today about the tests?" Amanda asked, though Cindy's bad mood seemed to be their answer. Cindy nodded slowly with tears in her eyes. "I'll bet that was tough to hear."

Cindy's chin quivered, and she looked away from them and out the window. "He thinks I'm a retard." The pain on Cindy's face showed that this was not the first time she had heard that term.

"I'm sure he didn't use that word," Leah said.

Cindy's head snapped around to glare at Leah. "Yeah, he did! He keeped saying all this garbage just to confuse me. People always do that to mess me up."

Tears were streaming down her face and her nose was running like a faucet. Amanda held out a tissue, but Cindy just swept her arm across her dripping face, leaving a thick smear across her cheek and on her forearm. "I told him he wasn't making no sense. So then he said I was retarded, and retarded ladies can't be mamas unless someone helps them. But I ain't got no one to help me. Then I cried so hard, he gave me tea and told me it was gonna be okay. What did he mean that it's gonna be okay? Is he gonna let 'em come home anyways?"

Leah and Amanda exchanged looks. "What he means," Leah began, "is that I'm sure there are lot of things you are good at, but being a mom isn't one of them. No. They won't be coming home. Ever."

Cindy slumped forward with a wail and sobbed into her arms loudly. Amanda glared at Leah, but Leah just threw her arms in the air like she had no choice.

"ARE YOU SURE you're ready to be back? That was awfully harsh." Amanda said as she threw the file in the back seat and wrestled with the door handle to the front seat.

"Well I'm sorry for telling the truth," Leah snapped, wrestling with the passenger's side handle.

"Did you need to be quite that blunt about it? We are fifteen steps away from saying that her kids won't be going home. We've only been in court a couple months. We're still just getting started on her case plan, and who knows what she might do with support? And even if she can't do it, we still may be able to find a relative to help her." Amanda said, finally winning the battle and getting the car door open. She climbed in and opened Leah's door from the inside.

"I don't know why we would sugarcoat it for her. She needs the information, and she's not going to understand subtlety."

Amanda held the wheel with one hand and ran her fingers through her hair—she had been letting it grow in preparation for her wedding French twist. "So if I said your brother's a rapist and is probably going to prison for ten to twenty years and you better get used to that idea, am I just doing you a favor by not 'sugarcoating' it?"

Leah's mouth dropped open.

"Hey, I'm not trying to be mean," Amanda said. "I just don't think you needed to be so harsh with Cindy. The road ahead for her is going to be harsh enough."

Leah pulled in a breath and tried to find words. "I'm not good at being soft."

"Being kind doesn't mean you're soft." Amanda pulled the car over and looked at her friend. "We're all really worried about you. Are you okay?"

Leah stared ahead. "No."

"Is there anything—"

"No," she barked. "There's nothing you can do." Leah looked out the window dismissively so she couldn't see Amanda's frustration swell.

"You know what?" Amanda growled. "You act like we're the same because we grew up with messed-up families. But I'd never treat people the way you do. Never. I spent my whole life feeling alone and lost. I would've given anything to have people care about me, and when I finally found people, I sure didn't push them away." It took a lot to rattle Amanda, but Leah had found a way.

"Really? I thought you left Jake in the middle of the night after you two hooked up." Leah said feebly, forcing a smile, hoping to lighten the mood. It didn't work.

"I was eighteen years old! How old are you, Leah? How long are you going to keep pushing people away? You're so damn prickly to all of us you better be careful, or you'll end up getting what you act like you want." Amanda started up car #5 and jerked them onto the highway.

The day wasn't supposed to go like this. Leah had been so grateful to get a reprieve from basement duty and from her miserable thoughts. But she ruined the mood because she was too harsh and prickly, again. Amanda was right—if she wasn't careful she was going to push her friends away and would be left with no one.

Leah stared out the window with a lump in her throat, unable to keep the worry and memories away any longer. Their shockless car bumped and jumped through the rolling bluffs that led back to Terrance. The leaves were just starting to turn, the maples a deep red and birches a fluttery yellow. Those leaves were holding on to life against a brisk wind that could bring the fall colors to a quick end. Leah had a random thought that she hoped the leaves would last through Jake and Amanda's wedding because she knew they wanted the backdrop of autumn color. Then tears welled up, relieved she was still capable of thinking of someone besides herself. Raised by two selfish, flawed people, she wanted to do better.

But who was she to judge her parents when she'd failed Luke so badly?

Raising Luke was her job. She was the one who poured his cereal before school, she made sure he got on the bus in time, and she walked seven blocks from her middle school to his elementary school to make sure he walked home the right way after school. But these weren't the things that got stuck spinning in her head. It was that unbearable memory of Luke when he was thirteen, the one she'd been fighting off for weeks. It persisted and was there every time she closed her eyes.

When they pulled back into their parking spot at the office, Amanda turned off the car. Leah didn't move.

Amanda closed her eyes, "Oh, gosh, Leah . . . I'm sorry if I . . ."

Leah couldn't speak above a hoarse whisper: "Luke . . . what he did . . . it's my fault."

Amanda shook her head. "That's not–"

"Shut up . . . please . . . just listen to me. Somebody . . . hurt Luke, too." Leah couldn't feel her tears. She was back to that day, seeing it all again.

> *The game was always played in the same way. Uncle brought the little man to his place, and they played his games first to get him relaxed. Toys when he was young. Benadryl when he fought. Weed when he was older. When it all went wrong, it had been smoke. Uncle was fully baked that day, bleary and horny. And the little man was just about ready to get out of his little briefs when she opened the door and screamed. And screamed. And screamed.*

"I didn't do a thing." Leah was ashamed hearing the words and her failure out loud. "Luke followed me out the door, all messed up and high. He told me it wasn't what I thought, and he begged me to drop it. So I did. He was thirteen."

"But just because it happened to him . . . we both know most people who are abused don't become abusers . . ."

"I know that," Leah whispered, unable to look at her friend. "But all of it together . . . ? How many more times can I say that these terrible things . . . the ID, the mask, his . . . history . . . don't mean anything before I just need to accept the truth?"

There wasn't anything else to say, so Amanda grabbed her hand and held it tight. Prickly, lonely, heartsick Leah, for once, didn't pull away.

chapter twenty-five

EVEN WITH THE NAME CHANGE, the Danco Defense Fund Fundraiser was grossly inappropriate. Leah had told her mother repeatedly there was no way she would attend. But somehow, in the way that can only happen in families, Leah was there, hiding her face as she sold walking tacos and sloppy joes at the food table set up at the entrance of John C. Terrance Park.

Luckily, the only attendees for the Defense Fund Fundraiser were Maggie and Beverly's AA friends, so it turned into an endless twelve-step meeting, complete with sharing stories, hugging and crying. Leah thought she would have preferred going to prison herself.

"Oh, Bevvie, what a beautiful day!" Maggie announced. John C. Terrance Park was sadly neglected—dilapidated play equipment and a fenced-off wading pool half full of sludgy green water. Only those who had "taken the cure" could find beauty in John C. Terrance park on a windy, overcast September Sunday.

"It's good, isn't it, hon," Beverly said. Leah, who was loading up her third walking taco in two hours, nodded. The tip jar at Leah's table had the twenty Maggie threw in to get things started plus a few random coins, but Beverly was undeterred. She happily milled among the dozen AA friends as they checked out the food table, the raffle table (first prize was a spray tan package and a set of throw pillows with the serenity prayer crudely needlepointed on them), and the dunk tank that had so far remained empty.

When Coolie arrived, Leah wasn't prepared. She had been pretending, ignoring, and denying what she knew for so long that the truth felt like poison. All she saw when she looked at Coolie was the lecherous, stoned expression on his face when he and Luke were together. She shoved spoonfuls of taco in her mouth so she couldn't scream at him when he approached.

"Carl," Beverly purred. "I knew you'd come." Beverly flushed and smiled. Maggie looked at her shoes and stepped away.

"I'll take a couple of those," he muttered, motioning at the sloppy joes.

Beverly looked at Leah expectantly, but Leah had no intention of serving him. Leah backed away from the table. "Why don't you take over, Mom." Beverly hustled behind the table and picked up a plate. Leah grabbed her purse and decided she had tolerated this nonsense long enough.

Leah was halfway to the parking lot when she saw something that made her cringe and smile at the same time—Amanda and Zoe were unloading Zoe's twins from her minivan, Olivia in a pink windbreaker with the hood tied tightly around her head and Dylan holding large plastic dinosaurs in each hand. Leah was touched, but did not want them to witness the embarrassing spectacle that was her family. Amanda saw Leah approaching them and waved.

"Oh, guys, no. You don't want to be here . . ." Leah said, but Zoe looked up then and waved, unable to hear Leah's plea. The twins made it through the parking lot, saw the rundown playground, and ran for the swings. Leah's head dropped. There was no turning back now. Leah looked over her shoulder—two older women scrubbed the outside of the murky dunk tank and a couple of aged addicts tuned their guitars on the makeshift stage. It was humiliating to be part of this. She headed to the swings to tell her well-intentioned friends they needed to go home.

Dylan was madly flailing his legs around to get his swing moving.

"Hey there, kiddos!" Leah went up behind Dylan and gave him a push, but he scrambled down.

"No! My do it myself!" Stubborn Dylan stopped his swing, hopped back up on the seat and madly flailed his legs again.

"Dylan," Zoe warned. "Tell Auntie Leah 'thank you' for the push."

"Dank you," he breathed, his swing only swaying a few inches side to side.

Amanda was behind Olivia, pushing her as she went higher and higher, much to her brother's frustration.

"How's it going?" Zoe asked, digging in her purse. "I'm going to go get us some food."

Leah shook her head. "It's a fundraiser for a rapist. How do you think it's going? Please just go home, you guys. This is so embarrassing."

"You don't need to be embarrassed in front of us," Amanda said, zipping up her sweatshirt to protect against the chilly wind.

"But seriously, this is a whole new level of insane," Leah groaned. "They're acting like this is a regular old Sunday picnic. The older guys are playing horseshoes and talking about 'Nam while the women are fussing around trying to get everyone to eat. But then you go to this table where they're selling raffle tickets with a big sign that says, *All Proceeds go to Defending an Innocent Man.*"

Zoe cringed. "Okay, yeah, it's weird. But we're here for you."

Leah fought the tears out of her eyes. "I know . . . but please. Just let the kids play for a few minutes and then go. This is a freak show."

As if on cue, Maggie trotted over, a rotund spectacle in a yellow floral sweater and lime-green capris. "Leah?"

"Hi, Maggie," she managed a thin smile, hoping Maggie wouldn't try to hug her. "What do you need?"

Maggie wrung her hands and pursed her lips. "It's your mother . . ."

"*Madge?!*"

Maggie flinched and turned around. Amanda's eyes were huge. Maggie let out a strange, nervous laugh.

"Hel*lo*, Amanda," Maggie said softly, her eyes flitting around like she wanted to escape. Zoe and Leah looked back and forth between Maggie and Amanda, waiting for an explanation. Amanda just stood with her mouth hanging open. "Still working at the county?" Maggie asked in a flat voice Leah had never heard before.

Amanda nodded, snapped her mouth closed and tried to compose. "Yeah . . . I am. It's going well. I like it . . ."

Zoe stepped in. "I must be the only one who doesn't know you, then." Zoe stuck out her hand. "I'm Zoe. I work at the county with these two." Maggie accepted Zoe's hand daintily and gave her a little old lady handshake.

"I'm Maggie." She eyed Amanda, who had finally reined in her facial expressions and smiled stiffly.

"Remember that experiential education program I did at the high school?" Amanda said carefully. "We worked with teenagers with truancy problems . . ." Zoe and Leah both nodded. "Madge . . . Maggie was the teacher in the classroom for the kids we worked with. She and I worked together for a semester . . ." Amanda trailed off, not wanting to explain how the program ended when several of the kids got in a fistfight. The fight rattled Maggie, or Madge as she was called then, when she was fifty pounds lighter and was all about clean eating and healthy living. The program fell apart, and Madge along with it.

"Yes . . . well . . ." Maggie straightened to her full four feet, eleven inches. "My life was confused back then. I didn't know who I was . . . I . . . uh . . . went back to pills and had a hard time for a while. But I'm here now, healthier and happier than ever." Maggie never forgot this inappropriate gathering was still an AA meeting.

"That's great," Amanda said with an uncomfortable smile. "Are you still at the school? I thought I heard that you left . . ."

"Oh, no," Maggie said, giggling frenetically now. "I'm opening a bakery in a few weeks, specializing in cupcakes and fancy treats."

"Abby's Bakery!" Olivia yelled from her swing, famous for listening to the adults when everyone forgot she was there. "Yummy minnimon wolls!"

Maggie frowned but recovered quickly. "Not Abby's Bakery, kids. *Maggie's* Bakery."

"We getting minnimon wolls, Mama?" Dylan asked, still barely moving on his swing.

"Maybe we'll try Maggie's Bakery," Zoe said and Maggie beamed at her.

"No no! Abby's Bakery!" Dylan and Olivia both sing songed.

Maggie's smile crumbled. "Leah, I actually came over here to talk to you . . ."

"That's fine. I think we'll probably be heading out soon," Zoe said over her kids continuing cries for "minnimon rolls."

Leah waved at her friends and walked with Maggie back through the park.

Maggie took a deep breath. "I want to talk to you about your mother and . . . that man."

"Coolie's an asshole," Leah said, digging through her purse for her keys.

"I know," Maggie snapped, her voice dropping out of its usual syrupy octave. "There's something seriously wrong with him." Maggie's voice descended another octave, so low she sounded like a drag queen who'd dropped the act. Leah did a double take, looking Maggie up and down like she wasn't sure what she was seeing anymore. "Don't look at me like that," Maggie growled. "I'm complex, okay?"

Leah held her hands up, showing she meant no harm. After hearing that Maggie used to be Madge, she shouldn't be surprised by anything. "You're right," Leah said. "There is something wrong with that guy."

"Listen to me," Maggie said quickly. "He's making her do things. Sexual things."

"Oh, God, come on." Leah's face contorted. "I don't need to hear this."

"Yes, you do," Maggie snapped. "You don't understand. He's *making* her do things. Forcing her. I think he's getting her stoned and then he does it. Bev's pretty sure he's videotaping her, too." The thought of a video of her mother and Coolie having sex made Leah retch so violently she choked and started a coughing fit. Maggie shushed her and looked at Bev, petting the rhinestones on her neon-yellow bedazzled sweatshirt that read *Danco Defense Fund Fundraiser* in metallic letters. Leah pulled a bottle of Diet Coke out of her purse and took a long swallow to calm her cough.

"So he's getting her high against her will? It sure doesn't seem like it . . ." Leah's mind turned with possibilities. She knew Coolie had been getting Luke high when he did the horrible things he did. It fit he was getting her mother high now.

"Do you have any idea how fragile your mother is?" Maggie barked. "I'm former army, okay? I've seen a lot of things. Things that'd make your small town CPS job look like a cakewalk." Leah shrugged, but Maggie glared. "Carl's got dead eyes. There's nothing in there. And the guy doesn't care about your mother. He's using her, and not like you think. She needs help getting away from him. I'm trying to get her to see that." Maggie spoke with such possessiveness and affection that the friendship between Maggie and Beverly suddenly made sense.

Leah said as gently as she was capable, "Are you jealous, Maggie?"

Maggie took a step back and looked back at Beverly, as if she could have overheard. Beverly was clutching her purse and looking around anxiously while Coolie looked straight ahead and stuffed the last of his sandwich in his mouth. "Not the point," she said under her breath, making her voice sound strangely deeper.

"Then what is the point?" Leah asked with a weary sigh. Across the park, a few AA devotees had their arms around each other, swaying and singing "Yesterday." Days like this made her feel like she was a hundred years old.

"Look out for your mother. Tell her to dump Carl."

"Believe me, I would be thrilled if Carl vaporized, drowned, froze, or was drawn and quartered. But he's been around my family my whole life. He's not going anywhere." Leah looked at her mother and Coolie again. She saw her mother's desperate clinginess, and Coolie's aloof boredom. They were an odd couple, but really not a couple at all. Maggie gave Leah a final terse look, rearranged herself back into the prissy baker she was pretending to be, and trotted back to the picnic.

Leah examined Coolie with new eyes, looking for his angle. What *did* Coolie get out of this relationship? Leah knew Coolie's real interest had been in Luke, but now that Luke was in jail, why was Coolie still hanging around?

Leah walked as quickly as she could to her car without raising suspicion, but her mother was too focused on trying to get Coolie to try one of Maggie's cupcakes to notice. Leah slid into her car and drove straight to her mom's home.

THE FOURPLEX WAS ODDLY QUIET for a Sunday afternoon. Leah entered her mother's apartment with authority, so as not to raise suspicion in the likely event any of the neighbors were watching. The ever-present scent of antibacterial wipes and Pine Sol mingled with the odor of marijuana that was so strong she wondered if she could be getting high from the smoke that lingered. The apartment was unusually messy—socks on the floor by the couch, a glass on the end table, a dirty frying pan on the stove. Signs Beverly was not stable.

With a deep breath and a sense of foreboding, Leah entered her mother's bedroom.

KEMP SWORE, AS HE had been doing steadily since noon when the Vikings gave up a touchdown in the opening drive to the Packers. No one bothered him during Vikings games, at least not since the 2009 divisional playoff when the Saints put a bounty on Brett Favre, mangled his ankle, and took (another) Superbowl away from the Vikes. Kemp had watched the game with a bunch of cops at Shorty's Bar, lost his mind when they fell apart, and threw a beer sign at the urinal in the men's room. Shorty forgave him only because he was a cop, and Kemp learned he needed to suffer through the Vikings games on his own.

Kemp cursed all the way to the front door until he opened it, and Leah shoved the door back and pinned him against the wall.

"You tell me everything you know about Coolie right now!" Her eyes were wide and frantic.

Kemp shook off his surprise and ran his hand down her arm, squeezing her hand, trying to calm her down. In the middle of her rage, she noted that his cast was gone after only a few weeks. She suspected he cut it off himself. "Hey babe, what happened?"

"Don't you fucking 'babe' me," she spat at him. "Start talking."

Kemp closed the door and led Leah to the living room, motioning for her to sit on the leather couch. He could feel her tremble as he rested his hand on her back. "I will talk. But just tell me what happened."

Leah reached into her purse, fighting back the tears that were ready to break through, and took out a small, portable video camera, the kind sold for $100 at drugstores with little storage and poor picture quality. Kemp fiddled with the power button and was finally able to make it play. Leah shuddered, leaned back on the couch, and looked away.

The picture was grainy, but Kemp was able to make out what Leah had already seen: the yellow haloed glow of lamps on either side of a bed, covers removed other than a bare sheet. An older woman, perhaps sixty years old on the bed, naked, with a ski mask covering her face and most of her head. A man came into view, hiked up her mask to her nose and held a joint up to her lips while she inhaled deeply. The man was wearing white briefs and a black ski mask with graying stringy hair sticking out the back. A mask just like the one she had pulled out of Luke's closet. Kemp watched for a few moments with the detachment of a cop examining a crime scene, until Leah said, "Shit, Kemp, are you going to watch the whole thing?"

Kemp looked up at Leah, who was sitting and clasping the sides of her head with her hands like she was trying to hold it together.

"Where did you get this?" he asked. "Why do you have it?"

"It's my mom," Leah said, her voice catching.

Kemp looked back at the video for a second and grimaced. "Oh, that's effing awful," he said. "No kid needs to see their parent like this."

"That's not the point," she snapped. "It makes me want to pull my eyeballs out and scrub until that image goes away. But the issue is the damn guy! That's Coolie."

Kemp's eyes bulged. "No way. There's just no way . . ." He held the camera up close to his face and looked again. "How certain are you that this is him? Anything identifying about him?"

Leah dug a bottle of ibuprofen out of her purse and popped two pills with no water. "I just know."

"I need you to tell me everything," Kemp said, running his hand over his hair and scrutinizing the screen.

"You need to start talking to *me* or I'm not telling you shit." Leah hopped up and took the camera out of his hand. "I'm sick of being treated like I'm the problem here. You tell me what you know. I'll tell you what I know, and we'll work together."

Kemp squinted and hesitated, choosing his words carefully. "I can't really talk to you . . ." Leah's eyes grew wide. "I mean I know this is creepy and messed up—"

Leah's eyes popped and she clenched her jaw. "You don't understand. The masks! That's Coolie's MO, and he taught it to my brother. Or maybe he set up my brother. Maybe he did it himself, I don't know. But he's *in* this. Somehow Coolie is in this."

"I know that, Leah. I've known for a very long time."

KEMP FOUND A DIET COKE leftover from their weekend on the river, so he brought it to Leah and said he'd tell her what he could if she swore she'd never tell anyone or use what she knew. Gordy had told him he couldn't talk to Leah, so he could get fired for this. Kemp scrubbed his head and paced, making sure Leah understood the risk. Leah agreed to keep quiet, but they both knew she was lying.

Kemp frowned at the TV (Vikings down by fourteen), and then explained the case that he had been pursuing against Carl for eight years. It started when Kemp noticed a lot of the drug traffic in town led back to a house on West Ninth Street. It was a typical drug house frequented by crappy cars making quick visits. He had arrested Luke coming from that house on a traffic stop with enough marijuana in his car to earn him one to three years in prison.

"I remember that," Leah said, pulling in another deep breath. "I was back in college my second time around, and I was working on a huge paper. He called me to bail him out."

"I remember you bailing him out," Kemp admitted. "You dropped him off at this dumpy apartment over Gramp's Bar. You got out with him, and you two were yelling at each other. I followed your car, and I went up and met with him right after you left."

In spite of herself, Leah asked, "You remember someone bailing him out, or you remember me?"

Kemp gave her his half grin. "I remember you. You were wearing skin-tight jeans. I was surprised he had such a hot girlfriend."

"Whatever," she said, backing out of the conversation.

"So I gave him the typical offer," he continued. "I told him he could be looking at some serious jail time, but we were more concerned with getting his dealer. Your brother spilled everything, and he started working for us the next day. He was collecting what he could about Carl's dealer, but Carl was pretty careful about what he told anybody."

"You mean he's paranoid," Leah said.

"All dealers are paranoid," Kemp countered. "Carl was careful, too. But we got lucky on a garbage search."

"You dug through Coolie's garbage? Not for a million dollars would I touch that man's trash."

"Yeah, well, disgusting or not, garbage searches get us a lot of information. They're legal, and they don't require a search warrant. "Kemp looked over at the TV just as the Packers scored another touchdown. "God, I hate the Packers."

"Focus, Kemp."

He shook his head and turned back to Leah. "Luke told us the bigger dealer was in St. Louis, and we found a number written on a scrap of paper that tracked back to a dude who had just been indicted in St. Louis for big-time drug trafficking. We got the feds involved at that point. Barb Cloud agreed to a search warrant and got Carl's phone records connecting him to this dealer. *And* we found about a dozen different types of pills and a brick of marijuana—enough to arrest him on the spot." Kemp's face grew dark. "I interviewed Carl, and I read him his goddamn rights." Leah pondered this—the Miranda case that got Kemp demoted was against Coolie. "I'll go to my grave saying I gave him the Miranda. But when Sheila transcribed the interview tape, it wasn't there. So we went back and watched it, and it wasn't there. I must not have done it, even though I swear I did. Barb Cloud went ape shit. The feds begged off the case. And I looked like a complete imbecile and almost got fired."

"Hmm." Leah was processing what Kemp had told her so far. "So what happened with Luke?"

"Barb had already given Luke a deal for cooperating with us. He did a few weekends in jail and was done. Carl got thirty days on a plea bargain for the brick of weed. And I got demoted to welfare fraud and child protection investigations. Bottom of the barrel."

"Poor you, stuck working with social services." Leah had heard this grumbling a hundred times and had no patience for it.

"Gordy went to bat for me. Again. He's the one who kept me from going back to patrol. He got me another shot on some decent cases, and I've been able to prove I know what the hell I'm doing. Eventually I started doing drug cases, and still everything led back to West Ninth Street."

"Because Coolie is a complete piece of shit."

"Agreed," Kemp said, and then bellowed at the TV as the Vikes got sacked and lost twenty yards, "What's it going to take to get a quarterback for this run-down, third-rate, piece-of-shit football team!"

Leah shot up and turned off the TV.

"What the hell?!" Kemp yelled. "You don't turn off the Vikings!"

Leah stood in front of the television. "I want ten minutes of your undivided attention or I'll put my foot through your $2,000 flatscreen."

"Fine. Bastards are going to lose anyway." He ran his hands over his head again, taking a minute to get back to his train of thought. "So I contacted Luke, and he agreed to work with me again. He'd been in and out of dealing for Carl ever since he got released. Carl's network is bigger, and we had him connected to a *major* supplier from Mexico. He's been dealing way more than weed for years now. The feds were willing to take a look, and I thought we had something huge. But when they reviewed the case, they said it was too risky because it all hinged on Luke. And I don't think they trusted me, either. When I told Luke the case against Carl fell apart, he spilled the other stuff." Kemp stopped talking and looked uneasy for the first time.

Leah stared hard. "What other stuff, Kemp? That 'other stuff' is the whole point I'm here, right? Keep going."

Kemp stood up and walked around his living room, constantly running his hands through his thinning hair. "Aw, geez, babe. It's hard to tell you this."

Leah found that Kemp's affection only made the conversation harder. "Call me 'babe' one more time and I will hurt you."

Kemp sat back down and leaned forward, elbows on his knees. "Carl was . . . 'doing stuff' to Luke for years. Sexual stuff."

Leah knew it was coming. She had all but seen it happening years ago. But hearing it from Kemp in his detached cop mode made it real. They both sat quietly, and Leah let out a long breath and fought her tears away. "Okay. Yeah. I kind of knew that."

Kemp sat back. "How did you know?"

"I just did." She wouldn't meet his eyes. "Go on."

Kemp studied Leah's face for a minute but kept talking. "He was ready to talk. You know how it is for some victims when they start telling their story. It just comes spilling out. Carl had been doing it to him for basically his whole life. He bribed him when he was young. Drugged him when he was older. And then he did anything and everything." Leah grimaced and Kemp slowed down. "We were within the statute of limitations because it was crim sex. Jake was ready to do the complaint when Luke got arrested." She thought she was ready to hear the worst of it, but still the guilt was smothering. All the years that Luke was fetching Coolie and their parents beer, getting high off of their pot smoke, sitting on Coolie's lap. Coolie called Luke his "little man."

It was unbearable. Leah tried to pull herself out of those memories and process the way Kemp did, just looking at the facts to understand what could have happened.

"So," she started, tears in her eyes. "Since, he was getting . . . hurt . . . for so many years, that's why he became what he is . . ." Her face hardened. "Or was it Coolie? Could it have been him? Is that even possible . . . ?"

Kemp came back and sat down next to Leah. "Maybe." He rubbed his hands together hard.

Leah let out a shaky sigh. "What are you saying?"

"I'm saying I think Carl might be behind all of it . . . Ben . . . Annika . . . all of it."

THEY LEFT THE RECORDER on the coffee table next to the remote control with one minute and nineteen seconds left to play. Those seventy-nine seconds would have answered every question they had. But the recorder and all of its answers sat on the table for the next thirteen days, until everything exploded.

chapter twenty-six

Monday morning, and Beverly was awake before dawn. Carl was already gone, which always made her feel cheap. Years ago when it was just the three of them, before Beverly had made her choice, Carl had always been there all night. Of course, they were usually doing it all night, but at least it saved her from waking up in a cold bed.

Lately Beverly thought of those early days more often, with longing and nostalgia. Beverly was waitressing when she met Carl and Roger, and it took only a few nights of serving them omelets at 2:00 a.m. before they became fast friends. The three of them took road trips in Carl's van, sleeping in a row on the mattress in the back. Beverly "attended" to both of them, depending on the night, how drunk they were, and who passed out first. Carl was adventurous in every way, and he expected as much from her. Beverly still grew warm when she thought of all the ways he turned her inside out while Roger slept (could he have really been sleeping through all of that?) next to them in the back of that smelly old van.

But it was Roger's heart that had eventually won her over. Where Carl was aggressive, Roger was tender. Carl was titillating, but Roger was steady. Roger was also odd, rigid, and obsessive, but he meant well. The partying—three-day acid trips, the rainbow of pills, and the perpetual hangovers—wore Roger out first. So when Roger settled down and rented a basement apartment from his stepbrother, Beverly moved in and her choice was made.

Carl went from being her favorite tryst to being the third wheel. Roger and Beverly's relationship grew serious, and they daydreamed about having twins and taking road trips as a family. Carl was irritated by their homeyness and was always trying to coax them back into their old lifestyle.

Ironically, it was pregnancy that gave Carl a way back in. Beverly was ill every minute of those nine months, so Carl and Roger renewed their friendship and left Beverly trying to sleep and smoke away her nausea. Beverly was angry that

Roger continually abandoned her, and Roger was overwhelmed by the impending responsibility. By the time Leah was born, there was a permanent rift between Roger and Beverly, created and perpetuated by Carl.

Beverly tore her thoughts out of the past and dragged her sorry self out of bed. Her body was sore, and she ached between her legs. She couldn't remember anything happening last night after those first few hits. Carl had been bringing such strong stuff she was always blacking out now.

Beverly showered, wincing at the smears of blood she brought up on the washcloth. She dressed in lavender sweatpants and a beige sweatshirt embroidered with ladybugs and dragonflies, hoping the whimsical insects would improve her mood.

She pulled a filter out of the box and was preparing to make coffee when she paused, hearing a noise, or perhaps a voice. Her heart pounded hard and she froze, waiting for the sting of a knife between her shoulder blades or the sharp thud of a brick on the back of her skull, just like she had always feared. For a full five minutes, Beverly stood motionless, the coffee filter growing damp in her sweaty hand, nose running, tears streaming. Her throbbing heart sent blood gushing throughout her body, and she felt her pulse everywhere—from her throat to the tips of her fingers and all the way down to her toes. Eventually Beverly was able to pull herself back, away from her racing thoughts and exploding fears, avoiding a full-blown episode.

But the experience took its toll, and Beverly's craving for escape had returned. She looked at the clock, calculating when Carl, and his stash, might return.

LUKE WAS FINALLY HIGH AGAIN. Thank God. The shots smoothed out the stabbing prongs of the nightmares that hovered and haunted and stayed all day. Nightmares seemed to cling to the walls of this old place. Luke had no idea what was real anymore, but the shots offered enough lucidity to know that he had a problem.

The first problem came in the form of the gorgeous lawyer who kept visiting him. He always wore white shirts and loose ties, and Luke couldn't tear his eyes away from the man's throat—the way it was encased by his shirt collar. He looked like Han Solo, or actually more like Indiana Jones when he was teaching, all dressed up and respectable.

Luke *liked* this guy, but that kind of thing made his head hurt.

The attorney was babbling, never asked questions, and didn't want to hear what Luke had to say. He was confusing, and Luke didn't need any more of that, either.

"You're pretty banged up," the guy said, his eyes light and looking over Luke's face and hands. Luke didn't answer because the guy didn't like to hear him talk. "I'm going to get a motion for a Rule 20 eval right away." Luke nodded though he didn't know what that meant. "The detention deputies say you're talking all the time to people who aren't there, like you really don't know what's going on." The guy was talking fast. "Did that happen to you before? Did you hear voices?" The guy waved his hands in the air. "Never mind. Don't answer that. The issue is that you are clearly hearing voices now, and you're seeing things that aren't there. It means you're probably psychotic, and that's good for us, Mr. Danco. We've just gotta get someone to say it."

The guy left and Luke sat in the visiting room alone. *Psychotic.* Luke knew that word—it meant he didn't know what was real. He struggled through the pea soup that clogged his brain and tried to think, but it was so hard. His mind didn't work right anymore. He had gotten some bad dope . . . he was sure that had to be it . . . and everything went dark. All he knew was that he was in jail because everyone said he beat up a girl. Luke slumped and laid his head on the cold, dirty table. He tried to remember, but the fog was thick again.

LEAH WAS DISTRACTED during their Monday morning staff meeting. As much as she would love it to be true, the idea that Coolie was behind everything was so implausible it was almost embarrassing. The more Kemp talked, the more obvious it became that he needed it to be true. Really it was paranoid, and Leah knew paranoia when she saw it. It was like everyone said—Kemp was so hung up on Coolie he had lost his focus.

Unfortunately, Leah wondered if Kemp really was to blame for the lack of progress on both cases—Ben and Annika. It was striking how little evidence they had found, other than what Leah found in her home. No one had seen or heard anything of note in either case. How was that possible?

"I think this whole wedding is actually an elaborate scheme to drive me away," Amanda announced, yanking Leah back to the present. Jill had been describing the sexual abuse investigation that had taken most of the last week, but Amanda had interrupted her mid-sentence. Amanda looked around the table at her coworkers' confused faces and frowned. "I love that woman—my mother-in-law. Truly I do. But a father-daughter dance? 'Pick a song' she says. 'It will become so meaningful between the two of you, the first time you dance together as father and daughter,'" Amanda sing-songed in a perfect imitation of Trix's squeaky voice. She stared at the legal pad in front of her, scribbling in hard circles. No one responded, but Zoe patted her arm, and Jill eventually went back to describing her case.

Their staff meeting ended early because no one could focus, including Max, who sent them all back to their desks and said they could reconvene later if necessary. Leah wandered back to her cube to find a pile of waiting paperwork and phone calls. Leah let Kemp's theory fade from her mind. Thoughts of Coolie made her crave liquor and that was the last thing she needed right now. Reports were streaming in, and Max was finally letting her get back to investigations on her own.

That afternoon Leah found herself back in therapy, and she was almost in a good mood with only one session left after today's hour in hell. Nick was as handsome as ever in a navy v-neck sweater that highlighted his eyes, and dark jeans.

"Have you thought about my questions?" Nick asked, sitting up straight on a hot pink stability ball he was using instead of a chair. Leah slumped in the recliner, ignoring the ball to avoid giving Nick the opportunity to educate her on how effectively the stability ball could strengthen the core muscles.

"I already answered your questions," Leah answered lightly. "Nothing to discuss."

"You gave the first thoughts off the top of your head," Nick countered. "Helpful, sometimes, but I really wanted you to take some time to mull this stuff over."

Leah blinked at Nick, buying some time. "Your theory is that buying the liquor is a bigger deal than drinking it."

"I'm just wondering what triggered you to buy it," Nick said. He inhaled and exhaled deeply, like he was in yoga class. It was annoying he was using her therapy time as a workout.

"You want me to say it was the bats?" Thankfully, the bat dreams had subsided. Actually, they were replaced by nightmares about Luke being sent to the electric chair with Leah flipping the switch.

"Was it the bats? Is that why you bought it?"

"No." Leah slumped. "I don't know. I don't think so."

"So then . . . why?"

Leah's anger boiled up. "I. Don't. Know. What do you want from me?"

Nick sat up even straighter, and then leaned in. "Honesty."

Leah leaned in and met his gaze. "I am honestly sick of meeting with you."

"And I honestly think you are headed for another relapse." Nick shifted and the stability ball made a farting sound under his weight. Leah snickered. Nick looked hard at Leah and then closed his eyes, steadying himself on the ball while holding his body completely still.

Leah shrugged, and they sat in silence. Five minutes passed. Then ten.

Finally, Leah couldn't stand it anymore. "You're not asleep, are you?"

Nick opened his eyes slowly. "I'm in recovery. Seven years."

Leah eyed him, waiting for his angle.

"I'm HIV positive," Nick said, looking past Leah, his words coming out quickly, so different than his usual measured diction. "I was married and miserable. I'm gay and couldn't get myself to come out and just be who I am. I was getting drunk on the weekends, finding ways to leave town, and then I would hook up. I got infected, and then gave it to my wife. I overdosed." He sat very still and pulled a large breath in and out. Leah gaped at him, not knowing what to say. "I went to Hazelden and got my head together. It's the only way I could get through every day." Nick stood and rolled his shoulders back, forcing himself to slow back down. "Honesty," he said walking back to his desk chair. "Your turn."

Leah looked up at Nick, who was shaken by his disclosure, but he held her gaze. Everyone had their secrets. The difference was Nick wasn't afraid to admit his.

"Why did you tell me that?" she finally asked, trying not to be unkind, but wanting to understand. "Therapists aren't really supposed to self-disclose, are they?"

"You wanna know why I told you that? Because we're getting to the end of your mandatory therapy, and all you've done is dodge your garbage. So you want some more honesty?" Nick sat in the chair across from Leah, close enough for her to see the shine in his unblinking, strikingly blue eyes. "You are not the kind of alcoholic who can have a drink here and there. You are the kind of alcoholic who goes on benders until you're eventually found dead in a hotel bathroom. "

He was trying to get a reaction. Leah forced herself to sit still and avoid his bait.

"You think so, huh?" Leah asked.

"Yes, Leah, I think so, and I'm scared for you. You don't have a tolerance anymore, so when you chug hard liquor you can get alcohol poisoning and die. You need to grow up and quit screwing around." His serenity was back, but he looked tired. "You set yourself up for that relapse. I really think it could have been Luke's arrest or something else, but you were going to get yourself in trouble. I'm worried you'll do it again, but next time you won't be so lucky."

Leah deflated. Nick raised his eyebrows and smiled sadly.

"I don't like you," Leah said softly.

"Yeah. I know."

AS LEAH LAY IN BED that Monday night, her thoughts swam in circles around Luke and Kemp and why she bought that stupid liquor. Leah thought back to the first night Kemp stayed over at her house. She was happy all day as she prepared for her guests, but when they arrived she couldn't enjoy herself. That was the first night she had craved drinking in years.

Leah felt so . . . flawed. Did her family make her this way? Her experiences? Her biology? And what made Luke into what he was?

Leah knew that, when she was drinking, she still had some control. Driving to that hotel room in Apple Falls was a choice. Drinking the whole bottle of whiskey was her choice, too, a very conscious one she made to shut down and disappear. She also chose not to drive and get more liquor when she was bombed out of her mind, and thus she chose to sober up and return to reality. What were Luke's choices?

Leah let herself wonder about Luke. Since his arrest, she had barely allowed herself to think about him lying in a jail cell. Was he still in pain from the beating he got from the guard? Was he sad? she wondered. Was he sorry?

And another thought . . . was he innocent?

The video was running. Uncle pulled her mask up and gave her a long draw on a fat blunt. She let out a throaty giggle, and through the slits in the mask he could see her eyes roll. He slid the mask back down so she was breathing the nitrous again. Her joints were spiked with PCP, acid, or sometimes grittier stuff. Uncle had soaked the mask with enough nitrous oxide to knock out a horse, but she was so high she didn't notice it. Beverly took one more deep breath, and then slumped against him. He pushed her back on the bed, naked and ready. Uncle stepped away and nodded at the Boss, who was hovering by the door in his usual position, watching and primed. Uncle grabbed his clothes and stepped out, bored by the things the Boss would do with her. Uncle wasn't jealous, just annoyed, so he dressed quickly and left. The Boss moved forward, ready to take what was his.

chapter twenty-seven

THE WEDDING, IN ALL of its miracle and awkwardness, was in two days. Jake was a distracted, crabby groom. Amanda was a distant, anxious bride. And Amanda's future mother-in-law flitted and fussed and turned away from their dark faces, planning the wedding that someone needed to want.

But Jake couldn't even pay attention to the wedding. It was day two of Joe's trial, and Kemp was scheduled to testify. Kemp and Jake found a conference room outside their courtroom and reviewed Kemp's testimony. They had barely seen each other in the past few weeks since Kemp had been removed from the Danco investigation. Jake had been working sixteen hours a day, and he was out of patience.

"I'm just going to take you through the day," Jake said, resting his forehead on his fist. "The ER doctor's testimony yesterday set up that there was a report from the hospital. I'll question you about the interview with Jenny, and then we'll go into the interview with Joe. We won't go line by line because I just need to get enough to introduce the video, and then the judge has already agreed to allow the full video, including his confession." Jake sat back in his chair and messed with his tie.

"What about my second interview with Jenny?" Kemp said.

Jake clenched his jaw. "We talked about this. I'll ask one question. You'll keep your answer brief."

"And what if Joe's attorney asks me if I think he did it?" Kemp raised his eyebrows.

"You know damn well he's not going to ask you that. Knock it off." Jake gathered his files and dropped them into his boxy trial briefcase.

"I'd say I don't think he did it." Kemp pulled himself up to his full height, his expression grim but firm.

Jake set his briefcase down and looked up at his friend. "You know what, buddy, you need to listen to me because I am saying this as your friend." Kemp glowered. "You need to get your head on straight. People are talking about you and how they don't trust your judgment anymore. And now that Jordan's doing investigations, the attorneys would prefer to work with him. He knows his stuff, and he doesn't bring any baggage."

Kemp snorted. "You know what, *friend*—"

Jake leaned in and pointed hard. "No, Kemp, I'm serious. I'm trying to help you here. Your obsession with that dealer has turned your brain to mush and your work is suffering. I told you I would consider a case against him if you could bring me evidence. And you haven't brought me anything because there isn't any evidence. People think Gordy's been carrying you because they don't know your work, but it's getting to the point that Gordy can't defend you anymore, and neither can I."

Kemp looked away, then looked back. "*People* think that, huh . . . *buddy*?"

Jake threw his hands in the air. "I gotta get in the courtroom," he muttered. Kemp watched him go, shrugging off Jake's sharp words that had been whispered around the county for months. He knew what people had been saying, but he was used to being the screw-up.

KEMP SPENT MOST of the day in court. The judge began by ruling in their favor on the defense's motion, saying that Kemp's Miranda warning was sufficient. Kemp was too distracted to gloat at being vindicated. The defense tried to bring it up during testimony anyway, which prompted a weary objection from Jake that was sustained. Next the attorneys argued the admissibility of Kemp's recorded interview with Joe. Since the issue was addressed with the judge only, the attorneys were less theatrical, but more brutal with each other. Jake's neck and ears flared deep red while the defense attorney went on the offensive with several complex motions to attempt to keep the interview out of court. Again, the judge ruled in favor of the state. The interview was admitted, and Joe's interview was played for the jury.

Kemp watched the video with detachment and none of his usual swagger. At the end, when Joe crumpled and agreed he must have assaulted Ben, Kemp's stomach dropped. Jake asked a few follow-up questions after the video was played, but he was brief. Kemp knew Jake was trying to get him off the stand as soon as he could.

The questions from the defense were more pointed and probing. Kemp agreed with a simple "yes" every time he asked about additional evidence that connected Joe: "Isn't it true you do not have any witnesses who observed my client assault the child?"

"Yes," Kemp agreed with an eagerness that made Jake shift in his chair, fighting to keep his expression neutral.

When he was finally done testifying, Kemp was more determined than ever to get his answers about Carl. He went straight to Gordy's office, two doors down from Kemp's, where he spilled his theory and put it all on the line.

"Aw, geez, man," Gordy said. The office chair wailed under his weight, and Gordy scratched at his neck where his eczema was flaring, purple and raw. "Why are you still on this guy?"

"Just hear me out," Kemp said, weary but intense. "I know it's a stretch, but just think about it for a second. Both Joe and Luke are dealing for Carl, and they were both trying to get out. Both of them are accused of horrible crimes, and neither one of them has a damn clue about what happened. I think he drugged them so they couldn't get in the way, and so they didn't have any alibi, either." Kemp paused for Gordy's reaction, but Gordy remained silent except for his raspy, shallow breathing. "So, I want to get a search warrant. I want his DNA."

Gordy let out a thick sigh. His breathing was always audible, but lately there was so much sputum rattling around in his trachea that it was a miracle he was getting any air through.

"You know what? I don't know what else to do with you. I'm getting pressure to get some real production out of you. Some proof there's a reason we keep you on, because lately you've needed someone to back you up on every investigation you've done. And now this . . . this?" Gordy's face grew red with the effort of his long-winded speech, and with anger. "You could ask a ten-year-old kid if there's enough to request a search warrant and that kid would call you a fucking idiot."

"Come on–"

"NO!" Gordy stood up, with effort, and pointed at Kemp. "You're on suspension for one month. Get the hell out of here. And when you come back, I don't ever want to hear you utter the name Carl Vole again."

"Suspension," Kemp laughed in disbelief.

"I'm not fucking kidding!" Gordy bellered. "Go fishing, Kemp. Go sleep for a week. Get laid. Clear your damn head. We want you on this team, but not like this."

"I'm in the middle of a bunch of cases . . ." Kemp scrubbed his forehead with both hands.

"Rick Jordan will take your cases." Gordy turned away from Kemp with finality and scratched his neck, sending a shower of dead skin flying.

"Jordan?!" Kemp paced around the office shaking his head. "Well, isn't that what you've wanted all along? To get rid of me and get him in here instead?"

Gordy slapped his desk with his hand, the smack echoing around the brick walls of his office. "Shit no! For *years* I've been putting my neck on the line to keep you in here, but I can't keep defending you." He pointed up at Kemp. "You're making all of us look bad, and I'm getting you out of here before you can try to sell your cockamamie theory to anyone else." Gordy lumbered around his desk, panting with effort, and leaned on the edge. "You've got enough time saved up that you can take the month off with pay. It's a vacation, man. A gift. Just take it."

Kemp just looked at his boss, feeling like the ground was crumbling under him, and then slowly turned around and walked out.

BEVERLY'S CHECK WAS LATE this month, so their first Wednesday tradition of shopping had to be done on Thursday. It was an opportunity for Leah to talk to her mom about Coolie and whether she was safe, and figure out what else her mom knew about him. But she wasn't sure how to begin that conversation without going down a dozen different paths Leah didn't want to touch. Plus, Leah was hoping to get done early enough tonight to go drop off her mom and go back to Target, alone, to find a bra that would work under that miserable bridesmaid dress. She had two days to find a more positive attitude for the wedding, and getting the ungodly task of bra shopping out of the way would help.

As Leah pulled into the driveway, she willed her mother to be watching out the kitchen window so she wouldn't have to go in. Leah parked but left the engine running, sitting through two songs on Cities 97 before admitting to herself she was going to have to go inside.

Beverly was a compulsive door locker, of course, so Leah used her key to go in the front door. The apartment was still and quiet.

Leah walked through the kitchen and cramped dining area. A cereal bowl rested in the sink with a half inch of milk and some bloated rice krispies floating in it. Leah pushed the bathroom door open, but it was dark and empty, with all of her personal items put away.

The floor creaked in its typical spot outside of Beverly's bedroom. The door was closed, and Leah was afraid of what she might walk into. She knocked softly. Silence.

"Mom?" The word sounded foreign on her lips as Leah realized how rarely she actually called her mother anything. More silence. Leah promised herself if she walked in on her mother and Coolie having sex that she would kick him in the nuts. She held her breath and opened the door.

The bed was rumpled with the Wal-Mart bedspread slid partly on the floor. The geometric pattern in the sheets played tricks on her eyes and seemed to be vibrating. Glancing around the room, it was disrupted but empty. And the smell of marijuana hung in the air, along with another odor she couldn't identify. She checked on her mother's stash on the dresser, but this time there was nothing but a roach clip.

Beverly had asked Leah to pick her up at 5:00 p.m. The clock on the nightstand said 5:23.

Leah sat on the edge of the bed and pulled out her phone to call her mom, and then something caught her eye. A spot, or rather a smudge, on the sheet. Leah brushed her hand across the sheet and found the spot was hardened. And it was bigger than she thought.

It was like déjà vu—her gut knew before her head could catch up. Her heart sped up, and a part of her wanted to run. But instead, with her hand shaking, she pulled back the bedspread to find an enormous bloodstain.

Uncle had met the Boss when the Boss was vulnerable—tweaking like crazy—and Uncle had the upper hand . . . at first. Uncle got him the best of the best, and the Boss was happy and hooked. It all changed when Uncle got busted and almost destroyed. Now the Boss was in charge, and Uncle owed him. And the Boss never let him forget it.

chapter twenty-eight

THE TERRANCE HOTEL was built in 1902 by wealthy entrepeneurs who settled in the town because of its proximity to Minneapolis and to the Mississippi. The builders had a penchant for glitz, so the hotel was styled in art deco—pink tile, painted mirrors, and fountains everywhere. Trix knew it would be the perfect wedding venue and put down the deposit money before asking Jake and Amanda how they felt about it. Two days to go before the wedding, the wedding party was meeting on the hotel's historic seventh floor to set up and decorate.

Amanda waited until she was alone in the mirrored elevator with Lucy, returning from their mission to find tape, to let her resentment fly.

"This place looks like *My Little Pony* exploded all over it," Amanda groaned, slumping against the mirrored wall and holding her hands over her eyes. "It's so pink! When have you ever known me to like pink?"

"Never," Lucy answered obediently.

"I really thought this was going to get easier, but we're two days from the wedding and when I think about it I just cringe!"

"Amanda . . ." Lucy began carefully. "Can I be honest?"

Amanda uncovered one eye and looked at her friend. "What?"

"You need to get over yourself." She said it softly, but her tone was scolding.

Amanda stood up straight. "Are you turning on me, too?"

"Amanda!" Lucy was stern, near tears. "So many hard things have happened to you in your life, but having your future in-laws throw you an elaborate, beautiful wedding is not one of them."

Amanda gaped at Lucy, her face covered in growing embarrassment.

The elevator doors opened to the seventh floor, interrupting Amanda's uneasy pout. Zoe was waiting for them, concern in her eyes.

"Leah's mom is missing."

ZOE, AMANDA, AND LUCY left Trix at the hotel and arrived at the Beverly's apartment to find two squad cars in the driveway and Leah sitting on the front step.

"This can't be real." She shook her head and stared at her hands, like the answer was hidden on her palms. "Not real. None of this is happening. I wanna go back, rewind to before any of this started. We were grilling in my backyard. Kemp burned the chicken. Remember that?" Leah looked up at her three friends, but their worried faces showed Leah it was real.

"What happened?" Zoe asked, sitting next to Leah on the step.

Leah shook her head as a chubby young officer came outside. "Excuse me, Ms. Danco?" Leah's head snapped around. "We can do some basic checking, but like we told you inside, it hasn't been twenty-four hours."

"Whatever," Leah said, standing up slowly. "Just go away." The officer looked between Leah and Zoe.

"Leah, this is scary," Lucy said. "What happened?"

Another officer, tall and thin, came outside. "I would suggest you just leave everything in the house 'as is,' and contact us tomorrow if she's still missing. Most of the time people show up . . ." Leah's withering look made him stop, and the officers shuffled back to their cars and drove away.

"My mom's gone," Leah said in answer to Lucy's question. "I was supposed to take her shopping, like we always do every other week. I got here, and she wasn't here. I found a huge blood stain on her bed."

Lucy gasped and looked at Amanda and Zoe.

"Honey, that's horrible," Zoe said.

"Yep," Leah said, suddenly standing and putting her hands on her hips. "That pretty much sums it up." She pasted on a grim, saccharine smile.

"So the police really aren't going to do anything?" Lucy asked. "How's that possible?"

"Blood in a woman's bed is not necessarily an emergency," Leah recited, glassy eyed and nauseous, but still with a sick smile. "There was no sign of struggle. No *splatters*," she dragged out the word, "or anything that would indicate that she was hurt. It may just be, and I quote, 'rough sex or woman problems.' That was the answer I got from our men in blue." All three women cringed.

Zoe stood and brushed off her hands. "We need Kemp."

AMANDA WAS AFRAID to let go of Leah. All the way to Kemp's house, Amanda sat in the back seat with Leah and held onto her arm, as if she could keep her from retreating into despair with her touch.

Zoe knocked on the front door with authority and urgency. No response.

Amanda went to the door, knocking and yelling, "Kemp, let us in!"

When he finally opened the door, he looked like such holy hell that Leah wanted to turn around and leave. His hair was oily and greasy, slicked back, and made worse from his nervous habit of running his hand over his head. His eyes were half closed, revealing his drunken haze. And he was wearing nothing but his typical gray boxer briefs, bringing her back to every time they had been together. It felt like an egg beater churned in her already-scrambled brain.

"You're drunk," Amanda spat. "You told Jake you were going to lay off the booze."

Kemp made a face at her. "Do you two lovers share everything now?" he slurred. "I s'pose I should just know that anything I say to him goes right to you, huh?"

Zoe stepped up before Amanda could escalate any further. "Kemp, we need to talk to you about a situation."

"Is my man Jake screwin' around?" His mouth contorted while he talked like he couldn't make it work. "You wan' me to rough him up?"

"You're being an asshole, Kemp. I told you you'll never get—" Amanda glanced at Leah and stopped talking.

"Kemp," Zoe started again, trying to keep him on track. "Leah's mom is missing."

Kemp's face drooped, and he moved aside and let them in.

AFTER CLEARING AWAY ABOUT ten empty beer bottles, a plate full of hot sauce and chicken wing bones, and an empty bag of Doritos, the women sat in a row on the couch with Lucy still cleaning up as unobtrusively as possible. Kemp had put on a pair of faded, twenty-year-old jeans that had been draped over a chair, but he was still shirtless, and Leah couldn't stop staring at a tuft of chest hair by his chin. Trying to forget what it felt like to run her hands along his chest.

Kemp collapsed into a well-worn recliner and accepted a tall glass of water from Lucy, downing half of it. He scrubbed his face with his hands.

"So tell me again . . . you were s'posed to pick her up, and when you got there she was gone and there was this big ol' bloodstain on the bed?"

Leah nodded, still unable to find words, still locked onto the tuft of hair.

"The uniformed guys said they couldn't do anything now," Zoe said.

Kemp's head snapped over to Zoe. "Sure they can . . ."

Zoe shook her head. "That's the thing. They said they can't do anything for twenty-four hours. Can you make some calls and get them to start the investigation right away?"

Kemp slumped back on the couch. "Yeah . . . well, that's where we got a problem. They gave me the 'gift' of a one month suspension . . . so . . . no. Nobody's taking any calls from me." Kemp reached for the beer Lucy had quietly just taken away, so Kemp took a long swallow of water instead.

"They suspended you?" Amanda asked, shocked. "For what?"

Kemp shrugged. "Doesn't matter, does it? They get to do what they want." His typical swagger had been replaced by a sadness that dragged down his whole face.

Leah pulled her eyes away from the chest hair to meet Kemp's pained eyes. They had both fallen so far.

Zoe and Amanda looked at each other. "So tell us what to do. Should we call Gordy?" Zoe asked. "What should the cops be doing right now?"

"We need to call all the hospitals in the area." Kemp said, warming into investigator mode. "Last time she was all the way at Hennepin County Medical, so if you include all the hospitals in the metro, that's a couple dozen phone calls," Leah had seen him worked up like this so many times when they were on cases together.

Zoe was writing notes and nodding, relieved they were making a plan. "I can do that," she said. "And we can drive around and look, too."

Kemp agreed, but Leah said, "She's not just going to wander around. She'll go with people she knows."

"So who does she know?" Amanda asked.

Leah slapped her knee. "Maggie! I can't believe I didn't think of her before. We need to call Maggie." Leah pulled out her phone and scrolled through old messages.

"She's a friend of your mom?" Lucy asked.

"I guess you could call her that," Leah said, still focused on her phone. "She's . . . odd." Leah called but Maggie didn't answer.

Kemp slowed his pacing and sat on his recliner, leaning forward with his elbows on his knees and turned to Leah. "Doesn't your mom have . . . you know . . . mental health issues?"

"She's got generalized anxiety disorder, with psychotic features at times of stress," Leah recited like she was reading from her psychological evaluation.

"In other words, she loses it sometimes . . ." Kemp said.

". . . and she disappears," Leah finished. "Yeah, I know it's possible she took off. But that doesn't explain the blood."

Kemp tilted his head in acknowledgement. "Carl explains that."

"Exactly," Leah said louder, and with finality. "Once again, all roads lead back to Coolie." Leah jumped up and started pacing around the room. "I don't know what to believe anymore."

Kemp stood up quickly, swayed for a second, and then went into the kitchen. Amanda looked at Leah with apprehension.

"What's he talking about?" Zoe asked, looking back and forth between Leah and Amanda.

Leah felt like her brain had just switched back on after being dormant, probably in shock, since she found the bloodstain in her mom's bed. "*Coolie*," she spat. "His real name is Carl Vole, and he's the piece of shit who's been hanging around my family my whole life. He . . . messed with my brother, and he's been getting my mom high and screwing her for months. Mom acts like she's in love. It's the most painful, pathetic thing I've ever seen. He's a frigging psychopath."

"You think he hurt your mom?" Lucy asked, finishing her cleaning and sitting on the edge of the couch. Amanda glanced up at Leah, still uneasy.

"I *know* he did," Leah said, her jaw set.

"Leah . . ." Amanda started.

"What?" Leah felt her agitation growing and knew she wasn't going to be able to hold it in very long. She paced faster, circling the couch and small dining room table covered with weeks of mail and junk.

Amanda glanced at the kitchen where Kemp was banging around, opening and closing the refrigerator. She lowered her voice. "Isn't this the guy Kemp is a little nuts about?"

Leah stopped and glared at Amanda. "Well, you two really do share everything, don't you?" Leah sneered.

"Leah . . ." Zoe said with warning.

"You know what?" Leah snapped. "I don't need—"

"Here we go," Kemp announced, bounding back in the living room holding a plate full of hastily made sandwiches. He stood in front of Leah with his back to the other women, and handed her a sandwich. “Come on, babe,” he said under his breath. “Don’t take it out on them.” He was still shirtless, still giving her those intense eyes, still calling her babe. Leah was barely holding on through the roller coaster of emotion.

So Leah grabbed the sandwich out of his hand—white bread with deer sausage (last year’s six-point buck he still bragged about) and half an inch of mayo. It was Kemp’s favorite. They had eaten it several times during their July Fourth weekend on his boat, and she couldn’t hold back a tiny smile.

“I thought I told you I would never eat this again,” she muttered.

He sat back in his recliner and winked at her. “You know you love it.”

Leah probably did. But she knew it wasn’t good for her—the sandwich and everything that came with it.

Kemp finished off the plate of sandwiches since everyone else declined. Leah ate hers, not realizing until then that she hadn’t eaten for hours. It settled her churning stomach briefly until she got heartburn from the spicy sausage. At least the food and the work were helping Kemp sober up.

“Okay, gals,” Kemp announced, slowing down his pacing and standing in front of the women on the couch. “I think you should call all those hospitals tonight, but I also know that Jake’s mom is going to pop her gourd if she doesn’t get some help from you bridesmaids pretty soon.”

“I was kind of thinking the same thing,” Lucy said. “I mean, Leah, your mom is way more important than centerpieces, but I think we at least need to tell her where we are.”

“I would *much* rather be here . . .” Amanda began.

“Yeah, toots, everyone knows how excited you are to put on that dress,” Kemp said. “But here’s the deal. There’s a pretty decent chance Leah’s mom is having a psychotic episode, so that’s really where we need to put our energy right now.”

Leah looked at Kemp, incredulous. “Are you *kidding* me?”

“No, babe, I’m not. I’ve been thinking about this, and the uniform cops were right. There isn’t any sign of a struggle, and your mom does have a history of problems. It makes sense to call the hospitals, but otherwise I think we’re done for tonight.”

Zoe and Amanda stood, and Lucy retrieved their jackets. Leah hadn’t moved. “We came here for your help!”

"Yeah, you and I need to talk about that, actually," Kemp said. Lucy's eyes widened, and Zoe and Amanda both stopped to look at Kemp. "You girls go ahead, but leave Leah here."

"Oh I don't think that's a good—" Zoe began.

"Hey!" Leah snapped. "You're all talking about me like I don't exist! Do you really think I'm that helpless?"

"No, hon, of course not. We just want to be sure you're okay," Zoe said, accepting her jacket from Lucy.

"And I just want to talk to you," Kemp said, hands on his hips, flexing his pecs.

"*Fine,*" Leah snapped. "I'll stay here for a few minutes and talk."

"How are you going to get home?" Lucy asked.

Leah looked at Kemp. "She can take my truck," he said. "I'll get it back tomorrow, or sometime before the wedding. It'll be fine."

Zoe looked back and forth between Kemp and Leah, pondering whether she would give her blessing to this plan.

"Just go," Leah said, dropping back onto the couch. Zoe ducked into the kitchen, and Leah knew she was looking at Kemp's supply of booze. A few cupboard doors closed, and Zoe came out. Leah could barely contain her irritation as her friends reluctantly shuffled out the door. Leah watched them through the bay window, and then turned to face Kemp, ready to let her anger fly.

"Finally," Kemp announced, digging through a drawer in the dining room hutch. "Take off your shirt."

That stopped her cold. "Huh?"

Kemp pulled a coil of wires out of the drawer. "We're gonna get you miked up, and we're gonna finish this with Carl once and for all."

As the years went by, the Boss gained more influence. More control. *It was the control he enjoyed the most. He played both sides—the game fed him. With the Boss in charge now, the game grew and evolved. Even for Uncle's tastes, it had gone too far.*

chapter twenty-nine

KEMP'S HANDS WERE COLD. Leah perched on the edge of the heavy dining room table, unbuttoned her flannel top and slipped it off. Kemp tried to tape the wire to her cotton camisole, but the duct tape wouldn't stick to the soft fabric.

"Come on, babe," he said, pulling off the loose strips of tape. "I've seen a whole lot more of you than this. You gonna get shy on me now?"

Leah glared. "You're still drunk."

Kemp threw up his hands. "Hey, I drank a gallon of water and ate a pound of sausage. I'm barely buzzed anymore." Kemp pointed to her chest. "Now come on. If Carl sees a big lump in your top he's gonna know something is up, and then we're screwed."

Leah exhaled hard and pulled her cami off, glad she was wearing a decent bra, the front-hooking one she'd bought for easy access during their quickies in his office.

"That's the stuff," he said under his breath, but he had lost his swagger. Leah couldn't look at him and found it hard to breathe with his hands all over her, fumbling around her cleavage. Even with all that had happened, she couldn't help being a self-conscious girl, sucking in and trying to make it look like she had firm abs. He was breathing hard. His familiar hands slid the mic under the front hook and ran the wire along the underwire of her bra, taping the small recording box on the middle of her back.

"It's bluetooth," he said as he patted the last strips of tape around the box, "so as long as I'm close, and I promise you I will be, I'll be able to hear everything." He stepped back while she pulled her camisole back on, and he smoothed the fabric over the wires. "Hey." he cleared his throat. "I just wanted to say that I'm sorry . . ."

Leah looked around for her shirt, still avoiding eye contact. "Don't."

Kemp's smile dropped, and he ran his hand down her arm and squeezed her hand. "Okay, babe."

Leah found her shirt and buttoned up while Kemp gathered up the used tape and extra wire. "Let's just focus on how we're going to do this."

Leah hopped up and paced while Kemp explained his plan. She was going to barge in the door and start screaming that her mom was gone and it was his fault. Kemp said she needed to be as hysterical as possible to get him worked up, and he'd be more likely to blurt something out.

"This seems like such a shot in the dark," Leah said.

"You'd be surprised how often tactics like this work. It's kind of like those phone calls when we get the victim wired up and have them call the perp and start yelling. They get flustered and admit to all kinds of shit."

"I mean, it's better than doing nothing, so I'll try it. I'll try anything."

"Remember, you need to stay back," Kemp cautioned. "Don't get within an arm's length of him."

Leah scoffed. "He better not get within an arm's length of me."

COOLIE HAD LIVED IN an eighty-year-old house on the same side of town as Leah and Amanda, but closer to the train switching station. Leah had been there once, many years ago, when they were loaded in her parents' conversion van on their way to a Star Wars convention in Chicago and needed to make a "quick stop." Luke had been about seven, Leah eleven, and the two of them waited in the van until curiosity got the better of them. Luke, who knew the house all too well, led her to the back door. They sneaked inside and wandered through the filthy kitchen, but both stopped short as they saw their mother, sprawled on the couch, set a tiny paper square on her tongue. As the minutes passed, her eyes got wide and rolled back. Leah lunged forward, but Luke pulled her arm and held her back. And so Luke and Leah huddled in the kitchen and watched their parents giggle and moan their way through an acid trip.

Leah remembered that day as she explained to Kemp she was going to use the back door. They drove slowly past the front of the house, and Kemp agreed there was so much junk in the front porch it was unlikely the door would even open.

"Typical dealer," Kemp said. "Barricading the front door." Leah, who had insisted on driving, steered the car around the corner and into the alley behind the house. The dark was oppressive–the area was too old and poor for street lights. She parked two houses down, next to a garage nearly tipping over. They jogged down the alley and crouched behind a row of buckthorn bushes just starting to drop their leaves. Every house on the block was dark, possibly vacant, and the only light for 100 yards was the blue glow of television in Coolie's front room.

Kemp grabbed Leah's arm and pulled her close to him.

"Maybe this isn't a good idea . . ." he whispered, the cold wind whistling above them in the trees drowning out his voice, his face inches from hers.

"What? No way. We're not backing down now." Leah patted the mike on her chest and exhaled heavily. "I'm ready to go in."

Kemp looked at the house for a long moment. "Okay," he finally said. "But I'm going to be right by the window. If he does anything sketchy, I'm going in."

"Fine," she snapped. "You get in position first, and I'll go in thirty seconds."

Kemp reached out and grabbed both of her hands. "Be careful, Leah. Don't get close. Don't engage him too much. If he gets agitated, get out of there right away. Deal?"

"Yes, deal. Now go." He was making her nervous, and she wanted him to leave so they could get this over with. He scurried through the tall grass behind the house with surprising speed, and then slowed down and crept past the kitchen door to the front of the house where the blue light shone through the blinds. After a few more seconds, she assumed he was in position, so she stood up, smoothed her khakis, and walked through the yard. Summoning every bit of fear, anxiety, and grief she had felt in the past month, she churned it all into anger and stomped to the door. She pounded twice with her fist, and then grabbed the door knob, surprisingly unlocked, and she shoved her way in.

"Coolie!" she bellered. The kitchen was every bit as garbagey as it had been twenty years before, so she had to kick aside beer and soda boxes and fast food bags. "Where the *fuck* are you and what did you do with my mother?"

"Huh?" he grunted from the front room.

"You heard me," she screeched, stomping through the hallway and banging her fist on the wall. "Where is she? What did you do to her?" Coolie was stretched out in an oversized office chair in front of three computer monitors and a laptop. When he saw Leah he automatically snapped the laptop closed and switched off all three screens, leaving the two of them in almost total darkness.

Coolie sat back in his chair and crossed his arms with an unsettling smirk. "Whatta you want, kid?"

Finally facing off with Coolie alone in the dark staggered her for a second, and she flashed back to the image of Luke as a spindly-legged preteen, nearly naked in Luke's bedroom. Then she summoned back her courage—and her fury.

"I asked what you did with my mother," she spat, pointing hard at him while he remained maddeningly still. "We both know you've been screwing her for months, probably years. Now she's gone, and I know you're responsible."

Leah had convinced herself she would be able to pound her way into Coolie's house and intimidate him until he spewed some answers. It played in her head like an episode of *Law and Order*. But hearing her jittery accusations out loud, she sounded naive and just plain stupid. Leah stood with her pointed finger wavering in the air, waiting for a response.

Through the dim light from the partially closed laptop, Leah could barely see Coolie sneer at her. "God, I never liked you. From the day you were born you annoyed the shit out of me. But, hey, none of us liked you." He drained his beer, crushed the can and dropped it next to him on the floor. "Shit, your own mother can't stand you."

It was just Coolie, and he was being cruel, as usual, his hatred for Leah always there. Hearing that her own mother felt the same way knocked the wind out of Leah. Images of Luke flashed through her head in those lime-green prison scrubs. Leah felt her composure cracking from memories, anger, and loss.

But she forced herself to keep going. "*Where is she?*"

"I don't have any idea where that woman is. You know your mother is bat-crap crazy." He snickered at his own joke. "*Bat*-crap crazy. You do love bats, don't you." He leaned back in his chair, and now that her eyes were adjusting to the dark, Leah could see Coolie clasp his hands behind his head. Like he was enjoying himself. "Bat-crap crazy . . . I always liked that one . . ."

Leah shuddered, as she would for the rest of her life any time someone mentioned bats. She couldn't think with her heart pounding in her ears so hard that it was drowning out Coolie's sneers. She needed to find a way to throw him off balance and regain her own.

"I was at her apartment. Maybe that's your blood all over . . ." Leah blurted.

His eyes narrowed, and she could see her shot had landed. "Your mama knows how to have a good time," he said with a shrug, but his entire demeanor had changed. "Maybe she's got herself a boyfriend and things got a little kinky." Leah hadn't said anything about the blood, where it was, or what it looked like.

It could have been anything—splatters or drops or a blood bath from a murder scene. She didn't even say it was on the bed, but he went right to something "kinky." It felt like he knew what she was talking about.

"I think *you* were doing something kinky. That's how you roll, right, Carl? But maybe it got out of hand, didn't it, Carl?" She was falling into an old investigative technique, trying to lead him into an admission a piece at a time. "And then you hurt her. Didn't you?"

Coolie let out a snort. "You need to get out of my house, little girl. I've had just about enough of you." Coolie pushed away from his desk and pulled himself up to stand. Leah backed up a shaky step. He was rattled, and that meant she was getting somewhere. Her determination grew, and not only to find her mother. Coolie took away her brother, and every time she thought of Luke her anger deepened. "Not until you tell me where my mom is."

"Get. Out." He warned, moving closer to her, reeking of weed and filth.

"Or what?" Leah snapped. "What are you gonna do, *Uncle*? Are you gonna mess with me the way you messed with my mom? With my brother?" Her heart pounded harder as she looked in Coolie's face and into his dead, blue eyes. "Where is she? *Where is she?!*"

A sharp rapping on the window pulled their attention away from each other, but Leah had seen something else in Coolie's face and couldn't relent. He looked afraid.

"What did you do, Carl? Did you finally go too far?" Leah persisted, her voice rising with the pounding in her ears.

"You need to watch yourself." He was standing over her now, but Leah held her ground.

"Maybe you need to watch yourself!" She waved her finger in his face, and he grabbed it and twisted hard.

"You point your bony little finger at me and I'll rip it off . . ." Leah's knees buckled with the pain. His grip was tight and she couldn't free her hand.

The back door banged open, and Kemp was in the living room a second later. Coolie dropped her hand in shock. Kemp grabbed Leah around the waist, picked her up like she was a doll, and put her behind him.

"You keep your filthy hands off of her," Kemp snarled and Carl stepped back, never taking his eyes off of Kemp.

"*Seargent* Kemper," Carl growled, and Kemp snapped. He charged at Carl until he had him backed against the wall with Kemp's arm against Carl's throat. The older man coughed and sputtered, his face darkening as he was losing oxygen, his eyes bulging in panic.

Leah lunged at his back. "Kemp! You're gonna kill him!"

Kemp held his nemesis up against the wall, able to win the war of strength. "What did you do to her?" Carl coughed but couldn't answer. He pawed at Kemp but was growing weak. Kemp finally lifted the pressure on Carl's neck enough for him to breathe. "Where is she?"

Carl gasped and panted, Kemp still inches from his face. "I don't know," he breathed, his eyes narrowing. "And I don't care."

Kemp shoved Carl to the floor and hovered over him as Carl writhed like the snake he was. Before he could do anything else, Leah grabbed Kemp's arm and pulled him through the house and back into the alley.

The night was still pitch black and the wind was picking up, threatening a cold fall rain. Leah broke loose from Kemp and started running.

"Hey! The truck is back this way," Kemp yelled. Leah veered for the truck but kept running. Kemp was right behind her, jogging and swearing. They reached the truck at the same time. "Did you see all those computers? Why does that dirtbag need all those computers?"

"I don't know!" Leah paced back and forth by the truck, banging on the hood with her fist, her finger still aching and pounding from Carl's grip. "What the hell, Kemp? You coulda killed him! As much as I want that bastard dead, how would that help anything? What were you thinking?"

"What was *I* thinking?" Kemp unlocked the door and climbed in the driver's seat. "What about you?" Kemp gripped the steering wheel and shook his head. "I can't believe I let you go in there."

Leah jumped up in the passenger seat and slammed the door. "I'm not yours to *allow* to go anywhere. " Kemp fired up the truck and squealed out of the alley. Still too angry to speak, Leah stared out the window as Kemp drove around Terrance looking for Beverly and burning off steam.

After several minutes of silence, Kemp said, "Check your phone. See if Zoe has found your mom yet." Leah pulled out her phone but didn't have any messages. She shook her head.

Kemp pulled off the road near Grafton Park and parked at a scenic overlook with a stunning view of the river valley during the day. At night they could barely see the shimmer of the water. He put his head down on the steering wheel and closed his eyes. Leah kept looking out the window, but it was too dark to see anything but street lights and the moon as it peeked out from the clouds. They both sat without speaking, listening to the hard splats of a fall rain on the windshield, their anger gradually deflating.

"I'm sorry I sent you in there." He didn't open his eyes as he said it.

It hurt to see him look so defeated. "You didn't make me go in there. He's taken everything from me. I had to try."

"He knows something," Kemp said. "The bastard knows something."

Leah sighed heavily. "Do you really think Coolie could have pulled off what you're saying? That he could have forced two people to commit these awful, violent crimes? Or did he actually do it himself with no evidence, no trace? No anything? On his own?"

Kemp didn't lift his head, but turned to look at Leah. "I don't know, babe. I don't know how he did it. But, yeah, I think he's responsible for it all, and I think he knows where your mom is now." He reached out and held her hand, and, surprising herself, Leah let him. They sat like that, holding hands and taking the comfort they could from that gesture, knowing there would be no comfort when they went back outside.

Uncle pulled himself off the floor, his hip throbbing from the fall. He muttered and swore as he went to the kitchen, double locking the back door. He wandered back through the dark house, checked the computer monitors, and then dropped on the couch and called the Boss. "What did you do to her?" Uncle listened for a minute, shaking his head the entire time. "You're outta control." Uncle hung up and looked around again. It was time to get out of the game. There was no way this would end well anymore, and he had no intention of getting caught or going to prison. He had to figure out how to cover his tracks, because the Boss wouldn't hesitate to take him down.

chapter thirty

"WHAT A GLORIOUS DAY!" Trix Mann announced over brunch with the bridesmaids. Her shaky smile revealed her angst about how to balance the day she had been awaiting most of her life—or at least since Jake met Amanda—with the knowledge that Leah's mom was mentally ill and missing. She didn't want to be insensitive. She landed on unrelenting positivity, hoping it would be contagious, praying Leah's mother would return. Both for Beverly's sake and the wedding's.

Amanda wore a wooden smile since they sat down at Gloria's, a lovely restaurant with a windowed wall overlooking the river. Trix had planned a day of primping and pampering for the bridesmaids and the mother of the groom, of course.

Beverly had been missing for at least eighteen hours.

Leah and Kemp had driven around until midnight with no sign of her. They went back to the house so Kemp could see the bedroom. He concurred there was no sign of a struggle, but it was a lot of blood and had to mean Beverly wasn't well. After seeing the stain, they went back to the police station. Kemp pitched a fit with the sergeant on duty to no avail. Zoe had texted Leah that they had called nine hospital emergency rooms. No sign of Beverly.

On only a few hours of sleep, Leah went to brunch, staring out the window and watching the clock. Trix, in overdrive, overcompensated for the gloomy, anxious faces at the table.

"You're going to be the most gorgeous bride I've ever seen," Trix announced as the waitress refilled their coffee and brought orange juice. "I mean, along with my girls, of course," she added with a blush. Jake's sisters had been absent from the wedding preparations. Amanda explained they both had busy careers and families, but the bigger reason was that they found weddings to be frivolous and overblown. The tension with their mother over all this had kept them away from most of the events and seemed to add to Trix's desperation to make it all perfect.

It felt frivolous to Leah, too, but she didn't know how to say no. Amanda had apologized repeatedly for the spa day Trix had scheduled—manis and pedis and massages for all of them. Amanda was embarrassed by the expense until Zoe said she'd be paying for all of them—her gift to the group.

The spa was on the main floor of the hotel, so they finished their brunch with silence around Trix's excited ramblings and headed down the gilded hallway to the spa. Leah cringed when the massage therapist led her to her room that smelled of patchouli and where soft Asian flute music played.

Leah did not want a massage. Even on a good day she didn't want people touching her. She tried to say so, got the look from Zoe, and ended up gritting her teeth through another painful wedding ritual.

Leah was self-conscious in the empty room as she undressed and quickly wrapped herself in a soft sheet. The therapist, a tiny woman in her sixties with a cap of white hair, knocked softly, waited for Leah to say, "Come in," and then entered. She introduced herself as Naomi. As she bustled around the room, Leah rolled over and tried to get comfortable with her face in the padded holder.

In Leah's family, they didn't touch. The Dancos were anxious, paranoid people. A simple touch at the wrong time could set off panic attacks. When Naomi ran her hands along Leah's spine and massaged the rigid muscles around her neck, Leah didn't know how to react. Her first impulse was to turn and bite her.

Leah fought herself the entire hour. When she let her guard down and started to relax, her thoughts drifted to her mother and brother, and her whole body stiffened with grief and near panic. Naomi shushed and patted Leah, tolerant of Leah's sadness that couldn't be contained unless Leah was consciously holding it in.

"It happens all the time, dear," Naomi whispered. "Releasing muscle tension also lets loose a stream of emotion. Just go with it." With that, Leah's tears started and wouldn't stop, running down her nose and splatting on the floor.

Finally over, Naomi rested her hands on Leah's shoulders. "I wish you peace, dear. I prayed for answers for you." Leah lay motionless until Naomi finally left the room. Leah dressed slowly, exhausted, and dragged herself back into the reception area where Zoe, Lucy and Amanda were waiting and laughing. They quieted when Leah came out, silenced by her haggard expression.

Trix burst into the room, invigorated by her massage and facial. "On to our next adventure, ladies!"

THE DAY CONTINUED that way for Leah, choking back tears, biting back angry rants, and stumbling through sentimental rituals.

The actual rehearsal was a blur. Leah and Kemp were paired to walk down the aisle together. Leah couldn't even look at him, and missed the pained expressions from most of the wedding party who knew of her "situation." Kemp was quiet, other than promising they would go back out and look later.

The pastor from Trix's church was affable and relaxed. When it was time for Matt to practice walking Amanda down the aisle, they both hesitated. Amanda's cheeks reddened. She could barely look at her dad. Both tall and lanky, they looked alike in so many ways it was surprising they didn't figure out the family connection from their first meeting. With a prompt from the pastor, Matt took Amanda's arm and threaded it through his. He whispered something in her ear, and she laughed out loud, taking his arm and relaxing into her father for the first time in her life.

Trix cried. Leah checked her watch.

THE REHEARSAL DINNER was so full of sentiment, speeches and tears, Leah felt like she was at another AA meeting. By the time it was over, Leah had checked with the police department a half dozen times and learned there was no progress on finding her mother. She'd go to the police station tonight as soon as she could get away.

As the dishes were cleared, Amanda and Jake wandered around the room visiting with friends and family. Jake had grown into something of a politician, adept at small talk and making people feel at home. Amanda's father, Matt, looked almost comfortable as he chatted with Jake and Kemp.

For Leah, the room was stifling with heat and emotion. She needed air. Finally it had been over twenty-four hours her mom was missing, she could leave soon and make the formal police report. Winding through mirrored hallways giving the illusion of a maze, Leah backtracked twice before she found the bar with a restroom nearby.

The bar was less art deco, but still gaudy. And it was quiet. The temptation to have a quick shot of whiskey to settle her nerves was overwhelming. With only one other patron in the bar, she could be in and out in less than a minute.

It would probably have to be vodka, the guilty voice in her head told her, because sometimes the odor of whiskey lingered. She glanced around the bar again, noticing the familiar face in the corner. He made eye contact, and they nodded at each other. Strange that *he* would be here. Did he think he would be able to crash the party when the wedding group inevitably arrived in the bar?

Seeing a familiar face made her pause. She went to the restroom to clear her head. The room was mirrored floor to ceiling, and images of herself seemed to bounce back and forth, growing smaller and smaller in each reflection. The illusion added to her dizziness and made her crave a vodka shot even more . She crouched over the sink and patted cold water on her cheeks, not hearing the door open.

When she stood up, he was behind her. She had a second to register the shock before he grabbed her around the neck with surprising speed and held a cloth over her mouth. A smell, acrid and sharp, overtook her, and her knees buckled. Panicked, Leah flailed and grasped at the cloth, but he held it tight as the room swayed and rocked around her. She dropped to the floor. His reflection was everywhere, like she was being jumped by a gang. Her limbs grew heavy, and the cold floor tile on her cheek gave a bit of relief as she finally gave in and all went dark.

AS THE REHEARSAL DINNER was wrapping up and the guests were moving to the bar, Lucy noticed first that Leah wasn't back yet.

"Do you think she's okay?" Lucy asked Zoe as they watched the guys push tables together in the bar.

Zoe shrugged. "She'd been checking in with the cops every hour. I think she was going to leave early and file the official report on her mom." They looked around the dark room.

"I'm glad she's not hiding out in here," Lucy said.

"I know, right?" Zoe said. The wedding party and family members took seats around the table. Will went to the bar and brought back two pitchers of beer. Jake pulled up to the table and kept his arm around Amanda, and her smile was growing more genuine as the night went on. "I'll text her," Zoe said. "But I'm guessing she left to file the report. Not much we can do now."

KEMP HAD PULLED UP an empty chair next to him at the table and rested his arm across the back. He was on his third beer when he looked around and said, "Where the heck is Leah? Shouldn't she be back by now?"

Leah had been gone two hours.

The Boss expected Uncle to help, and he couldn't argue. Again the Boss went too far. Uncle headed home to pack up his house–the dope and all the equipment. Not a lot of weed right now, but plenty of heavy stuff. He gathered every zip drive, recorder, screen, and laptop. The video the Boss would make tonight would be worth a lot, but he wasn't in it for that. The Boss cared about the "productions." Uncle just wanted to keep selling–to keep the little man close. Now that he was gone, Uncle had lost interest in the business. He didn't care about anything anymore. He just wanted out.

chapter thirty-one

KEMP WAS WORRIED. He had texted Leah with no response, and his buddy Nate, the head dispatcher, said her last call to check for updates on her mother came in at 7:00 p.m. Kemp knew Leah rode to the hotel that morning with the bridal party and didn't have a car there. She was going to walk to the police station to meet with officers again and officially make a missing persons report. She never showed.

Kemp dialed her number, but her phone went straight to voicemail. Their table in the bar had cleared out, but Kemp stayed and wandered through the hotel lobby, back to the dining room where they had dinner, and the bar. Leah was nowhere to be found.

"Sorry to bother you," he said to the bartender capping bottles and putting away garnishes. "Did you see a tiny little blonde lady in here earlier . . . kinda frizzy hair, wearing a hot black dress?"

The bartender, a balding man with huge eyebrows, nodded and motioned to the hallway. "Yeah, she walked by here a few times. Never came in, though."

"So which way did she go?"

The bartender pointed down the long hallway toward the restrooms.

"Thanks, man." Kemp jogged out of the bar and searched the hallway, including knocking on the restroom door and then pushing it open tentatively. "Terrance PD!" he announced. The restroom was empty. Some paper towels were scattered on the floor, and there was a faint chemical smell. Kemp left the restroom and did one more lap around the main floor of the hotel, but it was quiet. He asked the front desk staff if they had seen Leah come through, but they hadn't. Troubled, he headed for his truck, assuming she must have left the hotel.

SO COLD. HER EYES were fused shut. Crushing pain in her skull. And the cold . . . Curled in a ball trying to find warmth . . . smooth fabric under her. Sheets?

What's happening?

Still unable to open her eyes, Leah felt around. She ran her hand along her back, her shoulder. Along her waist, hips . . . bare skin. *Oh, God . . .*

KEMP FUMBLED WITH THE LOCK until he lost his patience and shoved the weak door in with his shoulder, pulling the whole doorframe loose. Leah's house was dark and cool. Kemp went straight for Leah's bedroom but it was still, no sign she had been there for many hours. The sheets were cold.

Kemp was kicking himself for not maiming, arresting, or killing Carl when he had the chance last night. Whether Leah had gone off searching for her mom by herself, or something worse, this was Carl's fault.

Kemp went by Luke's room and pushed the door open. Apparently Leah had closed the door and ignored the mess made by the BCA less than a month ago as they turned the room over looking for evidence. He looked over the pile by the closet. Hiking shoes, steel-toed boots . . . no athletic shoes. It was a stupid piece of evidence, but it was there. His gut told him all along Luke couldn't have attacked Annika. But as always, Kemp was one step behind and could never prove it. How could he always be one step behind?

He peeled out of Leah's driveway and headed for Carl's house, afraid of what he would find when he got there. The bastard had eluded him for most of his career, but this had to end tonight.

TEETH CHATTERING, the cold was seeping into her bones. Her mind had cleared enough to recognize the black ski mask over her head. Leah choked back her panic and forced herself to think. She had to be on a bed–what bed? Whose bed? She could hear his breathing–heavy, diseased, rattled breathing.

THE WHEELS OF HIS PICKUP screamed his return to the alley behind Carl's house. Kemp repeatedly dialed Leah's number with no response, growing more concerned by the second. Kemp drove up on the lawn, erupted from the truck and threw himself into the kitchen door, splintering another doorframe. He raced through the house to the front room.

Empty. A heavy layer of dust coated the dining room table, with clean squares outlining where the computers used to be.

Kemp froze, forced himself to think. What the hell would Carl be doing with all of those computers? And why did he suddenly need to get rid of them?

Kemp flashed back on the hand-held video recorder Leah had shown him days ago.

Computers . . . video . . . *holy hell*. It all came together.

Kemp bounded for his truck and tore out of the alley.

In the old days, with just the three of them, Uncle had almost been happy. At least, as happy as someone like him knew how to be. He laughed back then. It had been so long since Uncle had laughed he was sure he didn't know how anymore. There were some good times with the little man, too, but the laughter was eventually replaced by the foggy haze required for compliance. And then, when the little man wasn't so little anymore, the game had changed. It was his only choice, really. Backed into a corner, busted, *Uncle did what he had to do. He bought into the new game in exchange for his freedom. There was no way Uncle was going to jail.*

Uncle had met the Boss when they each had a problem. The Boss was sick and Uncle was in trouble. That damn cop finally had enough to bring him down, so the Boss took care of it. And the Boss needed more help than any doctor could give, so Uncle found a way to get what he needed. And so their partnership started.

But the Boss had bigger plans than pills and weed (and acid and ecstasy and whatever else he could get his hands on).

It was straight up porn at first. Uncle had no interest, but the Boss didn't give him a choice. And there was a market he couldn't believe. With the feds clamping down, he had to get away from selling for a while, so Uncle went along with it. It got more messed up, more violent, and way too risky. Uncle was almost ready to run when he found out that the little man had betrayed him–he told about their game. And the Boss had come up with a way to bring him down just like they had taken care of Joe and the kid. Blinded with rage, Uncle went along with it: setting the little man up, demolishing the girl himself, and feeling the last piece of his soul break off and drift away.

And so Uncle was empty now. The little man was gone, the game had to end, and Uncle had nothing left.

Uncle had been driving his old van in circles around town, packed to the top with screens and laptops, baggies and pills. He pulled up to an overlook of the river, at least forty feet above the water where the river made a sharp turn to the north. He stared out at the water, black and glossy in the moonlight, choppy with wind and bone-chilling rain. He took a long hit on the last of his joint, holding the smoke in his lungs until they burned. Without another thought Uncle Coolie rolled down his windows, pressed the gas pedal to the floor and propelled the van over the weak curb. It rolled down the steep hill and into the river, where it sank in less than a minute.

Game over.

chapter thirty-two

AFTER CHASING THIS DIRTBAG for eight years, nothing should have surprised him anymore. Carl was making porn. Kemp kicked himself again for missing what was right in front of his face. Carl got Beverly high and had sex with her on video. For years he had gotten Luke high and had sex with him, and if he looked there'd probably be video of that, too.

Kemp was convinced, more than ever, Carl had assaulted Annika. And somewhere there had to be video.

For now, he just needed the video of Carl and Beverly. He would use it to convince Jake, a judge, or anyone who'd listen, that every cop in the county needed to be searching for Carl. If they found him, he knew they would find Leah.

Back at his house, he rifled through the junk on his table to find the recorder he'd left there days ago. He found it under the sports section and played it again, seeing it in a different light this time. His hatred for Carl swelled as he watched him violate Beverly, but he was unprepared for what came next. Carl held another blunt up to her lips, and she barely inhaled before she collapsed. But then Carl backed away, and someone else stepped into the picture and climbed onto the bed.

Someone else?

He watched with revulsion, and then nearly dropped the recorder when he realized who it was.

"Oh, fuck no . . ."

Gordy Hoffbrau.

Gordy was working with Carl?!

In seconds Kemp was back in his truck and drove straight to Jake and Amanda's house. He pounded on the door until Jake opened it, half asleep, his curly hair wild around his head.

"I'm getting married in like sixteen hours, dude," Jake muttered, wearing a t-shirt and boxers, his eyes barely open. "You're very lucky that Amanda's at Lucy's. If you're here to take me to a strip club I'm gonna punch you in the face."

"Hoffbrau! Fucking Gordy Hoffbrau! Oh, my God, I can't believe this. I can't believe this!" Kemp pushed his way in, dripping wet from rain, pacing maniacally.

Jake jumped out of the way. "Kemp, what's your problem? What the hell is going on?"

"Gordy has been working with Carl Vole. I saw it with my own damn eyes. Do you know what this means?! How far back this has to go?" Kemp froze. "The Miranda Warning eight years ago. It was Gordy! He got rid of it and fucked me over."

Jake closed his eyes. "You're losing your mind." He started for his bedroom when Kemp grabbed his shoulder and pulled him back.

"I'll show you!" Kemp fumbled with the buttons on the camera.

"Calm down, Kemp," Jake snapped. He grabbed the video out of his hand, looking between Kemp and the recorder. "Come on. What is this?" Jake asked warily, squinting at the tiny screen.

"Leah brought it to me days ago. She found it in her mom's bedroom. It's her mother and Carl . . ." Shaking, Kemp took the camera back and messed with the buttons until he could get the video to move forward. As if the video wasn't heinous enough, seeing their naked limbs flail crazily on that tiny screen was madness. Jake shook his head at Kemp, turning away until Kemp slowed the recording just as Gordy came into view.

Jake recoiled. "Holy shit," he breathed. Gordy was unmistakable—huge and heavy, coated in purple and red blotches and sores. And doing unspeakable sexual acts to a drugged, unconscious woman.

"You see?" Kemp's pacing resumed. He ran his hands through his hair.

"We can get a warrant with this," Jake stammered. "We're going to arrest the assistant chief of police." He dropped into a chair. "On my wedding day."

"That's not even the problem!" Kemp bellered. "I can't find Leah."

Jake looked up, incredulous. "Now *she's* gone? What the hell's going on here?"

JAKE THREW SOME CLOTHES on while Kemp tried to explain what he knew about Carl and why he thought Carl, and now Gordy, were connected to Leah's absence. Again, he went through his theory about Joe and Luke trying to get away from dealing for Carl, reminding Jake only once he told him this weeks ago. Jake told him to move on. When Kemp described Leah and Kemp's trip to Carl's house, Jake interrupted and told him he was an idiot.

"Desperation," Kemp barked back. "It happens to cops when their attorneys don't trust their judgment or believe what they say. They end up doing stupid shit and getting their girlfriends hurt."

"Okay, fine, keep talking," Jake said. "I didn't know she was your girlfriend."

Kemp's stomach dropped. "We need to call the girls. If she's not there, then Hoffbrau's got her."

"We don't know that," Jake said. "But, yeah, call them."

Kemp took a breath and dialed Zoe's cell.

"Hey, Kemp," Zoe answered sleepily. "Did you guys find Leah's mom?"

"No. Is Leah with you?"

"No," Zoe said, awake now. "We thought she was with you. What's going on?"

"I don't know." Kemp looked over at Jake, who was shaking his head.

"Don't scare them yet," Jake whispered at Kemp. "She could be anywhere."

Kemp hesitated, knowing Jake could be right even though his gut told him something was wrong. "Yeah, uh, I was just checking in . . . to see how you ladies are doing tonight. That's all."

"Yeah, right, Kemp. You called after midnight for no good reason. Is she off drinking somewhere?" Zoe sighed.

"Maybe. I'm sorry for bugging you. Just, uh, give me a call if you hear from her." Kemp set his phone down. "I know something's wrong."

"Yeah. . . you may be right, buddy," Jake agreed. But we've gotta do this the right way. We might be able to get a crim sex charge against both of them, just on the video of Leah's mom alone."

"I'm not worried about charges," Kemp snapped. "I'm worried about her."

"I know," Jake said. "We're trying, and an arrest warrant will get us in the door just as well as a search warrant. We need to get the squad working with us, and they're not going to go after their boss without a judge's signature."

Jake threw together the evidence for an arrest warrant on both Carl and Gordy for the incident with Beverly on video. Criminal sexual conduct laws were complicated. Getting a warrant without a statement from the victim was going to be tough. But with both Leah and Beverly missing, Jake argued that a judge would sign it. Kemp still thought it was a waste of time, but it was the best they had for now.

CONSCIOUSNESS EVADED LEAH like a balloon caught in the wind. She could reach for it and think she had taken hold, only to have it slip through her fingers while darkness fell again. She dreamed of her father looking at stars, of Jedi Knights, and of her brother begging for her help.

When Leah awoke her mind was clearer. Her throat burned and she tasted a constant, bitter bile in the back of her throat. She lay as still as she could, straining to hear any sound, but the room was silent, and she didn't know what that meant. Was Gordy gone? Injured?

The struggle against him in the restroom was foggy and surreal. She was stronger, but he had drugged and overpowered her, just like he had done to Annika. Or maybe it was Coolie who had drugged Annika, and Gordy covered it up. She couldn't think through her haze and rage. All she knew was that Gordy, the next in line for the chief of police, had fooled them all. She clenched her teeth to hold back a furious sob as she thought of what he might do to her while she was still so weak.

But the room felt empty, so with great effort she took a risk and pulled the mask off. No sign of anyone else in the room. She blinked and strained to focus: gilded wallpaper, mirrored tile, pink carpet. She was still in the Terrance Hotel.

Leah felt her first surge of hope.

KEMP'S RINGING PHONE cut through the howl of the wind and rain and startled him. He ducked through the heavy bushes around the back of Gordy's dark and silent townhome and ran back for his truck. Jake had warned Kemp to stay away from Gordy's house and wait for the warrant, but they both knew he wouldn't. As soon as Jake was out the door, Kemp was back in his pickup and at Gordy's townhome on the newer side of town. Kemp had pressed his face against every window, but they were heavily covered so he couldn't get a glimpse of anything. His cop instinct told him the place was empty, but he was afraid to be wrong. The warrant wasn't going to do them any good if they didn't know where to look.

It was just after 3:00 a.m., and there was still no sign of her.

Kemp had made a report to dispatch, so the uniformed cops were looking for her, too. But he had stopped short of telling the dispatchers about Gordy and Coolie. Kemp was still the unstable detective on administrative leave, and Jake was right—making accusations without proof wasn't going to get them anywhere. As soon as the warrant was signed, Jake would bring it to the police department and the full search would begin for the assistant chief.

Kemp hopped back in his truck, mopped his face with an old fast food napkin, and pulled his buzzing phone from his pocket. It was so damp he was afraid it would be dead, but it lit up with the number for sheriff's dispatch.

"Hey, Kemp," Nate said.

"Is she there?" Kemp interrupted.

"No . . ." Nate's voice was professional, but pained. "You should probably head out to the river overlook on the north end."

Kemp recognized the tone immediately. "Why? What's out there?"

"A van registered to Carl Vole was found partially submerged," Nate said. "It looks like it crossed the overlook and rolled down the hill and went under."

"And Carl?" Kemp asked flatly, his eyes fixed on Hoffbrau's front door, wishing stupidly that somehow Leah would emerge and run to his truck.

"They want you to ID him."

Carl was dead. Kemp had envisioned arresting him so many times he had never considered Carl could end up killing himself, one way or another. But there was no satisfaction—just fear escalating into panic at what this might mean for Leah.

LEAH HAD BLACKED OUT again, but when she awoke she grabbed the string of her consciousness and wouldn't let go. She just needed to get across the room and to the hallway, and someone had to find her.

Leah forced her brain to think. The mask was off, and her clothes were in a heap next to her. He had drugged her the same way Annika was drugged. The bad smell, as Annika had called it in her interview, had made everything go dark, and her limbs wouldn't work now.

The struggle with Gordy played in her head like a nightmare—distorted and terrifying. More so because it was Gordy. All that time they had been focused on Coolie, and Gordy had been there undermining them at every turn. He was under their noses, pretending to be a good guy. Leah had learned years before that criminals, especially sex offenders, got off on what researchers called "duping delight." They were actually aroused by the trust they gained and subsequently destroyed in their victims. Her rage was swelling, but if she gave in to her anger she wouldn't be able to think. Right now her priority had to be getting away.

Leah sized up her surroundings. The covers were pulled off the large bed just like they were in the video of her mom she had seen days before. She pulled her arm under her, aching with the effort, and pushed up on one elbow, blinking and straining to look around the hotel room. The bathroom door was around the corner and was closed and dark. The rest of the room was strangely bright, and she turned her aching neck to look up at a lamp that seemed to dangle over her. Not a hotel lamp. A red light blinked in front of her. Was that a camera?

KEMP STOOD AT THE EDGE of the river where the back bumper of the van protruded like the tip of an iceberg, with the remaining mass submerged and ominous. All he could do was stare at the water, his feet rooted to the rocky shore, his breathing shallow and fast.

The river was swarming with uniformed officers, EMTs, and a team in wetsuits had just arrived to start the retrieval.

"It looks like it's just the guy," one of the officers said. "And about $20,000 in computer equipment. What the hell is an old man doing with all that shit?"

Kemp wandered back to his truck. Renewed fear washed over him. He was at a loss for what to do next when his phone buzzed again. He swiped the phone to answer the number he didn't recognize.

"Seargent Kemper?"

"Who is this?"

"I have Beverly Danco," a deep, female voice said with a sniffle. "We're at the hospital. She's hurt so bad."

The Boss was slipping . . . struggling . . . and losing. He gave up on his doctor when he told him his trio of autoimmune diseases were winning. Nothing helped him anymore–not his meds, not pills, not weed. The fevers came more often at night, signs of the infections his body couldn't fight off any longer. The sores on his body were on fire. His lungs were thick and barely pulled in enough oxygen to breathe. He sputtered and coughed all the time now. And his brown frothy urine meant his kidneys were failing, too.

But the itch was still there. The need to be serviced. He deserved *what came so easily to everyone else. What Kemp had the nerve to do, sweaty and moaning, next door to his office and pretend it was nothing. The itch built slowly at first, and he got off whenever he could. Whoever Carl would bring to him was enough for a long time.*

He had been stuck with Carl for years. When his meds were failing him, the opportunity with Carl presented itself. Carl could supply him what he needed, and in exchange he could keep the guys away and keep Carl in business.

But then business grew slower, and he got sicker, so he needed more stuff. Stronger stuff. The Boss got creative and took care of several problems all at once. They started the new business, with the girls and the video, and holy fuck it was good for a while. His pain all but gone, the itch satisfied . . . it was good for a while.

KEMP WAS MET at the hospital by a short, round woman in a knee-length pink raincoat. She had the hood pulled up over her head to protect from the relentless, cold rain.

"I'm Maggie, a friend of Beverly's," Maggie said in a gravelly voice, leading him to the room where Beverly had been admitted for the night. "Leah told us once that she trusts you."

They entered her room quietly. Beverly was sleeping, milky pale, and her mouth slack and pained. Kemp looked her over with a cop's lens—broken blood vessels around her mouth and all over one cheek. Darker bruising around her ear and across the left side of her face. Her right hand was above the covers, her nails coated in blood. Defensive injuries.

"She's hurt so badly." Maggie fell into the chair beside her bed, pushing aside a sparkly, hot pink sweatshirt.

"What the hell happened to her?" Kemp rubbed his head viciously.

Maggie set her hands on her blocky hips. "Carl. That's what happened to her."

Beverly stirred, and they both stopped and looked down at her. "I t-t-told you it wasn't him," she whispered.

"I know what you said, Bevvie." Maggie knelt by Beverly and stroked her arm. "But of course it was him."

Beverly sat up with great effort and shook her head hard. "No. It wasn't him. The one who hurt me was different. Carl loves me . . ." Beverly crumpled back in bed, holding her sides like it hurt to cry. Beverly looked up at Kemp in agony.

"I think you're right. It wasn't just Carl." Kemp leaned down over Beverly. "Mrs. Danco? Can you describe who hurt you?"

Beverly clamped her hand over her eyes like she was shielding herself from seeing him again. "No," she wailed. "I don't want to."

"I'm very sorry, Mrs. Danco, but this is important. We need to know who hurt you. I already have a good idea, but I need to hear it from you." Kemp fought to keep his voice steady when he was ready to scream at her.

"It can wait," Maggie snapped. "She's been through enough."

"Leah's missing," Kemp blurted. "And I'm afraid the man who attacked her has her right now."

Beverly's eyes flew open, and she grabbed Kemp's wrist. "NO!"

KEMP USED EVERY OUNCE of energy he had left to calm Beverly, or she'd never be able to give a coherent statement. Maggie helped Beverly move the head of the bed up, and she laid back on a pile of pillows, holding a crumpled tissue against her lips. Kemp found his digital recorder and started asking questions. They sped through the basics, and then got to Beverly and Carl's relationship.

"It started when we were all just barely grownups. Me, Carl, and Roger. We were the three amigos. And sometimes we were more like a threesome. But I chose Roger, and Carl never forgave me. He's been in love with me all these years." She mopped the tears off her cheeks.

"Bevvie," Maggie said in a thick voice. "What he's been doing to you isn't love." Beverly's head snapped over at Maggie.

"He loves me. And he's been taking care of people like me for years." She stuck out her chin. "I need more than what a regular doctor can get me. But Carl wants me to feel better. He gets me what I need." She glanced at Kemp nervously. "You don't understand what it's like to have my kind of anxiety. It's worse than other people's, and I can't use regular medicine. "

Maggie sat forward on her chair. "He's been giving her so much marijuana she has to be high every minute of the day. Every time I'm there I check out her stash, and it's stronger and heavier than the last time I looked. I don't know if it's synthetic pot, or if it's mixed with harder stuff, but she's high all the time. And then he takes advantage of her. Sexually. Half the time she doesn't even know what happened." They didn't know Kemp had already seen the whole thing on a five-inch screen.

Beverly hung her head, an odd expression on her face, and Kemp realized she didn't mind Coolie doing whatever he wanted to her.

"Mrs. Danco, can you explain how you learned someone else was hurting you?"

"I woke up, or whatever you call it when you're high. He was there, and everything hurt. I thought I was wetting myself because I could feel it all over. But it was blood." She shuddered and the tears started again. "He was over me . . . on me . . ." Beverly squinted like she was seeing it, but afraid to see it.

Kemp's heart sped up, but he forced himself to stay calm and get the information. "What did he look like?"

"Big." She stared and grimaced. "Cruel."

"That's enough," Maggie barked in a deep voice. "She can't do any more."

"Just a few more questions," Kemp said, fighting the urge to yell at the strange woman with a voice that seemed to range from a squeaky mouse to bear.

Beverly nodded.

"Describe him, please, as best you can."

Beverly took a new tissue and blew her nose. "He was large, naked and hairy. And something is wrong with him. He has them sores all over his body. And I mean all over." Maggie grimaced and turned away. "Something else ain't right about him. It's like he can't breathe. He was angry I woke up, so he smacked me in the face, but it made him tired to hit me. I kicked at him, and he howled. That's all I remember." She fell back against her pillows, exhausted.

"I found her later that day," Maggie said. "Yesterday. How could it just be yesterday?" she said absently. "And she's been with me ever since. I brought her to the hospital an hour after she started to bleed so much."

"And we've been looking for her ever since," Kemp said with a frown. "Leah's been worried sick. She found blood in her room and her mother gone."

"I knew she loved me," Beverly said with a triumphant smile that was soon replaced by more tears. "You have to find her! He's dangerous . . . but sick, too. If he has her, he couldn't have taken her far. Go, now. Find her!"

"We're working on it." Kemp gathered the recorder and his jacket, handed her his business card, and headed for the door. "Stay in touch, Mrs. Danco. I'll let you know as soon as I find her."

Kemp was on the phone with Jake before he made it to the hallway, describing her statement. "It's enough," he said. "Judge Knox is still reviewing it. She's already pissed off that I woke her up in the middle of the night, and to arrest a cop, no less. But she can't say it's weak anymore. I'll add it to the warrant and we'll have everything we need."

Leah grabbed for her clothes, shame overcoming the fog. Her black dress, chosen on a shopping trip with Amanda and Zoe that seemed like a lifetime ago, was shredded. Her body shuddered in a visceral reaction, subconsciously recalling the dress being sliced off in a violent haze. Leah covered herself as best she could and crawled off the bed, rolling onto the floor with a sick thud.

As she crawled toward the door, the mirrored wallpaper reflected her brokenness. Wild frizzy hair, thick black smudges around her eyes, naked and draped in rags. Alone. She thought of her friends and how they had been there for her more times than she could ever count. And images of Kemp ran through her head, and how she pushed him away, desperately trying to prove she didn't need him, or anyone.

In this moment above all others, she knew how stupid and pointless that was. Terror shook her as she feared she may not get back to everything she loved.

Leah summoned the strength that had carried her through years of abandonment, loss, and drunkenness. The same strength had helped her find her work, her friends, and a life she desperately wanted to keep.

Leah reached up to the doorknob and grabbed on, wailing with the effort, and was ready to pull herself up when a heavy foot stepped on her back hard.

"I don't think so, little lady," he said, gasping with the effort of holding her down. "You and I are just getting started."

The Boss knew he was getting soft. His life would end soon. All he wanted anymore was someone to lie with him when it hurt too much and he was afraid.

Bev was good for that. He tried it the regular way first, just meeting and talking to her. But like all the women, all *of them, she was repulsed by him. So he knocked her out, and then he could lie with her all night. He would fuck her first, as hard as he could, proving that he wasn't weak. Proving she was his and he was strong. Afterward he held her and laid with her all night.*

But then she screamed. She just had *to wake up and scream, like he was a monster, like she wasn't his. She ruined everything. Something snapped in him, and he had to punish Beverly the best way he knew how.*

The plan was genius, of course. Carl would go along because it took care of all of his problems at once. This time the Boss would take the girl, fuck her within an inch of her life, and leave her there. Carl would get Kemper and drag him back with whatever it took, back to the hotel. The Boss would set him up and do the honors himself, arresting Investigator Pete Kemper for first degree criminal sexual conduct against Leah Danco, who'd nearly die from her injuries.

And with the two of them out of his way, done with their fucking and flirting and taunting for good, he would spend whatever days he had left taking Carl's sloppy seconds with Beverly. It wouldn't be a great end, but it was what he wanted, and for once he should get what he deserved.

KEMP SPED ACROSS TOWN to the Terrance Hotel. Beverly had unknowingly pointed them there when she described how sick Gordy was. Kemp felt like a fool for not figuring it out himself. Gordy had to be at the hotel, somewhere, with Leah. She'd disappeared so quickly last night because he pulled her into a guest room before anyone could see them. A huge man carrying a tiny blonde would have attracted attention. Plus Gordy was too sick to carry anyone, and they all knew the only way Leah would have left the hotel with him was kicking and screaming, or drugged. He had to be right. She had to be at the hotel, because the alternative was worse. That possibility was unbearable.

Kemp called Jake on his way there and told him to get every cop in Terrance County over to the Terrance Hotel.

"I'll call the chief right now," Jake said, always one to stick with the rules. "We'll get the damn squad."

"I'm going to murder him." His voice was ice, and they both knew he meant it.

LEAH WRITHED UNDER his weight, rage and panic clearing her head.

"Get off me!" He pressed his heel further into her back, and she wailed in pain. She slapped around at her back trying to shrug him off, but he had leverage and held his ground.

"Does it hurt?" Hoffbrau taunted, coughing and sputtering as he pressed down harder. "You and I need to finish the show."

"You're . . . a lunatic," Leah strained to get the words out as the air escaped her lungs.

He leaned on her harder. "You think so?" He was heaving with the effort of holding her down and talking. "You think I'm untouchable? Like you're so much better than me? Who's better now?" In the mirrored wallpaper she could see he was struggling to maintain his balance, and sweat was dripping down his blotchy neck. Leah knew she had to be stronger.

Her right arm was pinned under her, pressing on her sternum, but her left arm was free. She flailed her arm around and then hit hard against his other foot. He was panting harder now, gasping for air, but so was she. Leah drove her knuckles into his Achilles tendon. It was enough to throw him off balance. He stumbled and then crashed backward onto the bed with a great thud.

Leah tried to pull herself up on her elbows but the crushing pain in her ribs was unbearable and she collapsed. He was thrashing around on the bed above her, and Leah had to find a way to move. She screamed as she rolled onto her back, clenching her teeth hard as she tried to sit up, feeling her ribs pop. Explosions went off in front of her eyes. She managed to sit up against the wall while Gordy grabbed something off the bedside table and was up again, coming at her with a syringe in his hand. He was going to knock her out again. Leah pawed at the door in panic, but couldn't reach high enough to grab the knob.

Suddenly there was pounding at the door. Gordy's head shot up, and his face contorted.

"Terrance Police! I need you to open this door immediately." They could hear officers pounding on other doors in the hallway and voices, confused and scared, going into the hallway. Gordy stared at the door, wheezing hard.

"Help me," Leah tried to yell, but it came out a breathy wail.

"Open this door or we will come in," the officer insisted. Gordy glared at the door, and then his face went slack.

His last thought was of Beverly and how she could have almost loved him some day . . .

He closed his eyes, turned the needle on himself, and plunged it into his chest. Gordy Hoffbrau, assistant chief of police, fell back on the bed and sputtered and coughed until he breathed his last.

WHEN THE DOOR FINALLY OPENED, Leah was struggling again to hold onto her consciousness. Images swirled in her head of her dad pointing out constellations on warm summer nights . . . of eating cinnamon rolls and laughing with her friends . . . of Luke walking out of jail. And she thought of Kemp with his arm around her as they rocked in his boat watching fireworks . . . he was caressing her hair, and telling her that she was going to be okay, and thanking God that they found her in time.

chapter thirty-three

WEDDING PREPARATIONS USUALLY take a year, if not more. Flowers and food, dresses and decorations—every detail considered, weighed out, and finalized. Finding a dress could take months by itself, not to mention deciding on a meal, a reception site, the DJ—the process can put a strain on the best of relationships.

What is often forgotten is that weddings and marriage are two different things, and a perfect wedding has no bearing on the strength of the relationship.

Jake and Amanda were indifferent about their wedding—neither could summon interest in daisies vs. begonias, chicken vs. beef. Amanda chose a dress in an hour, and Jake agreed to his tux sight unseen.

So on the day they had been planning for months, they both knew exactly where they wanted to be.

Jake spent the night obtaining warrants, locating perpetrators, and releasing an innocent man. Luke Danco walked out of jail shaken and confused. A woman named Maggie picked him up and drove him back to her house, where his mother hugged him and cried. They spent the day on the couch watching Star Wars movies while Maggie served them soup and cupcakes. All three of them cheered when Luke Skywalker, Jedi Knight, blew up the Death Star.

Releasing the other innocent man would take more work, but they were all committed to doing right by Joe, too.

Amanda awoke to the news that Leah was in the hospital after a night in hell. Amanda, Zoe, and Lucy rushed to the hospital and brought Leah home, all of them whispering and tidying while she rested.

Promptly at 4:00 p.m., when the wedding was set to begin, most of the wedding party, including Jake and Amanda, made their way back to the church and into the pews. And then Michael Mann escorted his wife, Trix, of fourteen years down the aisle, and they renewed their vows in a ceremony Trix had dreamed of her whole life.

epilogue

LATE FALL FOOTBALL in Minnesota meant cheerleaders in turtlenecks and windpants. Bright lights illuminating shredded grass fields. And high schoolers gathering under blankets in frosted bleachers. The Terrance Warriors were playing for the conference championship, and the whole school was there.

Annika followed her friends to the freshman section of the bleachers, and they climbed to the top. A ninth grader named Zach watched Annika as she passed by in a down jacket and white fuzzy hat, her hair whipping around her face. And then he made up an excuse to get his friends to move up higher, too.

MOST OF THE NURSES and therapists in the rehab unit tried not to get too attached, but everyone had fallen in love with Ben. He was ticklish, so he giggled through his stretches, walking practice with his braces, and PT exercises. His silliness brought Jenny's smiles back through so many painful days. And his resilience would get them through that amazing, terrifying day when they finally got to go home.

THE WEST COAST SUNSET brought spectators to the beaches most nights. Families gathered on blankets to roast marshmallows, teenagers played frisbee until the dark took over, and couples walked hand in hand with the water lapping at their ankles. The orange-and-pink sky cast a magical glow, and most watched for the moment when the sun flashed green as it fell below the watery horizon. A sunset wedding near the waves gathered a smiling crowd, none more giddy than the bride and groom.

"ZACH AND HIS FRIENDS are coming up here . . ." Annika's friend whispered in her ear. Annika watched him climb the stairs casually. He and his friends filed into the row in front of Annika and her friends. Zach and Annika were science partners, and he smelled good, like shampoo and deodorant. Clean, unlike many of the boys in their grade.

Annika breathed in and out slowly, the way she practiced with her therapist. It didn't take the nightmares away, but she hardly had panic attacks anymore, and it definitely got her through moments like this.

She was an island among these normal teens who were laughing about Stevie's new braces and bemoaning the impossible geometry test. For months, Annika had watched them do regular things and wondered if her time of normalcy was over. Her therapist said no. The nightmares would fade, and the feeling of being chased all the time couldn't last forever. Her therapist promised, as they talked or played cards when talking was too much, that it would get better.

There were days it seemed impossible. When the guy they had in custody was released, and Sergeant Kemper said the man who had actually hurt her was dead, the panic attack lasted for a full hour. *They could be wrong again,* she told them through shallow, hysterical breaths. *He might come back again.* Kemper stayed at her house well after her panic subsided, and he explained over and over, until they were convinced, that the man who hurt Annika was gone for good.

The kids in school knew she was the victim, the girl who was found half naked in the street. While she had never been identified, the rumors spread fast. No one was mean, exactly, but most people just stayed away.

Except for Zach. For some reason, he wasn't scared of Annika and her disease of trauma. They had been in many of the same classes for years, both on the honor track, so they were used to chatting over tests and sharing notes. But this was the first year he talked to her like a friend. It was nice.

BEN'S LEG WAS HELD together by pins and a plate, and he still had many surgeries ahead to ensure that the bone would grow with him. He walked with a limp, swinging his bad leg around because he couldn't get his knee to work right. The physical therapist told Jenny it still might come.

Ben didn't seem to care. He marched down the hallway of the rehab unit high-fiving nurses and unit aides. He understood he was going home for good this Friday evening, and he was giddy.

Jenny was anxious, afraid of what was next for her. Life on the unit was safe and predictable. The nurses had become her friends, and Jenny didn't need to face co-workers, family members, or anyone else who wondered how she had chosen such a monster for a boyfriend.

And when the real monster was found dead, and Joe was released hours later, Jenny could hide on the unit, not facing any of it. No one asked or seemed to care what Jenny would do about her falsely arrested boyfriend.

Joe actually contacted her first, asking if he could see Ben, just once. He needed to know Ben was okay. Jenny agreed, knowing Ben had grown so accustomed to people in and out of his room she thought Joe's visit would be uneventful. She was unprepared when Joe slunk into the room and Ben's eyes lit up. He scrambled out of bed as best he could and wrapped himself around Joe's leg. Joe wasn't prepared for Ben's forgiveness, the forgiveness he didn't know he needed until that moment, for his failure to protect Ben from the man who actually hurt him.

Joe stayed through dinner that evening, his eyes meeting Jenny's every time Ben couldn't hear something, or when his injured brain stumbled over words he used to know. When it was time to leave, Ben and Joe hugged for a long time, until Ben's little t-shirt was soaked with Joe's tears.

Surprising herself, Jenny invited Joe to the hospital for Benny's discharge. He showed up early and helped pack his clothes, toys, and cards into hospital-issued plastic bags. Jenny and Joe barely talked, words still eluding them, but Jenny found his presence soothing, and occasionally she looked over at him and smiled.

JAKE AND AMANDA WERE in a full sprint, followed closely by Zoe and Sam, William and Lucy. They reached a fenced overlook with stairs down to the beach, and they paused to breathe.

"I see her!" Lucy pointed at their friend, who looked even smaller from above.

"Thank God!" Zoe panted.

"Now where's Kemp? Let's find him so you gals get settled down." Jake said, wrapping his arms around Amanda and resting his chin on her shoulder.

"Hey!" Amanda said, grabbing at his hand. "Weddings are meant to be shared with the people you love."

"Ha! That's big talk coming from such a reluctant bride yourself," Will teased.

"Our wedding was beautiful!" Amanda grinned at him. "The reception filled Crabby Dan's entire restaurant and deck!"

Below them, Leah drew in the sand with her toes, her sandals tossed aside, the air still warm despite the fading sun. She breathed in and out slowly, the way Nick had taught her, until her heart rate slowed to normal again. The waves rolled in at a predictable, soothing pace helping her feel calm.

"So she's just standing there, staring out at the water," Amanda said. "Where is he? Did they do it? Don't tell me he left her . . ."

"No, my cynical bride," Jake said, pointing down the beach at the marina. "That's gotta be him loading up that boat." They watched him for a moment, and Jake wrapped his hand around Amanda's, clinking their wedding rings together.

"Do you think they're already married?" Lucy asked with a touch of sadness. "Do you think we missed it?"

"I'm not sure if they even went through with it," Zoe said as she leaned her head on Sam's shoulder and he kissed her forehead.

"They went through with it," Jake said with conviction. "There's no way he was gonna let her slip away again."

ZACH BUMPED ANNIKA'S knee with his elbow, and then turned around with a grin. "Oh, hey, sorry! I totally didn't see you back there."

Annika smiled and breathed, slowly in and out. The game below them was nearing halftime, and the Terrance Warriors were ahead.

Zach climbed up a row to sit next to Annika.

"Do you mind if I sit here?" he asked.

"Sure," she said through chattering teeth. She stared straight ahead.

"So . . . that geometry test was terrible, huh?" Zach rubbed his hands up and down his jeans trying to warm them up. His knee was almost touching hers.

Annika nodded slowly. "Yeah. It was." He asked about geometry and only knew of normal things. For Zach, a bad day was a B- on a math test. Annika's heart raced and she wanted to run.

But another voice in her head told her to breathe, to stay on the bleachers next to Zach, and to let herself chat about school.

Zach took a deep breath in and out, still rubbing his hands up and down his pants nervously. Annika looked over at him, wondering what he was so scared of. Then he reached over and held her hand, lacing his fingers with hers.

Zach let out a big breath and glanced over at her. "Um . . . is this okay?"

Was it okay to sit in the bleachers at a football game with goofy, kind Zach, who worried about his grades and whether he had gone too far by holding her hand? To be with friends and struggle through geometry? To do normal things?

Annika trusted and nodded.

"Awesome," he said under his breath, and then stared at the football field, too nervous to say anything else.

Annika sat in that moment as she held hands with a boy for the first time, letting herself believe that she might actually be okay.

JOE CARRIED MOST of the bags so Jenny could give hugs to the people who took such good care of both of them—Ben and Jenny. So many hugs, high-fives, and fist bumps. And so many tears.

"Ooooh! Dark outside!" Ben had only left the unit a handful of times and always during the day. They stood outside the hospital, Ben holding his mother's hand on one side and his father's hand on the other.

Jenny wasn't sure about anything anymore. She has talked with the social workers and chaplains about all of her fears—her panic about the future and what life might bring for Ben. There were other fears, too—going back to regular life in a great big world full of danger, finding a way to go back to work and trust someone else to take care of Ben, figuring out what to do about Joe. They taught her to pray, to hope, to trust, and above all to breathe.

Ben loved him. After all that time and everything he had been through, Ben still loved Joe. Jenny didn't know how she felt or what to do next, but on that night when they ventured into their new life, it felt right to have him there.

Jenny, Ben, and Joe paused there, none of them ready to take the next step yet. Ben was quiet, but held on tight to the two people who loved him most. Jenny was afraid, but it was time to move on. She breathed in and out, daring to trust and ready to move on.

KEMP WAVED HIGH IN THE AIR and Leah picked up her sandals and walked across the beach, weaving around couples, clumps of teens, and families clustered around bonfires. She climbed up on the dock and stood in front of the boat with her hands on her hips. Kemp held his arms out wide.

"So this is it?" Zoe said wistfully as they spied on their friends from the cliff above. "We really came all this way and we're not going to tell them we're here?"

The group watched as Leah leaned into Kemp and he wrapped his arms around her.

"No . . ." Amanda sighed. "They're good."

Kemp and Leah stood there together for a moment, and then he held her hand and helped her onto the boat. Leah settled into a seat in back while Kemp pulled the rope off the post and pushed away from the dock.

As they headed toward the harbor, Leah thought of Nick. While she had completed the obligatory therapy, she returned once more on her own.

"I can't get away from the nightmares," Leah had told him. "And I'm afraid most of the time . . ."

Nick assured her that the nightmares would fade. They chatted a while, and he shared a photo of his latest adventure parasailing with his boyfriend. And he taught her that when she was overwhelmed, she needed to breathe.

Kemp stood behind the wheel and steered the boat out of the marina several hundred yards ahead, far enough from shore so they could drop the anchor for the night.

When the boat was secure, Kemp settled in next to his bride, teasing and grinning in that easy way of his. As the sun set and with her husband's arm on her shoulder, Leah relaxed into him and looked up at the sky, pointing out the constellations she had learned long ago.